Please re
You ma
You can

Maids Under the Mistletoe

...omoted: from maids to Christmas brides!

...aids Emma, Ashleigh, Grace and Sophie
...work for the same elite London agency.
...d with Christmas just around the corner,
...'re gearing up for their busiest period yet!

...t as the snowflakes begin to fall, these
...tmas Cinderellas are about to be swept off
...r feet by romantic heroes of their own...

11/16
Blake
11/21

A Countess for Christmas
by Christy McKellen
(October 2016)

Greek Tycoon's Mistletoe Proposal
by Kandy Shepherd
(November 2016)

Christmas in the Boss's Castle
by Scarlet Wilson
(December 2016)

Her New Year Baby Secret
by Jessica Gilmore
(January 2017)

D0300989

CHRISTMAS IN THE BOSS'S CASTLE

BY
SCARLET WILSON

All rights reserved including the right of reproduction in whole or in part in any form. This edition is published by arrangement with Harlequin Books S.A.

This is a work of fiction. Names, characters, places, locations and incidents are purely fictional and bear no relationship to any real life individuals, living or dead, or to any actual places, business establishments, locations, events or incidents. Any resemblance is entirely coincidental.

This book is sold subject to the condition that it shall not, by way of trade or otherwise, be lent, resold, hired out or otherwise circulated without the prior consent of the publisher in any form of binding or cover other than that in which it is published and without a similar condition including this condition being imposed on the subsequent purchaser.

® and ™ are trademarks owned and used by the trademark owner and/or its licensee. Trademarks marked with ® are registered with the United Kingdom Patent Office and/or the Office for Harmonisation in the Internal Market and in other countries.

First Published in Great Britain 2016
By Mills & Boon, an imprint of HarperCollins*Publishers*
1 London Bridge Street, London, SE1 9GF

© 2016 Harlequin Books S.A.

Special thanks and acknowledgement are given to Scarlet Wilson
for her contribution to the Maids Under the Mistletoe series.

ISBN: 978-0-263-92040-6

23-1216

Our policy is to use papers that are natural, renewable and recyclable products and made from wood grown in sustainable forests. The logging and manufacturing processes conform to the legal environmental regulations of the country of origin.

Printed and bound in Spain
by CPI, Barcelona

Scarlet Wilson writes for both Mills & Boon Cherish and Mills & Boon Medical Romance. She lives on the west coast of Scotland with her fiancé and their two sons. She loves to hear from readers and can be reached via her website, www.scarlet-wilson.com.

This book is dedicated my favourite little people,
Taylor Hyndman, Noah "Batman" Dickson,
Lleyton Hyndman and Luca Dickson.
Let's hope you're all on Santa's nice list this year!

CHAPTER ONE

GRACE BRUSHED THE snow from her shoulders as she ducked in the back door of the exclusive Armstrong hotel in Chelsea, London. It was just after six in the morning, the streets were still dark and she could see her footprints in the snow outside.

Frank, the senior concierge, came in behind her. A wide grin lit up his face as he saw her looking at the snow outside. 'Finally,' he muttered as he shook the snow from his coat and started to sing the words to *It's Beginning To Look A Lot Like Christmas*. The words of the song floated from his lips. He gave her a nudge. 'You're too young to remember this one.'

She raised her eyebrows. 'Frank, you should know, I know every version of every Christmas song that's ever existed.'

They walked into the changing room. 'What version do you want to go for? Johnny Mathis, Frank Sinatra, or Michael Buble?' She started singing alongside him as she wound her long brown hair up into a loose bun and tied on her white chambermaid's apron over her black shirt and skirt.

Christmas was her absolute favourite time of year. It brought back great memories of the Christmases she'd spent with her grandmother in the little flat they'd shared in one of the poorer parts of London. But what they didn't have in wealth, they'd certainly made up for in love. This would be her first Christmas without her gran and she was determined not to be sad and gloomy—her gran would never have wanted that for her.

Frank slid his arms into his dark green and gold jacket and started fastening the buttons. 'I swear this thing shrinks every night when I put it into my locker.'

Grace laughed and closed her locker, walking over to Frank and pulling his jacket a little closer across his wide girth, helping him with the buttons. He kept singing the whole time. She finished with a sigh. 'I wish those words were true.'

Frank frowned as he glanced at his reflection in the nearby mirror and straightened his jacket. They started walking down the lower corridor of the hotel together. She shrugged. 'I wish it was beginning to look a lot like Christmas.' She held out her hands. 'Because it certainly isn't in here.' She gave a shake of her head. 'I don't get it. All the other big hotels in London have huge Christmas trees in their reception area and garlands and holly wreaths everywhere.'

The Armstrong hotel was part of a luxurious chain across the world. Locations in London, Paris, Tokyo, Rome and New York were regularly used by statesmen, politicians, rock stars and Hollywood celebrities. They were the epitome of glamour, renowned for their exclusivity, personal touches and attention to detail. It was a far cry from the small flat that Grace lived in and over the past few months she'd secretly loved seeing how the other half lived their lives. She knew one pop star that never laundered their underwear and instead just threw them away. A politician who had a secret interest in romance novels and a statesman that only ate red-coloured candy.

They reached the stairway up to the main reception. Frank held the door open for her and pressed his lips together. But now Grace had started, she couldn't stop. 'I mean, I know this place is exclusive, but the minimalist Christmas decorations?' She gave another shake of her head. 'They just look—well…cold.'

Frank sighed as he headed over towards his granite-topped desk. He spoke quietly as he glanced around the reception area. Everything was sleek and shades of black or grey. 'I know.' His eyes took in the small black and glass sign on the main reception desk.

The Armstrong wishes you
a Merry Christmas.

It was the only concession to Christmas on show. He checked the ledger on the desk in front of him and handed Grace an envelope. 'The Armstrong used to have beautiful Christmas decorations and lights. All exclusive. All extortionate. But they added colour to the place. Vibrancy.'

Grace started to automatically open the envelope with her day's assignments. She glanced upwards. 'So, what happened?'

Frank paused for a second before finally answering. Her gaze narrowed. Although she'd only been working here a few months, Frank had been here for ever. He was thoroughly professional, good at his job and for the guests who returned time after time—a most welcome sight. 'They had a rebranding,' he said finally.

Grace frowned. She wanted to ask more, but, like most good concierges, Frank had always been the soul of discretion. It was unlikely she'd get any more out of him.

She waved her assignment at him. 'I wish they'd let me do the rebranding around here. I could sprinkle some Christmas fairy dust.' She held out her hands and spun around. 'Some silver lights up here, some red ones over there. A tree near the glass doors. How about some garlands at the reception desk? And a huge pile of beautifully wrapped presents in the little alcove, just as you go through to the bar.' She stopped spinning, closed her eyes and held her hands to her chest. For a few seconds she could actually see in her head what this place could look like. The welcome. The warmth. The festivities.

Frank let out a wry laugh. 'Keep dreaming, Grace.'

Her eyelids flickered back open. Grey. Sleek. Blackness everywhere. She leaned forward across Frank's desk. 'I could even make this place *smell* like Christmas. Cookies. Cinnamon sticks. Cranberries. Pine trees and Christmas spices. And *not* from some tacky candle.'

Frank arched an eyebrow and leaned over towards her. 'There's a lot to be said for candles. And I'm sure we've got a whole host of those things packed up in the basement somewhere.' He shook his head. 'But I doubt very much we'll ever see them again.' He gave her a careful nod. 'You should take some home with you. Make good use of them.'

She gave a half-smile. He knew. He'd heard from some of the other girls that she was on her own. Grace didn't like people feeling sorry for her. But Frank had only the best of intentions. She knew that. So, she couldn't be offended by his good intentions. In fact, she was quite sure that some time, some place he might actually dress up as Santa.

Truth was, while The Armstrong hotel was opulent, its biggest asset was actually the staff. There were no 'bad pennies' as her gran used to call them.

Everything here was luxurious. From the bed sheets, to the furnishings, the Michelin-starred restaurant, even the heavy-duty stationery that her daily work assignment was printed on.

It was a world away from what she'd been brought up in. Working with the Maids in Chelsea agency had been a blessing in disguise. When her grandmother had died almost a year ago after a long battle with cancer, Grace had realised it was time to stop putting her own life on hold. Her gran had been the biggest part of her world. For a few years she'd only managed to take temporary part-time jobs that fitted in around being full-time carer for her gran. Working as a chambermaid might not be many women's dream job, but the salary was good and her work colleagues had turned into the best bunch of friends a girl could have.

As it was one of London's exclusive hotels, work at The Armstrong varied. There were a few guests that stayed here permanently. Some of the city's big businesses always had rooms on hold for their overseas visitors. A few of the suites seemed to be permanently vacant. Then, there were the celebrity guests.

In the space of a few months Grace had seen enough scandal and impropriety to keep the tabloid presses in headlines for the next year. But confidentiality was part of the contract for Maids in Chelsea—and she would never have breathed a word anyway.

Today's assignment was a little different. She headed over to the reception desk. 'Anya, can I just check? I've to clean the Nottingdale Suite? The penthouse? No one has stayed there in the whole time I've worked here.'

Anya checked the computer system. 'Yes, it's going to be used later. We're expecting the guest around five.'

'Who normally stays there?'

Anya smiled. 'I'm not sure. I did hear a rumour it was the reclusive tycoon who owns the whole chain.'

Grace tried not to let her mouth hang open. 'Really? Is it a man or a woman? What's their name?'

Anya held up her hands. 'You tell me. You've worked here longer than I have.'

Grace shook her head. 'I haven't paid that much attention. And I've never been in the penthouse.' She winked at Anya. 'This could be fun.'

* * *

The morning flew past. And it was fun. She cleaned a few rooms. Made a few special request orders for guests. Unpacked seven giant cases for a guest who was staying for only two nights. Then spent nearly an hour with Mrs Alice Archer, her favourite long-term guest who was eighty-nine going on twenty-one. Mrs Archer needed special soft sheets for her bed due to a long-term skin condition that affected her back, legs and arms. Grace was happy to give her a hand applying cream to spots she couldn't quite reach and helping her into whatever fabulous outfit she'd picked for the day. Alice's walk-in wardrobe was every girl's fantasy. It was full of original nineteen-forties clothes—all completely immaculate. Gorgeous full skirts, waist-cinching jackets, gingham dresses, a rainbow array of neckerchiefs, fitted sweaters and a few rarely worn satin evening gowns. There were a handbag and shoes to match every outfit.

Alice Archer had her hair styled twice a week, was fastidious with her make-up, favouring bright red lipstick, and drank lemon tea that Grace prepared for her most mornings, once she'd been helped into her clothes. In a way she reminded Grace of her grandmother. Oh, her grandmother had certainly never had the lifestyle that Alice had experienced. But both had the same quick wit, sharp minds and big hearts. Grace finished fastening Alice's shoes as she sipped her lemon tea.

'What are you doing today? Lunch or afternoon tea?'

Alice patted her hand. 'Thank you, Grace. It's Thursday. So it's afternoon tea at the Ritz. I'm meeting an old colleague.' She nudged Grace. 'He proposed to me once, you know.'

Grace looked up. 'He did? Now that sounds interesting. Why didn't you marry him?'

Alice let out a laugh. 'Harry? Not a chance. Harry was

a cad. A man about town. He would have broken my heart. So I had to break his first.'

Grace blinked. It was the throwaway way that she said it. There was a trace of something else behind those carefully made-up eyes. Did Alice regret her choice?

She hoped not. A man about town. Definitely not the type of guy that Grace was looking for. She'd never want a relationship with a man who only wanted a fling, or something meaningless. She'd suffered rejection enough. It was pretty much the worst thing in the world to be abandoned by your mother; hers had moved to another continent, married another man and created the family she'd really wanted, instead of the unexpected teenage pregnancy she'd ended up with.

Grace had always been determined that would never be her. She wasn't prepared to hand her heart over to anyone. Least of all a man that wouldn't value and respect her. She wanted everything: the knight on the white horse, the total commitment and someone with eyes only for her.

Hence the reason she was still on her own.

She rested back on her heels and looked up at Alice. 'Well, I'm sure that you couldn't have broken his heart too much, or all these years later he wouldn't still be meeting you.'

Alice sighed and leaned back in her chair. 'Or maybe we're the only ones left,' she said wistfully. Grace reached up and put her hand over Alice's frail one, giving it a gentle squeeze. 'I bet he'll be delighted to see you.'

After a second Alice seemed to snap out of her thoughts. 'What do you have planned? Tell me you've finally decided it's time to say yes to one of those nice young men that keep asking you out.'

Grace felt her cheeks flush. Alice's favourite hobby seemed to be trying to pair her off with a 'suitable' young man. She wasn't quite sure any of the men that had asked her out recently would be Alice's definition of suitable though. Lenny, the biker, had been looking for somewhere cheap to stay and thought asking Grace out might solve his problems. Alan, the banker, had earned another nickname in her head—as soon as darkness had surrounded them he'd turned into the eight-handed octopus. Ross from college had merely been looking for someone who might do the shopping and make him dinner. And Nathan? He'd seemed perfect. Handsome, hard-working and endearingly polite. But when he'd leaned in for that first kiss they'd both realised there was absolutely no spark.

She was still searching for her knight on a white horse.

In a way it made her sad. Her friends at Maids in Chelsea seemed to be pairing off at an alarming rate. Emma had just reunited with Jack—the husband nobody had known she had. Ashleigh seemed to have fallen under the spell of her gorgeous Greek, Lukas. Even Clio, their boss, had just announced her engagement to her old boyfriend Enrique and was currently planning an intimate New Year wedding. Then two nights ago her fellow singleton Sophie had mysteriously disappeared. Grace was beginning to feel like the inevitable spare part.

She shook her head at Alice and stood up. 'No men for me, I'm afraid. Maybe we can make a New Year's resolution together to try and find some suitable beaus.'

Alice let out a laugh. 'Now, that would be fun.' She glanced at the clock. 'What are you doing next?'

Grace glanced at the clock too and gave a start. Where had the time gone? 'Oh, I'll have to rush. I'm going to make up the penthouse suite—the Nottingdale. I've never even been in it before. I heard it belongs to the owner.'

Alice stared at her for a second with her bright blue eyes.

'What? Do you know him? Or her?'

Alice pressed her lips together. She seemed hesitant to

speak. Finally she gave a little smile. 'I've stayed here a while. I might know *him* a little.'

Grace grinned. She was instantly intrigued. 'Go on, then. Tell me about him. He's a bit mysterious. No one seems to know much about him.'

Alice shook her head. 'Oh, no, Grace. Sometimes mystery is good. I'm sure you'll meet him in good time.'

Grace narrowed her eyes good-naturedly as she headed towards the door. 'Alice Archer, I get the distinct impression you could tell me more.' She shook her head. 'But I'd better get on. Have fun with your afternoon tea.'

She closed the door behind her and took out her staff key for the elevator to the penthouse.

The elevator didn't just move. It glided. Like something out of the space age. It made her want to laugh. The rest of the hotel used the original elevators and Grace actually loved them. The little padded velvet love seat in the back, the panelled wood interior and the large brass button display inside. This private elevator was much like the front entrance. Shades of smooth black and grey. So silent that even her breathing seemed to disturb the air. When the doors slid open she almost jumped.

She stepped outside pulling her little trolley behind her. The entrance to the penthouse was different from the rest of the hotel. Usually the way to guest rooms was lined with thick carpet. The entrance way here was tiled, making the noise of the trolley bumping from the elevator echo all around her.

There was a huge black solid door in front of her with a pristine glass sign to its right: 'The Nottingdale Suite'.

She swallowed. Her mouth felt dry. It was ridiculous. She was nervous. About what?

She slid her staff card into the locking mechanism at the door. An electronic voice broke the silence. *Grace Ellis, Housekeeping.* She let out a shriek and looked around. In the last few months that had never happened anywhere in the hotel. It took a few seconds for her heart to stop clambering against her chest. Her card had actually identified her?

She pulled it out and stared at it for a second. Her befuddled brain started swirling. Of course, her staff card probably identified everywhere she went in the hotel. That was why she had it. But it had never actually said her name out loud before. There was something quite unnerving about that. Something a little too futuristic.

Hesitantly, she pushed open the door. It swung back easily and she drew in a breath. Straight in front of her were the biggest windows she'd ever seen, displaying the whole of Chelsea—and lots of London beyond around them. Her feet moved automatically until her breath misted the glass. The view was spectacular.

Kings Road with its array of exquisite shops, Sloane Square. If she looked in the other direction she could see the Chelsea embankment with Battersea Park on the other side and Albert Bridge. The view at night when everything was lit up must be spectacular.

Beneath her were rows of beautiful white Georgian town houses, mews cottages, streets lined with cherry trees. Houses filled with celebrities, Russian oligarchs and international businessmen. Security at all these houses probably cost more than she earned in a year.

She spun around and began to tour the penthouse. The still air was disturbing. Almost as if no one had been in here for a long time. But the bedroom held a large dark travel case. Someone had been here. If only to drop off the luggage.

She looked around. The bed was bare—waiting to be made up. It took her a few minutes to find the bedding— concealed inside a black gloss cupboard that sprang open as she pressed her fingertips against it. It only took a few minutes to make up the bed with the monochrome bedding. Underneath her fingertips she could feel the quality but the effect still left her cold.

She opened the case and methodically unpacked the clothing. It all belonged to a man. Polished handmade shoes. Italian cut suits. Made-to-measure shirts. She was almost finished when she felt a little lump inside the case. It only took a second to realise the lump was from something hidden in an inside pocket.

She pulled out the wad of tissue paper and unwrapped it carefully as she sat on the bed. The tissue paper felt old— as if it had wrapped this item for a number of years. By the time she finally peeled back the last layer she sucked in her breath.

It was gorgeous. A sparkling Christmas angel, delicately made from ceramic. Easily breakable—no wonder it was wrapped so carefully. She held it up by the string, letting it dangle in the afternoon light. Even though it was mainly white, the gold and silver glitter gave it warmth. It was a beautiful Christmas tree ornament. One that should be decorating a tree in someone's house, not being hidden in the pocket in a case.

Her heart gave a little start as she looked around the room. Maybe this businessman was having to spend his Christmas apart from his family? Maybe this was the one thing that gave him a little hint of home?

She looked around the cold, sleek room as ideas started to spark in her brain. Frank had told there were decorations in the basement. Maybe she could make this room a little more welcoming? A little bit more like Christmas?

Her smile spread from ear to ear as her spirits lifted a little. She didn't want to be lonely this Christmas. She certainly didn't want anyone else to feel that way either.

She hurried down to the basement. One thing about The Armstrong, it was super organised. She checked the ledger book and quickly found where to look. Granted, the room she entered was a little cluttered and dusty. But it wasn't impossible to find all the cardboard boxes. The tree that once stood in the main entrance was twenty-five feet tall. How impressive it must have looked.

She found some more appropriate-sized decorations and put them into a box to carry upstairs.

Two hours later, just as the sky had darkened to shades of navy blue and purple, she'd finally achieved the effect she wanted.

Tiny white sparkly lights lit up a tree in the corner of the main room. A gold star adorned the top. She'd found other multi-coloured twinkling lights that she'd wrapped around the curtain pole in the bedroom. She'd even strung a garland with red Christmas baubles above the bathroom mirror.

Each room had a little hint of Christmas. It wasn't over-whelming. But it was cute. It was welcoming. It gave the room the personal touch. The thoughtfulness that could occasionally be missing from even an exclusive hotel like this.

She walked around each room once again, taking in the mood she'd created. The Christmas style potpourri she'd found added to the room, filling it with the aroma of Christmas spices and adding even more atmosphere. She closed her eyes for a second and breathed in. She just loved it. She just loved everything about it.

Seeing the sky darkening with every second and snow dusting the streets outside, she gave a little smile.

Just one more touch.

She lifted the Christmas angel from the tissue paper and gently placed it on the pillow in the bedroom. She hadn't felt this good in a long time.

'Perfect,' she whispered.

'Just what do you think you're doing?' The voice poured ice all over her.

* * *

Finlay Armstrong was tired. He was beyond tired. He hadn't slept in three days. He'd ping-ponged between Japan, the USA and now the UK, all while fending off concerned phone calls from his parents. It was always the same at this time of year.

When would they realise that he deliberately made things busy at this time of year because it was the only way he could get through the season of goodwill?

He'd already ordered room service in his chauffeur-driven car on the journey from the airport. Hopefully it would arrive in the next few minutes then he could sleep for the next few hours and forget about everything.

He hadn't expected anyone to be in his penthouse. Least of all touching something that was so personal to him—so precious to him.

And the sight of it filled him with instant anger.

He hated Christmas. *Hated it.* Christmas cards with happy families. Mothers, fathers and their children with stockings hanging from the fireplace. The carols. The presents. The celebratory meals. All yearly reminders of what he had lost.

All reminders of another year without Anna.

The tiny angel was the one thing he had left. Her favourite Christmas decoration that she'd made as a child and used to hang from their tree every year with sentimental pride.

It was the one—and only—thing that had escaped the purge of Christmas for him.

And he couldn't even bear to look at it. He kept it tucked away and hidden. Just knowing it was there—hidden in the folds of his bag—gave him a tiny crumb of comfort that others clearly wouldn't understand.

But someone else touching it? Someone else unwrapping it? The only colour he could see right now was red.

Her head shot around and her eyes widened. She stepped backwards, stumbling and making a grab for the wall. 'Oh, I'm sorry. I was just trying to get the room ready for you.'

He frowned. He didn't recognise her. Didn't recognise her at all. Her shiny brown hair seemed to have escaped from the bun it was supposed to be in with loose strands all around her face. There was an odd smear across one cheek. Was she dirty?

His eyes darted up and down the length of her body. An intruder in his room? No. She was definitely in uniform, but not quite *his* uniform. She had a black fitted shirt and skirt on, a white apron and black heeled shoes. There was a security key clipped to her waist.

'Who are you?' He stepped forward and pulled at her security badge, yanking it from the clip that held it in place. She let out a gasp and flattened against the wall, both hands up in front of her chest.

What? Did she think he might attack her in some way?

He waved the card. 'Who on earth are the Maids in Chelsea? Where are my regular housekeeping staff?'

She gave a shudder. *A shudder.* His lack of patience was building rapidly. The confused look on her face didn't help. Then things seemed to fall into place.

It was easy to forget how strong his Scottish accent could become when he was angry. It often took people a few seconds to adjust their ears to what he was saying.

'Maids in Chelsea is Clio Caldwell's company. I've worked for her for the last few months.' The words came out in a rush. She glanced around the room. 'I've been here for the last few months. Before that—I was in Knightsbridge. But I wasn't here.' She pointed to the floor. 'I've never been in here before.' She was babbling. He'd obviously made her nervous and that hadn't been his intention.

He pointed to the angel on the pillow. He could hardly even look at it right now. 'And is this what your work normally involves? Touching things you have no business touching? Prying into people's lives?' He looked around the room and shook his head. He couldn't help himself. He walked over to the curtains and gave the annoying flickering lights a yank, pulling them so sharply that they flickered once more then went out completely. 'Putting cheap, tacky Christmas decorations up in the rooms of The Armstrong?' The anger started to flare again. 'The Armstrong doesn't do this. We don't spread Christmas tat around as if this were some cheap shop. Where on earth did these come from?'

She looked momentarily stunned. 'Well?' he pressed.

She seemed to find her tongue again. 'They're not cheap. The box they were in said they cost five hundred pounds.' She looked at the single strand of lights he'd just broken and her face paled. 'I hope that doesn't come out of my wages.'

The thought seemed to straighten out her current confusion. She took a deep breath, narrowed her gaze at him and straightened her shoulders. She held up one hand. 'Who are *you*?'

Finlay was ready to go up like a firework. Now, he was being questioned in his own hotel, about who *he* was?

'I'm Finlay Armstrong. I'm the owner of The Armstrong and a whole host of other hotels across the world.' He was trying hard to keep his anger under control. He was tired. He knew he was tired. And he hadn't meant to frighten her. But whoever this woman was, she was annoying him. 'And I take it I'm the person that's paying your wages—though I'm not sure for how much longer.'

She tilted her chin towards him and stared him in the eye. 'I'd say it's a pleasure to meet you, Mr Armstrong, but we both know that wouldn't be true.'

He almost smiled. Almost. Her dark brown eyes were deeper than any he'd seen before. He hadn't noticed them at first—probably because he hadn't been paying attention. But now he was getting the full effect.

He still wanted to have something to eat, crawl into bed, close the curtains and forget about the world outside. But this woman had just gained his full attention.

The tilt of her chin had a defiant edge to it. He liked that. And while her hair was a little unkempt and he still hadn't worked out what the mark was on her cheek, now those things were fading.

She was quite beautiful. Her hair must be long when it was down. Her fitted shirt showed off her curves and, although every part of her body was hidden, the white apron accentuated her slim waist and long legs.

She blinked and then spoke again. 'Clio doesn't take kindly to her staff being yelled at.'

'I didn't yell,' he replied instantly.

'Yes, you did,' she said firmly.

She bent down and picked up the broken strand of lights. 'I'm sorry you don't appreciate the Christmas decorations. They are all your own—of course. I got them from the basement.' She licked her lips for a second and then spoke again. 'I often think hotels can be a little impersonal. It can be lonely this time of year—particularly for those who are apart from their family. I was trying to give the room—' she held up her hands '—a little personality. That's all. A feeling of Christmas.' It was the wistful way she said it. She wasn't trying to be argumentative. He could tell from the expression on her face that she meant every word.

His stomach curled. The one thing he was absolutely trying to avoid. He didn't want to feel Christmas in any shape or form. He didn't want a room with 'feelings'. That was the whole point of being here.

He wanted The Armstrong to look sleek and exclusive. He'd purposely removed any sign of Christmas from this hotel. He didn't need reminders of the time of year.

For the first time in a long time he felt a tiny pang of regret. Not for himself, but for the person who was standing in front of him who clearly had demons of her own.

She pressed her lips together and started picking up the other decorations. She could move quickly when she wanted to. The red baubles were swept from above the bathroom mirror—he hadn't even noticed them yet. She stuffed the small tree awkwardly into the linen bag on her trolley. The bowl with—whatever it was—was tipped into the bin.

Her face was tight as she moved quickly around the penthouse removing every trace of Christmas from the room. As she picked up the last item—a tiny sprig of holly—she turned to face him.

'What is it you have against Christmas anyway?' She was annoyed. Upset even.

He didn't even think. 'My wife is dead and Christmas without her is unbearable.'

No one asked him that question. Ever. Not in the last five years.

Everyone tiptoed around about him. Speaking in whispers and never to his face. His friends had stopped inviting him to their weddings and christening celebrations. It wasn't a slight. It was their way of being thoughtful. He would never dream of attending on his own. And he just couldn't bear to see his friends living the life he should have with Anna.

The words just came spilling out unguarded. They'd been caught up inside him for the last five years. Simmering under the surface when people offered their condolences or gave that fleeting glance of pity.

'I hate Christmas. I hate everything about it. I hate seeing trees. I hate seeing presents. I hate seeing families all happy, smiling at each other. I don't need any reminders of the person missing from my life. I don't need any at all.

I particularly don't need some stranger digging through my belongings and taking out the last thing I have of my wife's—the only thing that I've kept from our Christmases together—and laying it on my pillow like some holy talisman. Will it bring Anna back? Will it make Christmas any better?' He was pacing now. He couldn't help the pitch of his voice. He couldn't help the fact that the more he said, the louder he became, or the broader his Scottish accent sounded. 'No. No, it won't. So I don't do Christmas. I don't want to do it. And I don't want to discuss it.'

He turned back around to face her.

She looked shell-shocked. Her eyes wide and her bottom lip actually trembling. Her hand partially covering her mouth.

He froze. Catching himself before he continued any further.

There were a few seconds of silence. Tears pooled in her eyes. 'I'm s…sorry,' she stammered as she turned on her heel and bolted to the door.

Finlay didn't move. Not a muscle. He hadn't even taken his thick winter coat off since he'd arrived.

What on earth had he just done?

He had no idea who the Maids in Chelsea were. He had no idea who Clio Caldwell was.

But he didn't doubt that as soon as she found him, he could expect a rollicking.

CHAPTER TWO

ONCE THE TEARS started she couldn't stop them. They were coming out in that weird, gasping way that made her feel as if she were fighting for every breath. She stopped in front of the elevator and fumbled for her card.

No! She didn't have it. He still did.

She looked around. Fire exit. It was the only other way out of here. There was no way she was hanging around.

As soon as she swung the door open she started upwards instead of down. Her chest was tight. She needed some air and she must be only seconds away from the roof. The grey door loomed in front of her. Was everything in this place black or grey? She pushed at the door and it sprang open onto the flat roof.

The rush of cold air was instant. She walked across the roof as she tried to suck some in.

She hadn't even thought about the cold. She hadn't even considered the fact it might still be snowing. The hotel was always warm so her thin shirt was no protection against the rapidly dipping temperatures on a late December afternoon.

But Grace couldn't think about the cold. All she could think about was the man she'd just met—Finlay Armstrong.

The expressions on his face. First of anger, then of disgust, a second of apparent amusement and then the soul-crushing, heart-ripped-out-of-his-chest look.

She'd done that to him. A stranger.

She'd caused him that amount of pain by just a few actions—just a few curious words.

She shivered involuntarily as the tears started to stream down her face. He'd implied that he'd sack her.

It was Christmas. She'd have no job. How could she afford to stay in the flat? As if this Christmas weren't already going to be hard enough without Gran, now she'd absolutely ruined whatever chance there was of having a peace-filled Christmas.

Her insides curled up and tumbled around. Why had she touched that angel? Why had she thought she had a right to decorate his room? And why, why had she blurted out that question?

The look on his face…the pain in those blue eyes. She shivered again. He'd lost his wife and because of that he couldn't bear Christmas. He didn't want to celebrate, didn't want to be reminded of anything.

The little things, the little touches she'd thought he might like, the tree, the decorations, the lights and the smells had all haunted him in a way she hadn't even imagined or even considered. What kind of a person did that make her?

She knew what it was like to find Christmas hard. A hundred little things had brought tears to her eyes this year—even while she was trying to ignore them. The smell of her gran's favourite perfume. The type of biscuit she'd most enjoyed at Christmas. Even the TV listing magazine where she used to circle everything she wanted to watch. But none of that—none of that—compared to the pain of a man who'd lost his wife.

Her gran had led a good and long life. His wife? She

could only imagine how young she must have been. No wonder he was angry. No wonder he was upset.

She squeezed her eyes closed. She hadn't managed to find someone she'd made that special connection with yet. Someone she truly loved with her whole heart. Imagine finding them only to have them ripped away. How unfair must that feel?

The shivering was getting worse. Thick flakes of snow started to land on her face. She stared out across London. The views from the penthouse were already spectacular. But from the roof? They were something else entirely.

It was darker now and if she spun around she could see the whole of Chelsea spread out in front of her. The Armstrong's roof was the highest point around. The streets below looked like something from a Christmas card. Warm glowing yellow lights from the windows of the white Georgian houses, with roofs topped with snow. There were a few tiny figures moving below. People getting excited for Christmas.

The tears flowed harder. Battersea Power Station glowed in the distance. The four distinctive chimneys were usually lit up with white lights. But this time of year, the white lights were interspersed with red—to give a seasonal effect.

Every single bit of Christmas spirit she'd ever had had just disintegrated all around her.

Perfect Christmas. No job. No family. A mother on the other side of the world who couldn't care less. And probably pneumonia.

Perfect.

The realisation hit him like a boxer's right hook.

What had he just done?

There was a roaring in his ears. He didn't behave like

this. He would never behave like this. What on earth had possessed him?

All thoughts of eating, pulling the blinds and collapsing into bed vanished in an instant.

He rushed out into the hall. Where had she gone? Her chambermaid cart was abandoned in the hall. His eyes went to the panel above the elevator. But no, it wasn't moving. It was still on this floor.

Something cut into the palm of his hand. He looked down. The plastic identity card. Of course. He'd taken it from her. She couldn't use the elevator.

He strode back into his room and picked up the phone. He hadn't recognised the new receptionist. Officially—he hadn't even checked in.

The phone answered after one ring. 'What can I do for you, Mr Armstrong?'

'Frank? Who are the Maids in Chelsea?'

There was a second of silence. The question obviously caught the concierge unaware.

He could almost picture the way Frank sucked the air through his teeth when he was thinking—he could certainly hear it.

'Staff from the Maids in Chelsea company have been working here for the last four months, Mr Armstrong. There were some…issues with some of our chambermaids and Mr Speirs decided to take a recommendation from a fellow hotel.' Frank paused and then continued, 'We've had no problems. The girls are excellent. Mrs Archer, in particular, really loves Grace and asks for her whenever she's on duty.'

He cut right to the chase. 'What were the issues, Frank?'

The sucking sound echoed in his ear. He would have expected Rob Speirs to tell him of any major changes in the way his prestigious hotel was run. But Speirs was currently in hospital after an emergency appendectomy. That was part of the reason that he was here at short notice.

'There were some minor thefts. The turnover of staff was quite high. It was difficult to know where the problem lay.'

'And Rob—where did he get the recommendation?'

'From Ailsa Hillier. The Maids in Chelsea came highly recommended and we've had no problems at all.' There was another hesitation. 'Mr Armstrong, just to let you know, I have something for you.'

'What is it?'

'It's from Mrs Archer. She left something with me to pass on.'

Now he was curious. 'What is it, Frank?'

'It's a Christmas present.'

Frank was silent for a few seconds. Just as well really. Every hair on Finlay's body stood on end. Of course, he'd received Christmas presents over the last few years. His parents and sister always sent something. But Mrs Archer? This was a first.

Frank cleared his throat again. 'Mr Armstrong, is there anything I can help you with?'

This time it was Finlay that paused. He liked Frank. He'd always liked Frank. The guy knew everything that happened in his hotel—including the fact that his manager had used a company recommended by their rivals at the Corminster—interesting.

'Keep a hold of the present, I'll get it from you later, Frank.' It wouldn't be good to seem ungracious. Then he asked what he really wanted to know. 'Have you seen Grace Ellis in the last five minutes?'

'Grace? What's wrong with Grace?'

Finlay really didn't want to get into this. He could already hear the protectiveness in Frank's voice. He should have guessed it would be there. 'Nothing's wrong, but have you seen her?'

'No, sir. Not in the last hour at least.'

Finlay put down the phone. She could easily have run out but he had the strangest feeling that she hadn't.

He walked back outside, leaving the penthouse door open behind him and heading towards the stairs. When he pushed the door open he felt a rush of cold air around him.

The roof. She'd gone to the roof.

He ran up the stairs, two at a time, pausing when he reached the top.

She was standing at the end of the roof, staring out over London. She wasn't thinking of…

No. She couldn't be. But the fleeting thought made him reluctant to shout her back in.

He crossed the roof towards her. As he neared he could see she was shivering—shivering badly.

He reached out and touched her shoulder and she jumped.

'Grace? What are you doing out here? You'll freeze.'

She must have recognised his voice but she didn't turn towards him. Her arms were folded across her chest and more wisps of her hair had escaped from the bun.

He walked around slowly, until he was in front of her, blocking her view.

Her lips were tinged with blue and her face streaked with tears.

Guilt washed over him like a tidal wave.

Him. He'd caused this. He'd made this girl cry.

Why? After five years he'd thought he was just about ready to move on. But Christmas was always the hardest time for him. He was frustrated with the rest of the world for enjoying Christmas when it only brought back what he had lost.

Thank goodness he still had his coat on. He undid the buttons and shrugged it off, slipping it around her shoulders.

She still hadn't spoken to him. She was just looking at him with those huge brown eyes. The ones that had caught his attention in the first place. The ones that had sparked the reaction he should never have had.

Why was that? He'd always kept things locked inside. His friends knew that. They knew better than to try and discuss things. They spent their lives avoiding Anna's name or any of the shared memories they had of her.

'I'm sorry,' he said hoarsely. 'I should never have shouted at you.'

She blinked. Her eyes went down to her feet. 'I should never have decorated the room. I'm sorry,' she whispered.

He shook his head. 'No, Grace. You were trying to do something nice. Something sweet.' The words made his insides twist a little. Was it really so long that someone had done something sweet around him?

She blinked again. The shivering hadn't stopped yet and he could tell why. The wind was biting through his thin knit black jumper. It didn't matter he had a shirt underneath. It had been a long time since he'd felt this cold.

She bit her bottom lip. 'I… I sometimes forget that other people don't like Christmas. I should have been more sensitive. I should have thought things through.' A tear slid down her cheek. 'Did you come up here to fire me?'

'What? No.' He couldn't believe it. That was the last thing on his mind right now.

She looked confused. 'But you said…you said—'

'Forget what I said,' he cut in. 'I was being an idiot. I'm tired. I haven't slept in three days. I'm sorry—I know it's no excuse.'

'I'm sorry about your wife,' she whispered.

It came out of the blue. Entirely unexpected.

Sweeping through him like the brisk breeze of cold air around him.

It was the waver in her voice. He'd heard this a thousand times over the last few years. Most of the times the words had seemed meaningless. Automatically said by people who were sometimes sincere, sometimes not.

This woman—Grace—hadn't known his wife at all. But there was something about her—something he couldn't quite put his finger on. It was as if she knew mourning, she *knew* loss. It was probably the sincerest he'd ever heard those words spoken and it twigged a little part inside him.

He stepped back a little. He stepped back and sucked in a breath, letting the cold air sear the inside of his lungs. She was staring at him again. Something about this woman's vulnerable eyes did things to him.

He wanted to protect her. He wanted to make sure that no one hurt her. There was something else. It wasn't sympathy in her eyes.

He couldn't stand the look of sympathy. It only filled him with rage and self-loathing.

A tear slid down her cheek and the wave of protectiveness that was simmering beneath the surface washed over him completely.

He couldn't help himself. He reached up with his thumb and brushed it away, feeling the coolness of her smooth skin beneath the tip.

He stepped closer again. 'Don't,' he said quickly, his voice rising above a whisper. 'I'm sorry I made you feel like this.' He wanted to glance away—to have the safety of looking out over the capital's skyline—but Grace's chocolate gaze pulled him in. His hand was still at the side of her face. She hadn't pulled away. 'I meant what I said.' He pressed his lips together. 'Christmas brings out the worst in me. It just brings back too many memories. And I know... I know that not everyone feels like that. I know that maybe…just maybe I should be able to get past this.' A picture swam into his head and he let out a wry laugh. 'As for the Christmas decorations in the hotel? They might be a little on the sparse side.'

It was the oddest situation. The most bizarre he'd ever found himself in. The irony of it almost killed him. If someone had told him twenty-four hours ago that he'd end up on the roof of his hotel, in the snow, with a strange, enigmatic woman who was causing the shades to start to fall away from his eyes after five years, he would have laughed in their face.

He wasn't joking about the sparseness of the hotel. Rob Speirs had emailed to say some of the guests were complaining about the lack of Christmas spirit. Rob had also dropped a few hints that it was bad for business.

Grace's eyebrows arched. The edges of her lips turned upwards. 'You think?'

He put his arm around her shoulders. 'It's freezing out here—and only one of us has a coat. Let's go back inside.'

She hesitated for the tiniest second then gave a shiver and a nod as they started walking to the door. 'So you can fire me in comfort?'

'Less of the firing thing. Are you going to bring this up all the time?'

She nodded. 'Probably.'

He pulled open the door. 'How about we go downstairs for some hot chocolate and you can tell me more about Maids in Chelsea? I have it on good authority you've got a fan in Mrs Archer.'

Grace nodded. 'I thought you were tired. You said you hadn't slept in three days. You don't need to talk to me. We can just call it quits and I'll go home now.'

He shook his head as they stepped inside and walked down the stairs. 'Oh, no. You don't get off that easy. We have things to discuss.'

'We do?'

She sounded surprised. He swiped a key fob next to the elevator and the doors swished open. He gestured with his hand for her to go inside. 'You don't want to have hot chocolate with me?'

He made it sound light-hearted. He wanted to try and make amends for his earlier behaviour. But the truth was his curiosity was piqued by Grace.

She gave him a cheeky stare. 'Only if there are marshmallows and cream. I get the impression you might be a bit of a cheapskate.'

He laughed as she walked into the elevator and for the first time in five years something happened.

It had been so long he almost didn't recognise it.

His heart gave a little leap.

Grace wasn't quite sure what to make of any of this. One minute Mr Film Star looks was firing her in his gravelly Scottish voice, the next minute he was apologising and making her heart completely stop when he touched her cheek.

It was the weirdest feeling. She'd been beyond cold— but the touch of his finger on her cheek had been like a little flame sending pulses around her body.

They stood in silence as the elevator moved silently to the ground floor. Frank caught sight of them as they walked out into the foyer, but Finlay didn't give them time to talk. He ushered her through to one of the private sitting rooms, speaking to a waitress on the way past.

They sat down on the comfortable black velvet-covered chairs. She ran her hand over the material. 'Black. Nice,' she said as she watched his face.

He shook his head. 'I feel that you might be going to make me pay.'

The strange wariness she'd felt around him had seemed

to vanish. She'd seen something up on that roof. Something she'd never seen in another person.

For a few moments it had felt as if she could see right into his soul. His pain. His hurt. His bitterness.

He seemed to be at a point in his life that she couldn't even begin to understand.

'Me? Make you pay? Whatever makes you think that?'

He put one elbow on the table and leaned on his hand. He did still look tired, but there was a little sparkle in those blue eyes. When Finlay Armstrong wasn't being so businesslike and generally miserable, he showed tiny glimmers of a sense of humour.

The good looks were still there. Now she wasn't so flabbergasted she could see them clearly. In fact, in the bright lights of the hotel his handsome features might even be a bit intimidating.

But there was something about that accent—that Scottish burr—that added something else to the mix. When she'd first heard it—that fierceness—its tone of *don't ever cross me* had had her shaking in her shoes. Now, there was a softness. A warmth about the tone.

He held out his arms to the room they were sitting in. 'I chose black and grey deliberately. I liked the smoothness, sleekness and no-nonsense look of the hotel. White would have been clinical. Any other colour just a distraction that would age quickly. Black and grey are pretty timeless colours.'

'If you can call them colours.'

The waitress appeared and set down steaming hot chocolates, adorned with marshmallows and cream, and long spoons. The aroma drifted up instantly. After the coldness of outside the instant warmth was comforting.

Finlay spooned some of the cream from his hot chocolate into his mouth and gave a loud sigh. 'I'm guessing you don't like my interior design selections.'

Grace smiled and tried to catch some of her marshmallows before they melted. 'I bet they cost more money than I could earn in ten years.'

He stopped stirring his hot chocolate and looked at her.

She cringed. Did she really mean to say that out loud?

The marshmallows-and-cream assortment was all sticking together inside her mouth. Any minute now she would start choking. She took another quick sip of the hot chocolate in an attempt to melt some of the marshmallows before she needed emergency treatment. Seemed as if she'd brought enough attention to herself already.

'How would you like to earn some more money?'

Too late. She coughed and spluttered everywhere. Did he really just say *that*?

As quickly as the words left his mouth and Grace started choking, Finlay Armstrong started to laugh.

He did. The guy actually started laughing. He leaned over and started giving her back a few slaps, trying to stop her choking. He was shaking his head. 'I didn't mean that. I didn't mean anything like that. It's okay, Grace. You don't need to fake a medical emergency and escape in an ambulance.'

The choking started to subside and Finlay signalled over to one of the waitresses to bring some water. He was still laughing.

Her cheeks were warm. No, her cheeks were red hot. Between choking to death and thinking completely inappropriate thoughts she couldn't be any more embarrassed if she tried.

Because she had thought inappropriate thoughts—even if it had been for just a millisecond.

She hadn't had enough time to figure out if she was mortally offended and insulted, or just completely and utterly stunned.

A bartender in a sleek black dress came over with a

bottle of water and some glasses with ice. She shot Finlay her best sultry smile as she poured the water for them both. Grace got a look of disdain. Perfect.

The water-pouring seemed to take for ever. She could almost hear some sultry backtrack playing behind them.

Finlay was polite but reserved. The bartender got the briefest of thanks, then he turned his attention back to Grace. It was hard not to grab the glass and gulp the water down. She waited until the water was finally poured, then gave her most equally polite smile and took some eager sips.

She cleared her throat. 'I didn't think that, you know,' she said quickly.

Finlay laughed even harder than before. 'Yes.' He nodded. 'You did. My bad. The wrong choice of words. I didn't mean that at all.'

She gulped again. Now they were out in public his conduct seemed a little different. He was laughing but there was more of a formality about him. This was his hotel and right now he was under the microscopic view of all his staff. He had a reputation to uphold. She got that. She did.

And right now his eyes didn't show any hint of the vulnerability she'd glimpsed upstairs. Now, his eyes seemed like those of a worldly-wise businessman. One that had probably seen and done things she could only ever dream of.

All she knew about Finlay Armstrong was the little he'd told her. But Finlay had the self-assured aura that lots of self-made businessmen had.

The knowledge, the experience, the know-how and the confidence that a lot of the clients she'd met through Maids in Chelsea had. People who had lived entirely different lives from the one she had.

She set down her water and tried to compose herself

again. Heat had finally started to permeate into her body. She could feel her fingers and toes.

She finally shook off Finlay's coat. She'd forgotten it was around her shoulders. That was what the bartender had been staring at.

She tugged at her black shirt, straightening it a little, and put her hand up to her hair, trying to push it back into place.

Finlay was watching her with amusement. 'Leave it— it's fine. Let's talk about something else.'

Grace shifted a little on the velvet chair. What on earth did he want to talk to her about?

His hands ran up and down the outside of the latte glass. 'I'd like you to take on another role within the hotel.'

She sat up a bit more. Her curiosity was definitely piqued. 'What do you mean?'

He held out his hands around the room. 'You mentioned the lack of Christmas decorations and I think you might be right. Rob Speirs, my manager, mentioned there's been a few complaints. He thinks it could be affecting business. It might be time to have a rethink.'

She tilted her head to the side. 'You want me to bring up the stuff from the basement?'

He shook his head. 'No. I don't want any of the old decorations. I want new. I want you to look around and think of a theme for the hotel, something that gives the Christmas message while keeping the upmarket look that I like for the hotel.'

Grace's mouth fell open. 'What?'

He started a little. 'And obviously I'll pay you. A designer fee, plus a company credit card to cover all the costs and delivery of what you choose.'

Grace was having trouble believing this. He'd pulled the few decorations she'd put up in the penthouse down with his bare hands. He'd called them tacky. Now, he wanted her to decorate the whole hotel?

She couldn't help the nervous laugh that sneaked out. 'Finlay, do you know what date it is?'

He wrinkled his nose. 'The sixteenth? The seventeenth of December? Sorry, I've crossed so many time zones lately I can't keep track.'

She shook her head. 'I don't know for sure, but I'm guessing most of the other hotels decided on their Christmas schemes months ago—and ordered all their decorations. They've had their decorations up since the middle of November.'

Finlay shook his head. 'That's too early. Even the first day of December seems too soon.'

Grace leaned across the table towards him. 'I'm not sure that what you have in mind and what I have in mind will be the same thing.'

'What do you mean?'

She sighed and tried to find appropriate words. 'Less than half an hour ago you told me you hated Christmas and everything about it. What's changed your mind?'

The hesitation was written all over his face. Just as she'd done a few seconds earlier, he was trying to find the right words. She could almost see them forming on his lips. She held her breath. Then, just when he looked as if he might answer, he leaned forward and put his head in his hands.

Now she definitely couldn't breathe. She pressed her lips together to stop herself from filling the silence.

When Finlay looked up again, it wasn't the polished businessman she'd been sitting opposite for the last twenty minutes. This was Finlay, the guy on the roof who'd lost his wife and seemed to lose himself in the process. What little oxygen supplies she had left sucked themselves out into the atmosphere in a sharp burst at the unhidden pain in his eyes.

'It's time.' His voice cracked a little and his shoulders sagged as if the weight that had been pressing him down had just done its last, awful deed.

She couldn't help herself. She didn't care about appropriateness. She didn't care about talk. Grace had always had a big heart. She always acted on instinct. She slid her hand across the glass-topped table and put it over his.

It didn't matter that the word no had been forming on her lips. It didn't matter that she felt completely out of her depth and had no qualifications for the position he wanted to give her. She squeezed his hand and looked him straight in the eye, praying that her tears wouldn't pool again.

He gave himself a shake and straightened up. 'And it's a business decision.' He pulled his hand back.

She gave him a cautious smile. 'If you're sure—and it's a business decision,' she threw in, even though she didn't believe it, 'the answer is yes.'

He leaned back against the chair, his shoulders straightening a little.

'I have to warn you,' she continued, 'that the picture you see in your head might not match the picture I have in mine.'

She glanced across the room and gave him a bigger smile. 'I can absolutely promise you that no matter how sleek, no matter how modern you think they are—there will be no black Christmas trees in The Armstrong hotel.'

The shadows fell a little from his eyes. 'There won't?'

There was the hint of a teasing tone in his voice. As if he was trying his best to push himself back from the place he'd found himself in.

'My Christmas could never have black trees. I'll do my best to keep things in the style you like. But think of Christmas as a colour burst. A rainbow shower.' She held up one hand as she tried to imagine what she could do. 'A little sparkle on a gloomy day.'

Finlay nodded in agreement. . 'I'll get you a credit card. Is there anything else you need?'

She licked her lips. Her throat was feeling dry. What had she just got herself into?

Her brain started to whizz. 'Use of a phone. And a computer. A space in one of the offices if you can.'

Finlay stood up. 'I can do that.'

It seemed the businessman persona had slotted back into place. Then, there was a tiny flicker of something behind his eyes.

He smiled and held out his hand towards her.

She stood up nervously and shook his hand.

'Grace Ellis, welcome to The Armstrong Hotel.'

CHAPTER THREE

'WHAT'S WRONG WITH you today?' asked Alice.

Grace was staring out of the window, lack of sleep making her woozy.

She turned her attention back to Alice. 'Nothing, I'm sorry. I'm just a little tired.'

Alice narrowed her gaze with a sly smile on her face. 'I've seen that kind of distracted look before—just not on you.'

Grace finished making the bed and turned to face Alice. 'I don't know what you mean.'

The last thing she wanted to do was admit to Alice the reasons that sleep had evaded her. It would be easy to say it was excitement about the job offer. Stress about whether she could actually *do* the job. But the truth was—while they might have contributed—the main sleep stealer had been the face that kept invading her mind every few seconds.

There was something so enigmatic about Finlay Armstrong. It wasn't just the traditional good looks, blue eyes and sexy Scottish accent. It was something so much more.

And there was no way she could be the only one that felt it.

A successful businessman like Finlay Armstrong must have women the world over trying to put themselves on his radar.

She had no idea how he behaved in private. Five years was a long time. Had he had any hook ups since his wife died? Probably. Surely?

She didn't even want to think like that.

It was just...that moment...that moment on the roof. The expression in his eyes. The way he'd looked at her when he'd reached up and touched her cheek.

Grace hadn't wanted to acknowledge how low she'd been feeling up there. She hadn't wanted to admit how she was missing her gran so much it felt like a physical pain.

But for a few seconds—up on that roof—she'd actually thought about something else.

She'd actually only thought about Finlay Armstrong.

'Grace?' Alice Archer had walked over and touched her arm.

'Oh, sorry, Alice. I was miles away.'

Alice raised her eyebrows. 'And where was that exactly?'

Grace bit her lip and pulled some folded papers from her white apron. 'I've to help choose some Christmas decorations for the hotel. I was up half the night trying to find something appropriate.'

Alice gave a little smile and reached her thin hand over to look at the printouts. Grace swallowed. She could see the blue veins under Alice's pale skin. A few of her knuckle joints were a little gnarled. They must give her pain—but she never complained. Another reminder of how much she missed her gran.

Alice glanced over the pictures, her eyes widening at a few. Grace had spent hours tracking down themes and stockists for particular items. All of them at costs that made her blink.

Alice gave her a thoughtful look as she handed the pictures back. She patted Grace's hand. 'I'm sure whatever you choose will be perfect. It will be nice to have some Christmas cheer around the hotel.'

Grace couldn't help but smile. 'Christmas cheer, that's exactly what I'm trying to capture. Something to make people get in the spirit.'

Alice walked over to her Louis XV velvet-covered chair and sank down with a wince.

'Are you okay? Are you hurting?'

Alice shook her head proudly and folded her hands in her lap. 'No. I'm not sore, Grace. I'm just old. I'll have some lemon tea now, if you please.'

'Of course.' Grace hurried over to complete their morning ritual. She sliced the fresh lemon and prepared the tea, boiling the water and carrying the tray with the china teapot and cup and saucer over to the table at Alice's elbow.

Alice gave a grateful sigh. Her make-up was still impeccable but her eyes were tired this morning. 'Maybe you should have some help? Someone to give you some confidence in your decisions.'

Grace was surprised. 'Do you want to come with me? You're more than welcome to. I would be glad of the company.'

Alice laughed and shook her head. 'Oh, no. I don't mean me. I was thinking more of someone else…someone else who could use a little Christmas spirit.'

Grace had poured the tea and was about to hand the cup and saucer to Alice but her hand wobbled. She knew exactly who Alice was hinting about.

'I don't think that would be appropriate. He's far too busy. He's far too immersed in his work. He wouldn't have time for anything like that.'

She shifted uncomfortably. She had a pink shirt hanging up in her locker, ready to change into once she'd finished her chambermaid duties. Alice was staring at her with those steady grey eyes. It could be a little unnerving. It was as if she could see into Grace's head and see all the secret weird thoughts she'd been having about Finlay Armstrong since last night.

Gran had been a bit like that too. She'd always seemed to know what Grace was going to say before she even said it. Even when she'd been twelve years old and her friend had stolen a box of chocolates from the local shop. The associated guilt had nearly made Grace sick, and she'd only been home and under Gran's careful gaze for ten minutes before she'd spilled everything.

Alice Archer was currently sparking off a whole host of similar feelings.

Her eyes took on a straight-to-the-point look. 'He asked you to get him some Christmas decorations, didn't he?'

Grace set the cup and saucer down. 'Yes,' she replied hesitantly.

'Then, he's reached the stage that he's ready to start living again.'

The words were so matter-of-fact. So to the point. But Alice wasn't finished.

'It's time to bring a little Christmas magic to The Armstrong, Grace, and you look like just the girl to do it.'

One hour later the black shirt was crumpled in a bag and her long-sleeved deep pink shirt with funny little tie thing at the collar was firmly in place. She grabbed some more deodorant from her locker. She was feeling strangely nervous. A quick glance in the mirror showed her hair was falling out of its bun again. She pulled the clip from her hair and gave it a shake. Her hair tumbled in natural waves. She was lucky. It rarely needed styling. Should she redo her lipstick?

She pulled her plum lipstick from her bag and slicked some on her lips. There. She was done. She took a deep breath, reaching into the apron that she'd pushed into her locker for her array of pictures. Her last touch was the black suit jacket—the only one she owned. She'd used it for her interview with Clio some months ago and thought of it as her good luck charm.

Finally she was satisfied with how she looked. She'd never be wearing designer clothes, but she felt presentable for the role she was about to undertake.

She pushed everything else back into the locker and did her final job—swapping her square-heeled black shoes for some black stilettos. She teetered for the tiniest second and laughed. Who was she trying to kid? She pulled open the locker again and slid her hand into the inside pocket of her black bag. There. Drop gold earrings that her gran had given her for her twenty-first birthday. She usually only wore them on special occasions but in the last few months, and particularly at this time of year, she missed her gran more than she could ever say. She slipped them into her ears and straightened her shoulders, taking a deep breath.

There it was. The little shot of confidence that she needed. She glanced down at the papers in her hand and smiled.

She was going to give this hotel the spirit of Christmas no matter what.

He could hear a strange noise outside his room. Like a shuffling. After more than a few seconds it was annoying.

Finlay's first reaction was to shout. But something stopped him. Maybe it was Alice Archer? Could she have come looking for him?

He sat his pen down on his desk. 'Is someone there?'

The noise that followed was almost a squeak. He smiled and shook his head. 'Well, it's obviously an infestation of mice. I'd better phone the exterminator.'

'What? No!' Grace's head popped around the door.

Grace. It was funny the odd effect that had on him.

She kind of sidled into the office. 'I'm sorry if I'm disturbing you, Mr Armstrong.'

He gestured towards the chair in front of him. 'It's Finlay. If you call me Mr Armstrong I'll start looking over my shoulder for my father.'

She shot him a nervous smile and walked hesitantly across the room towards the chair.

He tried his best not to stare.

Grace had already caught his attention. But now, she wasn't wearing the maid's outfit. Now, she had on a black suit and stiletto heels.

Finlay Armstrong had met a million women in black suits and heels. But he'd never met one quite like Grace. She had on a pink shirt with a funny tie at the neck.

And it was the colour that made him suck in his breath. It wasn't pale or bright, it was somewhere in the middle, a warm rose colour that brought out the colour in her cheeks and highlighted the tone of her lipstick. It suited her more than she could ever know.

Her hair swung as she walked across the room. It was the first time he'd seen it down. Okay, so the not staring wasn't going to work. Those chestnut curls were bouncing and shining like the latest shampoo TV advert.

Grace sat down in the chair opposite him fixing him with her warm brown eyes. She slid something across the desk towards him.

'I just wanted to check with you.' She licked her pink lips for a second. 'How, exactly, do I use this?'

He stared down at the company credit card. 'What do you mean?'

She bit her lip now and crossed one leg over the other. Her skirt slid up her thigh and he tore his eyes away and fixed on her eyes.

Big mistake.

'I mean, do I sign—can I sign? Or do I need a pin number or something?'

'You haven't used a company credit card before?' He hadn't even considered it.

She shook her head. He could see the slight tremble to her body. She was nervous. She was nervous coming in here and asking him about this.

'Sorry, Grace. I should have left you some instructions.' He'd just left the card for her in an envelope at Reception. He scribbled down some notes. 'This is what you do.'

She leaned forward on the desk as he wrote and a little waft of her perfume drifted towards him. He'd smelled this before. When he'd been inches from her in the penthouse he'd inhaled sharply and caught this same scent, something slightly spicy with a little tang of fruit. He couldn't quite place which one it was.

He finished writing and looked up. 'Have you had some ideas about what you need for the hotel?'

She nodded and lifted up some papers in her hand, unfolding them and sitting them on the desk. She still looked nervous. 'I know quality is important to you. But, because you've left things so late this year, I can't really pre-order or negotiate with anyone for a good price. We'll have to buy straight from the retailer. So...' she pressed her lips together for a second '... I've prepared three price ranges for you. You can let me know which one you prefer and we'll go with that one.'

He waved his hand. 'The price isn't important to me, Grace. The quality is.'

Her face fell a little. Wasn't that the right answer he'd just given her—that she had no limits to her spending? Any other designer he'd ever met would have cartwheeled out of the room at this point.

She shuffled her papers.

'What is it?'

She shook her head. 'Nothing.'

There were a hundred other things he could be doing right now. But since he had worked on the plane on the way home most things were up to date. Just as well really. After his experience last night, sleep hadn't come quite as easily as he'd expected.

Oh, he'd eventually blacked out. But he'd still managed to spend a few hours tossing and turning.

Her brown eyes were now fixed on those darn papers she was shuffling in her hands and he was strangely annoyed. He reached over and grabbed them.

It didn't take long to realise what he was looking at. He started to count them. 'Nine, ten, eleven, twelve... Grace, how many versions of these did you do?'

'Well, the first one was my absolute wish list. Then, I thought maybe you wouldn't want lights, or the big tree, or some of the other ideas I had, so I made a few other versions.'

He couldn't believe it. He'd only sprung this on her yesterday. The last company he'd worked with had taken three months just to give him a *quote* for something.

He shook his head. 'How long did this take you?'

She met his gaze again. It was clear she didn't really want to answer.

'Grace?'

She pulled a face. 'Maybe most of last night.'

'Until when, exactly?'

She pulled on her game face. 'I'm not sure exactly.'

He smiled and stood up, walking around towards her. She knew exactly how long it had taken her. He guessed she'd hardly had any sleep last night.

He put one leg on the desk, sitting just a few inches away from her. 'Grace, if I gave you free rein today, where would you go and what would you buy?'

She was silent for a few seconds. Then, her head gave a little nod. To his surprise she stood up.

Because he'd changed position she was only inches from his face. From close up, he had a much better view of her curves under her suit. He could see the upward and downward movements of her chest beneath the muted satin of her shirt.

Even more noticeable was her flawless complexion. There was a warmth about Grace. It seemed to emanate from her pores. Something trustworthy. But something else, a hint of vulnerability that just didn't seem to go away.

He'd seen other little glimpses. A spark of fire when he'd obviously annoyed her in the penthouse. She'd taken a deep breath and answered him back. Grace didn't like people treating her like a fool. She knew how to stand up for herself.

His smartphone buzzed and he glanced at it. An email he should deal with. But the truth was he didn't want to.

'What's your idea for the hotel?' he asked Grace.

She blinked at the suddenness of his question, but she didn't miss a beat. She held out her hands. 'I'm going to bring Christmas to The Armstrong. The hotel is missing something. Even you know that.' She raised her eyebrows. 'And you've given me the job of finding it.'

He picked up the phone on his desk and stared at her. 'Tell me where you're going and I'll order a car for you.'

She waved her hand and shook her head. 'I can catch the Tube.'

This time it was him that raised his eyebrows. 'Aren't you going to have some purchases to bring back?'

She put her hand up to her mouth. 'Oops.'

He asked again. 'So, where do you want the car to go?'

'First Selfridges, then Harrods, then Fortnum and Mason..' She didn't hesitate.

'You really think you can do all that in one day?'

She shook her head. 'Oh, no. I can do all that in an *afternoon*. You've obviously never met a professional Christmas shopper, Finlay.'

It was the first time she'd said his name. Actually said his name. And it was the way she said it. The way it rolled from her tongue with her London accent.

He spoke quickly into the phone on his desk, put it down and folded his arms across his chest. He smiled as he shook his head. 'No, I don't think I have.'

She wrinkled her brow. 'How old are you, exactly?' She matched his stance and stood in front of him with her arms folded across her chest.

It was almost like a challenge.

He stood up to his full height and stepped a tiny bit closer. He could take this challenge. 'Thirty-six.'

'Oh, dear.' She took a step backwards and put her hand up to her head. She looked out from under her hand with a wicked glint in her eye. 'Did you play with real live dinosaurs as a boy?' Her smile broadened as she continued. 'And shouldn't we watch the time? I guess you make all dinner reservations for around four-thirty p.m.—that's when all the early bird specials are, aren't they?'

He'd met a lot of people in this life—both before and after Anna—but he'd never met anyone who had the same effect as Grace. Even though she was officially an employee, he kept seeing glimpses of the woman underneath the uniform. Whether it was fun and jokes, a little melancholy or just a hint of real.

That was what it was.

Grace felt real. She was the only person who didn't seem to be watching how they acted around him—watching what they said. He liked the fact she was teasing him. Liked the fact she didn't treat him as if he were surrounded by broken glass.

'Seriously?'

She nodded. 'Seriously.' But it was clear she was teasing.

He laughed and shook his head and countered. 'You're probably not that much younger than me. You've just found some really good face cream.'

He handed over the company credit card as his phone rang. 'On you go and have some fun buying up any Christmas decorations that are left.' He answered the phone and put his hand over the receiver. 'I look forward to seeing what a professional Christmas shopper can do.'

Sixty minutes later Finlay Armstrong didn't look happy at all. He looked as if he were about to erupt.

Grace cringed as he strode across the store towards her. She was already feeling a little intimidated. Three security guards were standing next to her. She'd understandably almost been out on the street. That was what happened when you couldn't remember the pin number for the credit card you were using or answer any of the security questions.

Finlay walked over to the counter. 'What's the problem?'

Once she started talking she couldn't stop. She'd been having the time of her life. 'I've bought a huge Christmas tree for the foyer of the hotel, along with another two large trees for the bar and the restaurant.' Then she held her hand up towards the counter and the serious-faced woman behind it. 'Well, I haven't really bought them. I got here and...'

She held up the piece of paper that he'd given her. It had managed to get smudged and the numbers on it were indecipherable. She leaned forward. 'Please tell them I really do work for the hotel. I'm not on their list and don't know any of the questions they asked me.'

Finlay's jaw tightened, but he turned and addressed the woman with impeccable politeness. 'I'm Finlay Armstrong. I own the company. I can either use the correct pin, or answer any of the security questions you need.'

The woman gave a nod. 'I'm afraid you'll have to do both on this occasion. And, Mr Armstrong, if you add another member of staff onto the card—you really should let us know.'

Grace wanted to sink through the floor. This shopping trip definitely wasn't going to plan. She was behind already.

Finlay was finished a few minutes later. 'If I give you the number, do you think you can remember it again?'

The staff member cleared her throat behind them, 'Actually, Mr Armstrong, your card has already been flagged today. You might be asked security questions if you use it again.'

Grace gulped. 'What does that mean?'

Finlay glanced at his watch. 'How much longer will this take?'

Grace glanced down at the list still in her hands. She wanted to lie and say around five minutes. But London traffic would be starting to get heavy. 'Probably another couple of hours.'

Finlay rolled his eyes. He stared off into the distance for a second. 'We need the decorations for the hotel,' he muttered. 'Okay, let's go. The car's outside.'

The cold air hit her as soon as they came outside and she shivered. 'Where's your coat?' he asked.

She shrugged. 'I just got so excited when you gave me the card and told me there was a car outside, I forgot to go and get my coat and gloves.' She shook her head. 'It doesn't really matter. We'll be inside for most of the time.'

The car pulled up and he held the door as she slid inside and he climbed in next to her. He was talking on the phone—obviously still doing business.

It wasn't deliberate. But all her senses seemed on alert.

The wool from his black coat had brushed against her hand sending weird vibes everywhere. The aroma of his after-shave was slowly but surely drifting towards her in the warm atmosphere of the car. And even though it was cold outside, she was praying her pink shirt wouldn't show any unexpected perspiration marks.

It was only early afternoon but the sky already had a dark purple tinge at its edges.

Finlay glanced at his watch. There was a tiny shadow around his jaw line. The hint of a little stubble. Mixed with those unusual blue eyes it was enough to make any warm-blooded female catch her breath.

Part of her heart was going pitter-patter. So many expectations. What if he hated her ideas? What if he couldn't see how they translated to The Armstrong?

He closed his phone and leaned forward to speak to the driver. 'How much longer?'

'Just another ten minutes,' was the reply.

Grace felt nervous. Jumpy around him. Small talk seemed like the best solution.

'You mentioned your mum and dad earlier—are you spending time with them this year?'

He frowned. She wondered if he wasn't going to answer, then he shook his head. 'No. My parents are still in Scotland. My sister is expecting their first grandchild and will probably be fussed over non-stop.'

The answer was brisk. It was clear Christmas was still an issue for him—even if he was agreeing to decorations for the hotel.

As she went to speak again, her hand brushed against his. He flinched and then grabbed it. 'Grace, your hands are freezing.' He started rubbing his hands over hers. She was taken aback. After the frown it was a friendlier gesture than she might have expected.

His warming actions brought the aroma of the rose and

lavender hand cream she'd used earlier drifting up between them. She hadn't even thought about how cold her hands were.

The car pulled up outside one of London's oldest and most distinguished department stores, Fortnum and Mason. Grace was so excited she didn't wait for the driver to come around and open the door—she was out in a flash. She waved at Finlay. 'Come on, slowcoach. Let's get started. We need Christmas wreaths and garlands.'

She walked swiftly, darting her way between displays and heading for the elevators. But Finlay's footsteps faltered. It was like...*whoosh*!

Christmas everywhere. Every display. Every member of staff. Perpetual Christmas tunes piping overhead. Grace had even started singing along. Did she even notice?

It was like Christmas overload.

It was clear he'd unleashed the monster. He hadn't seen someone this enthusiastic about Christmas since his sister was five years old and thought she might get a horse. She did—but it was around twelve inches.

He pushed back the wave of emotions that was in danger of rearing its ugly head. He'd chosen to be here. He'd decided it was time to try and move forward. The perpetual little ache he felt would always be there. But should it really last for ever?

They walked through the tea hall that was jostling with people. 'I love the Christmas shop in here. There's so much to choose from.' She kept talking as they darted between shoppers.

The lifts were small and lined with wood. He found himself face to face with her, their noses inches away from each other. In this confined space he felt instantly protective, his hand reaching up and resting on her hip.

She smiled and tipped her head to one side. 'Did you listen to a single word I said?'

He shook his head as the doors closed and the piped music continued. 'Not a single word,' he admitted.

She gently slapped his chest. 'Shocker. Well, remember only these words: *I will not complain about the price.*'

He rolled his eyes. 'Grace, what are we buying in here?'

She still looked happy. It was obvious Christmas decorations were something that she just loved. 'I told you. Christmas wreaths and garlands to decorate the foyer, the bar, the corridors, the restaurant and the elevators.' She counted them off on her fingers.

He blinked for a second. Wreaths. He'd forgotten how often they were used as Christmas decorations now. It was almost as if the world had misplaced what they actually were.

They were lucky: no one else rode to the top floor with them. The elevator pinged and she looked over her shoulder. 'This is us.' She wiggled around, her backside pressing straight into him.

Finlay felt numb. No matter how she'd joked, he was still a young guy. And like any young man, his body reacted to a woman being up close and personal—even if it was unintentional.

Grace seemed not to have noticed anything. She dodged her way through the bodies.

As soon as they stepped outside the lift Grace almost started skipping. She handed him a basket and picked up a few delicate glass and white tree decorations. Then, she walked over to the counter. 'I phoned earlier about a special order. Wreaths and garlands—you said you'd put them aside for me.'

The clerk nodded. 'They're through here. Do you want to see them before you pay?'

Finlay let Grace work her magic. She was loving this. This wasn't the vulnerable woman that he'd seen on the rooftop. This was in control and in her element Grace.

Within a few minutes he'd handed over the company credit card and heard her arrange for delivery in a few hours' time.

Grace let out a squeal. 'My favourite ever Christmas song—"Last Christmas"—let's sing along.'

He looked at her in surprise. 'This is your favourite song? It's not exactly cheery, is it?'

But Grace was oblivious and already singing along. A few fellow shoppers gave him an amused stare. She really was singing and didn't seem to care who was listening. The fleeting sad thoughts disappeared from his head again. Grace had a little glance at her lists and made a few random ticks before folding them up again and belting out the main part of the song.

The pink flush in her cheeks suited her. But what caught his attention most was the sparkle in those dark brown eyes. He wouldn't have thought it possible. But it was. He sucked in a breath. If he didn't watch out Grace Ellis could become infectious.

Grace came back and pressed her hand on his arm. 'I've seen a few other things I like. You stay here or it'll spoil the fun.' She waved her hand. 'Have a look around. I'll only be five minutes.'

He frowned as she disappeared. Fun?

He wandered around, watching people gaze in wonder at all the decorations. The garlands in store were beautiful. They had a whole range of colours and they covered walls, shelves and the Christmas fireplaces that had been set up in store. Next to them was a whole range of wreaths: some holly, some twisted white twigs, some traditionally green decorated with a variety of colours. He stopped walking.

He was looking at wreaths and not automatically associating them with Anna. Guilt washed over him. Shouldn't she always be his first thought?

But she hadn't been. Not for the last few months. It was

as if his head was finally lifting from the fog it had been in these last five years. But Christmas time was a little different. It seemed to whip up more memories than usual. It made the thought of moving on just a little more tricky.

A little girl walked into him as she stared at a rocking horse. He bent down to speak to her. She was like something from a chocolate box. A red double-breasted wool coat, a little worn but clearly loved, dark curls poking out from under a black hat. She hadn't even realised she'd walked into him—her eyes were still on the white rocking horse with a long mane decorated with red saddle. She let out a little sigh.

'Come along, Molly,' said a harassed voice. 'We just came here for a little look. It's time to go.'

He lifted his head instantly. The woman looked tired— her clothes even more so. Her boots were worn, her jacket was missing a few buttons and the scarf she had wrapped around her neck looked almost as old as she was. But it was her accent that drew his attention.

He straightened up and held out his hand. 'Hi, Finlay Armstrong. What part of Scotland are you from?'

She was startled by his question and took a few seconds to answer. He could almost see the recognition of his own accent before she finally reached over and shook his hand. 'Hi, I'm Karen. I'm from Ayrshire.'

There was something in the wistful way she said it that made him realise this wasn't a visit.

He kept hold of her hand. 'Have you been in London long?'

She sighed. 'Three years. I had to move for work.'

He nodded his head towards the rocking horse. 'Your little girl was admiring the rocking horse.'

Karen winced. 'I know. I asked for one every year too as a child.' She glanced down at her child again then met his gaze. 'But we can all dream.'

He sucked in a breath. When was the last time he'd done something good? He'd been so wrapped in his own mourning for the last five years he hadn't really stopped to draw breath. Even when it came to Christmas presents he normally gave his PA a list and told her what kind of things his family preferred. That was as much input as he'd had.

He thought about the prettily wrapped present that Mrs Archer had left for him at reception. He hadn't even opened it yet.

He kept his voice low. 'How about Molly gets what she wants for Christmas?'

Karen looked shocked, then offended. He knew exactly how this worked. He shook his head. 'I work for a big company. Every year they like us to do a few good deeds. A few things that no one else finds out about.' He pulled the card out of his pocket, still keeping his voice low. 'There's no catch. I promise. Give the girl at the desk an address and time for delivery. That's all.'

Karen sucked in a breath. 'I don't want to be someone's good deed.' He could see her bristle.

He gave a nod of acknowledgement. 'Then how about a gift from a fellow Scot who is also missing home?'

Her eyes filled with tears and she put her hand to her throat. 'Oh…oh, then that might be different.'

He glanced down at Molly and smiled. 'Good. Just give the girl at the desk your details. I'll arrange everything else.'

'I don't know what to say, except thank you. And Merry Christmas!'

He gave her a nod. 'Happy Christmas to you and Molly.'

He ruffled Molly's curls and walked away, not wanting to admit to the feelings that were threatening to overwhelm him. That was the first time he'd wished anyone Happy Christmas in five years. Five long, horrible years.

What had he been doing? Had he been ignoring people around him like Karen and Molly for the last five years?

He heard an excited laugh and Grace walked through with one of the sales assistants from another room. Grace's cheeks were flushed pink with excitement and she was clapping her hands together again.

The girl really did love Christmas.

One part of him felt a selfish pang, while the other dared itself back into life. In a way, he'd felt better sticking his head in the sand for the last few years. Some of this Christmas stuff made him feel decidedly uncomfortable. Parts of it were making him relive memories—some good, some bad.

But the thing that he struggled most with was feeling again. *Feeling.*

The thing he'd tried to forget about.

He touched the saleswoman's arm as she was still mid-discussion with Grace. 'I need you to add something to the order.'

Grace's head shot up. 'What?' Then her expression changed. 'Really?'

He gave a nod and gestured to the white rocking horse. 'The lady in the dark coat, her name is Karen. Can you make delivery arrangements with her?'

The saleswoman shot a glance from Grace, to Finlay and then to Karen, who was still standing in the distance with Molly.

'Of course,' she said efficiently, adding the purchase to the bill.

What was he doing? All of a sudden Finlay was feeling totally out of his depth. 'Let's go,' he said to Grace abruptly.

She looked a little surprised but glanced at her watch. Did she think he wanted to beat the traffic? 'Thanks so much for your assistance. I'll be back at The Armstrong for the delivery.'

She rubbed her hands together again. Something sparked into his brain. The one thing he'd thought to do back at the hotel.

He pulled out his phone and spoke quietly as they hurried back outside to the car. The light had almost gone completely now and most of London's stores were lit up with Christmas displays. The journey to Harrods didn't take quite as long as he'd imagined.

Grace gave a sharp intake of breath as soon as the gold lights of the store came into view, lighting up the well-known green canopies.

He touched her elbow. 'We need to do something first in here before we go to the Christmas department.'

She looked surprised. 'Do you need some Christmas gifts for your family?'

He shook his head. Thick flakes of snow were falling outside. 'That's taken care of. This was something I should have done earlier.'

They stepped outside as the chauffeur opened the door and walked in through one of the private entrances.

A woman in a black suit with gold gilding met them at the entrance. 'Mr Armstrong?'

He nodded. She walked them towards some private lifts. 'This way, please.'

The journey only lasted a few seconds before the doors slid open on women's designer wear. Grace frowned and looked at him. 'We need to go to the Christmas department.'

He waved his hand. 'In a few minutes. I need to get something here first.' He turned to the personal shopper. 'Do you have anything the same shade as her shirt? And some black leather gloves please, lined.'

Grace was still frowning. 'Who is this for?'

He turned to face her. 'You.'

'What?' It was a face he recognised. Karen had worn

the same expression thirty minutes earlier. 'What on earth are you talking about?'

Finlay held out his hands. 'Look at me. I've dragged you halfway across London in the freezing cold with snow outside.' He touched her arm. 'You're only wearing your suit and a shirt. You must be freezing. I feel like an idiot standing beside you in a wool coat.'

She tipped her head to the side. 'Then take it off. It's too hot in here anyhow.'

She said it so matter-of-factly. As if he should have thought of it himself.

He shook his head. 'But once we get back outside, you'll freeze again. You were rubbing your hands together the whole time we were in the last two stores. It was obvious you were still cold.'

The personal shopper appeared carrying a knee-length wool coat in the exact shade of pink as Grace's shirt. She held it up. 'Is this to your taste?'

He smiled. 'It's perfect.' He gestured towards the coat. 'Go on, Grace, try it on.'

She was staring at it as if she didn't quite know what to say. Then she shook her head. 'You are not buying me a coat.'

He took the coat from the personal shopper and held it open. 'You're right. I'm not buying you a coat. The Armstrong hotel is. Think of it as part of your official uniform.'

She slid her arms along the black satin lining of the coat as he pulled it up onto her shoulders. The effect was instant. The coat brought out the darkness of her chestnut hair and dark eyes while highlighting her pink cheeks and lips. It was perfect for her.

He felt himself hold his breath. Grace turned and stared at her reflection in a mirror next to them. Her fingers started automatically fastening the buttons on the double-breasted coat. It fitted perfectly.

The sales assistant brought over a wooden tray of black leather gloves. Grace stared down in surprise and looked up at Finlay. 'They're virtually all the same. How am I supposed to choose?'

The personal shopper looked dismayed. She started lifting one glove after another. 'This one only skims the wrist bones. This one has a more ruffled effect, it comes up much further. This one has a special lining, cashmere. We also have silk-lined and wool-lined gloves all at different lengths. Do you have a specific need?'

Finlay could tell by the expression on Grace's face that she was bamboozled. He reached out and ran his fingers across the gloves. Some instantly felt softer than others. He selected a pair and turned them inside out. 'These ones must be cashmere lined. The leather feels good quality too. Want to try them?'

He had no idea what size or length they were. Somehow he thought his eyes might be similar to Grace's—all the gloves looked virtually identical. But they didn't feel identical.

She slid her hands into the pair he handed her and smiled. 'They're beautiful...' She gave them a little tug. 'But they seem a little big.'

In an instant the personal shopper handed her an alternative pair. Grace swapped them over and stretched her hands out. 'Yes, they feel better.'

'Perfect. Add this to our bill, please,' he said. 'We're going to the Christmas department.'

'But... I haven't decided yet.' Grace had her hand on the collar of the coat.

Finlay shrugged. 'But I have—the coat is perfect. The colour is perfect. The fit is perfect and the length is perfect. What else is there to say?'

He started to walk away but Grace wasn't finished.

'But maybe I'm not sure.' Her voice started to get louder

as he kept walking, 'What if I wanted a red coat? Or a blue one? Or a black one? What if I don't even *like* coats?'

People near them were starting to stare. Finlay spun around again and strode back over to her, catching her by the shoulders and spinning her back around to face the mirror.

'Grace. This is you. This is your coat. No one else could possibly wear it.' He held his hands up as he looked over her shoulder.

Her dark brown eyes fixed on his. For a second he was lost. Lost staring at those chocolate eyes, in the face framed with chestnut tresses, on the girl dressed in the perfect rose-coloured coat.

There was a tilt to her chin of defiance. Was she going to continue to fight with him?

Her tongue slid along her lips as her eyes disconnected with his and stared at her reflection. 'No one has ever done something like this for me,' she whispered at a level only he could hear. She pulled her hand from the leather glove and wound one of her tresses of hair around her finger as she kept staring at her reflection.

'Just say yes,' he whispered back.

She blinked, before lowering her gaze and unwinding her finger from her hair. She pulled off the other glove and undid the buttons on the coat, slipping it from her shoulders.

She handed it to the personal shopper. 'Thank you,' she said simply, then straightened her bag and looked in the other direction. 'Right,' she said smartly, 'let's hit the Christmas department. We have work to do.'

She wasn't joking. The Christmas department was the busiest place in the entire store.

And Grace Ellis knew how to shop.

She left the personal shopper in her wake as she ping-ponged around the department, side-stepping tourists, pensioners, kids and hesitant shoppers.

He frowned as he realised she was picking only one colour of items. 'Really?' He was trying to picture how this would all come together.

She laid a hand on his arm as she rushed past. 'Trust me, it will be great.' Then she winked and blew into her fingers, 'It will be magical.'

She was sort of like a fairy from a Christmas movie.

He was left holding three baskets and feeling quite numb as she filled them until the contents towered. Lights. Christmas bulbs. Some weird variation of tinsel. A few other decorations and the biggest haul of snow globes. He hadn't seen one since he was a child.

'Really?' he asked again.

She picked up a medium-sized one and gave it a shake, letting the snow gently fall around the Santa's sleigh above a village. 'Everyone loves a snow globe…it's part of our theme.'

Our theme. She was talking about the hotel. Of course she was talking about the hotel. But the way her eyes connected with his as she said the words sent involuntary tremors down his spine. It didn't feel as if she were talking about the hotel.

Maybe this wasn't such a good idea after all. Maybe he should have started much smaller. Grace's enthusiasm for Christmas had only magnified as the hours increased. Was he really ready for such a full-on Christmas rush?

She tugged at his sleeve. 'Finlay, I need you.'

'What?' He winced. He didn't mean for the response to be so out of sorts. The truth was, he wasn't quite sure what he was doing here, or how he felt about all this.

Five years ago he'd still been numb. Five years ago he'd spent September and October sitting by his wife's bedside.

The year before that he'd been frantically searching the world over for any new potential treatment. On a bitter cold November day, he'd buried her.

Anna had been so much better than him at all of this. She'd been devastated by the news. Devastated by the fact no treatment had worked. But she'd been determined to end life in the way she'd wanted to. And that was at home, with her husband.

No one should have to watch the person they love fade a little day by day. But Finlay knew that every day the world over, there were thousands of people sharing the same experience he had.

Grace was standing in front of him, her face creased with lines. 'What's wrong?'

'Nothing.' He shook his head. 'Nothing. What do you need?'

She nodded to the snaking line in front of them. 'We've reached the front of the queue. I need you to pay.'

Pay. Something he could manage without any thought.

He walked to the front of the line and handed over the credit card. The personal shopper was putting all the purchases into some trolley for them to take to the car. He stopped her as she started to wrap the coat in tissue paper. 'Don't,' he said. 'Just take the tags off. Grace should wear it.'

There was a moment's hesitation on Grace's face as he handed the coat over. But after a few seconds she slid her arms back inside. 'Thank you.'

'No problem.'

By the time they got outside the air was thick with snow. It was lying on the pavements and surrounding buildings and roads.

Grace fastened her coat and slid her hands into the leather gloves while all their packages were stored in the boot of the chauffeur-driven car.

The journey back to the hotel was silent. He'd started

this afternoon with the hope of a little Christmas spirit. It wasn't that he wasn't trying. But sometimes memories flared. Tempering his mood with guilt and despair.

Grace's fingers fumbled over and over in the new gloves. She was staring at the passing shop windows. Her face serious and her eyes heavy. What was she thinking about?

When they reached the hotel he couldn't wait to get out of the car. 'I have an international videoconference,' he said as he climbed out.

'Good.'

He stopped mid-step. 'What?'

She walked around to the boot of the car. 'I don't want you to see anything until I've finished. It's better if you have something to do. I'm going to get Frank and some of the other Maids in Chelsea to help me set things up. I'd prefer it if you waited until I was finished—you know, to get the full effect.'

It was almost as if somehow she had switched gears from her sombre mood in the car. Grace seemed back on point. Focused again. Ready to complete her mission.

And right now all he felt was relief. He could retreat into his office. He could stop asking himself why he'd bought a stranger's child a rocking horse and an employee a coat and gloves that were way outside her pay range.

Two of the doormen from the hotel started lifting all the purchases from the car. One of them gave her a nudge. 'Frank says there's a delivery at the luggage door for you.'

She was busy. She was engaged. She didn't need him around.

Finlay walked back through the reception without acknowledging anyone. He had work to do.

It was finished. It was finally finished. Grime and sweat had ruined her pink shirt and black skirt. She'd swapped back from the stilettos to her lower shoes and spotted a hole in her black tights. Her hair had ended up tied in a ponytail on top of her head as it kept getting in the way. She must look a complete state.

Emma gave a sigh as she looked up at the giant tree. 'If you'd told me this was what you had in mind when you asked for a hand...'

Sophie rolled her eyes. 'As if you would have said no.'

Ashleigh was leaning against the nearby wall with her arms folded. 'I think it looks spectacular. It was worth it.'

Grace couldn't stop pacing. 'Do you think so? What about those lights over there? Should I move them?' She pressed her hands to her chest. 'What about the colour scheme? Is it too much?'

The girls exchanged amused glances.

But Grace couldn't stop with her pacing. 'I'll need to go and get him. I'll need to make sure that he's happy with it.'

Sophie walked over and put her arm around Grace's shoulder. 'Well, whoever *he* is, he'd be crazy if he didn't like this.'

Ashleigh stepped forward. 'I hope you've been paid for this, Grace. I'd hate to think this guy was taking advantage of your good nature.'

Emma folded her arms across her chest. 'Who is he, exactly? You haven't exactly been forthcoming.'

Grace hesitated. She wasn't even quite sure what to say. She tried to slip the question by giving Emma a big hug. 'Thank you for coming today. You're not even a Maid in Chelsea any more. Should I start calling you by your fancy title?'

But Emma was far too smart for that. She returned the hug then pulled back. 'I'm going to ask Jack if he knows anything about Finlay Armstrong.'

Grace shook her head—probably much too quickly. 'I

don't think he will.' She turned and looked at the finished decorations again. 'I can't thank you girls enough. I owe you all, big time.'

'I think that's our cue to leave, girls,' said Ashleigh. 'Come on. Let's get cleaned up. I'm buying the drinks.'

They all gave Grace a hug and left by the main entrance of the hotel while she went to retrieve her jacket from behind the reception desk.

Should she wait? The hotel reception was quiet. She wasn't even sure of the time. She'd asked the staff to dim the main lights a little to give the full effect of the tree.

Her stomach gave a flip-flop. He'd asked her to do this. He'd asked her. Surely he'd want to see that she was finished?

She walked slowly towards his office door, listening out to see if he was still on his conference call. She couldn't hear anything and the office door was ajar.

She gave the door a gentle knock, sticking her head around it. Finlay was staring out of the window into the dark night. His office had a view of the surrounding area—not like the penthouse, of course, but still enough to give a taste and feel of the wealth of Chelsea. It was a wonder they didn't ask for credentials before they let you off the Tube around here.

He looked lost in his thoughts. She lifted her hand and knocked on the door again—this time a little more loudly.

He jumped. 'Grace.' He stood up; his actions seemed automatic. He started to walk around the desk and then stopped, the corners of his mouth turning upwards.

'What on earth have you done with your hair?'

She'd forgotten. She'd forgotten her hair currently resembled someone from a nineteen-eighties pop video.

She glanced down at her shirt too. Random streaks of dirt.

It wasn't really the professional look she'd been aiming for.

She gave her head a shake. 'I've been busy. This stuff doesn't put itself up.' Nerves and excitement were starting to get the better of her. 'Come and see. Come and see that you like it.'

He raised his eyebrows, the hint of a smile still present. 'You're already telling me I like it?'

'Only if you have exceptionally good taste,' she shot back.

He had no idea how much her stomach was in knots. This was the guy who hated Christmas. This was the guy that had pulled down a single strand of lights she'd put in his room.

This was a guy that was trying to take steps away from his past Christmas memories. If she'd got this wrong...

She stepped in front of him. 'It might be better if you close your eyes.'

'Nervous, Grace?' He was teasing her.

'Not at all.' She made a grab for his hand. 'Close your eyes and I'll take you outside. I'll tell you when you can open them.'

For a moment she thought he might refuse. She wasn't quite sure how long she could keep up the bravado. She stuck her hands on her hips. 'Hurry up, or I'll make you pay me overtime.'

He laughed, shook his head, took her hand and closed his eyes.

His hand in hers.

She hadn't really contemplated this. She hadn't really planned it. His warm hand encompassed hers. Was her hand even clean?

The heat from his hand seemed to travel up her arm. It seemed to spread across her chest. She shouldn't be feeling this. She shouldn't be thinking thoughts like...

'Are we going?'

'Of course.' She gave his hand a tug and started walking—too quickly to begin with, then slowing her steps to a more suitable pace.

Magda at Reception raised her eyebrows as they walked past. Grace couldn't think straight for one second. This was it. This was where he would get the full effect. The effect that every customer walking into The Armstrong would get from now on.

She spun him around to position him exactly where she wanted him. Far enough away from the traditional revolving door at the entrance way to stop him getting a draught, but still with enough distance between him and the display.

She tapped his shoulder. 'Okay. Open your eyes.'

Maybe he'd been hasty. Maybe he shouldn't have made any of the suggestions about Christmas decorations. He didn't know what he was doing. He'd spent the last few hours trying to get the image of Grace in that pink coat out of his head.

He opened his eyes.

And blinked.

And blinked again.

His hotel was transformed. In a way he could never have imagined.

The lights in the main reception area were dimmed. In normal circumstances the black and grey floor, walls and reception desk would have made it as dark as night.

But it wasn't.

It was purple.

Purple in a way he couldn't even begin to find words for. He started to walk forward, straight towards the giant Christmas tree at the end of the foyer that was just pulling his attention like a magnet.

The traditional green tree was huge. It was lit up with purple lights and a few white twinkling ones. The large purple baubles and glass snowflake-style tree decorations reflected the purple light beautifully. The strange-style purple tinsel was wrapped tastefully amongst the branches. Along either wall were more purple lights. It was a strange effect. They drew you in. Drew your gaze and footsteps towards the tree. At intermittent points all along were snow globes of various sizes.

There was a choking noise beside him. Grace's face was lit up with the purple lights, her hands clenched under her chin and her eyes looking as if they might spill tears any second.

'What do you think?' Her voice was pretty much a squeak.

He couldn't speak yet. He was still getting over the shock.

Christmas had come to The Armstrong hotel.

She'd captured it. She'd captured the Christmas spirit without drowning him in it.

The tree was giant, but the effect of only having one colour made it seem more sleek and exclusive than he'd expected. The intermittent snow globes were focal points. Something people could touch, pick up and hold.

The dimmed lights were perfect. It bathed the whole area in the most magical purple light.

'Finlay?' This time there was a tremor in her voice.

He kept looking, kept looking at everything around him, before finally turning and locking gazes with Grace.

'I think Santa got everything wrong,' he said.

Her eyes widened. 'What do you mean?'

Finlay laughed and opened his arms wide. 'His grotto. Clearly, it should have been purple.' He spun around, relishing the transformation of his hotel.

He didn't just like it. He loved it.

Never, even in a million years, did he think he'd feel like this.

He picked up Grace and swung her around.

She was still in shock. She put her hands on his shoulders and let out a squeal. She was still looking for verification. She needed to hear the words out loud.

'You like it? You think it's good?'

He set her feet back down on the slate floor. 'I don't think it's good—I think it's fantastic!' He shook his head. 'I can't believe you've done this. I can't believe you've managed to capture just what I wanted for The Armstrong without...'

His voice tailed off. That wasn't something to say out loud. That was part of his private thoughts.

She stepped in front of him again. This time the tension on her face and across her shoulders had disappeared. The expression on her face was one of compassion, understanding. She touched his arm. 'Without taking you back to where you don't want to be.' She nodded. 'I wanted this to be about something new for you. Something entirely different.' She lowered her gaze. 'Not that there's anything wrong with memories. Not that there's anything wrong with taking some time.'

His heart swelled. He knew so little about Grace. This woman, that he'd almost threatened to fire, that had stood up to him, teased him, and shown him compassion and made him feel things he hadn't in years.

He was thinking things and feeling things that had been locked away inside for a long time.

He'd been so shut off. So determined not to let anything out—not to open himself up to the world of hurt that he'd felt before.

But things felt differently than he'd expected. The world

outside didn't feel quite so bad as before. He recognised things in Grace that he hadn't expected to.

It was time to start making connections. Time to start showing interest in those around him. And he knew exactly where to start.

He reached down and took her hand. 'I owe you more than a coat.'

She shook her head automatically. 'No, you don't. And that coat is beautiful. Completely impractical and the kind of thing I wear in one of my dreams. Thank you for that.'

Her dark brown eyes met his. 'Every girl should get to be a princess some time.'

There was a little pang inside his chest. 'Come to the staff party with me.'

She dropped his hand. 'What?' She looked truly shocked.

'I mean it.'

Her mouth opened and then closed again.

'Every year there is a pre-Christmas staff party at the hotel. I haven't gone for the last five years. This year— it's time for me to attend again.' He shrugged. 'I can't promise I'll dance. I can't promise I'll play Santa Claus.' He gave her a serious nod. 'But I can promise you there will be music, spectacular food and champagne. If you want to be treated like a princess, then come to the party with me.'

She still looked a bit stunned. 'I've heard about the staff party. I just wasn't sure if I was going to go. What will the rest of the staff think if I go with you?'

He waved his hand. 'Who cares?'

'I care.' She looked serious.

He shook his head and took both her hands in his. 'Grace, they will think I'm saying thank you for the way you've decorated the hotel. The way you've managed to bring Christmas to The Armstrong in such a classy, stylish way. And they'd be right.'

She glanced over at the Christmas tree and finally smiled again.

She tilted her head to one side. 'Well, when you put it like that...'

76

She shut the book and wondered why the manuscript wouldn't leave her alone.

She glanced her head to one side once more when you could ...

CHAPTER FOUR

ALICE ARCHER COULD sniff out a problem from forty paces away. 'What's wrong with you today, Grace? One minute you're talking non-stop, next minute you're staring out of the window in some kind of daze. All with that strange expression on your face.'

Grace started back to attention. 'What expression?' she said quickly as she hung up another of Alice's coats.

Alice gave a knowing smile. 'That I'm-thinking-of-a-special-man kind of smile.'

Heat instantly seared her cheeks. 'I have no idea what you mean.'

But Alice wasn't put off. She merely changed the subject so she could probe another way. 'The decorations are beautiful.' She leaned back in her chair and gave a wistful sigh. 'I doubted I'd ever see Christmas in The Armstrong again. But you've captured the spirit perfectly.' She gave Grace a careful glance. 'Who knew that purple could be such a festive colour?' She picked up the individual snow globe that Grace had brought up to her room this morning, tipping it over so the snow swirled around in the liquid, then setting it back down on the table and watching it with a smile on her face.

'It's nice to see things changing.'

Grace was concentrating on the clothes hanging on the

rails. She'd started arranging them into colour schemes.
'He's asked me to the staff party,' she said without thinking.

'He's what?'

Darn it. She'd played right into Alice's hands.

Alice pushed herself up from the chair and stood next
to Grace. 'Finlay asked you to the party? He doesn't seem
the type to do parties,' she added.

Grace turned to face her. 'He doesn't, does he?' She
hadn't slept at all last night. The excitement of the day, the
success of the decorations, the long hours she'd worked.
The truth was she should have been exhausted and collapsed into bed. Instead, although her bones had been
weary and welcomed the comfort of her bed, her mind
had tumbled over and over.

Even though she'd been so busy, as soon as she'd stepped
inside the flat last night a wave of loneliness had swamped
her. It had been there ever since her gran had died, but
this time of year just seemed to amplify it. She'd ended
up texting Clio and asking for extra shifts. She couldn't
bear to be inside the house herself. Keeping busy was the
only thing she could think of.

She wasn't quite sure how she felt about all this. Finlay had been straight with her. He was still mourning his
wife. Christmas was hard for him. He was her boss. He'd
been angry with her. He'd almost fired her.

But he hadn't felt like her boss on the roof when she'd
been contemplating an even lonelier Christmas than she
was already facing. For a few minutes he'd felt like someone she'd connected with.

Again, when he'd held her hand and those little tingles
had shot straight up her arm.

Again, when he'd given her that look as he'd stood behind her in the shop and stared at their reflection in the
mirror.

Again, when she'd seen joy on his face as he'd seen the purple Christmas decorations.

But she was probably imagining it all.

What did she know? When was the last time she'd been on an actual date?

Wait? Was this a date?

'He asked me to go to the party,' she said out loud again. 'It's only a thank you for the decorations.'

Alice gave a brief nod. 'Is it?' she said knowingly.

Grace made a little squeak. Panic was starting to wash over her. 'It's just a thank you.'

Alice turned and walked back to her chair. 'I don't know that he's ever taken anyone else to the party—or to *a* party.'

'No one else has done Christmas decorations for him,' Grace said quickly, sliding the doors closed on the wardrobe.

She had to stop overthinking this. He'd been clear.

'He said we might not even stay long. And he said he doesn't dance. But the food will be good and there will be champagne.'

Alice's smile grew broader. 'So, if you're not staying long at the party, what *exactly* are you doing?'

Grace replied automatically. 'I guess I'll just go home.' Her hand froze midway to the rubbish bag attached to her cart. Would she just be going home? Or would Finlay expect them to go somewhere else?

'What will you be wearing?'

'Oh, no!' Grace's hand flew to her mouth. She hadn't even thought of that. Her mind had been too busy trying to work out what an invite to a party meant. Her stomach in a permanent knot wondering how *she* felt about everything.

Truth was, there was no getting away from the fact that Finlay Armstrong was possibly the best-looking guy she'd ever seen.

That voice, those muscles, and those blue, blue eyes...

She swallowed and stuffed the rubbish in the bin. She'd seen women looking at him on their shopping trip. She'd seen the glances that already said, *What is he doing with her?*

Her mind did a quick brain-raid of her wardrobe. A black dress from a high-street store. A pair of skinny black trousers and fuchsia semi-see-through shirt. A strange kind of green dress with a scattering of sequins that she'd worn four years ago to a friend's wedding.

Nothing suitable for the kind of party she imagined it would be.

'I have no idea what I'll wear,' she said as she slumped against the wall.

Alice gave her a smile and tapped the side of her nose. 'Why don't you leave it with me? I don't have all my clothes in that wardrobe and I think I might have something in storage—' she glanced Grace up and down '—that might just be perfect.'

'Really?'

Alice smiled. 'Just call me the Christmas fairy. Come and see me on the day of the party.'

Finlay wasn't quite sure what he should be doing. His inbox had three hundred emails. There was a thick pile of mail on his desk. His PA had left some contracts to be reviewed. A few of his other hotels had staffing issues over Christmas. He'd also had an interesting email from Ailsa Hillier at the Corminster, asking how things were working out with her recommended company, Maids in Chelsea.

She'd probably already heard about the Christmas decorations. Someone at The Armstrong seemed to tell their rivals all they needed to know. Just as well it was a friendly rivalry. Ailsa had lost her sister to cancer some years ago and when Anna had died she'd sent a message with her condolences and telling Finlay she would take care of The

Armstrong until he was ready to return. In the end, that had only been eight days—the amount of time it had taken to bury Anna—but he always remembered the kindness.

He picked up the phone, smiling as Ailsa answered instantly.

'I hear you've gone all purple.'

He choked out a laugh. 'It's a very nice colour.'

There was a moment's silence. 'I'm glad, Finlay. It's time.' Her voice was filled with warmth so the words didn't make him bristle. 'I might need to steal your designer though.'

Now he did sit straight in his chair. Ailsa couldn't possibly know about that, could she? He didn't give anything away. 'Your designer didn't pick purple this year?'

She sighed and he imagined she was putting her feet on the desk at this point. 'No. If they had then I could accuse you of copying. We are all white and gold this year and it already feels old. Tell me who you used and I'll poach them next year—after all, I did give you the Maids.'

He could sense she had a pen poised already. She was serious. And she didn't realise the connection. 'The Maids have worked out well, thank you. I'll ask Rob to have a look in the New Year about recruiting more permanent staff.' He leaned back in his chair. 'Or maybe I won't.' He drummed his fingers on the table as he thought. 'Some of our permanent residents seem to really like the Maids in Chelsea.'

'I think the truth is, Finlay, we get what we pay for. The Maids might cost more, but, in my experience, they are a polite, friendly, well-mannered bunch of girls. They want to do a good job and most of them seem to hide their light under a bushel. One of the girls I met yesterday has a degree in marketing, another has worked with four different aid agencies across four different continents. I like that.'

He liked that too. Hiding her light under a bushel

seemed to fit Grace perfectly. The work she'd done here was great. Maybe it was time to find out a little bit more about the woman he'd invited to the staff party?

'You still haven't given me the name of the interior designer,' Ailsa reminded him.

He smiled. 'Her name is Grace Ellis, but you can't have her, Ailsa, she's all mine.'

He put down the phone with a smile, imagining the email he'd get in response.

He stood up and walked through to the main reception; Frank was just waving off some guests. 'Frank, do you know where Grace is?'

Frank gestured off to the left. 'Back down in the basement. She's had some more ideas.'

Finlay looked around. Even though it was daytime the decorations still looked good. He could smell something too, even though he had no idea what it was. It reminded him of walking into one of those winter wonderland-type places as a child.

Grace was still working on this? He'd have to pay her overtime. And bonuses.

He walked down to the basement. It was well lit and everything stored was clearly labelled. But that didn't help when he walked into the room he heard rustling in and found Grace upended in a large storage barrel. All that was visible was black kicking shoes and a whole lot of leg.

'Grace?' He rushed over to help.

'Eek! Finlay! Help.' He tried not to laugh as he reached inside the barrel and grabbed hold of her waist, pulling her out.

'Finlay,' she gasped again as she landed in a heap on the floor. Blue. She was wearing a blue shirt today. Not as cute as the pink one. But she'd just managed to lose a button on this one so he might like it even more. Her hair must have been tied with a black satin ribbon that was now trailing over her shoulder.

He burst out laughing. And so did Grace.

She thumped her hands on the floor. 'Well, *that* wasn't supposed to happen.' She followed the line of his vision and blushed, tugging at her skirt.

He peered into the barrel. 'What was supposed to happen?'

She pointed to the label. 'As I left the hotel last night I realised that although it was gorgeous when people walked inside, there was nothing outside. Frank told me there used to be lights outside. I was looking for them.'

He frowned, trying to remember what the lights had looked like. They'd been made by some American company and had cost a fortune. 'We did have. Is this where they've been stored? What makes you think they even work any more?'

She shrugged. 'I figured it was worth a try. I can always check them first. Then I was going to try and order some purple light bulbs—you know, carry the theme outside.'

Wow. She thought of everything.

He held out his hand to help her up. 'Grace, can I ask you something?'

He pulled a little harder than he should have, catapulting Grace right forward crashing into his chest. 'Oh, sorry,' she said, placing both hands on his chest. She looked up at him. 'What is it you want to ask?'

He couldn't remember. Not for a second. All he could concentrate on were the warm palms causing heat to permeate through his shirt. Grace lifted one finger. 'Oops,' she said as she stepped back.

Finlay looked down and sucked in a breath. Two hand prints on his white shirt.

To the outside world it would look amusing. To him?

A permanent imprint that he was in a place he wasn't quite sure of.

What exactly was he doing here? He'd deliberately come down here to find Grace. There was no point in him denying it to himself. He wanted to find out more about her. But was this a betrayal of Anna? He now had another woman's hands imprinted on his chest. And for a few seconds, he'd liked the feel of them being there.

He was exasperated. Exasperated that he was drawn to this woman. Confused that he felt strangely protective of her. And intrigued by the person beneath the surface. There seemed to be so much more to Grace than met the eye. But how much did he really want to know?

Her hands were now clenched in front of her. He'd been quiet for too long.

'Finlay?'

He met her gaze. 'Are you free for lunch?'

'What?'

He glanced at his watch. 'Are you free for lunch?'

She looked down at her dishevelled clothing and pointed at his shirt. 'I don't think either of us can go anywhere like this.' He actually thought she looked fine.

He shrugged. 'I have other shirts.'

She shook her head. 'I only have what I'm wearing.' She bit her lip. 'But I think I might be able to borrow one of the bartender's black dresses.'

He gave her a nod. 'Five minutes, then?' He started to walk to the door.

'Finlay?' Her voice was quite serious.

'Yes?'

'Can I pick where we go?'

'Of course.' He was amused. He had no idea where he'd planned to take her. His brain hadn't got that far ahead.

'See you in five, then.'

* * *

Grace was trying hard not to breathe. The only female bartender she could find was a size smaller. She'd managed to do up the zip on the dress but there wasn't much room. Lunch could be an issue.

Why had he asked her to lunch? Did he want to talk more decorations? And now she was late. After he'd left she'd grabbed the end of the lights to check they worked. They did.

Then she'd phoned a rush order for purple light bulbs. They would be delivered in a few hours. She'd need to find out how the lights normally got up there. This could be a disaster if she needed scaffolding. Maybe one of those funny little cherry pickers would do the trick?

Finlay was waiting for her at the front door. She tried not to notice the obviously interested looks they were getting from other members of staff.

She pulled down her woolly black sequined hat. She'd got it in the bargain bucket at the supermarket and it was the least likely match for her designer pink coat and gloves. But it was all she could afford at the time.

He smiled at her. He'd changed his white shirt for a blue one. Her stomach gave a little somersault. Yikes, it just made those blue eyes bluer.

'Where are we going?' he asked.

'What do you like for lunch?'

She still hadn't quite worked out why they were going for lunch. She assumed he wanted to talk about the decorations some more. And that was fine. But she intended on doing it somewhere she was comfortable.

'I'm easy.' He shrugged his shoulders. 'What do you like?'

They started walking along the street. 'Are you okay with the Tube?' she asked.

'You want to go someplace else?'

She licked her lips. 'I don't normally eat around here.' It was best to be upfront. There were lots of pricey and ultra-fashionable places to eat around here. Artisan delicatessens where a sandwich generally cost three times as much as it should.

She veered off towards the steps to the underground. Finlay just kept pace with an amused expression on his face. She pulled out her card to use while he fumbled around in his pockets for some change and headed for the ticket machine. She shook her head. 'Just scan your credit card. It will just deduct the payment.'

He frowned but followed her lead. They were lucky— a train had just pulled into the station. She held onto one of the poles and turned to face him as the train started to move. 'I'll give you a choice of the best breakfast around or some fantastic stuffed croissants.'

He looked at her warily. 'What, from the same place?'

She laughed. 'No, silly. They're two different cafés. I'm just trying to decide which one we go to.'

'I had breakfast at six. Let's go for the croissants.'

She gave him a solemn nod. 'I warn you—you might get angry.'

'Why?'

She stood on her tiptoes and whispered in his ear. 'Because the coffee in this place is *miles* better than it is in the hotel.'

She could see him bristle. 'No way.'

'Way.' The train slid to a halt. 'Come and find out for yourself.'

There was almost a skip in Grace's step as she led him from the Tube station and across the road to a café much like every other one in London. But as soon as he opened the door he could smell the difference. The scent of coffee beans filled the air, along with whiffs of baking—apple tarts, sponge cakes and something with vanilla in it. If you weren't hungry before you entered this café, you'd be ravenous ten seconds after crossing the threshold. He'd need to remember that.

They sat at the table and ordered. As soon as the waitress left, Grace started playing with a strand of hair. 'I might have done something,' she said hesitantly.

'What?' he asked cautiously.

'I might have ordered some purple light bulbs. And some white ones. I figure that if we can get the lights up outside the hotel it will give people an idea of what it looks like inside.'

He gave a nod. 'I had a call from the manager of another chain of hotels today. She was asking about you.'

Grace's eyes widened. 'Asking about me?'

He nodded. 'She wanted to know the name of the designer I'd used because she'd heard how good the hotel looked.'

Grace leaned across the table towards him. 'Already? But I've only just finished.'

'I know that and you know that.' He held up his hand. 'But this is London, word travels fast.'

She shook her head. He could almost see her shrinking into herself. 'But I'm not a designer. I'm just one of the Maids in Chelsea.'

'We need to talk about that.'

'Why?'

Finlay reached into his jacket pocket and pulled out the cheque he'd written. 'I need to pay you for your services.'

Grace looked down and blinked. Then blinked again. Her face paled. 'Oh, no. You can't give me this.'

'Do you want to get Clio to bill me, then? I'm not sure why, though—this is different from the work you do for the agency.'

Her fingers were trembling. 'You can't pay me this much.'

Ah. He got it. It wasn't how he was paying her. It was how much he was paying her.

'I can increase it,' he said simply.

Her eyes widened even further. 'No.'

It almost came out as a gasp.

Ah. Now he understood.

'Grace, I based this on what we paid our last interior designer, plus inflation. That's all. As far as I'm aware, this is what I'd normally pay for these services.'

The waitress appeared and set down their plates. She'd caught the tail-end of the conversation—and glanced at the cheque under Grace's fingertips before making some kind of strangled sound.

Grace was looking distinctly uncomfortable. Finlay waved his hand and looked at the food in front of him. 'Take it, it's yours. You did a good job. You deserve it.'

He'd decided to follow Grace's lead. The croissant in front of him was stuffed with tuna and melted cheese. Salad and coleslaw were on the side and the waitress came back with steaming cups of coffee. She winked at him. 'Try the rhubarb pie after this, it's to die for.'

He almost laughed out loud. She'd seen the cheque and would expect a decent tip. He could do that.

'I think I might have to lie down after this,' he said, taking in all the food on the plate.

Grace was still watching the cheque as if it would bite her. He picked it up again and looked under the table, slid- ing it into her bag.

'Let's lunch.' He said the words in a way he hoped she'd understand. The amount wasn't open to debate. 'Where do you live?'

'What?' That snapped her out of her dreamlike state. 'Why?'

He shrugged. 'I'd like to know a bit more about the woman I'm having lunch with.'

Didn't she want to tell him where she lived?

She lifted her knife and fork. 'I live in Walthamstow,' she said quietly.

'Did you go to school around there?'

She nodded but didn't add anything further.

'How long have you worked for Maids in Chelsea?'

Her shoulders relaxed a little. That seemed a more acceptable question. 'Just for a few months.' She met his gaze, 'Truth is, it's the best job I've ever had. Clio, the boss, is lovely and the rest of the staff are like...family.'

Family. Interesting choice of word for work colleagues.

'What did you do before?'

She smiled. 'You name it—I've done it.'

He raised his eyebrows and she laughed. 'Okay, there are certain things I've never done. But I have had a few jobs.' She counted off on her fingers. 'I worked in the local library. Then in a few temp jobs in offices. I worked on the perfume counter of one of the department stores. Then I got poached to work on the make-up counter.'

'You got poached?' Somehow, he could see Grace with her flawless complexion and friendly personality being an asset to any make-up counter.

She nodded. 'But it wasn't really for me. I had to eventually give up due to some family issues and when I needed a job again Maids in Chelsea kind of found me.'

'Family issues? You have children?'

She shook her head and laughed. 'Oh, no. I'd want to find a husband first.'

He hadn't even considered the fact she might have children, or a husband! What was wrong with him? He tried to tease out a few more details. 'So, you haven't found a husband yet?'

She shook her head again. 'I haven't had time.' She looked up and met his gaze. 'I've dated casually in the last few years, but haven't really had time for a relationship.'

Due to her family issues? He didn't feel as though he could press.

'I take it you were brought up in Scotland?'

He smiled. 'What's the giveaway?'

She laughed and took a sip of her coffee. 'Is Sean Connery your father?'

'Sean Connery wouldn't have got a look-in. My mum and dad were childhood sweethearts. They lived next door to each other from the age of five.'

Grace set down her knife and fork. 'Oh, wow. That's so nice.'

It was nice. His mum and dad's marriage had always been rock solid, even when half the people he'd gone to school with seemed to have more step-parents than grades at school.

'Are they still in Scotland?'

'Always. They'll never leave.'

She gave him a fixed stare. 'Why did you leave?'

He hesitated then spoke quickly. 'Business.' There was so much more to it than that. He had a home—a castle— in Scotland that had been his pride and joy. He hadn't set foot in it for over a year. The penthouse in The Armstrong was where he now called home. He needed to change the subject—fast.

'Tell me about the Christmas stuff?'

She quickly swallowed a mouthful of food. 'What do you mean?'

He sipped his coffee. Then stopped and connected with her gaze. 'Wow.'

A smile spread across her face. 'I told you.'

He kept his nose above the coffee and breathed in the aroma, then took another sip. The coffee was different from most of the roasts he'd tasted. Finlay was a self-confessed snob when it came to coffee. This was good.

He looked over his shoulder to where the coffee machine and barista were standing. 'I have to find out what this is.'

She was still smiling. 'You'll be lucky if they tell you. The coffee in here has been this good for years. My gran and I used to come here all the time.'

Her voice quietened. He wanted to ask some more but it felt like prying. Could he really go there?

He went back to safer territory. 'The Christmas stuff. You seem to really enjoy it.'

She gave him a careful stare. Her voice was soft. 'I do. I've always loved Christmas. It's my favourite time of year.' She stretched her fingers across the table and brushed them against his hand. 'I'm sorry, I know you said you didn't like it.'

He took a deep breath. The coffee was excellent in here. The food was surprisingly good. And the company...the company was intriguing.

Grace was polite, well-mannered and good at her job. She was also excellent at the unexpected job he'd flung on her the other day. She'd more than delivered.

It was more than a little distracting that she was also incredibly beautiful. But it was an understated beauty. Shiny hair and a pair of deep dark brown eyes that could hide a million secrets. But it wasn't the secrets that intrigued him. It was the sincerity.

Grace didn't feel like the kind of person who would tell lies. She seemed inherently good. All the staff at the hotel liked her. Frank was strangely protective of her.

He took a deep breath. 'It's not that I don't like it. I know I said that—'

She touched his hand again. 'No, you said you hated it.'

He nodded. 'Okay, I said I hated it. And I have. For the last five years. But I didn't always hate it. I had great Christmases as a kid. My sister and I always enjoyed Christmas with our mum and dad.'

Grace pressed her lips together. 'I've spent all my Christmases with my gran. My mum...' She paused as she searched for the words, 'My mum had me when she was very young. My dad was never on the scene. I was brought up by my gran.'

'Your mum wasn't around?'

Grace shook her head. 'Not much. She's married now—lives in Australia—and has a new family. I have two half-brothers.' Her gaze was fixated on her plate of food. 'She's very happy.'

'Do you talk?'

Grace looked up. 'Yes. Of course. Just...not much. We have a relationship of sorts.'

'What does that mean?'

Grace sighed and gave a shrug. 'I'm a twenty-eight-year-old woman. There's not much point in holding a grudge against someone who couldn't cope with a baby as a teenager. I had a good life with my gran. And we had the best Christmases together.'

He got the feeling she was taking the conversation away from her family circumstances and back onto Christmas.

'Is that where your love of Christmas came from?'

She smiled again and got a little sparkle in her eyes. 'Gran and I used to watch lots of black and white films, and we especially loved the Christmas-themed ones. We had a whole load of handmade ornaments. Spray-painted pine cones were our favourites. We did a lot of Christmas baking. We couldn't afford a real tree every year but we always had a holly wreath and I loved the smell.' There was something in her voice. Something in the tone. These were all happy memories—loving memories. But he could hear the wistfulness as she spoke.

He'd told her the biggest event in his life. It didn't matter that he'd blurted it out in anger with a whole host of other things. Grace knew probably the most important thing about him.

Him? He knew very little about her. It was like peeling back a layer at a time. And the further he peeled back the layers, the more he liked her.

She looked out of the window. 'I love Christmas—especially when it snows. It makes it just a little more magical. I love when night falls and you can look out across the dark city and see snow-covered roofs. I always automatically want to watch the sky to see if I can spot Santa's sleigh.'

'Aren't you a little old for Santa?' Her eyes were sparkling. She really did love the magic of Christmas. The thing that for the last five years he'd well and truly lost.

It made him realise how sad he'd been. How much he'd isolated himself. Sure, plenty of people didn't like Christmas. Lots of people around the world didn't celebrate it.

But, when it had been a part of your life for so long, and then something had destroyed it, the reminder of what it could be circulated around his mind.

She set down her knife and fork. 'Finlay Armstrong, are you telling me there's no Santa?' She said it in such a warm, friendly voice that it pulled him back from his thoughts without any regrets.

He pushed his plate away. 'Grace Ellis, I would *never* say something like that.'

She wagged her finger at him as her phone beeped. 'Just as well. In that case I won't need to tell you off.' She glanced at her phone. 'Oh, great, the light bulbs have arrived.' She reached around for her pink coat and woolly hat. Her eyes were shining again. 'Come on, Finlay. Let's light up The Armstrong!'

How on earth could he say no?

CHAPTER FIVE

'I HAVE THE perfect dress for you.' Mrs Archer clapped her hands together. 'You'll love it!'

'What?' Grace was stunned out of her reverie. She'd spent the last few days in a fog. A fog named Finlay Armstrong.

He'd managed to commandeer staff from every department and they'd spent two hours—Finlay included—replacing the light bulbs on the external display. Five specially phoned-in maintenance men had hung the purple and white strips down either side of the exterior of The Armstrong.

As they'd stood together on the opposite side of the street to get a better look, Finlay had given her a nudge. 'It does look good, Grace. You were right.' He took a deep breath. 'Thank you.'

The closed-off man who apparently had a reputation as a recluse was coming out of his shell. Except Finlay hadn't been in a shell. Grace got the impression he'd been in a dark cave where the only thing he'd let penetrate was work.

He was smiling more. His shoulders didn't seem quite so tense. Since their first meeting he'd never shouted, never been impolite. Only for the briefest second did she see something cloud his eyes before it was pushed away again. Even Frank had commented on the changes in the last few days.

She nudged Finlay back. 'Just wait until next year. I'll pick a whole new colour scheme and bankrupt you in light bulbs!' She'd been so happy, so excited that things had worked out she'd actually winked at him.

Winked. All she could do right now was cringe.

But the wink hadn't scared him off. Every time she'd turned around in the last two days, Finlay had been there—asking her about something, talking to her about other pieces of interior design work she might be interested in. Getting her to sit down and chat.

They'd had another lunch together. Around four coffees. And a makeshift dinner—a Chinese take-away in the office one night.

She'd even found herself telling him about the Elizabethan-style chairs she'd found in a junk shop and spent weeks re-covering and re-staining on her own.

Last night she hadn't slept a wink. Her brain had been trying to work out what on earth was going on between them. Was she reading this all wrong? Had it really been *that* long since she'd dated that she couldn't work out the signals any more?

'Ta-da!'

Mrs Archer brought her back to the present day by swinging open a cupboard door and revealing what lay behind it.

Wow.

It glimmered in the early-morning winter light. A full-length silver evening gown in heavy-duty satin with a bodice and wide straps glittering with sequins. Around the top of the coat hanger was a fur wrap. She was almost scared to touch it.

'Don't worry,' said Alice Archer. 'It's not real fur. But it probably cost ten times as much as it should.'

Grace's heart was pounding in her chest. She'd forgotten Alice had offered to find her something for the party.

When Finlay had given her that exorbitant cheque the other day she'd almost squealed. Bills had been difficult since her grandmother had died.

Her grandmother and late grandfather had had small pensions that had contributed to the upkeep of the flat. Keeping up with bills was tough on her own. There was no room for any extras—any party dresses. She'd actually planned on going to some of the charity shops around Chelsea later to see if she could find anything to wear tonight.

'It's just beautiful,' she finally said. Her hand touched the satin. She'd never felt anything like it in her life.

'The colour will suit you marvellously.' Alice smiled. 'I had it in my head as soon as you told me about the party.'

'When did you wear this, Alice? It's just stunning.'

Alice whispered in her ear. 'Don't tell Finlay Armstrong, but I wore it at a New Year ball in The Ritz the year my Robin proposed to me.'

Grace pulled back her hand. 'Oh, Alice, I can't wear your beautiful dress. It has such special memories for you—and it's immaculate. I would be terrified about something happening to it.'

Alice shook her head. 'Nonsense, I insist.' She ran her fingers down the fabric of the dress with a far-off expression in her eyes. 'I always think that clothes are for wearing. I think of this as my lucky dress.' She gave Grace a special smile. 'And I'm hoping it will bring you some luck too.'

Grace stared in the mirror. Someone else was staring back at her. Whoever it was—it wasn't Grace Ellis. Ashleigh had come around and set her hair in curls. Sophie had helped her apply film-star make-up. She'd never worn liquid eyeliner before and wasn't quite sure how Sophie had managed to do the little upward flicks.

Around her neck she was wearing the silver locket her

grandmother had bought her for her twenty-first birthday and Emma had loaned her a pair of glittery earrings.

They were probably diamonds. But Emma hadn't told her that. She'd just squealed with excitement when she'd seen Grace all dressed up and said she had the perfect thing to finish it off.

And she'd been right. Right now, Grace Ellis felt like a princess. It didn't matter that the only items she was wearing that actually belonged to her were her locket, her underwear and her shoes.

The party was being held in one of the smaller main rooms in the hotel. The music was already playing and she could see coloured flashing lights. Her heart started beating in tempo with the music. Her hands were sweating. She was nervous.

But it seemed she wasn't the only one.

Finlay was pacing up and down outside the room. She couldn't help but smile. Just that one sight instantly made her feel better. Although the girls had helped her get ready they'd also plied her with questions.

'What's going on with you and Finlay Armstrong?'

'Is this a date?'

'Are you interested in him?'

'Do you want to date him?'

By the time they'd left her head had been spinning. She didn't know the answer to the first two questions. But the last two? She didn't want to answer them. Not out loud, anyway.

'Grace. You're here.' Finlay covered the distance between them in long strides, slowing as he reached her. At first he'd only focused on her face, but as he'd neared his gaze had swept up and down her body. He seemed to catch his breath. 'You look incredible.'

'You seem surprised.'

He shook his head. 'Of course I'm not surprised. You

always look beautiful. But…' He paused and gestured with his hand. 'The dress and—' He reached out to touch the stole. 'What is this thing anyway? You look like a film star. Should I phone the press?'

He leaned closer, giving her a whiff of his spicy after-shave. She tried not to shiver. He tilted his head to the side. 'What have you done to your eyes?'

She touched his jacket sleeve. 'It's called make-up, Finlay. Women wear it every day.' She made a point of looking him up and down too. The suit probably cost more than she even wanted to think about. But it was immaculate, cut to perfection. 'You don't look so bad yourself.'

His gaze fixed on hers. 'Grace?'

'Yes?'

'Thank you for saying you'd come with me.' The tone of his voice had changed. He wasn't being playful now, he was being serious. 'You know I haven't come to one of these in the last few years.'

She licked her lips and nodded, trying not to let her brain get carried away with itself. 'Why have you come this year?' she asked softly.

She was tiptoeing around about him—trying not to admit to the rapidly beating heart in her chest. She liked this man a whole lot more than she should. She didn't even know what this was between them. But Finlay was giving her little signs of…something. Did he even realise that? Or was this all just in her imagination?

'It was just time,' he said, giving his head a little nod.

Her heart jumped up to the back of her throat. Time.

Just as it had been time to think about Christmas decorations. What else might it be time for?

The serious expression left his face and he stuck out his elbow towards her. 'Well, Ms Ellis, are you ready to go to The Armstrong's Christmas party?'

She slid her hand through his arm as all the little hairs on her arm stood on end. 'I think I could be. Lead the way.'

The party was fabulous. She recognised lots of faces. Other chambermaids, bar staff, porters, reception staff and kitchen staff. Frank the concierge had dressed as Father Christmas and looked perfect.

There was a huge table laid with appetisers and sweets. A chocolate fountain, a pick-and-mix sweetie cart and the equivalent of an outside street cart serving burgers.

Finlay nudged her. 'What? Did you think it would all be truffles and hors d'oeuvres?'

She gave him a smile. 'I wasn't sure.'

He shrugged. 'The first year it was. Frank discreetly told me later that the staff went home hungry. After that, I gave Kevin, from the kitchen, free rein to organise whatever he thought appropriate for the Christmas party. I don't think anyone has gone home hungry since.'

She laughed as he led her over to the bar. 'Which of the Christmas cocktails would you like?' he asked.

She was surprised. 'You have Christmas cocktails?'

'Oh, yes. We have the chocolate raspberry martini, the Festive Shot, with peppermint schnapps, grenadine and crème de menthe, then there is the Christmas Candy Cane, with berry vodka, peppermint schnapps and crème de cacao—or, my personal favourite, Rudolph's Blast: rum, cranberries, peach schnapps and a squeeze of fresh lime.'

Grace shook her head and leaned her elbows up on the bar. 'You know what's in every cocktail?'

He gestured to the barman. 'We'll have two Rudolph's Blasts, please.'

He leaned on the bar next to her and leaned his head on one hand. 'Okay, that dress. You kind of caught me by surprise. Where did you get it?'

She waved her hand. 'Did you expect me to come in uniform?'

He hadn't taken his eyes off her and the smile on his face—well, it wasn't just friendly. It seemed...interested. 'Of course I didn't. But you look like something the Christmas fairy pulled off the tree.'

Her eyes narrowed and she mirrored his position, leaning her head on one hand and staring straight back. 'And is that good—or bad?'

He didn't answer right away, and the barman set their cocktails down in front of them.

She leaned forward and took a sip of the cocktail. She licked her lips again as the mixture of rum and fruit warmed her mouth. He was focused on her mouth.

And she knew it.

She ran her tongue along her lips again then bit the edge of her straw.

'I only have the dress on loan,' she said quietly. 'And I've promised to take very good care of it.'

He leaned a little closer, obviously trying to hear her above the music playing around them. Had she lowered her voice deliberately? Maybe.

As he moved a little closer she was still focused on those blue eyes. Only they weren't as blue as normal. In the dim lights his pupils had dilated so much there was only a thin rim of blue around them. Was it the light? Or was it her?

'Who gave you the loan of the dress?'

'A good friend.'

'A designer?'

Ah...he was worried she'd been loaned the dress by a male designer. She could tell by his tone. She took another sip of her cocktail. It was strong. But it was warming lots of places all around her body. 'Someone much closer to home.'

His brow furrowed. She was playing games with him.

His hand reached over and rested on her arm. 'Someone I know?'

She smiled. 'Someone you respect. Someone I respect.' Grace lifted her hand and placed it on her chest. 'I'm told it's lucky. Her husband proposed to her when she was wearing this dress.'

Something flitted across his eyes. It was the briefest of seconds but it made her cringe a little inside. That might have come out a little awkwardly. She wasn't dropping hints. She absolutely wasn't.

Then, it was almost as if the pieces fell into place. 'Alice Archer?' His voice was louder and the edges of his mouth turned upwards in a wide smile as he shook his head in disbelief, looking Grace up and down—again.

She was getting used to this.

'This was Alice Archer's dress?'

She nodded. 'This *is* Alice Archer's dress. She offered to give me something to wear a few days ago when she heard I was coming to the party.' Grace ran her palm across the smooth satin. Just the barest touch let her know the quality of the fabric. 'I had forgotten. When I walked in this morning she had it hanging up waiting for me.'

He moved closer again, his shoulder brushing against hers as he lifted his cocktail from the bar. 'Well, I think it's a beautiful dress. I have no idea how old it is, but it looks brand new.'

Her heart gave a little soar. The dress was definitely a hit. She'd need to buy Alice a thank-you present. A Christmas song started playing behind them, causing the rest of the people in the room to let out a loud cheer. The dance floor filled quickly. Grace sipped her drink.

'Do you want to dance?'

She shook her head. 'Not to this. I prefer to spectate when it's something wild. I prefer slow dances.'

She hadn't meant it quite to come out like that, but as her gaze connected with those blue eyes the expression on his face made her suck in a breath.

She could practically feel the chemistry between them sparkling. She wasn't imagining this. She just wasn't.

It wasn't possible for the buzz she felt every time he looked at her, or touched her, not to be real.

'I'll take you up on that,' he said hoarsely, before turning back to the barman. 'Can we have some more cocktails?'

His senses were on overload. Her floral scent was drifting around him, entwining him like a coiling snake. His fingertips tingled where they'd touched her silky skin. The throaty whisper of her voice had sent blood rushing through his body as if he were doing a marathon. His eyes didn't know whether to watch the smoky eyes, the tongue running along her succulent lips, the shimmer of the silver satin against her curves or the way her curls tumbled around the pale skin at her neck. As for taste? He could only imagine...

What was more, no matter how hard he tried, he couldn't shut his senses down.

It wasn't as if he hadn't spent time with women since Anna had died. On a few occasions, he had. But those encounters had been courteous, brief and for one purpose only.

There had been no attachment. No emotional involvement.

But with Grace? Things felt entirely different.

He wanted to see her. He wanted to be around her. He was interested in her, and what she thought. He didn't want to see her a few times and just dismiss her from his life.

It had been twelve years since he'd really dated. One date with Anna had been enough to know he didn't need to look any further. And right now, with his stomach tipping upside down, he wasn't sure he knew what to do any more.

Oh, he knew what to *do*.

He just couldn't picture doing it with emotions attached.

All of those memories and sensations belonged to Anna. He knocked back the last of the cocktail and lifted the Festive Shots that had appeared on the bar. He blinked, then tipped his back and finished it before turning to Grace.

Wow. Nope, nothing had changed in that millisecond. She was still here with her tumbling curls, sensational figure and eyes that looked as if they see down into his very soul.

She gave him a suspicious look as she eyed the shot glass. 'Who are you trying to get drunk, you, or me?'

He signalled to the barman again, who replaced his shot. He held it up and clinked it against her glass. 'This is only my third drink and it's only your second. Somehow, I think we can cope.'

She clinked her glass against his, then tipped back her head and downed her shot too. It must have hit the back of her throat because she laughed and burst out coughing. He laughed too and gave her back a gentle slap. 'It hits hard, doesn't it?'

She nodded as her eyes gleamed a little with water. 'Oh, wow.' She coughed again. 'Festive? More like dynamite.'

The music slowed and she glanced over her shoulder. 'Something you like?'

She tipped her head to the side as if she were contemplating the music. 'Actually, I really love this song.'

He didn't think. He didn't hesitate. He held his hand straight out to hers as Wham's Last Christmas filled the room. 'Then let's dance.'

She slid her hand into his. Her fingers starting at the tips of his, running along the palm of his hand and finishing as her fingers fastened around his wrist. His hand slid around her waist, skimming the material of the dress as they walked across the dance floor. He gave a nod to a few members of staff who nodded in their direction.

They were attracting more than their fair share of attention. He should have known this would happen. But the truth was, he didn't really care. This wasn't about anyone other than them.

Grace spun around as she reached the middle of the dance floor. Her hesitation only showed for a second before she slid her hands up around his neck.

It wasn't exactly an unusual position. This was a Christmas slow dance. All around them people were in a similar stance. If they'd stayed apart it would have looked more noticeable.

He kept his hands at her waist as they moved slowly in time with the music. Grace was already singing along with her eyes half closed. 'Hey, isn't this a little before your time?'

Her eyes opened wider. 'Of course. But I don't care. I just love it. I loved the video even more. I watched it a hundred times as a teenager.'

Finlay wracked his brains trying to remember the video. For the first time he actually heard the words to the familiar tune. 'You like this? Isn't this the video where the girl dumped him and came back the next year with someone else?'

She threw back her head and laughed, giving him a delightful view of the pale skin at the bottom of her throat. His teeth automatically ground into his bottom lip. He knew exactly where he wanted his lips to be right now.

'Yes, that's the story. But I liked the snow in the video. It looked romantic. And I like the tune.'

Her body was brushing against his as she moved in time to the music. He pulled her a little closer as he bent to whisper in her ear. 'I can't believe this is your favourite Christmas song.'

She stepped back a little, grabbing his hand and twirling underneath it, sending the bottom of her silver dress spinning out around her, with the coloured lights from the disco catching the silver sequins on her bodice and sending sparkles around the room.

Her eyes were sparkling too, her curls bouncing around her shoulders. Grace was like her own Christmas decoration. When she finished spinning her hands rested on his chest.

He almost held his breath. Would she feel the beat of his heart under her fingertips? What would she make of the irregular pattern that was currently playing havoc with any of his brain processes—that must be the reason he couldn't think a single sane thought right now?

She finished swaying as his hands went naturally back to her hips. He could see a few staff members in the corner of the room looking at them and whispering. He might be the boss, but Grace worked with these people. She did a good job. She brought a little life into the hotel. She deserved their respect. He didn't want to do anything to ruin that.

As the music came to an end he grabbed hold of her hand and pulled her towards the exit. All of a sudden the room felt claustrophobic. There were too many eyes. Too many whispers. He didn't want to share Grace with all these people.

He wanted her to himself.

'Hey, Finlay—what's wrong?'

He leaned into the coat check and grabbed her stole, leaving some cash as a tip. He could hear Grace's feet scurrying behind him as he lengthened his stride to reach the exit as quickly as possible.

They burst outside into the cold night air. He spun around and put the stole around her shoulders. She was breathing heavily; he could see the rise and fall of her chest in the pale yellow light of the lamp post above them. 'What are you doing?' Her voice was high. She sounded stressed.

He took a deep breath. He had no idea what he was doing. But could he really admit that?

He reached out and touched her cheek—just as he had on the roof that night.

'I needed to get out of there.'

He kept his finger against her cheek. It was the slightest touch of her skin. The tiniest piece beneath his fingertip. But it was enough. Enough to set every alarm bell screaming in his brain. Enough to let his senses just explode with overload.

He was past the point of no return.

Grace reached up and captured her hand around his finger, leaving it touching her cheek. 'Why, Finlay? Why did you need to get out of there?'

He could hear the concern in her voice. She didn't have a clue. She thought this might be about something else. She didn't realise that every tiny part of this was about her.

Guilt was racing through his veins in parallel to the adrenaline. Feeling. He was feeling again. And the truth was that scared him.

Guys would never admit that. Not to their friends. Not even to themselves. But most guys hadn't loved someone with every part of their heart, soul and being and had it ripped out of them and every feeling and emotion buried in a brittle, cold grave.

Most guys wouldn't know that they didn't think it could be possible to ever get through that once. Why would they even contemplate making any kind of connection with another person when there was even the smallest possibility they could end up going down the same path?

Once had felt barely survivable. He couldn't connect with someone like that again. How could he risk himself like that again?

Where was his self-preservation? The barriers that he'd

built so tightly around himself to seal his soul off from that kind of hurt again.

Somehow being around Grace had thrown his sense of self-preservation out of the window. All he could think about right now was how much he wanted to touch and taste the beautiful woman in front of him.

She was still watching him with those questioning brown eyes. She was bathed in the muted lamplight— her silver dress sparkling—like an old-fashioned film star caught in the spotlight.

He stopped thinking. 'Because I couldn't wait to do this.'

He pulled her sharply towards him, folding his arm around her waist and pulling her tightly against the length of his body. He stopped for a second, watching her wide eyes, giving her the briefest of pauses to voice any objections. But there were none.

He captured her mouth in his. She tasted of cocktails and chocolate. Sweet. Just the way he'd imagined she would. One hand threaded through her tumbling curls and the other rested on the satin-covered curve of her backside. He'd captured his prize. He wasn't about to let her go.

After two seconds the tension left her body, melding it against his. Her hands wound their way around his neck again, her lips responding to every part of the kiss, matching him in every way.

This was what a connection felt like. He hadn't kissed a woman like this since Anna died. This was what it felt like to kiss a woman you liked and respected. It had been so long he hadn't even contemplated how many emotions that might toss into the cold night air.

Her hand brushed the side of his cheek, running along his jaw line. He could hear the tiny scrape of his emerging stubble against her fingernails. The other hand ran through his hair and then down to his chest again. He liked the feel of her palm there. If only it weren't thwarted by the suit jacket and shirt.

Their kiss deepened. His body responded. He knew. He knew where this could potentially go.

Grace pulled her lips from his. It was a reluctant move, followed by a long sigh. Her forehead rested against his as if she were trying to catch her breath. He could feel her breasts pressed against his chest.

His hand remained tangled in her soft hair and for a few moments they just stood like that, heads pressed together under the street light.

He eventually straightened up. Should he apologise? It didn't feel as if the kiss was unwanted. But they were right in the middle of the street—hardly the most discreet place in the world for a first kiss. He could ask her up to the penthouse but somehow that didn't feel right either—and he was quite sure Grace wouldn't agree to come anyway.

'Thank you for coming tonight,' he said quietly.

Her voice was a little shaky. 'You're welcome.'

He took a step back. 'How about I get one of the chauffeurs to drop you home?'

He had no idea what time it was—but whatever time it was, he didn't want her travelling home alone. He trusted all the chauffeurs from The Armstrong. Grace would be in safe hands.

She gave a little nod. 'That would be nice, thank you.' This time her voice sounded a little odd. A little detached. Had she rethought their kiss and changed her mind?

He put his arm behind her and led her back to the main entrance of the hotel, nodding to one of the doormen. 'Callum, can you get one of the chauffeurs to take Grace home?'

She shivered and pulled the stole a little closer around her shoulders. 'Do you want me to get you another coat?'

She shook her head, not quite meeting his gaze. 'I'll be fine when I get in the car. That'll be warm enough.'

For a couple of minutes they stood in awkward silence. Finlay wasn't quite sure what to do next. He wasn't quite sure *what* he wanted to do next. And he couldn't read Grace at all.

The sleek black car pulled up in front of them and the driver jumped out to open the door. Grace turned to face him with her head held high. 'Thank you for a lovely evening, Finlay,' she said as she climbed into the car.

'You too,' he replied automatically as he closed the door, and watched the car speed off into the distance.

One thing was for sure. Finlay Armstrong wouldn't sleep a wink tonight.

CHAPTER SIX

SHE COULDN'T DESCRIBE the emptiness inside her. It was impossible to put into words.

She stared at the texts on the phone from her friends, teasing her about the party and assuming she'd had the time of her life.

She had—almost.

But last night when she'd opened the door to the cold and empty flat, everything had just overwhelmed her.

Silence echoed around her.

Unbearable silence.

The home that had once been filled with love and happiness shivered around her.

She actually felt it happen.

Even when she flicked the light switch, the house was dark. Emptiness swamped every room. She'd started to cry even before she'd made it to bed, wrapping herself in her gran's shawl, her own duvet and wearing the thickest pair of flannel pyjamas imaginable—but nothing could keep out the cold. Nothing at all.

That feeling of loneliness was enormous. Somewhere, on the other side of the planet, her mother was probably cuddled up to her husband or sitting around a table with her two children. Children she actually spent time with.

It wasn't that she didn't understand. Getting pregnant at sixteen would be difficult for any teenager. But to move away completely and form a new life—without any thought to the old—was hard to take.

It made her more determined. More determined to never feel second best with any man. She'd spent her whole life feeling second best and a cast-off. Although her relationship with her gran had been strong and wonderful, there had still been that underlying feeling of…just not being enough.

For the briefest spell tonight, under that lamp post, she'd felt a tiny bit like that again. All because of that kiss. Oh, the kiss had been wonderful—mesmerising. The attraction was definitely there. But the connection, or the sincerity of the connection? She just couldn't be sure if when Finlay kissed her he was thinking only of her.

She shivered all night. The heating was on in the flat and it didn't matter how high the temperature was —it just couldn't permeate her soul.

The night with Finlay had brought things to a precipice in her head.

Alone. That was how she felt right now.

Completely and utterly alone.

She'd thought being busy at Christmas would help. She'd thought decorating the flat the way it always used to be would help.

But the truth was nothing helped. Nothing filled the aching hole that her grandmother's death had left.

A card had arrived from her mother. The irony killed her. It was a personalised card with a photo of her mum with her new husband, Ken, and their two sons on the front. They were suitably dressed for a Christmas in Florida. It wasn't meant to be a message. But it felt like it.

Her mother had moved on—playing happy families on another continent. She'd found her happy ever after. And it didn't include Grace. It never had.

She received the same store gift card each year. Impersonal. Polite. The sort of gift you sent a colleague you didn't know that well—not the sort of gift you sent your daughter.

As she rode the Tube this morning people seemed to be full of Christmas spirit. It was Christmas Eve. Normally she would be full of Christmas spirit too.

But the sight of happy children bouncing on their parents' knees, couples with arms snaked around each other and stealing kisses, only seemed to magnify the effect of being alone.

Tonight, she'd go home to that dark flat.

Tonight, she'd spend Christmas Eve on her own. There was no way she could speak to any of the girls. They were all too busy wrapped up in their own lives, finding their own dreams, for Grace to bring them down with her depressed state.

The train pulled into the station and she trudged up the stairs to work.

This time last year her stomach had been fluttering with the excitement she normally felt at Christmas. Christmas Eve was such a special day.

It was for love, for families, for sharing, for fun and for laughter. Tomorrow, she would probably spend the whole day without speaking to a single person. Tomorrow, she would cook a dinner for one.

She'd pushed away every single thought about how she might spend Christmas Day. It had been easier not to think about it at all. That way she could try and let herself be swept along with the spirit of Christmas without allowing the dark cloud hanging above her head to press down on her.

But now, it seemed to have rushed up out of nowhere. It was here and the thought of being alone was just too much.

She pulled her phone out of her pocket and dialled. 'Clio? Are there any shifts tomorrow?'

She could almost hear the cogs whirring in Clio's brain at the end of the phone. 'Grace? What's wrong?'

Grace sucked in a deep breath to try and stop her voice from wobbling. She couldn't stop the tears that automatically pooled in her eyes. 'It's just the time of year...it's hard,' she managed.

'Your gran. You're missing her. I get it. But do you really want to spend Christmas Day working?' The compassion in Clio's voice made her feel one hundred times worse.

'Yes.'

There was a shuffle of papers. 'You can work at The Armstrong as normal. There are always lots of shifts at Christmas. I can put you on for that one.'

'Great, thanks.' The words came out easier this time; it was almost as if a security blanket had been flung over her shoulders. 'And, Clio? Congratulations on your engagement. Enjoy your time with Enrique.'

She hung up the phone and sighed. She meant it. She really did. Clio was over the moon with her new relationship and she deserved to be happy.

She changed quickly and started work. The Christmas themed music that she'd chosen was playing quietly in the background *everywhere*.

Other members of staff were smiling and whistling. No one was rushing today. The whole work tempo seemed to have slowed down for the festive season. And Grace noticed a few sideways glances from people who'd attended the staff party.

Her list was long. Lots of people had the day off. But Grace didn't care; it would keep her busy and give her less time to think.

It was surprising the amount of guests who checked in and out around Christmas. Something panged inside her again. People coming to visit families and friends.

Eight hours later her hair was back to its semi-normal

dishevelled state and she really wanted to get changed. One of the staff called her over. 'Can you do one more before you knock off tonight? I'm in a bit of a rush.'

Grace pressed her lips together. She knew Sally had four kids and would want to get home to them early. She held out her hand. 'Of course I will. No problem.'

Sally gave her a hug. 'Thanks, Grace. Have a great Christmas.'

Grace glanced at the list and her stomach did a little flip-flop. She had The Nottingdale Suite to clean—Finlay's place. She glanced towards the office. He'd be in there right now. If she was quick—she could get things done and get back out before he knew she was working.

It was a weird feeling. When he'd held her in his arms last night she'd felt…she'd felt…special. A tiny little fire that had been burning inside her for the last few days had just ignited like a firework—only to sputter out again.

The Nottingdale Suite didn't feel quite so empty as before. One of her Christmas snow globes was sitting on the main table, with a wrapped parcel on the slate kitchen worktop.

Grace couldn't help but pick it up. It was intricately wrapped in silver paper with curled red ribbon and a tag. The writing was copperplate. Grace smiled. She recognised it immediately and set it down with a smile. Mrs Archer had left a present for Finlay. How nice.

She made short work of cleaning the penthouse. The bathroom, kitchen area, bedroom and lounge were spotless in under an hour.

She stared out for a second over the dark London sky. In a few hours Christmas Eve would be over. By the time she got home, she could go straight to bed then get up early for her next shift. She squeezed her eyes closed for a second.

Please just let this Christmas be over.

* * *

'Grace?' She was the last person he expected to see at this time of night. 'What are you doing?'

The words were out before he even noticed the cart next to the doorway.

She jumped and turned around. 'Finlay.' The words just seemed to stop there.

She was wearing her uniform again. But in his head she still had on the silver dress from the last night. That picture seemed to be imprinted on his brain. Seared on it, in fact.

She still hadn't spoken. The atmosphere was awkward. He wasn't quite sure how to act around Grace.

That kiss last night had killed any ounce of sleep he might have hoped to get.

His brain couldn't process it at all. There was no box to put it in.

It wasn't a fleeting moment with someone unimportant. It hadn't been a mistake. It wasn't a wild fling. It hadn't felt casual. So, what did that leave?

Grace's eyes left his and glanced at the outside view again—exactly where she'd been staring when he came in. He heard a stilted kind of sigh. She moved over towards the cart.

This wasn't going to get any easier. Neither of them seemed able to do the casual and friendly hello.

He had a freak brainwave. This was Christmas Eve. Grace was the woman that loved Christmas. No—she lived and breathed Christmas. What on earth was she doing still working?

Grace picked up some of the cleaning materials and shoved them back in her cart. 'Merry Christmas, Finlay.' The words were stilted. Was this how things would be now?

'Merry Christmas, Grace.' His response was automatic. But something else wasn't.

The feelings that normally washed around a response like that. Normally they were cold. Harsh. Unfeeling and unmeant.

This was the first time in five years he'd actually meant those words as he said them.

He wanted Grace to have a merry Christmas. He wanted her to enjoy herself.

What if...?

The idea came out of nowhere. At least, that was how it seemed. He was flying back to Scotland on Boxing Day to see his family. Chances were, this would be the last time he would see Grace between now and then.

There were a dozen little flashes in his brain. Grace on the roof. Touching the tear that had rolled down her cheek. Drinking hot chocolate with her. The gleam in her eyes when she was cheeky to him. The expression on her face when she'd tried on the pink coat. The wash of emotions when he'd spotted the little girl and bought the rocking horse for her Christmas. Grace's ruffled hair and pushed-up shirt as she'd wound in hundreds of purple bulbs. The way she'd clapped her hands together when he'd first seen the tree.

And the feel of her lips on his. Her warm curves against his. The soft satin of her dress under the palm of his hand.

He'd felt more alive in the last week than he had in the last five years.

And that was all because of Grace.

He reached out to touch her arm. 'It's been nice to meet you. Enjoy Christmas Day.'

The words were nowhere near adequate. They didn't even begin to cover what he wanted to say or what was circulating in his brain.

Grace's dark brown eyes met his. For a second he thought she was going to say the same thing. Then, her bottom lip started to tremble and tears welled in her eyes. 'I'll be working as normal.'

He blinked. What?

Why would the girl who loved Christmas not be spending it with her family and friends?

'What do you mean—you're working? Don't you have plans with those you love?'

As soon as the words were out he realised he'd said exactly the wrong thing. The tears that had pooled in her eyes flooded over and rolled down her cheeks.

He reached out his arms to her. 'What on earth's wrong? Grace? Tell me?'

She was shaking and when the words came out it was the last thing he expected.

'There's no family. My gran…she died…she died a few months ago. And now, there's just no one. I can't face anything.' She looked at him, her gaze almost pleading. 'I thought I could do this. I thought I could. I thought if I kept busy and kept working everything would just fall into place. I wouldn't have time to miss her so much.' She kept shaking her head. 'But it's harder than I could ever imagine. Everywhere I go, everywhere I look, I see people—families together, celebrating Christmas the way I used to. Even Mrs Archer—I love her—but I'm finding it so hard to be around her. She reminds me so much of my gran. The way she speaks, her mannerisms, her expressions.' She looked down as she kept shaking her head. 'I just want this to be over.' Now, she looked outside again into the dark night. In the distance they could see the Christmas red and white lights outlining Battersea Power Station. 'I just want Christmas to be over,' she breathed.

Every hair on his arms stood on end. He got it. He got all of it.

The loneliness. The happy people around about, reminding you of what you'd lost. The overwhelming emotions that took your breath away when you least expected it.

He put his hands on her shoulders. 'Grace, you don't need to be here. You don't need to work at Christmas. It's fine. We can cover your shifts. Take some time off. Get away from this. The last thing you want to do is watch other families eating Christmas dinner together. Stay home. Curl up in bed. Eat chocolate.'

It seemed like the right thing to say. Comfort. Away from people under her nose.

But Grace's eyes widened and she pulled back. 'What? No. You think I want to be alone? You think I want to spend the whole of Christmas without talking to anyone, without seeing another living soul? Do you think anything looks worse on a plate than Christmas dinner for one?'

As she spoke he cringed. What he'd thought might take her away from one type of agony would only lead her to another. He hated this. He hated seeing the pain in her eyes. The hurt. The loneliness. He recognised them all too well. He'd worn the T-shirt himself for five years.

He squeezed her shoulders. 'Then what is it you want for Christmas, Grace? What is it you want to do? What would be your perfect Christmas?'

His agitation was rising. She'd got herself so worked up that her whole body was shaking. He hated that. He hated she was so upset. Why hadn't he realised she was alone? Why hadn't he realised she was suffering a bereavement just as he was?

Grace had always been so upbeat around him, so full of life that he'd missed the signs. He knew better than most that you only revealed the side of you that you wanted people to see.

He'd been struck by Grace's apparent openness. But she'd built the same guard around her heart as he had. It didn't matter that it was different circumstances. This year, she felt just as alone as he had over the last five.

He didn't want that for her. He didn't want that for Grace.

What if...?

The thought came out of nowhere. He didn't know quite what to do with it.

Her eyes flitted between him and the outside view. 'Tell me, Grace. Tell me what your ideal Christmas would be. What do you want for Christmas?' His voice was firm as he repeated his question. The waver in her voice and tears had been too much for him. Grace was a kind and good person. She didn't deserve to be lonely this Christmas. He had enough money to buy just about anything and he was willing to spend it to wipe that look off her face.

Her mouth opened but the words seemed to stall.

'What?' he prompted gently.

'I want a proper Christmas,' she breathed. 'One with real snow, and a log fire, and a huge Christmas turkey that's almost too big to get in the oven.' She took a deep breath. 'I want to be able to smell a real Christmas tree again and I want to spend all day—or all night—decorating it the way I used to with my gran. I want to go into the kitchen and bake Christmas muffins and let the smell drift all around.' She squeezed her eyes closed for a second. 'And I don't want to be alone.'

Finlay was dumbstruck. She hadn't mentioned gifts or 'things'. Grace didn't want perfume or jewels. She hadn't any yearning for materialistic items.

She wanted time. She wanted company. She wanted the Christmas experience.

He glanced out of the window again. He was a little confused. Snow dusted the top of every rooftop in London—just as it had for the last week.

'What do you mean by snow?' he said carefully.

She opened her eyes again as he released his hands from her shoulders. She held out her hands. 'You know—real snow. Snow that's so thick you can hardly walk in it. Snow you can lie down on and do snow angels without feeling the pavement beneath your shoulder blades. Snow that there's actually enough of to build a snowman and make snowballs with. Snow that, when you look out, all you can see is white with little bumps and you wonder what they actually are.' He could hear the wonder in her voice, the excitement. She'd stopped being so sad and was actually imagining what she wished Christmas could be like.

'And then you go inside the house and all you can smell is the Christmas tree, and the muffins, and then listen to the crackle of the real fire as you try and dry off from being outside.' She was smiling now. It seemed that Grace Ellis could tell him exactly what she wanted from this Christmas.

And he knew exactly where she could get it. The snow scene in her head—he'd seen that view a hundred times. The crackling fire—he had that too.

This was Grace. The person who'd shot a little fire into his blood in the last few days. The person who'd made him laugh and smile at times. The girl with the warm heart who had let him realise the future might not be quite as bleak as he'd once imagined.

He could do this. He could give her the Christmas she deserved.

'Pack your bag.'

Her eyes widened and she frowned. 'What?'

He started walking through the penthouse, heading to his cupboards to pull out some clothes. It was cold up north; he'd need to wrap up.

'I'll take you home to grab some things. I can show you real snow. I can light a real fire. We can even get soaked to the skin making snow angels.' He winked at her. 'Once you've done it—you'll regret it.'

Grace was still frowning. 'Finlay, it's after eight o'clock on Christmas Eve. Where on earth are you planning on taking me? Don't you have plans yourself?'

He shook his head as he pushed some clothes in a black bag. 'No. I planned on staying here and going up on Boxing Day to visit my parents and sister. My helicopter is on standby. We can go now.'

She started shaking her head. 'Go where?'

'To Scotland.'

CHAPTER SEVEN

THINGS SEEMED TO happen in a blur after that.

Her cart abandoned, Finlay grabbed her hand and made a quick phone call as they rode down in the elevator. The kitchen was still busy and it only took two minutes for him to corner the head chef.

'I need a hamper.'

The head chef, Alec, was in the middle of creating something spectacular. He shot Finlay a sharp look, clearly annoyed at being interrupted.

'What?'

But enthusiasm had gripped Finlay. 'I need a hamper for Christmas. Enough food for dinner tomorrow and all the trimmings.' He started opening the huge fridges next to Alec. 'What have you got that we can take?'

Grace felt herself shrink back. Alec was clearly contemplating telling Finlay where to go. But after a few seconds he gestured to a young man in the corner. 'Ridley, get one of the hampers from the stock room. See what we've got to put in it. Get a cool box too.'

Finlay had started stockpiling everything he clearly liked the look of on one of the counters where service was ongoing. The staff were dodging around them as they tried to carry on. She moved next to his elbow. 'I think we're getting in the way,' she whispered.

Prosciutto ham, pâté, Stilton and Cheddar cheese, oatcakes, grapes and some specially wrapped chocolates were already on the counter. Finlay looked up. 'Are we?' He seemed genuinely surprised about the chaos they were causing. 'What kind of wine would you like?' he asked. 'Or would you prefer champagne?'

Alec caught sight of her panicked face. He leaned over Finlay. 'Where exactly are you going?'

'Scotland.' It was all she knew.

Alec didn't even bat an eyelid, he just shouted other instructions to some of the kitchen staff. 'Louis, find two large flasks and fill them with the soups.'

Finlay still seemed oblivious as he crunched on a cracker. 'What are the soups?'

Alec didn't even glance in his direction; he was scribbling on a piece of paper. 'Celeriac with fresh thyme and truffle oil, and butternut squash, smoked garlic and bacon.'

A wide smile spread across Finlay's face. 'Fantastic.'

Ridley appeared anxiously with the hamper already half filled and looked at the stack of food on the counter. He started moving things between the hamper and cool box.

'Christmas pudding,' said Finlay. 'We need Christmas pudding.' Ridley glanced over at Alec, who let out a huge sigh and turned and put one hand on his hip and thrust the other towards Finlay.

Finlay frowned as he took the piece of paper. Alec raised his eyebrows. 'It's instructions on how to cook the turkey that's just about to go in your cool box.' He gave Grace a little smile, 'I'd hate it if you gave the lovely lady food poisoning.'

Finlay blinked then stuffed the paper into the pocket of his long black wool coat. 'Great. Thanks.'

Louis appeared with the soup flasks and some wrapped bread.

'We'll grab the wine on the way past. Is there anything else you want, Grace?'

She shook her head. Had she actually agreed to go to Scotland with Finlay? She couldn't quite remember saying those words. But somehow the dark cloud that had settled over her head for the last day seemed to have moved off to the side. Her stomach was churning with excitement. Finlay seemed invigorated.

A Christmas with real snow? It would only be a day— or two. He was sure to want to get back to work straight away. And the thought of a helicopter ride…

'Grace, are we ready?' He had the hamper in one hand and the cool box in the other.

She nodded.

It seemed as though she blinked and the chauffeur-driven car pulled up outside her flat. Her hand hesitated next to the door handle. This part of London was nowhere near as plush as Chelsea. She felt a little embarrassed to show Finlay her humble abode.

But his phone rang and he pulled it from his pocket. She slid out of the car. 'I'll be five minutes.'

He nodded as he answered the call and then put his hand over the phone. 'Grace?'

She leaned back in. 'What?'

He winked. 'Bring layers.'

She was like a whirlwind. Throwing things into a small overnight case, grabbing make-up and toiletries and flicking all the switches off in the house. She flung off her clothes and pulled on a pair of jeans, thin T-shirt, jumper and some thick black boots. The pink coat was a must. He'd bought it for her and it was the warmest thing that she owned.

She grabbed her hat, scarf and gloves and picked up the bag.

Then stopped to catch her breath.

She turned around and looked inside at the dark flat. The place she'd lived happily with her grandmother for years. This morning she'd been crying when she left, dreading coming home tonight. Now, the situation had turned around so quickly she didn't know which way was up.

The air was still in the flat, echoing the emptiness she felt there now. 'Love you, Gran,' she whispered into the dark room. 'Merry Christmas.'

She closed the door behind her. This was about to become the most unusual Christmas ever.

Grace squealed when she saw the helicopter and took so many steps backwards that he thought she might refuse to fly. He put his arm around her waist. 'Come on, it's fine. It's just noisy.'

Her steps were hesitant, but he knew once she got inside she would be fine. The helicopter took off in the dark night, criss-crossing the bright lights of London and heading up towards Scotland.

Once she'd got over the initial fear of being in the helicopter Grace couldn't stop talking. 'How fast does this thing go? Do we need to stop anywhere? How long will it take us to get there?' She wrinkled her nose. 'And where is *there*? My geography isn't great. Whereabouts in Scotland are we going?'

He laughed at the barrage of questions. 'We need to fly around three hundred and eighty miles. Yes, we'll need to stop to refuel somewhere and it'll take a good few hours. So, sit back, relax and enjoy the ride.'

Grace pressed her nose up next to the window for a minute. But she couldn't stop talking. It was clear she was too excited. 'Where are we going to stay? Will your family be there? Can I decorate again, or will they already have all the decorations up?'

Finlay sucked in a breath. His actions in the heat of the moment had consequences he hadn't even considered. His parents weren't expecting him until Boxing Day. He hadn't even called them yet—and now it was after ten at night. Hardly time to call his elderly parents. His sister was staying. He knew there was his old room. But there weren't *two* spare rooms. And his parents would probably jump to an assumption he didn't want them to.

This could be awkward.

He gulped. Not normal behaviour for Finlay. His brain tried to think frantically about the surrounding area. Although he stayed in the country they weren't too far away from the city. There were some nice hotels there. And, if he remembered rightly, there were some nice hotels in the surrounding countryside area.

He pulled out his phone to try and do a search. 'I haven't booked anywhere,' he said quickly as he started to type. 'But I'm sure we can find a fabulous hotel to stay in.'

'A hotel?' It was the tone of her voice.

'Yes.' His fingers were still typing as he met her gaze and froze.

'We're going to *another* hotel?'

It was the way she said it. He stayed part of the year at The Armstrong. The rest of the year he flitted around the globe. He hadn't set foot in his home—the castle—since Anna died.

Disappointment was written all over Grace's face. She gestured towards the hamper. 'Why did we need the food? Won't the hotel have food?' Then she gave a little frown. 'And are you sure you'll be able to find somewhere at this time on Christmas Eve when you don't have a reservation?'

There was an edge of panic to her voice. She hadn't wanted to spend Christmas alone—but she didn't want to spend it at the side of a road either.

She could be right. Lots of the hotels in the surrounding area would be full of families in Scotland for Christmas. 'Give me a second,' he said.

He made a quick call, then leaned forward to confer with the pilot. 'Snow is too heavy around that area,' the pilot said quickly. 'The hotel is too remote. Their helipad is notorious for problems.' He shook his head. 'I'd prefer not to, Mr Armstrong.'

Finlay swallowed. He'd used this pilot for years. If he said he'd prefer not to, he was being polite because Grace was here. He glanced at Grace. 'My parents aren't expecting me until Boxing Day. I don't want to appear early without letting them know.' He pulled a face. 'The hotel I'd thought we could go to has rooms, but—' he nodded to their pilot '—it's remote and our pilot doesn't recommend it.'

Grace's eyes widened. 'So, what do we do, then?'

He sucked in a breath. 'There is somewhere else we could stay.' As he said the words every bit of moisture left his mouth. Part of his brain was in overdrive. Why had he packed the hamper? Had he always known they would end up here?

'Where?' Grace sounded curious.

He hadn't quite met her gaze. He glanced out at the dark night. He had no idea where they were right now. And he had no idea what lay ahead.

Last time he'd been in the castle...

He couldn't even go there. But the practicalities of right now were making him nervous. What would they find at the end of this journey?

After a few years when he'd thought he'd never go back to the castle he'd let his staff go. His mother had made a few casual remarks. He knew that she must have been there. But he also knew that his family respected his wishes.

Grace reached over and touched his arm. Her warm fingers wrapped around his wrist. 'Finlay, where are you taking me? Where will we be staying?'

'My home,' he said before he changed his mind. 'Drumegan Castle.'

Grace pulled her hand back. 'What?' She looked from one side to the other as if she expected the castle to appear out of thin air. 'You own a castle?' Her mouth was practically hanging open.

It had been a while since he'd spoken about the castle. When they'd first bought it, he'd relished the expression on people's faces when he'd told them he owned a castle. But the joy and love for his property had vanished after Anna's diagnosis and then death.

'You own a castle,' Grace repeated.

He nodded. He had to give her an idea of what might lie ahead. 'I haven't been back there in a while.'

'Why?' As soon as she asked the question, realisation dawned on her and she put her hand up to her mouth. 'Sorry,' she whispered. 'Oh.'

'It's all closed up. I don't even know what it will be like when we get there. It will be cold. I hope the heating still works.' He leaned forward and put his head in his hands. 'Please let the electricity be working.' Then he looked upwards, 'Please let the water be working.' This was beginning to feel like a very bad idea. They might actually be better off at the side of the road than in the castle after five years. 'What am I doing?' He was talking to himself but the words came out loud.

Grace's hand came back. 'Finlay, we don't need to go there if you're not comfortable.' She bit her bottom lip. 'But five years is a long time. Maybe it's time to go back.' Her gaze was steady. 'Maybe it's time to think about whether you want to keep the castle or not.' She squeezed his hand again. 'And maybe it won't be quite as bad if you're not there by yourself.'

He could see the sincerity in her eyes. She meant every word. She wanted to help him. She didn't seem worried about the possibility of no water, no electricity or no heating. Just about every other woman in the world that he'd ever known would be freaking out right now. But Grace was calm. The excitement from the helicopter journey had abated now they'd been travelling for a few hours.

Something washed over him. A sense of relief. His stomach had been in knots. A long time ago he'd loved Drumegan Castle. Loved the approach and seeing the grey castle outline against the sky, towering above the landscape on the top of a hill. It used to give him tingles.

Then, for a while, it had given him dread. That had been the point of staying away for so long. He couldn't imagine coming back here himself. He couldn't imagine opening the front door and being swept away by the wave of emotions.

But even though those things were circulating around his brain, he didn't feel the urge at all to break the connection with Grace's steady brown gaze. There was something about being around her. A calmness. A reassurance he hadn't felt in…so long. He placed his hand over hers. 'I think you could be right.' She was trying so hard to help him, but how much had he done for her?

'You should have told me about your gran,' he said quietly.

She shook her head quickly. 'I couldn't. Once you'd told me about Anna… I just felt so guilty. My grief can't compare with yours. They're two entirely different things.'

She was trying so hard to sound convincing, to stop the tiny waver he could still hear in her voice. Her grief was still raw. His?

He kept holding her hand. 'It's not different, Grace. You lost someone that you loved. This is your first Christmas without that person. I get it.' He gave a rueful smile. 'Believe me, I do.'

He pulled her closer and she rested her head on his

shoulder. Next thing he knew the pilot was giving him a shout. 'Five minutes.'

He nudged Grace. 'Wake up, sleepy. We're just about to land.'

She sat up and frowned, rubbing her eyes and looking around. It was still pitch black outside. 'Where on earth are we landing?' she asked.

He smiled. 'At the helipad. The lights are automated.' As he said it they switched on, sending a stream of white light all around them. 'The helipad can be heated to keep it clear. It has its own generator.'

Grace pressed her nose up against the window. 'Is this near the castle? I can't see it.'

She turned and planted one hand on her hip. 'Finlay Armstrong, are you sure you have a castle? It's a caravan, isn't it? You're secretly pranking me and taking me to a forty-year-old caravan with no heating and electricity in the middle of nowhere.'

He raised his eyebrows. 'Don't forget the no water.'

She laughed. 'I couldn't possibly forget that.'

He pulled a face. 'Believe me, once you see the castle, you might prefer a forty-year-old caravan.'

She leaned back with a sigh as they approached the helipad. 'I bet I won't. Stop worrying.'

The helicopter landed smoothly and they jumped out into the biting cold air. 'Whoa!' Grace gave a start. 'I thought London was cold.'

He grabbed her bags. 'I told you to bring layers. Maybe I should have supervised the packing?' He was only half joking. He was curious about where Grace lived and was annoyed he'd been distracted by a business call. It might not have been the most prestigious part of London but he'd have liked to have seen the home she'd shared with her grandmother and had so many good memories of.

He gave a nod to the pilot and walked off to the side

as the helicopter took off again. There was a garage next to the helipad and he pressed a button to open the automated door. There was a squeak. And a creek. And finally it rolled upwards revealing a far too smart four-by-four.

Grace turned to face him. 'This is yours?'

'Last time I checked.' He felt up in the rafters of the garage for the keys, fingers crossed it would start. He knew that his father secretly used the car on occasion to 'keep it in running order'. He was just praying it hadn't been too long since he'd last borrowed it.

He put the bags in the boot and Grace climbed in. He waited until he was ready to get in next to her, then flicked another switch—the external lights of the castle.

She let out a gasp. 'What?'

It was almost as if the castle appeared out of nowhere. The white lights illuminating it instantly around the base, the main entrance, the turrets. At the same time more lights came on, picking out the long driveway between the landing pad and castle.

It might have helped that the whole area was covered in a thick layer of snow, making it look even more magical than normal.

Grace turned to face him, her face astounded. '*This* is your castle?'

'What did you expect?'

She pressed herself back against the leather seat as he started the engine. She was transfixed. She lifted up one hand. 'I don't know. I just didn't expect...that. Look at the snow,' she breathed.

He was fighting back the wave of emotions that was threatening to overtake him. The immense sadness was there. But it wasn't because he was grieving for Anna. It was the sudden realisation that he'd truly been away for too long. As soon as the lights had flashed on he'd been struck by how much he'd missed this sight.

Drumegan Castle had always made him so proud. It was every boy's dream to own a castle. According to Anna it had been every girl's dream too. Drumegan might not have been the pink of some Mediterranean castles, or the beige limestone of many English palaces and large houses. Drumegan Castle was built entirely of grey stone, making it look as if it just rose straight up from the green hill on which it was perched. But to him, just the sight of it gave him immense pride. He'd forgotten that.

It seemed he'd forgotten a lot of things.

He started the car and pulled away. 'What do you think?' It was the oddest sensation, but he wanted her approval. Why? He couldn't quite understand. It was important to him that she liked Drumegan Castle as much as he did.

'How many rooms does it have?' She sounded a bit spaced out.

'Rooms or bedrooms?' His reply was automatic. He'd answered so many questions about his home in the beginning he was practically a walking encyclopaedia on Drumegan Castle.

'Either.' She was still just staring at the structure ahead as they moved along the winding driveway.

'Well, it has wings really. Six bedrooms in each wing. Then two main kitchens. A scullery. A ballroom. Five sitting rooms. Three dining rooms. A few studies. And most bedrooms have separate bathrooms. Some of the top rooms have never been renovated. They're still the original servants' quarters.'

'Ah...so *that's* where you're putting me.' Grace had sparked back into life. 'No bed. No bedsheets. No curtains. And probably...' she pulled her hands around her body '...freezing!' She gave an exaggerated shiver.

He tapped the wheel. 'Hold that thought as you pray the heating is still working properly.'

The car moved up the final part of the drive towards the main entrance of the castle. Normally he would sweep around to the back where there were garages. But there didn't seem much point. He didn't expect anyone else to appear and they were both tired.

He pulled up directly outside the main steps and huge traditional carved double doors.

Grace stepped automatically from the car—she didn't need to be told twice. In the bright outside lights she looked pale. And a little nervous. Even though she was wearing the pink winter coat he could see the slight tremor in her body. He walked around to the back of the car and unloaded the cases, the hamper and the cool box. She came over to help and they walked up the flight of steps to the door.

His hand fumbled slightly as he reached for the lock. 'You'll need to give me a second to turn the main alarm off when we get inside. It should only take a few seconds.'

She nodded.

The lock creaked, then rattled as he twisted and jiggled the key. Finally the key turned around. He breathed a sigh of relief as he opened the iron door handle then shouldered the door completely open.

There was a whoosh. A weird kind of noise. Then an incessant little beep. The alarm.

He dumped the bags and walked to the right. The alarm panel was inside the cupboard at the side of the door. It only took a few seconds to key in the code. The light from outside was flooding in. He'd forgotten to mention the glass dome in the main entrance way. It had been put in by the previous owner—an architect and design engineer who obviously had been born before his time. Together with the lights reflecting from outside and the silver twinkling stars above filling the black sky it was a spectacular sight.

The hamper fell with a clatter from Grace's hand as she

walked forward under the dome. She held out her hands and spun around as her eyes stayed transfixed above. 'I've never seen anything like it,' she said as she turned slowly.

He smiled as he walked over next to her, moving close. 'It's amazing. It was the first thing I noticed when I came to view the castle.' He pointed above. 'At least I know the electricity is working inside as well as out.'

She gave him a curious stare. 'How do you know that?'

He kept looking upwards. 'Sensors. Think about it—the dome should be covered with snow—just like the rest of outside is. But the engineer who designed it knew that the weight of snow could damage it. He designed one of the first thermal sensors to pick up outside temperatures. The glass is heated—just barely—to stop snow gathering there. I had to have a specialist firm out around ten years ago to update the technology and they could hardly believe it.'

She stopped spinning and stared up at him. She didn't seem to notice how close they were—or she didn't seem to mind. She stared up with her chocolate-brown eyes. 'This place looks amazing. I can't wait to see the rest of it.' She touched his arm. 'Are you okay?'

Still thinking about him. Still showing concern. Anna would have loved Grace Ellis.

'I'm fine. Come on.'

They hadn't even closed the door behind them yet and the bitter winds were sweeping in behind them. He slammed the heavy door shut then walked to another small room to flick a few switches. 'Hot water and boiler should be on. But this place takes a long time to heat up. There are separate heating systems in the different wings so I've just put on the main system and the one for the wing we'll be staying in.'

Did that sound pretentious? He didn't mean it to. It was a big place, but it could be morning before they finally felt warm here.

He walked over, opening the door to the main sitting room, flicking on the light switch, then stopped in shock.

Grace walked straight into his shoulder.

The artificial light seemed harsh. What greeted them was even harsher. As soon as his foot hit the floor a white mist puffed upwards.

The five windows were shuttered from the inside. The whole room covered in dust sheets. The dust sheets were covered in dust. The dark wooden floor had its own special coating of dust. One curtain was half hanging from a rail. The things that hadn't managed to be covered in dust sheets were coated from head to foot in a thick layer.

Grace gave a huge sneeze. 'Oh, sorry.'

He spun around, sending up a further cloud. 'No. I'm sorry. I didn't realise it would be quite this bad.' He shook his head. 'I just… I just…' The words wouldn't form in his brain.

She reached up and touched his cheek. 'Finlay, it's fine. It's your home. It needs a bit of work.'

'A bit of work? Grace—how on earth can we stay here?'

She folded her arms and looked around. She flicked the edge of a dustsheet and sneezed again as the air clouded. 'It's like that film—you remember—when the spy comes back to the old Scottish mansion house he was brought up in.'

'Remember what happened to that house?'

She let out a laugh. 'Okay, let's go for another film. I could sing the Mary Poppins song as we cleaned up.'

'You honestly want to clean up?' He couldn't quite believe it.

'Why not?' It was quite ironic. There were no airs and graces around Grace Ellis. She took off her coat and started to roll up her sleeves.

She glanced around. 'Let's check out the kitchen. We have some things to put in the fridge.'

Finlay winced. If this was one of the sitting rooms he had no idea what the kitchen would look like.

But he was in for a surprise. The kitchen wasn't dusty at all. Grace ran her fingers along one of the worktops and looked at him in surprise. Then she started opening cupboards, followed by the larder and fridge.

'This place isn't so bad. Someone has kept it clean. Right enough, there isn't a single piece of food in this house. Just as well we brought the hamper.'

Something clicked in his brain. 'My mum. They did offer to look after the place and I said no.' He was almost ashamed to admit that. He walked around. 'But the main hall wasn't so dusty and in here has certainly been emptied and cleaned.' He gave a slow nod. 'All the other rooms have their doors closed. She hasn't gone into them. But the kitchen is open plan. She's only kept things tidy in here.'

Grace gave a nod. 'The surfaces just need a little wipe down.' She walked through a door off to the side then stuck her head back around. 'And there's enough cleaning products through here to clean this whole place a hundred times over.' She went to lift the hamper.

Finlay moved quickly. 'Slow down. Let me.' He picked up the hamper and then the cool box. She swung the door open on the fridge and started emptying the cool box straight into it. 'Why don't you find a cupboard to put some of the things from the hamper? Then we can get started on the main room.'

She was like a whirlwind. He had no idea what time it currently was but Grace seemed to have endless energy. He shook his head. 'I think we should look at the bedrooms.'

Her hands froze midway into the fridge. She dipped back and stared around the door at him. 'What?'

He shook his head and laughed. 'That didn't come out quite the way I meant it to. You must be tired. I'm tired. Let's put the food away, then go to the wing where I turned

the heating on. The beds will all be stripped down. I'll
need to find the sheets and bedding and make them up.'

She started restocking the fridge and looked amused.
'Do you have any idea where the bedding will be?'

He nodded. 'It's all vacuum-packed so I think it should
be okay. I'm just worried the rooms will be as dusty as the
sitting room.' He'd said rooms deliberately. He didn't want
to make Grace uncomfortable.

Grace closed the fridge door. 'Okay, then, let's go.'

He flicked the lights on as they walked down the corridors. Some cobwebs hung from the light fittings. 'This
place feels like the Haunted House at one of the theme
parks.'

Grace shivered. He stopped walking. 'I'm sorry, did I
scare you? I didn't mean to.'

She looked surprised. 'No, I'm not scared, silly, I'm
cold.'

Of course. She'd taken her coat off and left it in the
hall. The whole house was still bitterly cold. He opened
the first door and gulped. It was every bit as bad as the
sitting room. Grace instantly coughed.

'Let's try another,' he said.

So they did. The next room wasn't quite so bad. It only
took him a few moments to realise why. He walked over
to the fireplace. 'This room has a chimney—a real fire.
There's still a chimney sweep who comes in once a year to
clear all the chimneys. Between that—and the fact there's
still some air circulating means it's not quite so bad.'

He walked over to a cupboard and pulled out some vacuum-packed bedding. Then paused. There was only one
king-sized bed in here. He glanced between Grace and the
bed. 'We can find another room.'

She raised her eyebrows. 'How many others in this wing
have a fireplace?'

Realisation settled over him. 'Only this one.'

She sighed and held up her hands. 'How much energy do you have?' She stuck her hands on her hips. 'This place is still freezing. No one will be taking any clothes off.'

The way she was so matter-of-fact made him laugh out loud. He'd been a bit wary about saying something. He didn't want her to think he'd deliberately brought her up here with something in mind.

His stomach was flipping over and over. This had been his marital home. This room hadn't been the bedroom that he and Anna had shared—that was in another wing. But Grace was the first woman he'd ever brought to this house since Anna had died. All of a sudden he was in a bedroom, in his castle, with another woman, and he wasn't entirely sure how they'd got there.

Grace seemed unperturbed. She walked over to the curtains and gave them a shake. The little cloud of dust circulated around her like fairy dust from a film. She gave a sneeze and grabbed a chair. 'I'm going to take these down and throw them in the washing machine. If they come out okay, we can rehang them tomorrow.' She pointed to the fireplace. 'Why don't you see if you can light the fire? Once I've put these in the wash I'll make up the bed. If I don't get to sleep soon, I'll sleep standing up.'

She was already unhooking the curtains from their pole.

The uneasy feeling drifted away. She made things so easy. Things seemed to make sense around Grace. It was her manner.

He knelt down and checked the fireplace. It was clean and ready to be stocked. He knew exactly where the supplies were. It would only take a few minutes to collect them.

By the time he returned Grace had a smoky outline on her black jumper and jeans from the curtains. 'They're in the wash,' she said happily. 'But I think I'll need to get cleaned up once I've made the bed.'

She shook out the sheets and made up the bed in record time. It was bigger than the average king-size and Finlay tried not to think about how inviting it looked covered with the thick duvet, blankets and masses of pillows.

Grace put a hand on his shoulder as she wheeled her pull-along case behind her. 'You said the hot water would work?'

He nodded.

'Then I'm going to duck in the shower.'

He stood up quickly, brushing his hands. 'As soon as I light the fire I'll go and check out one of the other rooms.'

She shook her head again. 'Honestly, don't worry. I'm pretty sure we can sleep in the giant bed without either of us feeling compromised.' She gave him a smile, 'You've no idea how many layers I can wear.' She opened the door to the bathroom and dragged her case inside. A few seconds later he heard the shower start to run. She stuck her head back outside as he started trying to light the fire. 'But if you decided to go to the kitchen and make some tea I wouldn't object.' She frowned. 'Tea. We did bring tea, didn't we?'

He nodded as the fire sparked into life. 'Tea, milk and biscuits.' He arched his back, stretching out the knots from the long journey. 'Tea I think I can manage.'

Thank goodness he was tired. Thank goodness he was overwhelmed with stepping back inside the castle. If he hadn't been, he would have spent the whole time wondering how on earth he would manage to keep his distance from Grace while they were the only two people here. He shook his head as he headed to the kitchen. He should have thought about this beforehand. If he hadn't been able to resist kissing her under a lamp post in London, how on earth would he keep thoughts of touching her from his head now? He couldn't even think about that bare skin in the shower. No way.

By the time he came back Grace was sitting on the bed, her hair on top of her head, wrapped up in one of the giant duvets. She looked as if she had old-fashioned fleecy pyjamas on. He was pretty sure he was supposed to find them unappealing and unsexy.

Trouble was—he just didn't. Not when they were on Grace. He set the steaming-hot tea down on the bedside table along with some chocolate biscuits. She nodded towards the bathroom. 'I left the shower running for you. Figured you'd want to wash the dust off.' She leaned forward conspiratorially. 'Just don't tell the owner. I hear he keeps tabs on the water usage.'

He put his tea down next to hers. 'I think I can take him,' he said with a smile on his face.

In the dim light of the room all he could focus on was the warmth from her brown eyes. 'We'll see.' She picked up her tea and took a sip. 'Not bad.' She gave an approving nod. 'And just think, Alec didn't even give you written instructions.'

He laughed as he pulled his bag into the bathroom and closed the door behind him. It only took a few seconds to strip off his dusty clothes and step into the warm shower. Grace had left some shampoo and shower gel—both pink, both smelling of strawberries.

He started using them without thinking, let the water stream over his body along with distinctly female scent. His stomach started to flip-flop again.

She'd made things sound so casual. As if sharing a bed was no big deal.

And it wasn't—to most men.

It wasn't as if he hadn't shared a bed with a woman in the last five years. He had—if only for the briefest of moments.

But that hadn't actually been *sharing* a bed. That had been using a bed. Something else entirely. He hadn't slept next to another woman since Anna had died. He hadn't *woken up* with another woman.

That was what made him jittery. That was what was messing with his head.

He couldn't deny the attraction to Grace. His body thrummed around her. He couldn't pretend that it didn't. When he'd kissed her—he'd felt lost. As if time and space had just suspended all around them. His hands rubbed his head harder than they needed to, sending the shampoo over his face and eyes, assaulting his senses with the scent.

He leaned back against the bathroom tiles, adjusting the water to a cooler temperature. The house was still freezing. But the heat in this bathroom seemed ridiculously high. Steam had misted the mirror. It was kind of clawing at his throat, making it difficult to breathe.

He turned the dial on the shower once more; the water turned instantly icy, cooling every part of his body that had dared to think itself too hot. All breath left his body in shock as he turned the knob off.

He grabbed the already semi-wet towel and started drying himself vigorously. He didn't want to think that this was the same towel Grace had used to dry her silky soft skin. He didn't want to think that at all.

He glanced at his still-closed bag. Oh, no. He wasn't a pyjama kind of guy. Never had been. What on earth could he wear in bed with Grace?

He leaned against the other tiled wall and sighed. Boxers. That was all he usually wore. Maybe he should just stick to that because the room outside was so cold that any part of him that didn't behave might just drop off in the icy temperature. But he wouldn't be comfortable like that around Grace. He had a terrible feeling that in the weird space between almost sleeping and not quite he wouldn't have any control of his thoughts or body reactions. A suit of armour would probably help. Pity the castle didn't have any.

He rummaged through his bag and found a black T-shirt, clean boxers and then, stuck in a zip pocket, a pair of gym shorts. Baggy and mid-thigh-length. He'd obviously planned on visiting the hotel gym on his last trip and not quite managed it. He sent a silent prayer upwards. Thank goodness for being lazy.

He wiped down the mirror with the towel and brushed his teeth as his brain started whirring. What kind of presleep conversation would he have with Grace? What if he snored? What if she snored? He couldn't remember ever feeling this nervous around a woman. It was like being fourteen years old again.

He ran his fingers through his damp hair as he refused to meet his own gaze. He was being ridiculous. He was tired. That was all. That, and being back in the house again, was reviving a whole host of natural memories.

It wasn't quite as hard as he'd thought it would be. Having Grace here certainly helped. Seeing the house so desolate and neglected-looking had been a shock. He'd left it too long. He knew that now.

But now he was here. A thought flicked through his brain. It must be after midnight by now. It must be Christmas Day. At the very least he'd have to wish Grace Merry Christmas and thank her for accompanying him. It was time to stop delaying. Time to realise his duties as a host.

He pulled open the door and was surprised by the warm air that met him. The fire had certainly taken hold. He held his breath.

All he could hear was the comfortable crackle of the fire. And something else.

The noise of deep, soft breaths. Grace was sleeping. Her hair had escaped the knot on top of her head and her dark curls were spread across the white pillowcase. Her pink flannel pyjamas were fastened unevenly, leaving a gap at the base of her pale throat.

She looked exhausted. She looked peaceful. Turned out he didn't need to worry about pre-sleep conversation at all.

He walked over next to her and picked up his cup of now lukewarm tea. She shifted a little as his shadow fell over her and he froze. His fingers itched to reach out and brush a strand of hair away from her face. But he couldn't. He didn't want to do anything to disturb her. Anything to make her feel uncomfortable.

He walked back around to the other side of the bed, sitting down carefully, cringing as the bed creaked. One quick slug of the tea was enough. He shouldn't have spent quite so long in the shower. He slid his legs under the cool duvet, his skin bristling a little. The pillows were soft, the mattress comfortable under his tired muscles. He pulled the duvet a little higher as he turned on his side to face Grace.

The bed was huge. There was plenty of space between them. There would be no reason to end up on the wrong side of the bed, or touch arms or legs accidentally. He leaned his head on his hand and watched the steady rise and fall of her chest for a few minutes.

Even fast asleep Grace was beautiful. Her lips plump and pink, her pale skin flawless. In the space of a few days she'd woken him up. Woken him up to the world he'd been sleepwalking through these past five years.

Part of him was grateful. Part of him was scared. He didn't know what any of this meant. 'Merry Christmas, Grace,' he whispered as he laid his head on the pillow and went to sleep.

CHAPTER EIGHT

GRACE'S EYES FLICKERED OPEN. It took a few seconds for her to remember where she was. The bed was so comfortable. Her fingers and nose were a little chilled but everything else that was under the covers was cosy.

Her body stiffened. She'd fallen asleep last night while Finlay had been in the shower. She'd tried to stay awake, but as soon as she'd finished her tea and the heat from the fire had started permeating across the room her eyelids had grown so heavy that she couldn't keep them open a second longer.

Her eyes flitted around the room. She'd taken the curtains down last night. She'd need to hang them back up and let them dry. Now the pale light of day was filtering through the windows she could see the pale creams and blue of the room. It was much bigger than a normal bedroom, but the size didn't hide the most important aspect.

It was exquisite. Exactly the type of room you'd expect in a castle. The bed, tables and furniture were traditional and elegant. Cornicing on the ceiling and a dado rail around the middle of the room, with a glass chandelier hanging in the middle of the room. The two chairs next to the bed were French-style, Louis XVI, ornate with the thick padded seats covered in pale blue patterned fabric. Was it possible the rest of the castle was this beautiful?

Between the dim light last night and the clouds of dust she couldn't remember the details of the sitting room.

Now, she was conscious of the heavy breathing next to her. She turned her head just a little, scared to shift in the bed in case she woke him.

Finlay Armstrong's muscular shoulders and arms were above the duvet cover. She had a prime view. All of a sudden her mouth felt oddly dry. He was sleeping. For the first time ever, Finlay looked totally relaxed. There were no lines on his face. None at all. All the usual little stress lines around his forehead and eyes had completely vanished.

He almost looked like a different person. Finlay had always been handsome. But there was always some kind of barrier around him, some protective shield that created tension and pressure. This was the most relaxed she'd ever seen him.

His jaw was shadowed with stubble. Her eyes followed the definition of his forearms and biceps, leading up to his shoulders and muscled chest. He shifted and the duvet moved again. Crumpled next to his shoulder looked like a black T-shirt. Did he have anything else on under these covers?

She squirmed under the bedclothes. Her flannel pyjamas were uncomfortably warm. The heating had obviously kicked in overnight. She slid one foot out of bed then realised she hadn't brought any slippers. The carpet was cool. She'd need to find some socks.

How did she get out of bed without waking him?

Her phone beeped. Except it wasn't really a beep. The jangling continued to echo around the room.

Finlay's eyelids flickered open and he stretched his arms out, one hand brushing her hair.

Her heartbeat flickered against her chest as he turned his head towards her and fixed on her with his sleepy blue eyes. 'Morning,' he whispered.

'Morning,' she replied automatically. She felt kind of frozen—even though one of her legs was currently dangling out of the bed.

The edges of his lips turned upwards as the phone tune kept going. 'Or should I say Merry Christmas?'

It was like warm melted chocolate spreading over her heart. She'd had so many images in her head about this Christmas—all of them focusing on the fact she'd be alone.

This was the absolute last thing she'd expected to happen. Waking up in bed next to Finlay Armstrong in a castle in Scotland would never have found a way into her wildest imagination. She almost wanted to pinch herself to check she was actually here.

She couldn't help but smile. 'Merry Christmas, Finlay,' she said in a voice that squeaked more than she wanted it to.

He stretched again and pushed the covers back. If she'd been prepared—and if she'd been polite—she wouldn't have been caught staring at his abs and chest muscles as he jumped up in a pair of shorts and reached over for his T-shirt. He slid it easily over his head. Giving her a smile as she watched every movement. 'I take it the heating's kicked in at least. Not as warm as I might have hoped. The fire in here last night made me too warm. We'll need to try and find a happy medium.'

She swung her leg out of bed and stopped dead. She was facing the window—the one she'd removed the dusty curtains from last night. For as far as the eye could see there was thick white snow. It clung to every bump of the terrain. Every tree. Every fence. Every path. She stood up and moved automatically to the window. 'Oh, wow,' was all that came out.

She felt his presence at her shoulder and tried not to think about the fact there wasn't much between her and those taut muscles. 'You wanted snow,' he said quietly.

She nodded. 'Yes. I did.' She turned her head towards him. 'Just how wet are we going to get?'

He raised his eyebrows. 'How wet do you want to get?'

The air was rich with innuendo. She could play this either way. But she couldn't forget how they'd ended up here. She just wasn't sure where she was with Finlay. All she knew was that the more those deep blue eyes looked at her, the more lost she felt.

'It's snow angels all the way,' she said safely. 'But how about we find the Christmas decorations first?'

He nodded. 'Let's get some breakfast. Then, I think I might have a turkey to stick in the oven before we hit the hills. I know where the Christmas decorations are stored—but I've no idea what state they're in.'

Grace shrugged her shoulders. 'No matter. I'd just like to have Christmas decorations up when we eat dinner tonight. We'll need to clean up the sitting room too.'

He hesitated. 'Are you sure? This isn't a busman's holiday, you know. Just because it's the day job, doesn't mean that I expect you to help clean up around here.' He stuck his hands on his hips as he looked at the white view. 'I should probably get a company in.'

Grace shook her head. 'You can do that after Christmas—for the rest of the house. The kitchen is fine. I can rehang the curtains in here, and I'm sure between us we can sort out the other two rooms. It's just a bit of dust.'

It was more than a bit of dust. They both knew that. But Grace was determined to show Finlay that she wasn't a princess. Last night had been a bit of a dream. Ending up at a castle made her seem like a princess. But emotions ran deep.

This was her first Christmas without her grandmother. It was always going to be tough. But Finlay had already made it a bit easier. The change of scenery. The fact that someone had actually thought about her, and considered her, meant a lot.

Today would be hard. Every Christmas aroma would bring back memories of her gran. She'd worked so hard up until now to try and push the reality of today into a place there wasn't time to think about.

Past Christmases with her gran had also been a panacea for something else. It didn't really matter what age you were—being ignored by your mother would always cut deep.

It didn't matter that she'd reached adulthood intact and totally loved by her grandmother. The big gaping hole was always there. She could never escape the fact her mother had all but abandoned her to make a new life for herself. What kind of person did that?

In a way, it had strengthened the bond between her and her grandmother. Both of them trying to replace what the other had lost. But it also made it hard for her to form new relationships with other people. Grace struggled to make friends easily, because she struggled to trust. The girls from Maids in Chelsea were the closest friends she'd ever made. As for men? It was easy to blame her gran's illness and juggling jobs to explain why she'd never had a truly lasting relationship. She could just say it was down to poor taste in men. But the truth was, she'd always found it hard to trust anyone, to believe that someone would love her enough not to abandon her. It was easier to keep her feelings cocooned. At least then they were safe.

But now? Her biggest problem was that every second she was around Finlay she became a little bit more attached. Saw another side of him that she liked, that she admired, that she might even love a little. But he was her boss. They lived completely different lives. Her heart didn't even know where to start with feelings like these.

So why had they ended up here together?

Finlay's fingers intertwined with hers as they looked at the snow together. The buzz was instant, straight up her arm to her heart. There was so much she could say right now. So many tumbling thoughts.

'Let's get dressed,' said Finlay as he turned and walked away.

Grace folded her arms and smiled out at the untouched snow. This Christmas was shaping up to be completely different from what she'd ever imagined.

Her phone beeped and she pulled it from her bag. Sophie.

Where are you? I dropped by the flat.

Grace pressed buttons quickly, knowing exactly the response she'd get.

With my boss. In Scotland.

She smiled, added a quick, See you all at the Snowflake Ball, and tucked the phone into her bag, knowing it would probably buzz for the rest of the day.

It was like having someone with boundless energy next to you all day. Grace didn't seem to know how to sit down. Five minutes at breakfast was her record. After that, she'd rehung the curtains, then started to power around the dining room.

Meanwhile he'd been in the place he clearly wasn't destined for.

Finlay frowned at the instructions. They must have got a little wet in his pocket. They were a bit smudged. He'd found a suitable tray for the turkey and followed Alec's instructions. But this basting thing looked complicated. Would he even get to leave the kitchen at all today?

Grace appeared with a smudge on her nose, laughing, watching him squint at the instructions. 'How's the turkey?' She smiled with a hand on her hip.

He shook his head. It was too, too tempting. His thumb was up wiping the smudge from her nose instantly, the rest of his hand touching the bottom of her chin.

Whatever she'd opened her mouth to say next had been lost. She just stared at him with those big brown eyes. For a second, he couldn't breathe. He couldn't inhale.

Every thought in his head was about kissing her. Tasting those lips. Running his fingers through her soft hair, tied back with a pink ribbon. She'd changed into a soft pink knit jumper and blue figure-hugging jeans. Her face was make-up-free, but, although she was as beautiful as ever, today she looked different. She looked happy. She was relaxed.

He could almost sense a peaceful aura buzzing around her. His stomach turned over. He'd done the right thing. He'd done the right thing bringing Grace here—both for him, and for her.

It was as if she was caught in the same glow that he was. 'How's your Christmas going?' she whispered.

He couldn't tear his gaze away. 'Better than I could have hoped for.'

She put a hand over his at the side of the turkey tray. 'Then let's get this old girl in the oven. I've found the Christmas decorations, but I couldn't find the tree.'

'Oh.'

Her hand was still on his. 'What do you mean, oh?'

He picked up the tray—this turkey was heavier than it looked—and slid the tray into the oven. He picked up the other items that Alec had given them, onion, stuffing and chipolatas, and pushed them back in the fridge. 'We can put them in later.'

He closed the oven door with a bang and checked the

temperature. Grace folded her arms and leaned against the countertop. Finlay looked around the room for his navy jumper. It only took a moment to find it and pull it on. He glanced at Grace's feet. 'Do you have other boots?'

'Why?'

He walked around her and held the door to the main hall open. 'Because I don't have an artificial tree. I've never used one at Drumegan Castle.' He gestured with his hand. 'I've got a whole wood out there full of pine trees. All we need to do is go and get one.'

Her eyes widened. Even from this far he could see the enthusiasm. 'Really, you're going to cut down a real Christmas tree?'

He nodded. 'Snow angels, anyone?'

Her eyes sparkled. 'I'll race you!'

In the end she hadn't worn the very expensive pink winter coat that Finlay had bought her. He'd found old waterproof jackets in the cupboard and they'd worn them on their hike across the grounds, complete with wheelbarrow and electric saw.

'I'm kind of disappointed,' she teased as he wheeled it towards the wood.

'Why?' He looked surprised.

Her feet were heavy in the snow. It really was deep here. Finlay hadn't been kidding. She gave him a teasing smile. 'I kind of hoped you'd just stomp over here with an axe, cut down the tree then throw it over your shoulder and bring it back to the castle.'

He let out a laugh. 'Really? Just like that?' He stopped wheeling, obviously trying to catch his breath just at the edge of the wood. 'Well, I guess I could do that if you want.' He pointed to a tiny tree just at the front of the wood. It was about two feet tall. 'But this would be our Christmas tree. What do you think?'

She sidled up next to him. It had started to snow again and the snow was collecting on her shoulders with a few flakes on her cheeks. 'Finlay Armstrong, you know how much I love Christmas, don't you?'

She'd tilted her chin towards him. All he had to do was bend down a little.

He couldn't help the smile that automatically appeared. Grace's enthusiasm was infectious. 'Grace Ellis, I might have noticed that about you.'

'You did?' She blinked, snowflakes landing on her thick lashes.

His hand naturally went around her waist, pulling her closer. Her hands slid up the front of his chest. 'I might have. So, I want you to look around the wood and find your perfect Christmas tree. When you find it, it's all yours.'

She was watching him carefully. 'All mine, I like the sound of that.'

He licked his lips. A few weeks ago, if someone had told him he'd be standing in the castle grounds on Christmas Day, waiting to cut down a tree with a beautiful woman in his arms, he would have thought they were crazy.

That would never, ever happen for him again.

And yet…he was here. With Grace. And for the first time in years he actually felt happy. He wasn't imagining this. This was real. There was a real connection between them.

She gave her hand a little thump against his chest and looked upwards. 'Snow's getting heavier.' She winked at him. 'It must have heard I was here. Snow angels waiting. Let's find this tree, Finlay. We have a date in the snow.'

A date in the snow.

He knew exactly what she meant and the words were casual. A date. Hadn't they already had a few dates? Had he been dating without really knowing it?

She walked ahead and gave a shout a few minutes later.

Then she gave a squeal. He darted through the trees. She was jumping up and down, clapping her hands together. 'This is it. This is the tree. It's perfect. Don't you think? It will look gorgeous in the sitting room.'

She was infectious, truly infectious. She was right. She'd picked a perfect tree. Immaculately shaped, even branches and just the right height. 'It's not quite perfect,' he said as he stepped forward.

'It's not?' She leaned back a little, looking up as if she was trying to spot the flaw.

'No,' he said as he reached the tree and stretched his hand through the branches to catch hold of the trunk. 'Too much snow.'

He started shaking the tree as she screamed, covering them both in the tumble of snow from the branches. It fell thick and fast, sliding down his neck and making him shiver.

Grace fell backwards with a shriek, laughing as she fell.

She lay there for a few seconds, trying to catch her breath. He pulled his hand back and stepped over her. 'Okay down there?'

She was lying looking up at the sky. 'No,' she said firmly. 'I've been hoodwinked by a crazy Scots man.' She held her hand up towards him.

He grabbed it, steeling himself to pull her upwards. But Grace was too quick for him. She gave him an almighty wrench, yanking him downwards to her and the heavy snow.

He landed with a splat, face first in the snow next to her, only part of his body on hers.

Her deep, throaty laugh echoed through the wood. Once she started, she couldn't stop.

He sucked in a breath and instead sucked in a mouthful of snow, making him snort and choke. He tried to get up on his knees to clear his mouth, but Grace grabbed hold of his arm. 'Oh, no, you don't.' She was still laughing.

He spluttered again, this time getting rid of snow and starting to laugh himself. She'd got him. She'd got him good.

'You promised me something,' she said.

The laughing had stopped and she sounded deadly serious. He lay down next to her in the snow. 'Okay, then. What did I promise?'

She reached over and touched the side of his cheek. It was the tenderest of touches. 'You promised me snow angels,' she whispered. 'And I plan on collecting.'

He only had to move forward a couple of inches. Maybe she was talking about snow angels. But the heat between them had been rising all day; it was a wonder they hadn't melted all the snow around them.

He captured her sweet lips in his. Her cheeks were cold. The hat she'd pulled from her pocket earlier had landed on the snow, letting her hair fan out in the snow—just as it had on the pillow last night. That memory sparked a rush of blood around his body.

He pulled his hand from his gloves and tangled it through her hair. Her other hand caught around the back of his neck, melding her body next to his. It didn't matter that the ground was freezing and snow was getting in places it just shouldn't. He didn't care about anything other than the connection to this woman.

Somewhere deep inside him a little spark was smouldering. Willing itself to burn brighter and harder.

Grace responded to every movement, every touch, matching him step by step. He didn't have any doubt the feelings were mutual. He was surprised when she slowly pulled back and put one arm against his chest. She was smiling though.

'Parts of me I didn't know could get wet, are wet.' She

sighed. 'I guess this would be the right time to collect on the snow angels.'

He laughed and nodded. Kissing lying in the snow wasn't an ideal arrangement. He knew that. He just didn't care about the wet clothes.

He looked over at the piece of ground a little away from the trees. 'To make snow angels, we need to do it where there are no other marks. Let's go over there.'

He took her arm and pulled her up. They'd only walked a few steps when she stopped dead. 'Look!'

'What?' He looked around near the trees and bush she was pointing to.

'Holly,' breathed Grace. 'It's holly.'

She was right; the jaggy green leaves and red berries were poking out from underneath the snow. She grabbed hold of his arm. 'Can you cut some? Wouldn't it be gorgeous to have some fresh holly in the house?'

There it was again. That infectious enthusiasm. If she could bottle it and sell it she could be a millionaire. He put his arm around her waist. 'Snow angels first, then the tree, then the holly. You could freeze out here.'

She nodded and shivered. 'I think I already am.'

He took her hand and led her across the snow, turning around to face the castle. 'How about here?'

She nodded as she looked at their trail of footprints in the snow.

'Then let's do it.' Finlay grinned as he held out his arms and fell backwards in the snow, landing with a thud. *'Oof!'*

Grace looked a bit shocked, then joined in, turning to face the castle, holding out her arms and falling backwards. Her thud wasn't nearly as loud.

They lay there for a few seconds. The clear blue sky above them, the white-covered world all around them, with the majestic grey castle standing like a master of all it surveyed.

'It's just beautiful here,' breathed Grace.

Finlay wasn't thinking about the cold. His eyes were running over the hundreds of years old building he'd neglected for the last five years. It had stood the test of time, again and again. It had been here before him. And it would still be standing long after he had gone. 'Yes, yes, it is,' he agreed.

Pieces were starting to fall into place for him. The brickwork at one of the turrets looked as if it needed work. There were a few misaligned tiles on one part of the roof—probably the result of one of Scotland's storms. All things that could be easily mended.

The cold was soaking in through his jacket and jeans. All things could be mended. It just depended on whether you were willing to do the repairs.

'Hey? Are you going?'

He smiled again. Grace was the best leveller in the world. 'Yes, let's go.'

They yelled and shouted as they moved their arms up and down in the heavy snow. Grace started singing Christmas songs at the top of her voice.

He hadn't felt this happy in such a long time. He hadn't felt this free in such a long time. He turned his head and watched her singing to the sky with a huge smile on her face—this was all because of Grace. He just couldn't deny it.

When she finally stopped singing they lay in the snow for a few seconds.

'Thanks, Grace.'

She looked surprised. 'For what?'

He held up one damp arm. 'For this. For helping me come back here. For making something that should be hard feel as if I was meant to do it. I was meant to be here.'

She rolled over in the snow onto her stomach, facing

him. 'That's because I think you were, Finlay. Maybe it was just time.'

He nodded in agreement. 'Maybe it was.'

She pushed herself up onto her knees. 'Thank you too.'

'What for?'

She smiled. 'For making a Christmas that I thought I was going to hate, into something else entirely. Snow? A castle? What more could a girl ask for?' She shook some snow off her jacket. 'Except pneumonia, of course.'

He pushed himself up. 'You're right. Let's go. The tree will only take a few minutes to cut down and we can grab some holly along the way.'

From the second they'd got back in the castle and showered and changed, things had seemed different. This time, Grace had put on the only dress she'd brought. It was black with a few sparkles. She'd always liked dressing up on Christmas Day and she was hoping Finlay would appreciate the effort. There hadn't been time to do anything but dry her hair so she left it in waves tied back with the same pink ribbon as earlier. Finlay was in the kitchen, muttering under his breath as he basted the turkey—again.

She nudged him as she watched. 'What do you say we make this easy?'

'How?'

'That tray of roast potatoes, stuffing and chipolatas? Just throw them in next to the turkey.'

'You think that will work?'

She shrugged. 'Why not? Let's put the Christmas pudding on to steam. We might as well. We have a tree to decorate.'

Something flashed behind his eyes. She wasn't sure what, because it disappeared almost as soon as it appeared. He nodded. 'Yes, we do, don't we? Okay, then.' He threw the rest of the food into the turkey tray. 'At least if nothing

else works, we still have the soup. It's stored in the fridge.
At least it's safe.'

Grace put a pan of water on to boil and arranged the
steamer on top with the small muslin-wrapped Christmas
puddings. 'All done.'

She'd left the cardboard boxes full of decorations in the
sitting room. Finlay had already arranged the Christmas
tree on the stand—just waiting to be decorated—and lit
the fire to try and warm the room some more.

As they walked through to the room together she could
sense something about Finlay. A reluctance. A worry.

The aromas around her were stirring up a whole host of
memories. She was so used to making Christmas dinner
with her grandmother. While the Christmas pudding was
steaming they normally dug out some old board games
and played them together.

It was hard not to have her around. It was hard to face
the first Christmas without her. Her hand went automatically to her eyes and brushed a tear away. She wanted to
enjoy this Christmas. She wanted to know that she could
still love her favourite time of year without the person she
usually spent it with.

What scared her most was how much she was beginning to feel about the man she was secluded with in this
castle. That one kiss had stirred up so many hidden emotions inside her. Apart from a dusty castle, there were no
other distractions here.

It was just him. And her.

It was difficult to ignore how he made her feel. It was
difficult to fight against a build-up of emotions in an en-
closed space.

She rummaged through the box and heard a little tinkle
of bells. It reminded her of an old film she'd watched with
her grandmother. She looked upwards and smiled. It didn't

make her feel sad; instead a little warmth spread through her. 'Love you, Gran,' she murmured.

She pulled a strand of tinsel from one of the boxes, bright pink, and wrapped it around her neck. Then, she flicked the switch on the radio. The words of *Let it Snow* filled the room..

She turned to face him and held up her hands. 'Think they knew where we were?'

'Could be.' His voice seemed a little more serious than before; his eyes were fixed on the cardboard boxes.

She moved over next to him and put her hands on his chest. He'd changed into a long-sleeved black shirt, open at the neck, and well-cut black trousers. It would be easy to spend most of the day staring at his muscular thighs and tight backside. 'We don't have to do this, Finlay.'

He shook his head. 'No, we do. *I* do.' She stood back and let him open the flaps of the first box and start lifting out the decorations.

They were all delicately wrapped in tissue paper. He unwrapped one after the other. She could see the expression on his face. Each one brought back a different memory. She put her hand over his. 'If I was at home right now, I'd be feeling exactly the same way,' she said reassuringly. 'Some of the decorations my gran and I have had for years. Some of them we made together. There were several I just couldn't hang this year. I get it. I do.'

His grateful blue eyes met hers. There was pain in them, but there was something else too. A glimpse of relief.

His hands seemed steady as he handed each one to her to hang. Occasionally he gave a little nod. 'That one was from Germany. This one from New York.'

Her stomach twisted a little. She felt like Scrooge being visited by the ghost of Christmas past. All of these memories were wrapped around Anna. She didn't expect him to forget about his dead wife. But she needed to be sure that when he kissed her, when he touched her, he wasn't thinking of someone else. She wasn't a replacement. She wouldn't ever want to be. Lots of his actions made her think he was ready to move on. But this, this was eating him up. Her stomach flipped over. She'd brought something, lifted something on instinct in the penthouse in London. Maybe it hadn't been such a good idea after all.

She looked in the box and gave him a smile. 'Hey, I haven't found anything purple yet. Isn't there anything that will match our decorations down in London?'

He gave her a smile and shook his head. 'There's nothing in those boxes. But I did think about purple before we left. Give me a second.'

His footsteps echoed down the hall and she looked around. The fire was flickering merrily, giving off a distinctive heat. The smell of the turkey and Christmas pudding was drifting across the main hall towards them. Between that, and the Christmas tree, this place really did have the aroma and feel of Christmas.

Finlay came back holding a string of Christmas lights—the same ones they'd used in the hotel. Grace gasped. 'You brought purple lights?'

He nodded. 'I don't even know. I didn't think I'd planned to come here. But I know the lights we used to have here don't work any more. I liked the purple lights from the hotel so I brought some along.'

He started to wind them around the tree. It was almost finished. The lights should have gone on first, but Finlay managed to wrap them around the tinsel and hanging decorations without any problem. When he'd finished he flicked the switch to light up the room.

It had grown steadily darker outside, now the room was only lit with the orange crackling fire and the purple glowing lights. Together with the smells of Christmas it was almost as if some Christmas spirit had been breathed back into Drumegan Castle.

Grace felt her heart flutter. There was one last thing she had to do. She was doing it for the right reasons. Even if she did have a tiny bit of selfishness there too. She needed to know where Finlay was. She needed to know how ready he was.

'I brought something too. Give me a minute.'

She practically ran along the hall, finding the white tissue paper and bringing the item back. Finlay was standing looking around the room. She couldn't quite read the expression on his face.

So, she took a deep breath and held out the item with a trembling hand.

It was now, or never. Time to find out what the future might hold.

Finlay's breath was caught somewhere in his throat. He didn't need to unwrap the item to know what it was.

Grace's hand was shaking. He could see that. He reached up and put his hand under hers, taking his other hand to pull back the delicate tissue paper.

'You brought this?'

She nodded. It wasn't just her hand that was shaking. Her voice was too. 'I thought it might be important. I thought it might be important for you.'

He pulled back the tissue paper on the white ceramic Christmas angel. This time when he looked at it, he didn't feel despair and angst. He didn't feel anger and regret. He looked into the eyes of the woman that was holding it. It was almost as if she were holding her heart in her hand right now.

He knew exactly how she felt.

Grace had brought this. Even though she'd been feeling lonely and sad this Christmas she'd still thought of him.

He could see how vulnerable she was right now. It was written all over her face. He reached up and touched her cheek. A sense of peace washed over him.

Anna. She was here with him. He could almost feel her smiling down on him. It was as if a little part of him unravelled. Anna had made him promise he'd move on. He'd find love again.

He'd locked that memory away because he'd never imagined it possible.

But he'd never imagined Grace.

Did she know how gorgeous she looked in that black dress that hugged her curves and skimmed out around her hips?

He lifted the white ceramic angel and clasped Grace's hand as they walked over to the tree together. As he lifted the angel to hang it from the top of the tree there was the sound of fireworks outside. Bright, colourful, sparkling fireworks lighting up the dark Christmas night sky.

Everything about this just felt right. He reached up and gave the pink ribbon holding Grace's hair back a little tug. As it came away in his hand he rearranged her hair, letting the loose curls tumble all around her face. 'You always tie it back. I like it best like this,' he said. 'While you're in the snow, and while you're lying in bed.'

Grace's eyes were glistening. This time when she smiled the warmth reached all the way into her brown eyes. Her sadness was gone. Banished. 'We haven't sorted out our sleeping arrangements for tonight,' she said huskily. 'I think we forgot to clean the other bedroom.'

He pulled her closer. 'I think we did. But I've got another idea.'

She tilted her chin up towards him. 'What is it?'

He nodded towards the fire and rug in front of it. 'I was thinking of a picnic. A Christmas picnic with a mishmash of turkey, stuffing, potatoes, chipolatas and Christmas pudding, all in front of our real fire.'

She licked her bottom lip. 'Sounds good to me. In fact, it sounds perfect. Do we have any wine? Or any champagne?'

He lowered his head, his lips brushing against the soft delicate skin at the bottom of her neck. 'I think we might have brought some with us.'

She laughed, her fingers reaching for his chin and bringing it up next to hers. She met his lips with hers. 'How about you grab the food and champagne and I grab us a blanket?'

He didn't want to let her out of his grasp. Not when he could feel all her curves against his. 'How quick can you be?'

She winked. 'Quicker than you. Just grab an oven glove and bring the whole tray and some knives and forks.' She stood on her tiptoes and whispered in his ear. 'Last one back pays a forfeit.'

'What will that be?'

She raised her eyebrows as she walked backwards to the door. 'You'll find out, slowcoach.'

He loved that she was teasing him. He'd already decided she could win. 'Oh, and, Grace?'

She spun around at the door. 'Yes?'

He winked at her as his mind went directly to other places. 'Forget the flannel pyjamas. You won't be needing them.'

CHAPTER NINE

THIS TIME WHEN she woke up in the castle, underneath was hard and uncomfortable. The arms around her were warm and reassuring, as was the feel of Finlay at her back. His soft breathing against her neck and feel of his heartbeat against her shoulder sent waves of heat throughout her body.

She couldn't help the soft little moan that escaped her lips. Neither could Finlay; she smiled as she recognised the instantaneous effect it had on him too.

'How do you feel about a Boxing Day excursion?' he murmured in her ear.

She leaned back further into him, relishing the bare skin against hers. 'What do you mean?'

He cleared his throat. 'I'd told my mum, dad and sister I would visit today, remember? How do feel about coming along?'

She turned onto her back so she could face him. 'You want me to meet your mum and dad?' The tiny hairs on her arms stood on end. Last night had been magical. Last night had felt like a dream. She'd never, ever experienced a connection like that. For Grace, it had felt like coming home to the place she'd always meant to be.

Nothing had ever seemed as right to her. But she was worried about what it meant to Finlay. His inviting her to meet his mum and dad today was sending a million reassuring *go faster* signals through her body.

She snaked her arms around his neck. 'I'd love to meet your mum and dad. And your sister. Do you think they'll be okay about meeting me?'

He gave a gentle laugh. 'Oh, I think my mum will measure you for a pair of family slippers.' He dropped a kiss on her lips. 'Don't worry, my family will love you.'

It was easy to respond to his kisses. Even though her brain was focusing on the family-loving-her part. Everything about this Christmas was turning out to be perfect.

The expression on his mother's face when she opened the door was priceless. She flung her arms around his neck while the whole time she stared at Grace.

'This is Grace,' he said quickly as he slid his hand into hers for reassurance. 'We met at work and she came up for Christmas at the castle with me.'

His mother's chin bounced off the floor. 'Fraser!' she shouted at the top of her voice. 'Aileen!' He imagined his father pushing himself out of his chair at the pitch of his mum's voice. 'You spent yesterday at the castle? Why? You could have come here.'

He glanced at Grace and gave her a smile. Yesterday had been better than he could ever have imagined. Nothing could have matched that. He edged around his mother, who was still standing in the doorway in shock. 'You knew I was coming today. That seemed enough.'

His father walked through from the living room and only took a few seconds to hide his shock. He greeted Finlay, then Grace with a huge bear hug. He wasn't even discreet about the whisper in Grace's ear. 'Watch out for Aileen, she's pregnant, cranky and will ask a million questions.'

For Grace it was a wonderful day. The love between the family members was clear. It reminded her of the relationship she'd shared with her grandmother. Aileen didn't hide in the least the fact she was quizzing Grace. But it was all good-natured.

The family shot occasional glances between each other. But all of them were of warmth, of relief. It was obvious they were delighted that Finlay had brought someone to meet them. They obviously wanted him to be happy. Anna was mentioned on occasion. But it wasn't like a trip down memory lane. It was only ever in passing, in an occasional sentence. And she was glad; she didn't want them to tiptoe around her. Not if there was any chance that this relationship could go somewhere.

The board games were fiercely competitive. She paired up with Finlay's dad and managed to trounce him on more than one occasion. When it got late, Finlay's mum, Fran, gave her a little nod, gesturing her through to the kitchen where she was making a pot of tea. 'I've made up Finlay's room for you both. No need to go back to the castle. We usually drink tea, then move on to wine or port and some Christmas cake.'

Grace smiled. She liked the way Fran said it. It was like a warm welcome blanket. Letting her know she was welcome to stay, as well as introducing their family traditions. She picked up the tray with the teapot and cups. 'Thanks, Fran, will I just take these through?'

Fran picked up the port bottle and tray with Christmas and Madeira cake and gave Grace a nudge. 'Let's go.'

Finlay met her at the door; he opened his mouth to speak but his mother cut him off.

'I was just letting Grace know the sleeping arrangements. Now, we're going to have a drink.' She raised her eyebrows at Finlay. 'I believe there was some cheating going on at that last game. I mean to get my revenge.'

Finlay slung his arm around Grace's shoulder. 'Are you okay with this?'

She knocked him with her hip as she smiled back. 'Oh, I'm fine. I mean to defend my winner's crown by all means necessary.' She leaned forward and laughed. 'Brace yourself, Mr Armstrong. You haven't even seen my winning streak yet.'

Firsts. These last few days had been full of them.

It woke him in the middle of the night.

First time since Anna had died that he'd allowed the hotel to be decorated. First time he'd brought someone else to the castle. First time he'd kissed another woman and actually *felt* something. First time he'd introduced his family to someone. First time in five years he'd actually enjoyed a Christmas instead of working straight through.

First time he'd woken up in his mother's house with someone who wasn't his wife.

What was completely obvious was how much his family had relished having Grace there. He could almost see the relief flooding from his mum and dad that he might actually have met someone, and he might actually be ready to move on.

He could hear her steady breathing next to him. But instead of feeling soothed, instead of wanting to embrace the idea of listening to this time after time, he felt an undeniable wave of panic.

They headed back to London today. Reality was hitting. How on earth would things be when they got back to the real world?

He worked goodness knew how many hours a week. He spent most months ping-ponging around the world between various hotels. There was no way he had time for a relationship.

It was as if a cold breeze swept over his skin.

Guilt was creeping in around the edges of his brain. He'd brought another woman to Drumegan Castle and slept with her there. He'd let Grace decorate, feel at home, help clean up and make snow angels in the ground. Most of the time he'd spent with Grace at Drumegan he'd enjoyed. He'd only thought of Anna in fleeting moments. And Grace had been the biggest instigator of that when she'd brought out the ceramic angel. His last physical link to Anna.

The woman that he should have been thinking of. Not Grace.

He shivered as her warm eyes flickered open next to him. 'Morning.' Her sexy smile sent pulses through his body and he pushed the duvet back and stood up quickly.

'Morning. I've got some work to do. Some business calls to make. I might be a few hours. I'm sure my mum will fix you some breakfast.' He was slipping on his jeans and pulling a T-shirt over his head as he spoke. Grace sat upright in the bed, her mussed-up hair all around her face. She looked confused—and a little hurt. 'Oh, okay. No problem. I'm sure I can sort myself out.'

There was no excuse. None. But he couldn't help it. His head was so mixed up he just needed some space.

And that was easy. Under the fake guise of work his mum, dad and sister were delighted to entertain Grace for the next few hours. Right up until they were ready to head back to the helipad at the castle.

His mother's bear hug nearly crushed him. 'It's been so good to see you, honey. She's fabulous. I love her. Bring her back soon.'

His hand gripped the steering wheel the whole way back to Drumegan Castle's helipad. All of a sudden he didn't feel ready for this. It seemed rushed. It had come out of nowhere. Could he really trust his feelings right now, when he'd spent the last five years shut off?

He couldn't help the way he was withdrawing. It seemed like the right thing to do.

'I think I should be honest, Grace. The past few days

have been wonderful. But up here—in Scotland, staying in the castle—this isn't the real world. I'm sorry. I think I made a mistake asking you up here. I knew how you were feeling about Christmas, and I was dreading coming up here again, and I think I might have given you the wrong idea. I'm just not ready for another relationship. Not yet, anyway. I'm not going to be able to give you what you want, Grace, or what you deserve. You should have a partner who loves only you, who wants to settle down and can commit time and energy to your family. I'm sorry, but I'm just not that person.'

She'd stopped noticing the whirring of the helicopter blades. All she could hear right now was the quiet voice next to her. It was almost as if he was speaking in hushed tones so she'd have to lean closer to hear. But the truth was, these were words she'd never wanted to hear.

This morning had been awkward. This afternoon had been worse. She'd almost been relieved when they'd said their goodbyes to Finlay's lovely family and driven back to the helipad at the castle.

She hadn't been able to ask Finlay why he was on edge. And now that made her angry. She'd been close enough to get naked and make love to him, but she didn't feel secure enough to ask what was wrong. Now, after giving her a Christmas she could only have dreamed of, he was unceremoniously dumping her. And he wasn't even doing it that well. He might have waited until they'd landed at The Armstrong. At least then she could have walked straight down the stairs and into the bar.

She tried to push all the angry thoughts aside. Finlay looked terrible. He was pale and his hands were constantly twitching on his lap. He wasn't the cool, remote man she'd first met. But he wasn't the dashing businessman either. Who was it she'd actually fallen in love with?

Her heart stuttered. That was it. That was why those few words felt as if they were wrenching her stomach inside out. Slowly but surely over the last few days Finlay Armstrong had stolen piece after piece of her heart. From that first moment on the roof of The Armstrong, from that tiny stroke of her cheek. From the shopping trip for the decorations, the drinks at the staff party and that first kiss under the lamppost.

He'd recognised her aching and lonely soul and embraced it. She'd given him space. She'd understood visiting Drumegan Castle was hard. But she'd felt as if they'd stood shoulder to shoulder the whole way. When they'd made love on Christmas Day, and he'd taken her to meet his family on Boxing Day, everything had just seemed to be surrounded in pink clouds.

But the storm had swept in. Why? What on earth had she done wrong?

She nervously licked her lips. The last few days had given her something else. A confidence she'd never felt before. She'd had a glimmer of a job that she might love. She'd found something she enjoyed and could be good at. It was a path she wanted to explore.

But she'd wanted Finlay to walk that path alongside her.

She lifted her chin and looked at him. Losing her gran had taught her one thing: love was worth reaching for and holding onto. She deserved love. She deserved to find happiness. She couldn't accept anything less.

It was so hard not to reach for his hand. She took a deep breath. 'I understand this Christmas has been hard, Finlay—I do. I understand that visiting the castle took courage. And it must have whipped up a whole host of memories that maybe you'd forgotten. But I have to ask you this.' She met his gaze, even though it killed her to do so. 'It's been five years, Finlay. Five years that you've turned your back on love. How much longer will it take? Do you think you'll ever be ready to love someone again?'

He could barely meet her gaze. 'It's been an amazing few days, Grace, but no, I'm not looking for love again. I don't think I'll ever be ready.'

She breathed in slowly through her nose. She wanted to shout. She wanted to cry. She wanted to punch him right in the chest. Hadn't he looked at Drumegan Castle and said he'd left things far too long? Hadn't he said that in a few different ways to her?

She'd obviously misunderstood—and that was her own foolish fault. When he'd talked about the neglected castle she'd assumed there was some parallel to himself and his life.

But that was clearly all in her head.

Finlay Armstrong might be the most handsome man she'd ever met. He might be the only man she'd ever felt a connection like this with. He might be the only man who'd stamped all over her fragile heart.

She could almost hear her gran's voice in her ears. She straightened her shoulders and looked him straight in the eye. He'd been right. She deserved so much better than he could offer. She loved him completely, with her whole entire heart. The one that was currently shattered all around them. She had too much pride for this. She wasn't going to hang around waiting for any scrap of his attention when she was worthy of so much more.

She bit her lips as tears threatened to pool in her eyes.

No. She wouldn't let them. He wouldn't see her cry. He wouldn't know just how much this hurt.

She kept her voice steady. 'Then thank you for a nice Christmas, Finlay. But now we're on our way home—it's clearly best that we both resume our own lives.'

CHAPTER TEN

HE FELT WRETCHED. It was as if a huge cloud of misery had descended over his head in an air of permanence.

He'd been miserable before. He could buy the T-shirt and wear it. But this was different.

He hadn't lost his wife. That was an understandable misery.

This time, he'd lost Grace. The strong, proud woman he still saw walking about his hotel on a daily basis. She didn't look in his direction—not once. She didn't try and engage in conversation. His few 'good mornings' had been resolutely ignored.

But that wasn't the thing that made him feel wretched.

It was the fact that when she thought no one was watching, her shoulders would slump, her head would bow and she'd pull a tissue from her apron.

Grace. The girl with the sparkling eyes, gorgeous smile and biggest heart in the world.

He'd done this.

This morning he'd woken up and turned over in bed. The empty space beside him hadn't just felt empty—it had felt like a massive void.

He'd never considered himself a coward. But why had he retreated so quickly? Was he actually scared? He hated feeling like this. And he hated the way he'd made Grace feel.

The sunlight sparkled off something in the corner of

the room. Silver paper. The gift that Mrs Archer had left him. He'd forgotten to open it.

He stood up and walked over. It took a few minutes to unfurl the curling silver ribbons and unwrap the silver paper. Inside was a black box. He flipped it open. An engraved silver heart gleamed at him.

Memories are special in every single way,
But new memories can be made every single day.

A long red ribbon was attached at the top. It was a Christmas decoration. Ready to be hung on a tree.

Right alongside his ceramic angel.

There was noise outside her flat as she approached. Grace froze. The last thing she needed was trouble. All she wanted to do was get inside, pull on her pyjamas and make some toast.

As she took another step forward she recognised the voices. She straightened up and walked around the corner. 'Emma, Sophie, Ashleigh—what are you doing here?'

'Grace!' Their shouts were probably heard all up and down the stairwells of the flats. She found herself enveloped in a group hug. Tears prickled at her eyes.

'You missed Christmas with us.' Emma held up a bag that clinked.

Ashleigh held up another, her engagement ring gleaming in the dim hall lights. 'Let us in, we want to hear all your news.'

Sophie was clutching a huge trifle in a glass bowl. 'What happened with your boss?'

She couldn't hold it together a second longer. She'd tried so hard all day. Seeing Finlay at the hotel was torture. Because now she knew what they could share together, she was having trouble being anything but angry.

She dissolved into tears of frustration.

'Grace? Grace? What's wrong?'

The keys were fumbled from her hands, her door opened and she was ushered into the flat. Within two minutes glasses appeared, wine was poured and her jacket was pulled from her shoulders. She sank down onto the sofa as Ashleigh opened the biggest box of chocolates in the world and dumped them on her lap.

It just made her cry all the more. Right now she valued her friends more than anything.

One hour later they were all gobsmacked. Emma slid her arm around her shoulders. 'Why didn't you tell us how you were feeling? You could have spent Christmas Day with any one of us.'

Grace shook her head. 'I didn't want to put a dampener on anyone else's Christmas.'

Sophie narrowed her eyes. 'But what about your Christmas? Finlay's certainly put a dampener on that.'

Grace sighed. 'It's not his fault I fell hook, line and sinker. I knew right from the start that he was a widower. I should have known better than to fall in love.'

Ashleigh leaned forward and slipped her hand into Grace's. 'But we can't always control where our heart will take us. Finlay took you to the staff party, he kissed you, he took you to Scotland, he slept with you. Then he took you to meet his family.' She shook her head and leaned back on her heels. 'It doesn't matter what way I look at this, Grace. He led you on. He didn't guard your heart the way he should have.'

'People don't always love you back,' Grace replied flatly.

Sophie slammed her hand on the table. 'Then the man's a fool.' She lifted her glass towards Grace. 'Whatever happens next, we're here for you, Grace. All of us. We're your family now.'

The words made her heart swell. She looked around at her friends with love and appreciation. 'Thank you, girls. That means so much. But I know what I need to do. I know how to take things forward for me.' She gave her head a shake. 'I don't need a man to determine what to do with my life. I have plans. I need someone who can stand by my side and support my choices in life. If Finlay can't do that—then he isn't the right man for me.' She lifted her glass to raise a toast then paused. Something sparked in her brain. She turned towards Sophie. 'Ashleigh said you went for drinks with some gorgeous Italian. I haven't heard about it yet. Spill.'

Anything to distract her from the way she was feeling right now.

Because one thing was for sure. The next steps would be the hardest.

He couldn't take it. He couldn't take it for a second longer. Four days were already four days too many.

He'd only needed one glimpse of Grace to know that this situation couldn't continue.

She was standing at the lifts with her cart, waiting to go upstairs. He walked over purposely and caught her by the elbow. 'Come with me for a second.'

'What?' She looked shocked. He'd caught her off guard.

He steered her towards one of the nearby empty rooms. 'We need to talk.'

She lifted her chin determinedly and folded her arms across her chest. 'Do we? I thought everything had been said.'

He ran his fingers through his hair and tried to find the right words. 'I hate seeing you like this.'

'Like what?'

'I hate seeing you so miserable—especially when I know it's all my fault.'

'I'm glad there's something we can agree on.' The words had obviously been on the tip of her tongue. She gave a little shake of her head. 'I'm a grown-up, Finlay. And so are you.'

He stepped closer. Her perfume drifted around him, giving him agonising flashbacks to the Christmas party and to Christmas night. 'Maybe we should have a rethink? Maybe, now that we're back, we could see each other when I'm back in London? I mean, I'm away a lot on business. But we could have drinks. Dinner.' He was rambling. Words were spilling out.

Her face paled. 'Tell me that you're joking?'

Not quite the effect he was looking for. 'Why?'

He could see the bottom edge of her jaw line tremble. It was something he'd never seen before in Grace Ellis. Rage.

'Why?' She shouted so loudly he winced. Guests in the bar next door would have heard.

She marched straight up under his chin, her eyes flashing madly. 'I'll tell you exactly why, Finlay Armstrong.' She pushed her finger into his chest. 'I am so much better than this.' She shook her head fiercely. 'I am not having a three-way relationship with a ghost. You can't move on because you won't let yourself. I don't want to spend my life living in the shadow of another woman. I don't deserve it and I don't need this. Don't come in here and offer me a tiny piece of yourself, Finlay. I don't want that. It's not enough. It will never be enough.' The fury started to dissipate from her voice. She took a step backwards. Her hand was shaking.

He saw her suck in a breath and pull herself back up. The expression in her brown eyes just about ripped out his soul. He'd tried to conjure up some remedy, some patchwork arrangement that might work. But his misplaced idea had backfired spectacularly.

'I want a change of shifts. I don't want to be around

when you're here. I'm going to speak to Clio about a transfer. We work in the Corminster across town. I'll ask if I can do my shifts there instead.'

'What?' Panic gripped him like a hand around his throat.

Her eyes focused on the door. She started walking straight towards it. Her shoulders seemed straighter, her head lift stronger. 'You'll have my resignation in the morning. I'll make it official and keep everything above board.'

For the briefest of pauses her footsteps faltered. There was so much circulating in his head. This was exactly what he didn't want. This was the absolute opposite of what he wanted.

Grace's voice softened for a second. 'Goodbye, Finlay,' she said as she opened the door and left.

CHAPTER ELEVEN

HE'D BEEN ON the roof most of the night. It was Frank who finally found him.

'Mr Armstrong? What are you doing? Why—you're freezing.' Frank whipped off his jacket and put it around his shoulders.

He hadn't meant to stay up here so long. But the frustration in him had built so much that he'd punched a wall in the penthouse and knew he had to get outside and away from anyone. The roof had been the ideal solution. Too bad he hadn't thought to bring a coat.

One hand held the ceramic angel. He'd pushed it into his pocket when he'd closed up the house. The other hand held the silver heart from Mrs Archer. One symbolised a lost love, the other a new.

Looking out over the darkness of London, lit only by Christmas lights, had been haunting. Watching the sun start to rise behind Battersea Park and the Albert Bridge had been a whole new experience. It made him realise that the lights at Battersea Park should be purple instead of white and red. Purple seemed a much more festive colour.

Frank's fierce grip pulled him to his feet and over to the stairs. The heat hit him as soon as he stepped inside again. He hadn't realised he was quite so cold.

Frank walked him down to the penthouse and made a quick phone call. 'I've ordered you some breakfast and some coffee.' He paused. 'No, scrub that. Give me a second.' He picked up the phone again and spoke quietly before replacing it. 'I've ordered something more appropriate.' He walked over to the room thermostat and turned it up. He looked around the room, then left and scouted in the bathroom, coming back with a fleecy dressing gown that Finlay rarely wore. 'Here, put that on too. I'm going to deal with something else. But I'll be back up in ten minutes to check on you.'

Heat was slowly but surely starting to permeate his body. His fingers were entirely white with almost a tinge of blue. They were starting to tingle as they warmed up.

He was still staring at the Christmas decorations. He'd made so many mistakes. He just didn't know where to start to try and put them right.

He closed his eyes for a second, trying to wish away some of the things that he'd said. When Anna had died, he'd truly believed the biggest part of him had died too. It wasn't true. Of course it wasn't true. He just hadn't been able to face up to his grief.

Concentrating on business and only business had been his shield. His saviour. It had also been his vice.

He'd let relationships with friends deteriorate. He'd shunned any pity or sympathy. It was so much easier to shut himself off from the world. A wave of embarrassment swept over him as he realised he'd also shut out his mum, dad and sister.

His sister had got married two years ago. He hadn't participated at all. He'd hardly even been able to bear attending. The occasion when he should have been happy for his sister, and dancing her around the marquee floor, he'd spent nursing a whiskey at the bar.

Now, she was pregnant with her first child and clearly nervous. Had he even told her how delighted he was to be an uncle? How much he was looking forward to seeing her with her child in her arms?

What kind of a person had he become?

There was a ping at the door. Room service. The trolley was wheeled in. He lifted the silver platter. Pancakes, eggs and bacon. Unusual choice. He looked in the lower part of the trolley for the coffee.

But there was no coffee. Instead, there was a hot chocolate, piled high with cream and marshmallows and dusted with chocolate.

He sagged back into his chair. Frank. How did he know?

The first sip was all it took. Two minutes later he was tearing into the pancakes, eggs and bacon. He flipped open his computer and did a quick search, made a few calls.

Then he made another.

'Mum? Hi. Yeah… Yeah… I'm fine. Well, I'm not fine. But let me handle that. I wanted to ask a favour. How would you feel about supervising the staff from a cleaning and restoration company for me? They can be there on the sixth of January.'

It was amazing. Just one simple but major act made him feel as though a huge dark cloud had been pushed off into the distance.

She spoke for a long, long time. Finlay knew better than to interrupt. He just gave the occasional, 'Yes…yes… yes…thanks…'

Her final words brought tears to a grown man's eyes. He put the phone back down as Frank came into the room.

The room seemed brighter, the early-morning sun sending a yellow streak across the room. Frank looked approvingly at the empty plate. 'Good, you've eaten. You're looking a bit more like yourself.' He bit his lip.

Finlay stood up. He wanted to shower and get changed. The more his head cleared, the stronger his heart pounded.

For the first time in five years he had personal clarity. His business acumen had never been affected, but his own life?

It was time to finally get started.

Frank was still standing.

'What's wrong?'

'You have a guest. She wanted to leave something in your office. But I told her to come upstairs.'

Finlay caught his breath. Frank's face was serious. 'I'll take this,' he said briskly as he stepped forward for the empty tray. His face was impartial but his muttered words weren't. 'Don't you dare upset her. Just don't.'

Somehow he got the feeling that if he were the last man on a sinking ship right now, Frank wouldn't let him in the lifeboat. Frank's green coat disappeared.

There could only be one person that would cause this type of fatherly protection in Frank.

The heart that had already been pounding started to race to a sprint. 'Grace?'

He stuck his head out of the door. Grace was standing rigid, a white envelope clutched in one hand.

'Grace?'

Her steely gaze met his. He'd never seen her look quite so determined. His heart gave a little surge.

She straightened her shoulders. She was wearing a classy black wool coat, with an unusual cut. It emphasised her small waist. There were red skirts sticking out from the bottom of the coat and he could see the red collar at her neck.

But there was something else—a real assuredness about her. His heart swelled a little. Grace just got more spectacular every time he saw her.

She marched forward and thrust the envelope towards him. 'I just wanted to leave this for you, but Frank insisted I spoke to you. My resignation.'

It was as if all his best dreams and worst nightmares had decided to cram themselves into one hour of his life.

Grace's hair was styled a little differently and her lips were outlined in red.

She looked vaguely familiar and it took a few seconds to realise why. 'You look like Alice Archer,' he said quietly. His hand reached up to touch her hair but Grace flinched backwards. He swallowed. 'The only thing different is your hair colour. You look amazing, Grace.'

Her eyebrows shot up. 'Really?'

As he realised what he'd just said he gave a nervous laugh. 'I mean it, though. I do.'

She was still holding out the envelope towards him. She had her black leather gloves on that he'd bought her. He shook his head. 'I'm not taking it.'

Her brow furrowed. 'You have to. You can't stop me resigning.' His reaction seemed to spur her on. 'There's no way you can stop me. I've made plans. I'm transferring my shifts. I've enrolled at college to do interior design and Clio will give me shifts that suit. I'm moving on, Finlay. I'm not going to stay here and watch you walk about in a fog for the rest of your life.'

There were rosy spots on her cheeks. There was an edge of determination to her. He loved it. He loved everything about it.

He walked over and put his hands on her shoulders. 'Grace, that's the best thing I've heard this year. You will be a fantastic interior designer. You *are* a fantastic interior designer. I can't think of anything more perfect for you. But you don't need to leave here to do that.'

There was an almost startled expression on her face. 'Yes. Yes, I do. I can't be around you, Finlay. I *won't* be around you.'

His heart twisted inside his chest. 'Not even if I tell you that I love you? Not even if I tell you I've been a complete fool?' He stopped to draw breath. 'Grace, for the first time in years you've made me wake up and look around. I wasn't paying attention to life—oh, I thought I was, but not really, not the way I should have.' He ran his fingers through his hair. He wished he'd showered. He wished he'd changed out of the clothes he'd spent all night wearing on the roof. He put his hands on his hips. 'It wasn't just Drumegan Castle that I neglected. It was everything else too.'

'What does that mean?'

He reached out for her hands. 'It means everything, Grace. I think I have been ready to move on. The only person that hadn't acknowledged that was me.'

She shook her head as he clutched her hands even tighter.

'I'm sorry. I don't know how to do this any more. I've forgotten every rule of dating that I ever knew.' He pressed one hand against his heart. 'All I know is that ever since I met you, I've felt alive again. I've woken up and had something to look forward to. I'll never forget Anna, but, for a few days there, I felt guilty because I'd hardly thought about her at all. My mind was just filled with you, Grace. Every time you smiled, every time you winked at me, every time you looked sad. The way you loved Christmas. When you shared with me about your grandmother. But I looked at you, and your capacity to love, and wondered if I could ever meet that. Ever fulfil that for you.'

Grace blinked and licked her red lips. Her gaze was steady. 'What are you doing, Finlay? Where has this come from?'

He laughed and pointed to his head. 'In here.' Then his heart. 'And in here. I spent most of last night sitting on the roof trying to get my head in order. You know, after a while, you start to think the Battersea Power Station lights should be purple.'

The edges of her lips curled upwards for a few seconds. 'But I still want everything. I don't want half a relationship. Anna's gone, Finlay. But I'm not. I'm here. I won't share. Not with anyone dead or alive.'

She was deadly serious. It was written all over her face and it just made his heart ache all the more for the pain he'd caused her. 'I love you, Grace Ellis. How long does it officially take people to fall in love? Can it happen in a few hours, a few days, a few weeks? Because that's what it feels like to me. I'm sorry for what I said in the helicopter. I'm sorry for what I suggested yesterday. I don't want just to see you now and then. I want to see you every single day.' He reached over and touched her cheek. 'Every single day for the rest of my life.'

Her eyes were wet. He could see her struggle to swallow. 'I don't know, Finlay. I just don't know. You hurt me.'

His hands were shaking by now. 'I know. I'm sorry. I can't promise that I'm good at all this. But what I can promise is that every day, for the rest of my life, I'll try and show you how much I love you. How much you mean to me. Will you let me, Grace? Will you let me try?'

He pulled his hands back. He had to give her space. He had to respect her wishes. He'd already trampled all over her heart once.

She turned and looked out of the window, across the snow-dusted rooftops of London.

'How long were you up on that roof?'

'What?'

'How long were you up on that roof?'

He shook his head. 'I'm not sure. I went up to try and clear my head. It must have been the early hours. I was there until Frank found me this morning.'

'And you didn't freeze to death?'

He could see her watching his reflection in the glass. 'Not yet. There wasn't enough snow. And I didn't have anyone to make snow angels with. It didn't seem like the right place, or the right time.'

'How do I know any of this is true?'

He nodded and walked over to the kitchen counter. 'When I phoned my mother this morning about cleaning up the castle, she threatened me with grievous bodily harm if I came back to visit without you.'

She spun around. 'So, your mother wants you to date me?'

He smiled. 'No, my mother wants me to marry you. But I have to beg for forgiveness first.'

She sucked in a breath and pulled her hands around herself. She rocked back and forth a little. 'You're going to clean up the castle?'

He nodded. 'Starting January the sixth. Once it's clean, I will probably need to hire an interior designer to help me redecorate.' He raised his eyebrows. 'Can you think of anyone I might ask?'

She took a step closer to the counter. 'I might do. You should think about the person who thought purple was such a Christmas colour. She decorated one of the most exclusive hotels in London.' He nodded and smiled as she added, 'But I've heard she's expensive.'

He picked up the decorations from the counter top. 'There's one last thing I need to do. To make this official. To make this right.' He held out his hand towards her. 'Will you come with me?'

She looked at his hand for a second before finally reaching out and sliding her hand into his. He walked them over to the private elevator, pressing buttons to take them to the ground floor.

It was New Year's Eve. The hotel was busy with guests staying for the New Year's celebrations. Finlay ignored them all. He strode across the foyer with Grace's hand in his, only slowing down when they reached the main Christmas tree.

He took a deep breath. 'A few weeks ago you found

something and set it on my pillow.' He pulled the ceramic angel from his pocket and lifted it, hanging it on the tree. 'You also remembered to bring it to Scotland with us.' He lifted his hand towards it. 'It's a memory. One that I will treasure and respect.' He pulled something else from his pocket. 'But I have another gift.' He nodded his head and smiled. 'This one was left in my office. It's from a mutual friend. Discreet. Knowledgeable. With more finesse in her little finger than I can ever hope to achieve in my life.' He lifted up the silver heart and hung it on the tree in front of them. 'Alice gave me this before we'd ever met. She knew before I did, before *we* did, the potential that was in the air.'

He spun the silver heart around so Grace could see the engraving.

She read it out slowly. *'"Memories are special in every single way, But new memories can be made every single day."'* She gasped and put her hand to her mouth. 'Alice gave you that?'

He nodded as he turned Grace around and slid his arms around her waist.

'How do you feel about making some new memories, for The Armstrong, and for Drumegan Castle?'

She smiled and wound her arms around his neck. 'I think I might have to be persuaded.'

He caught the twinkle in her eye. 'And how might I do that?'

She laughed. 'I can think of a few ways.' Then stood on her tiptoes to whisper in his ear.

He picked her up and swung her around. 'Grace Ellis, we're in public!' He put her feet back on the floor. 'But we've got to start somewhere.'

And so he kissed her—again and again and again.

* * * * *

"Tonight," he whispered. "Eight o'clock."

She should have done what she always did when he pretended to put a move on her—given a shake of her head, stepped away, maybe let out a little chuckle of mingled amusement and annoyance. It was only a silly game between them and they'd been playing it the same way for months now, ever since she'd begun working with Bravo Construction, made friends with his sisters and started getting invited to Bravo family gatherings. They did this all the time and it didn't mean a thing. All she had to do was stick with the program.

Shake your head. Move away. Her mind told her what to do, but her body and her heart weren't listening. She had so much yearning all bunched up and burning inside her. The yearning had her hesitating, frozen on the brink of a dangerous emotional cliff.

Maybe it was her crazy Christmas-fling fantasy. Or his sweetness with the girls. It might have been loneliness stirred up and aching from too many years of self-control and strict self-denial.

Or maybe it was simply the perfect manly scent of him, the low, rough sound of his voice that had haunted her as a teenager and now, as a grown woman, stirred her way more than she ought to allow.

Whatever it was that finally pushed her over the edge of the cliff, she went. She fell. She turned her head back toward him behind her and whispered so low he probably shouldn't have been able to hear it. "Great. See you then. I'll be naked."

* * *

The Bravos of Justice Creek:
Where bold hearts collide under western skies

A BRAVO FOR CHRISTMAS

BY
CHRISTINE RIMMER

All rights reserved including the right of reproduction in whole or in part in any form. This edition is published by arrangement with Harlequin Books S.A.

This is a work of fiction. Names, characters, places, locations and incidents are purely fictional and bear no relationship to any real life individuals, living or dead, or to any actual places, business establishments, locations, events or incidents. Any resemblance is entirely coincidental.

This book is sold subject to the condition that it shall not, by way of trade or otherwise, be lent, resold, hired out or otherwise circulated without the prior consent of the publisher in any form of binding or cover other than that in which it is published and without a similar condition including this condition being imposed on the subsequent purchaser.

® and ™ are trademarks owned and used by the trademark owner and/or its licensee. Trademarks marked with ® are registered with the United Kingdom Patent Office and/or the Office for Harmonisation in the Internal Market and in other countries.

Christine Rimmer came to her profession the long way around. She tried everything from acting to teaching to telephone sales. Now she's finally found work that suits her perfectly. She insists she never had a problem keeping a job—she was merely gaining "life experience" for her future as a novelist. Christine lives with her family in Oregon. Visit her at www.christinerimmer.com.

For MSR.
Always.

Chapter One

The girls had been decorating Darius again.

Ava Malloy entered the Blueberry troop club-house to find him surrounded by ten laughing Blueberries, ages six through eight. He wore jeans, boots and a thermal work shirt. The girls had added a pink paper crown dusted with glitter, an oversize pair of red cat's-eye glasses and a giant purple pop bead necklace. And someone had tied a length of rumpled blue velvet around his neck—for a cape or possibly a royal robe.

Ava's seven-year-old daughter, Sylvie, caught sight of Ava at the door and crowed, "Mommy, look! Darius is king of the Blueberries!" as the other girls giggled and clapped.

Ava played along and sketched a bow. "Your Majesty."

Darius was already looking her way. He did that

a lot—watched her. Teased her. The man was born a shameless flirt. At her greeting, he lifted a dark eyebrow and returned a slow, regal nod that caused his paper crown to dip precariously near one gleaming blue eye.

He should have looked ridiculous. But no. Somehow, glittery paper crowns, tattered velvet capes and giant toy necklaces only made Darius Bravo seem more manly.

And he was so good with the girls. Ava hadn't expected that. She'd known him since high school, and he'd been with lots of women. He'd never settled down with any of them, though, never started a family. She'd always assumed that kids didn't interest him.

Yet somehow, he'd let himself get roped into helping out with the Blueberry Christmas project this year. For the last six weeks, he'd been supervising the troop as they assembled, painted and furnished five kit dollhouses for five local children's charities. He'd done most of the work, while at the same time managing to get each girl involved in a constructive way.

So yeah. Darius was hot and charming *and* he had a way with children. Ava's Sylvie adored him. And that made Ava like him more, made her more susceptible to the teasing glances he lavished on her and the jokingly suggestive things he said.

For so long, she'd considered herself totally over whatever had made him so tempting to her in high school. Now she feared she might be coming down with a slight crush on the guy all over again. She might even have fantasized about him once or twice.

Or a lot.

And so what? She needed her fantasies. When it

came to romance and passion and sex, fantasies were all she had.

And no, she didn't feel sorry for herself because she didn't have a man. Ava didn't want another relationship. She'd loved Craig Malloy and lost him, had the medals and the folded flag to prove it. Six years after the casualty notification officer knocked on her door, grief at Craig's passing still haunted her. It wasn't the clawing agony it used to be. However, it was bad enough that she didn't want to get serious with any guy. Not yet. Maybe never.

But was it so wrong to yearn for a little magic and passion? Ava wanted the shivery thrill of a hot kiss, the glory of a tender touch.

To put it bluntly, she would love to get laid.

A man for Christmas. Was that too much to ask? A lovely holiday fling. Yeah. That would work perfectly for her. No strings attached—and over and done by New Year's Day. Scratch where it itched.

And move on. To her, that sounded just perfect. But she had a daughter to raise and a demanding real estate business to run. Somehow, she never found the time to track down the right no-strings lover.

The door opened behind her, letting in a gust of icy November air. Chloe Bravo, one of Darius's sisters-in-law, slipped through. "Hey, Ava."

Ava dismissed her absurd Christmas-fling fantasy and smiled at Chloe, whose six-year-old stepdaughter, Annabelle, was also a Blueberry and Sylvie's best friend. Leaning close to Chloe, Ava asked softly, "How are we doing for Saturday?"

Chloe was tall, blonde and drop-dead gorgeous. She and Ava both worked with Bravo Construction, which was owned and run by two of Darius's half siblings, Garrett and Nell. "I'm still waiting to firm up the delivery on a sofa, two bedroom suites and most of the wall and table decor." An interior designer, Chloe was staging a Bravo-built home for the open house Ava would be holding on the weekend.

Ava pulled Chloe to the side of the mudroom/entry area, away from the laughing Blueberries and their blue-eyed king. "You know I'll help when it comes to the crunch."

Chloe removed her bright red beanie and shook off a light dusting of snow. "Thank you. There's way too much going on. Thanksgiving's in three days, and then there's Black Friday. I may have to skip the family shopping trip if I want to get it all pulled together by Saturday."

"You can't miss that." The Black Friday shopping trip was a Bravo family tradition. The Bravo women got up at three in the morning and caravanned to Denver. "Just give me your design plans at dinner on Thursday." Ava and Sylvie were having Thanksgiving with the Bravos this year. "I'll go in first thing Friday morning and set up whatever you didn't get to. Then you can come by after the trip to Denver and double-check that it's all ready to go."

"I couldn't. You have enough on your plate—and aren't *you* going to Denver?"

"Stop." Grinning, Ava shook her head. "I know you really want to go. I'll take care of the last-minute stuff, no problem."

"You're sure?"

"Positive."

Chloe beamed. "You're a lifesaver. And I owe you."

"All right, everyone." Out in the main area of the clubhouse, Janice Hayes, the troop leader, clapped her hands lightly for attention. "Moms and dads are arriving. Let's get everything picked up and put away."

Laughing and chattering, the girls set to work stuffing their cubbies and cleaning up their supplies and tools. Darius shrugged out of his regal finery and enlisted the aid of a few moms to help him move the five fully assembled dollhouses back to their assigned spots along one wall.

Ava helped, too. She put away paints and craft supplies.

Then Janice waved a bright pink clipboard for attention again. "We have three weeks until the Holiday Ball." The dollhouses would go on display in the ballroom lobby during the annual Haltersham Hotel Holiday Ball. After the ball, the dollhouses would be given to five different centers for disadvantaged or seriously ill children in the Justice Creek area.

"It may seem like plenty of time, but there's still a lot of painting, furnishing and accessorizing to do. And we all know how it is at the holidays. Everyone's busy and things get away from us. Anyone who can put in a few hours next week or the week after, let me know. I'm working out a schedule." Hands went up. Janice jotted down names and times as daughters and parents volunteered.

In the buzz of activity, Ava had almost forgotten the Blueberry king. But then, there he was, moving in just behind her left shoulder. She felt the air stir with his heat. His wonderful scent of leather, sawdust and soap tried to seduce her.

A shiver of yearning lifted the hairs on the back of her neck.

And all at once, she was fifteen again, turning from her hall locker, worn backpack sliding down one arm, to find him standing right behind her...

"Ava Janko." He'd said her name that day like he was daring her to do something crazy and thrilling and probably dangerous.

He might have saved his breath.

Ava didn't do dangerous, not ever again—not by choice, anyway. Her parents were dreamers. They'd always claimed they lived on love. The way Ava saw it, living on love just made you broke. Somebody had to consider the future, behave responsibly and remember to pay the rent. She was only fifteen, but she babysat, helped her aunt Rae clean houses and worked part-time at Deeliteful Donuts on Creekside Drive a few blocks from the family double-wide.

"Dare Bravo," she replied, wrapping both arms around her backpack, using it as a lumpy, faded shield between them, a shield she really needed. Because those blue eyes burned into hers, and that too-full bottom lip of his made her wonder things she shouldn't—like how it would feel to kiss him.

"Party Friday at Cal's house." Cal Flanders was a linebacker on the Justice Creek High football team. Everybody knew about the parties at Cal's. His parents didn't spend a lot of time at home. "Come with me. I'll pick you up at seven."

Her heart did something really scary inside her chest—kind of froze, twisted and then rolled. For a second or two *Yes* tried to jump right out of her mouth.

But she didn't let it.

Uh-uh. She tipped her chin higher. "No, thanks."

Her refusal didn't seem to faze him. "Why not?" he asked with a definite smirk.

So she lowered her voice to keep others from hearing and said, "Because you're the rich-boy quarterback of the Justice Creek High football team who's got a different cheerleader hanging on his arm every time I turn around—not to mention, I'm too young for you, and you know it, too."

He stuck his hands in his pockets and went on smirking. "You're too young for me? What girl thinks like that?"

"A smart girl." She clutched her backpack harder and refused to drop her gaze.

He leaned a little closer. "I know you like me. If you didn't, you wouldn't be keeping track of who I go with." His minty breath touched her cheek, and longing burned through her—to be like every other girl her age and take a chance now and then, to flutter her eyelashes, to blush and smile and say she would love to go to that party at Cal's.

But she had plans for her life, and they didn't include ending up where she was right now—in a double-wide at the Seven Pines Mobile Home Park. He was too popular and too good-looking, and it wouldn't last and she knew it. When it was over, he would move on to the next pretty girl, leaving her with her heart in tatters. She had no time for a battered, broken heart. She needed her focus on what mattered: a better life for herself.

She tried to explain. "It's just…a bad idea. You're nothing but trouble for a girl like me, Dare."

He scoffed. "'A girl like you.' I don't know what that means."

"I already told you. I'm too young for you, and I'm from the south side of town."

"I don't care where you live. And I'm not asking for anything that'll get either of us in trouble. I just want you to go to a party with me. You're putting limits on yourself because you're scared."

He refused to understand. But why should he? He was a Bravo and he had it all.

Of course she put limits on herself. Limits protected her from making the kinds of bad choices that could mess up her life all over again. "I am not scared." Her voice didn't shake at all. "I have no reason to be. 'Cause I'm not going to Cal's with you."

He leaned in even closer. She should have jumped back. But her pride wouldn't let her. "Liar," he whispered. "You *are* scared."

"How many times do I have to tell you? I'm. Not. Scared."

"Fine. Be that way. But someday you're gonna say yes to me, Ava."

To that, she set her shoulders and shook her head. Darius backed off then. He gave a low laugh, as though he knew things she didn't have a clue about and now she would never find out what those things were. And finally, with an easy shrug of those sexy broad shoulders, he turned and walked away.

She heard a week later that he took Marilyn Lender, head of the cheerleading squad, to Cal's party. Marilyn didn't last long. Dare was with someone else by Homecoming. And someone else soon after that. He didn't ask Ava out again, so she never got a chance to prove to him that he had it all wrong and she would never say yes to him.

And then that spring, he graduated and left town. She heard that he moved to Las Vegas for a while, of all things. And then to LA. Eventually, he returned to Colorado and got a business degree from CU. By the time he came back home to take over his father's metal fabricating business, she'd married Craig and moved to San Diego.

Seventeen years had passed since those few moments by her locker at Justice Creek High.

And yet somehow, today, as Dare stood at her shoulder in the Blueberry clubhouse on the Monday before Thanksgiving, seventeen years ago felt way too much like yesterday.

He moved, bending closer. She knew what was coming: a teasing fake pass. She was right.

"Tonight," he whispered. "Eight o'clock."

She should have done what she always did when he pretended to put a move on her, given a shake of her head, stepped away, maybe let out a little chuckle of mingled amusement and annoyance. It was only a silly game between them, and they'd been playing it the same way for months now, ever since she'd begun working with Bravo Construction, made friends with his sisters and started getting invited to Bravo family gatherings. They did this all the time, and it didn't mean a thing. All she had to do was stick with the program.

Shake your head. Move away. Her mind told her what to do, but her body and her heart weren't listening. She had so much yearning all bunched up and burning inside her. The yearning had her hesitating, frozen on the brink of a dangerous emotional cliff.

Maybe it was her crazy Christmas-fling fantasy. Or his sweetness with the girls. It might have been loneliness stirred up and aching from too many years of self-control and strict self-denial.

Or maybe it was simply the perfect manly scent of him, the low, rough sound of his voice that had haunted her as a teenager and now, as a grown woman, stirred her way more than she ought to allow.

Whatever it was that finally pushed her over the edge of the cliff, she went. She fell. She turned her head back toward him behind her and whispered so low he probably shouldn't have been able to hear it, "Great. See you then. I'll be naked."

Chapter Two

Darius heard her, no doubt about that.

She knew by the way his big body went dead still, by the sudden sharp intake of his breath.

Run away, run away fast! shouted the internal voice of smart, practical, everyday Ava, who knew better than to issue blatantly sexual invitations to a man she'd always promised herself she would never be foolish enough to fall into bed with.

But she didn't run away. Not immediately.

Instead, she compounded her own idiocy by turning fully toward him and looking him straight in the eye.

He gaped back at her, his expression pure deer-in-the-headlights. Clearly, she'd surprised him.

And not in a good way.

So then. In spite of what he'd said seventeen years ago, the last thing he really wanted was for her to finally say yes to him.

Her heart beat a sick, limping rhythm under her ribs as she accepted the fact that she'd just made a complete fool of herself.

Dear God, please let me sink right through this floor this very instant.

But God didn't come to her rescue and suck her beneath the surface of the earth. The world kept on turning. Behind her, Janice continued scheduling volunteers—and Dare Bravo stared at her like she'd just sprouted horns and a long, forked tail.

Behind her, Janice dismissed the group. "All right, everyone. Happy Thanksgiving. See you all next Monday."

Ava wheeled and made a beeline for her daughter. She had Sylvie in her coat, wool hat and mittens in seconds flat. Then, with a cheerful wave and a "Happy Thanksgiving!" she got the hell out of there.

"I don't see why you won't come with us." Kate Janko ate a bite of mashed potatoes and gazed reproachfully across the dinner table at Ava. "The weatherman's promised no more snow until next week. The roads will be clear for the drive tomorrow. Ava sweetie, everyone will be there." *There* was Coeur d'Alene, Idaho, where Ava's parents, her brothers and their families would all be attending a big Janko family reunion over the coming Thanksgiving weekend.

"Mom, I'm sorry, but I can't," Ava said for the umpteenth time. "I've got a closing on Wednesday and an important open house on Saturday. It's just not doable."

"You work so hard, honey." Her mother cast a wistful glance around Ava's dining room, with its gorgeous built-in cabinets and art glass chandelier. Ava was proud of the cozy two-story bungalow she'd bought when she first returned to Justice Creek from California. It might not be large, but she'd restored it meticulously, keeping true to its Arts and Crafts style. "I just don't see why you can't take a few days off and be with your family for Thanksgiving."

"Gramma, we just can't," Sylvie piped up. "We're having Thanksgiving at Annabelle's aunt Clara's house. And then Saturday night, I'm going for a sleepover at Annabelle's house."

Kate frowned. "Aren't you a little young for sleep-overs?"

Sylvie puffed up her thin chest. "Annabelle's too young 'cause she's only six." Every *s* had a soft, sweet little hiss to it. Sylvie had lost two front baby teeth, one in October and one just two weeks ago. "But I'm seven, and that is old enough." She glanced Ava's way. "Mommy said so. Right, Mommy?"

Ava hid a smile and gave her daughter a nod.

Kate opened her mouth to voice further objections. But Ava's dad, Paul, put his hand over his wife's. "Looks like our girls are staying home for Thanksgiving, Kitty Kat."

Ava's mother turned her hand over and gave her husband's fingers a squeeze. They shared a glance both tender and fond. They still called the double-wide at Seven Pines home. And all you had to do was look at them together to know they still lived on love. "Well, I wish you would change your mind," said Kate as Paul reluctantly took his hand back and both of them picked up their forks again.

"Sorry, Mom. But we just can't get away."

"We'll miss you," said her father.

"We'll miss you, too," Ava dutifully replied.

"May I please be 'scused till dessert?" asked Sylvie. "I ate everything, even my broccoli, and it was gross."

Biting her lip to keep her expression appropriately serious, Ava turned to her daughter. "That you ate your broccoli is excellent. Broccoli is very good for you."

"It doesn't taste like it's good for me. *Chocolate* tastes like it's good for me."

Ava bit her lip harder. Grandpa Paul made a faint choking sound as he tried not to laugh. Gramma Kate swatted him under the table.

Ava said, "Sylvie. What do you do when you don't like the taste of your food?"

"I eat it or I don't eat it," Sylvie replied obediently. "If I don't eat it, I don't get dessert. But I'm not s'posed to say that I don't like it because that is *rude*."

"Very good. And saying that your broccoli is gross is the same as saying that you don't like it."

Sylvie wrinkled her nose but conceded, "Yeah. I guess so. I s'pose I am sorry."

Ava nodded. "Excellent. You are excused. Clear off your place, please."

Sylvie beamed a giant smile, displaying the wide gap where her baby teeth had been. She jumped up, grabbed her plate and trotted through the arch to the kitchen.

As soon as she was gone, Kate lowered her voice and asked, "Did you hear about Nick Yancy?"

Ava didn't know Nick well. He was in his early twenties, a sweet cowboy and something of a star in the local rodeo. In the last few months, Nick and Jody Bravo, one of Darius's half sisters, had become friends. Jody swore it was only that—friendship. But everyone thought Nick wanted it to be more, even though he was six or seven years younger than Jody.

And the bleak expression on her mom's face alarmed her. "Did something happen to Nick?"

"Tractor accident," said her father somberly.

"Oh, no. When?"

"They found him just this afternoon. The story is that a spring locking pin failed. He got crushed in a rollover. They rushed him to Justice Creek General but he died on the way."

Ava pushed her plate away. "Now, that's just all wrong."

Her mom nodded. "He was a fine young man. They haven't said yet when the service will be. I'm guessing this weekend sometime. We should be there." Ava's mom and dad had gone to school with Nick's stepdad. "But we have the Idaho trip…"

Ava took the hint and volunteered, "I'll go if I can possibly manage it."

"That would be good." Her dad reached across and patted her hand.

And her mom had tears in her eyes.

Nick Yancy, gone. Suddenly, that Ava had embarrassed herself with Darius Bravo didn't matter in the least. A good man was lost. Life could be so cruel.

But then her mom said, "I saw that nice Ray Tucker at Safeway. He asked how you were doing." Ray was a CPA now. Ava had gone out with him twice years ago, when they were both at Mountain High Junior College, before she married Craig. "I told him you were going great guns with the real estate, and he said to be sure to say hi to you."

Ava knew where this was headed and didn't like it

in the least. She replied flatly, "If you see him again, tell him I said hi back."

"He's divorced now, you know. And I personally think he's still carrying a torch for you."

Ava leveled her sternest look on her mom. "Please don't."

"You should be dating. After what happened to poor Nick, it just brings it all home."

"Mom, I know Nick Yancy was a great guy, and it's awful that we've lost him so suddenly and so young. But it's just wrong for you to use his dying as an excuse for your matchmaking."

"I am not matchmaking."

"Oh, yes you are."

"I only meant that you never know what can happen, and you need to squeeze every drop of love and happiness from life while you can. Craig was a wonderful man, but it's been six years and you're still young, with so much to give. There's no reason you can't find a good man who—"

"Mom, can we just not go there tonight? Please."

Her mother sighed and shared another meaningful glance with Ava's dad. "I think you're cheating yourself," Kate said quietly at last.

"I'm very happy, Mom. I promise you. I have a brilliant, beautiful daughter, good friends and a loving family. I'm blessed with a fine house to live in. My business is booming. I don't need a man to make my life complete." As she spoke, she had a sudden, vivid image of Darius in his paper crown and pop beads. She felt her cheeks flame bright pink. Dear Lord, she would have to see him on Thursday at Clara's house. How awkward was that going to be?

Better not to even think about it.

Her mother asked anxiously, "Honey, are you okay? You look a little feverish."

"I'm perfect," Ava said firmly, and she reminded herself yet again that what she'd said to Darius didn't matter in the least. "Now, let me clear off. I'll get the coffee going and dish up the apple pie à la mode."

Her parents stayed until after Sylvie was in bed. As they went out the door, Ava pulled her mom back for a moment and pressed a check for six hundred dollars into her hand.

"Oh, honey. You don't have to do that," her mother protested softly.

"But I want to. Gas for the trip. And I know you're going to send flowers for Nick Yancy from the family. This should help with that, too." She'd been giving them money since she got her first babysitting job. At least now she could afford it. Back then, it had been tough to part with each and every one of those hard-earned dollars.

"You're the best daughter I ever had," said Kate, same as she always did when Ava helped her out a little.

And as always, Ava replied, "I'm your only daughter, so I'd better be the best."

Kate grabbed her close for a hug. "Thanks, baby."

"You're welcome. Love you, Mom…"

Thanksgiving with the Bravos. It should have been great.

Ava had been looking forward to all the warmth and good times of a big family get-together—but minus her bossy brothers and her mother's relentless attempts to get her to start dating again. However, no matter how often Ava lectured herself about keeping things in perspective, her own cringe-worthy behavior at the Blueberry troop clubhouse Monday afternoon had turned her anticipation to dread.

Through Tuesday and Wednesday and the first half of the big day itself, she kept up the internal pep talks. She told herself it was nothing. People said ridiculous things to each other all the time. She needed to get over it and move on.

And anyway, there would be a crowd at Clara's. It should be easy to steer clear of Darius. Given time, they would both forget her over-the-top comeback to his silly, meaningless flirting.

She and Sylvie arrived at Clara and Dalton Ames's house right on time at two.

Clara swung the door open, and the wonderful, savory smells of garlic, sage and roast turkey drifted out. She ushered Ava and Sylvie in and then enfolded each of them in a welcoming hug. "So good to see you."

"You, too," said Ava, admiring the garland of autumn leaves twined on the stair rail and the miniature pumpkins and gourds piled in a decorative bowl on the entry table. "Everything looks so festive, and dinner smells amazing."

Judging by the laughter and chatter coming from the great room down the hall, the beautiful old Victorian was already packed with Bravos. Franklin Bravo, the family patriarch, had fathered nine children—four by his first wife, Sondra. And five more by his then-mistress and eventually his second wife, Willow. Of those nine Bravo siblings and half siblings, four were married now and three of those had children. All of them were expected for dinner today, so avoiding Darius should be no problem.

"Toss your coats on the bed in there," Clara said, indicating the master bedroom off the front hall.

"Thanks." Ava shrugged out of her coat.

She was just about to help Sylvie with the tie on her favorite red wool hat when her daughter cried, "Darius! We're here!" and took off down the hall toward the tall, impossibly handsome man at the other end.

He wore a cream-colored sweater and black jeans, and even from the opposite end of the hallway, his eyes seemed bluer than usual. Damn him. Why did he have to be so good-looking? For a moment, she stared at him and he gazed back at her, and it was awful and wonderful, strange and exciting.

Sylvie skidded to a stop in front of him and wriggled in place, suddenly shy. "Hi."

"Happy Thanksgiving, Sylvie. Love your hat."

"It's red." She pointed at the cluster of knit daisies over her left ear. "With flowers."

"And very pretty."

"Mommy ties it double for me so it won't come undone."

"Ah." Darius shot Ava a glance full of humor—and something else that made her knees go weak.

"Would you please help me untie it?" Sylvie stretched her neck and pointed at the double-knotted bow.

"Let's see here…" He dropped to a crouch in front of her and went right to work.

At the same time, the doorbell chimed and Clara turned to let in the next guest, her half sister Jody. Ava willed her pulse to slow the heck down and made herself stride over to where Dare knelt before her little girl.

Those big hands with their long, clever fingers made short work of the knot. He pulled one end of the bow, and it fell open. "There you go."

Sylvie scooped off the hat, causing her caramel-colored hair to spark and crackle with static. She giggled, "I'm 'lectric!"

"You sure are." Dare's low chuckle set Ava's nerves humming.

Sylvie stuck out her little hand and patted his rock-like shoulder. "Thank you very much."

"You're welcome." He rose as Annabelle Bravo, all plump cheeks, thick dark hair and big brown eyes, raced down from upstairs. With a quick wave at Ava, she reached the main floor and headed straight for her best friend. "Sylvie! Finally. Come on. Aunt Clara let me make a fort with blankets upstairs in a spare room. Kiera helped." Kiera was Clara and Dalton's toddler.

Sylvie shed her coat and handed it and the hat to Ava. "Can I, Mom?"

"Sure." Annabelle already had Sylvie's hand and was pulling her toward the stairs at a run. "Okay, you two," Ava called after them. "No running in the house."

Annabelle slowed. "Sorry, Ava." The two girls giggled together and proceeded up the stairs at a slower pace, leaving Ava alone at that end of the hall with the one man she didn't want to be anywhere near at the moment.

But then Clara and Jody, who had disappeared into the makeshift coatroom, emerged and came toward them.

Ava thought of poor Nick Yancy, Jody's friend. "Jody! How are you?"

"Okay." Jody didn't look okay. Shadows rimmed her eyes, and her smile was forced.

Clara gave her half sister's arm a fond pat and went on into the great room, while Ava wrapped Jody in a hug and whispered, "My mom told me about Nick. I'm so very sorry."

Jody held on for an extra few seconds and admitted softly, "It's awful. He was such a sweet guy. I still don't really believe it..."

Ava murmured a few more soft condolences. She added, "I heard the funeral's Sunday afternoon." Her mom had called her yesterday with the information. "My parents know Nick's stepdad, but they're out of town for the holiday. I'm going to try to put in an appearance Sunday, represent the family..."

"That's good of you, Ava. Nick and I had only been friends for a few months..." Jody's voice trailed off as though she didn't know quite what to say next.

Who did in a situation like this?

Ava took her by the shoulders and held her gaze. "If I can do anything. *Anything.*"

"Thanks. You're a sweetheart." Jody put on a smile.

Ava released her.

Jody moved on to Darius, who greeted her with open arms and a fond, "Hey, little sister..."

Ava saw her opportunity to escape him and grabbed it. She turned for the relative safety of the master suite— after all, she needed to stash the outerwear, didn't she?

In the bedroom, she added the two coats and Sylvie's red hat to the growing pile on the king-size bed. And then, stalling a little to give Darius time to wander back to the great room, she popped into the bathroom

to smooth her hair and make sure she didn't have lipstick on her teeth.

Her hair looked fine and her teeth were lipstick-free.
But her eyes had a glazed sort of look and her face was
flushed all the way down to the scoop neckline of her
favorite cashmere sweater. Really, she needed to settle
the heck down.

"Chill," she whispered softly to her wild-eyed reflection. "Deep breaths." She took her own advice,
breathing slowly in and out through her nose, reminding herself that a good man had died on Monday and
so what if she'd said something ridiculous to Darius.
"Get over it. Move on."

There was a soft tap on the door. "Ava? You all
right?" *Darius. Oh. My. God.* Her face flamed anew.
"Ava?"

She gulped to clear her clutching throat and called,
"I'm great. Terrific."

"You sure?"

"Of course I'm sure."

"You sound strange."

"Darius, I'm fine."

"I'll just wait here until you come out."

She stifled a groan and glared at her reflection in
the mirror and knew she had to stop being an idiot and
open the damn door.

"Ava?"

She yanked it wide. "What?" she growled at him.

And he smiled that same slow, knowing smile he'd
given her seventeen years ago right after he told her that
someday she would say yes to him. "You look kind of
flushed. Are you sure you're okay?"

"I am fine. You can go."

He didn't budge. "About the other day, I—"

"Oh, please." She waved her hand so wildly, she almost hit her nose with it. "You know that was nothing."

"No." He said it way too softly. "I don't know that, Ava. In fact, I'm thinking it was definitely something."

"And I'm telling you it wasn't and you should forget it."

He leaned closer, bringing that scent of leather and wood shavings and something else, too, something wonderfully manly that she couldn't quite name. "Forget it?" he spoke softly, almost a whisper, his breath warm across her cheek and his eyes like the sky when night comes on. "You offered to be *naked*. There's no way I'm forgetting that."

Her heart felt like it would explode from her chest and splatter all over the room. Her pulse pounded loud and hard in her ears. How could she be so over-the-top about this? You'd think she was fifteen again, the way she was behaving.

She needed to cut it the hell out right now, start acting like an adult, for crying out loud. Drawing her shoulders back, she stared up at him defiantly and reminded him in a calm, even tone, "Look. This is stupid. Plus, it's all your fault. I mean, you're the one who's always flirting with me."

"So are you telling me you finally decided to flirt back?"

"Darius. Please. Can't we just forget what I said?"

"Are you kidding me? It's branded in my brain." He said that with real feeling—after which he grinned a slow, lopsided grin. "And we need to talk about it. In depth. At length."

How did he make that sound so dirty? She glared. "No, we don't."

He kept right on grinning. "Yes, we—"

"Is *this* bathroom taken?" The voice of old Levi Kenwright, grandfather-in-law to Dare's brother James, cut him off. The old man came toward them from the door to the hallway.

"All yours." Ava flashed Levi a giant smile, zipped around the old fellow on the side away from Darius and escaped out the open bedroom door.

She joined the others in the great room. Clara poured her a nice glass of Riesling, and they toasted the season. Then Chloe took her aside. They firmed up the open house staging she would be dealing with tomorrow.

An hour into the party, she went upstairs to check on the girls, who had taken over a guest room. They'd gathered a number of chairs from other rooms and draped blankets between them. Ava heard them giggling together inside the makeshift fort.

"Anybody in here?"

"Just us!" Sylvie answered.

Ava got down on all fours and stuck her head under the blankets to find Sylvie, Annabelle and little Kiera sitting in a circle pretending to drink from empty pink plastic teacups.

"How're you girls doing?"

"We're having a tea party," Sylvie replied.

"Ava!" cried Kiera gleefully. "Hi there!"

"Hi, Kiera."

Kiera made lip-smacking sounds, so Ava leaned closer, and the little sweetie pressed her lips against her cheek.

"Would you like a cup of tea?" asked Annabelle sweetly.

"I would love one." Ava crawled on in and joined their circle. Annabelle handed her a cup and a little plastic plate, and Ava proceeded to drink pretend tea and enjoy an imaginary cupcake. "Well," she said, once she'd sipped and chewed for a couple of minutes. "That was delicious." She pretended to blot her lips with an imaginary napkin. "And now, I must be on my way." The fort was perfect for the three girls, but things got tight with a mom included.

"Bye-bye!" chirped Kiera brightly.

"Dinner soon," Ava reminded them as she backed out the way she had come. "Don't eat too many cupcakes."

"Oh, Mom," Sylvie scoffed. "They're only 'magi-nary.'"

"Well, all right then. Have as many as you like." She emerged from the fort butt-first to find Darius leaning in the doorway to the upper hall.

Her heart did a silly forward roll, and her pulse went a little crazy. She shot to her feet. "This is getting ridiculous," she muttered as she straightened her skirt and smoothed her sweater.

He didn't say a word—probably because he knew if he spoke, the girls would hear him and demand that he crawl into their fort and have tea with them, too. Darius clearly had other plans. He stepped forward and grabbed her arm.

She should have jerked away, but she didn't. It felt too delicious, his warm fingers pressing into her skin through her sweater, the little thrill of excitement skittering down the backs of her knees to have him so close, touching her. He pulled her from the room, and she went a lot more willingly than she should have.

"No," he whispered for her ears alone once they were out in the upper hallway.

"No, what?"

"This isn't ridiculous. This is fun."

She almost giggled at that, which pretty much proved she was losing her mind.

"Come on," he said.

"Where?"

"In here." He ducked into the next bedroom, pulling her with him—and then shut the door. "Now. Where were we?"

She eased free of his grip and backed off a few paces. "I can't believe I let you drag me in here."

He folded those fine, hard arms across that broad chest and leaned back against the door. "Go out with me. Tomorrow night."

"That is not going to happen."

"Why not?"

"No dating. Not in this town. Not with our families."

"Ava. What's wrong with our families?"

She didn't even want to go into it. But he just stood there blocking the door, waiting for an explanation. So she gave in and provided one. "They're all up in my business, that's what. I've been out twice with nice men in the five years since I moved back to town. The first date was with a perfectly pleasant software designer. Afterward, all three of my brothers got me aside and told me I could do better. They're so overprotective they make me want to scream. Then a year ago, I tried again, with another Realtor who has his office in the same building as mine. Your sister Nell saw us together.

Later, there was endless discussion of if we would go out again and wasn't it great that I was finally seeing someone? That was when it came to me."

"What?"

"I don't want to go out with anyone. I like my life just as it is. I have the life I've always wanted, and I don't need the hassle of going on dates and all that." Was she overexplaining? Definitely. But now she couldn't seem to stop. "And then there's my mother…" Ava rolled her eyes so hard, she was lucky she didn't fall over backward. "I don't even want to get started on her. She's a hopeless matchmaker."

"Ava." He said her name slowly, as though he enjoyed the way it tasted in his mouth. "You have to know that what you're giving me here just sounds like a bunch of excuses for you not to have to take a chance with a guy."

She really hated that he was pretty much right, so she dug up another objection. "Well, *you* have to know that my brother Tom hates you." Tom used to work for Bravo Steelworks. It hadn't ended well.

Dare studied his boots for a second or two, then glanced back up at her. "I wouldn't say Tom hates me exactly."

"But you have to admit he doesn't like you very much."

"Ava." A weary little breath escaped him. "I don't care what our families say. I don't care what anyone says."

"Well, I do care. I love them, all of them. Dearly. But they all think they know what's good for me, and they simply don't. I don't want to go out because when I do, I never hear the end of it. So, well, if you and I were to, um, start seeing each other, I wouldn't want anyone to know, okay?" She backed up and dropped to the edge of the bed behind her. "Actually, I would prefer it if *you* didn't even know."

A low chuckle escaped him. "You're a difficult woman, you know that? You always have been."

"Which only proves you should show some good sense and stop chasing me all over your sister's house."

"But I like chasing you." God. The way he said that. Rough and low, with enough heat to make her feel she might burst into flame. He held her gaze for a long count of five. Electricity seemed to arc in the still air between them. "And I know you're offering *something*. I just can't figure out what it is."

Her throat clutched when he said that, and she realized he was right. She did want to offer him something: herself. Just for the holidays, just between the two of them.

Was there any chance he would go for something like that—and if he would, did she really want to follow through on it?

As she considered the very real possibility that she'd lost her mind due to long-term sexual deprivation, Darius left off leaning on the door and came closer. She watched him approach, her skin all prickly with awareness, her breath coming a little too shallow and too fast.

The bed dipped slightly as he sat beside her. "All right," he said. "If not dinner and a movie, then what?"

She turned her head, met his eyes—and put it right out there. "I just want a man for Christmas, okay? No strings, no dates, nobody else knowing about it. Just a Christmas fling. You, me and the holidays. And we're over and done on January 1."

Chapter Three

There was a moment that stretched into forever. Darius stared into her eyes. She knew he would look away any second.

But he never did.

She broke first with a low cry. "Oh, God." She face-palmed, because what else could a girl do at a moment like this? "Is that tacky and awful?"

"Not awful in the least," he said gently. Evenly. "Look at me, Ava." He waited until she lifted her head and faced him again. "You're on."

As she gaped at him in equal parts wonder and disbelief, there was a tap on the door. "Dinner in five," called a woman's voice. Ava wasn't sure who. And what did it matter who called them to dinner?

Nothing seemed real. She'd just made a deal with Darius Bravo to have a Christmas affair.

Darius called, "Be right out." And footsteps sounded, moving away from the door. He asked, "You okay?"

"Oh, I don't think so." She made herself stand, though her knees felt like rubber bands.

Before she could turn and race to the door, he caught her hand. "We're not finished here."

She gave a slight tug, but he didn't release her. Her skin felt on fire where he touched her. "I…have to check on Sylvie. Make sure her hands are washed before dinner."

"I'll help."

A weak laugh escaped her. "Really. I can manage. Just…let me go."

That did it. He released her, and she felt a sharp stab of regret as the connection broke.

Oh, she was a mess. She never should have told him her fantasy, never should have asked him to participate in it with her. Never should have even let him lead her into this room.

There were so many *nevers* running through her mind right now—starting with how she never should have said she'd be waiting for him naked.

Really, she didn't like herself much at the moment. She was acting like the kind of woman she despised, one of those girls who crooked her finger at a man with one hand and showed him the flat of her palm with the other. A *c'mere, c'mere—get away, get away* kind of girl.

"Ava."

"Mmm?"

"It's going to be fine," he promised. "Better than fine." How could he possibly know that? "We'll talk more later."

She should tell him never mind, should speak up

right now and say, *Forget it. I lost my mind for a second there, but I'm all better now...*

But then he instructed gently, "Go on. See about Sylvie."

And she thought how he was a much better guy than she used to give him credit for, that he was not only killer-hot, but also tender, sweet and funny—and maybe she should have given him a chance all those years and years ago. Truly, if she wanted a man for the holidays and he wanted to *be* that man for her, well, why shouldn't they both get what they wanted for Christmas this year?

"Go now," he warned, teasing and low. "Or I'm coming with you."

That did it. She turned and left him sitting there.

The rest of the afternoon and early evening went by without another word shared between her and Darius. They sat across and down from each other at the long dining room table, which was so packed with Bravos everyone had to be careful to tuck their elbows in close to their sides. The food was amazing. Clara put apples and chestnuts in the stuffing and a combination of spices that had everyone coming around for seconds and thirds.

Twice, Ava caught Dare watching her. But as soon as she met his eyes, he just smiled and looked away. She tried to forget about those moments in the upstairs bedroom, to put all that from her mind and enjoy Thanksgiving with the Bravos, but she kept zoning out during conversations.

Nell asked her twice if something was bothering her. Both times, she denied it.

The second time, Nell tossed her thick head of ginger hair and laughed. "Liar." She leaned close. "I'm always a phone call away if you want to talk about it— whatever it is."

Really, Ava was grateful to have a friend like Nell, who might be nosy and bossy, but who also really cared. "Thanks, Nell. You're the best."

During dessert, as they chowed down on absolutely perfect pumpkin pie with heavy dollops of freshly whipped cream, Elise Bravo announced her engagement to Jed Walsh, the world-famous thriller writer, who'd returned to Justice Creek the year before after almost twenty years away. Clara and Dalton brought out champagne, and Jed got up and made a really beautiful toast to his bride-to-be, one that had them all laughing through happy tears.

And finally, after the dessert was cleared away, most everyone lingered to visit a little longer. Dalton took Kiera off for her bath, and Sylvie and Annabelle played "Super Mario Kart" with Darius and Annabelle's dad, Quinn. Then the two girls went back upstairs for more fun in their fort.

At eight, when Ava went up to tell Sylvie it was time to go home, she found them both sound asleep in the cave of blankets. Gently, she folded back the covers and gathered her daughter into her arms. Chloe appeared then, looking for Annabelle. They carried the girls back down.

Sylvie fussed as Ava coaxed her into her coat and hat and then went right back to sleep as soon as Ava picked her up again. Clara appeared, and Ava gave her a one-armed hug of thanks as she went out the door.

Outside, a light snow was falling. Ava tipped her

head up to the dark sky and caught a snowflake on her tongue. She thought of Darius, and the strangest sort of calm settled over her.

Sylvie sighed in her arms. Ava gathered her closer and moved on to the car.

Half an hour later, just as she finished putting Sylvie to bed, her cell phone rang.

It was Darius. "Just checking to see that you got home all right."

"We're here. We're fine."

"You certainly are."

She laughed. "I'm not even going to ask who gave you my number."

"Like it's a state secret. I think there's a stack of your business cards at every restaurant and shop in town." It was true. She left a trail of business cards wherever she went, and she'd acquired more than one customer because they'd grabbed her card at a checkout counter. "Okay." All of a sudden, he sounded grim. "You're too quiet. Don't you dare back out on me, Ava."

"I'm not." She realized she meant it. The calm that had settled over her when she carried her daughter out Clara's front door had followed her home. "No stalling, I promise. We're making this happen."

"Come out to my place." He owned a beautiful piece of property a few miles from town—or at least, his sisters claimed it was beautiful. She'd never been there.

And she wasn't ready to go there quite yet. "Tomorrow," she said, without stopping to think it through. "I'm spending the morning finishing up the staging of a house for Chloe. It's out at that new Starview development, a Bravo Construction house. You take Mountainview west and—"

"I know where it is. What time?"

She would be there good and early and hoped to have everything done by lunchtime. "Noon?"

"I'll be there."

"Great—I mean, good. I mean..."

"Ava." His voice was like raw honey dripping fresh from the comb.

"Uh, yeah?"

"I'll see you tomorrow."

"Yes. Good. Perfect." She heard a click on the line, and he was gone.

The next day, Sylvie's sitter arrived at 8:30 a.m., so Ava got to the Starview house before nine.

Chloe had all the room plans uploaded to a private-access area of her website. She'd also come in early yesterday, unwrapped all the late-arriving stuff and had even gotten most of the furniture, art and accessories moved to the various rooms where each would be used. The beds, bureaus, larger tables and cabinets were all in place in each of the rooms.

And the three Christmas trees—one in the living room, one on the dining room sideboard and another in the family room—were up and fully decorated. Ava loved that Chloe had put such time and care into the Christmas stuff. Seasonal touches made potential buyers feel at home—and that was the whole point. Whoever finally bought this house had to experience it as the home they'd been looking for. Toward that end, Chloe had also provided acres of lighted garlands and some serious holiday table decor, which Ava would deal with today.

She turned up the heat a little, made a pot of coffee, plugged her old iPod into the dock Chloe had left on a side table and cranked up the Christmas tunes. Via her tablet, she accessed the room plans and got right to work.

By eleven thirty she had everything done. She stood in the beautiful living room with its giant Christmas tree that reached all the way to the vaulted ceiling and longed for a shower. Hanging pictures, draping garlands and moving chairs around was sweaty work. Her stomach growled with hunger.

And in half an hour, Darius would arrive to have sex with her.

Seriously, what had she been smoking to decide they should meet here and now?

She swiped a sweaty curl of hair off her forehead and pictured herself trying to seduce Darius all sticky from a hard morning's work as her stomach rumbled, demanding lunch. What was up with her? Usually, she thought of everything. But today, she couldn't even remember to bring a sandwich.

Her inexperience with casual sex was definitely showing. She had no time to go grab a burger or to run home for a quick shower.

Then again, she *had* hung gorgeous, thick designer towels in each of the bathrooms. And if, say, she was to pop into the shower for a quick rinse and then to use one of those pretty towels to dry off, she could easily take that towel home, run it through the washer and bring it back tomorrow with no one the wiser.

Ava headed for the master bath fast, before she had

a chance to rethink the appropriateness of any of this. By ten of twelve, she'd cleaned up a little, wiped down the shower, primped her hair and makeup and carried the soggy towel out to her Suburban so she wouldn't forget to take it home with her.

At a minute before noon, the doorbell rang.

Utterly breathless with her heart in her throat, she opened the door to him. He had a big white Dairy Queen bag and a box with two large soft drinks propped up in it. His face was freshly shaved, and he wore a shearling jean jacket over a gray sweater and a plaid shirt, blue jeans and lace-up work boots.

She couldn't decide which looked better—him or that white Dairy Queen bag, which gave off the incomparable aroma of burgers and fries. "You brought lunch," she whispered in wonder.

One wide shoulder lifted in a half shrug. "You said I wasn't allowed to take you out, and I thought you might be hungry." His breath plumed in the cold air.

"I'm starving."

"Well, good then. Cheeseburgers, fries and two Cokes."

"I worship you."

He grinned. "I like the sound of that."

She peered past his shoulder. "Where's your F-150?" She stepped back to let him in.

He followed her to the open-plan kitchen. "You said no one could know. I thought, what if some random family member showed up and saw my truck? So I left it around the corner."

"You're clearly quite the expert at sneaking around."

"That, I *don't* like the sound of much." At the breakfast

nook table, he set down the bag and the box of drinks, hung his jacket on the back of a chair and sat down.

She took the chair across from him. "About the sneaking around, I meant it in the best possible way."

"Right." He tore open the bag and distributed the burgers and fries. She grabbed one of the sodas and had a long, lovely sip. "So good. Thank you."

"Eat."

So she did. For several delicious minutes, neither of them spoke as they demolished the food.

Eventually he remarked on the Christmas music and all the decorations. "Nice house. And definitely holiday ready."

"Nell and Garrett build them right."

"Yeah, they do."

As her stomach had filled up, her jitters returned. She hardly knew what to say next. "So... You finished? Let me have all that." She gathered up the remains of the meal and carried it to the black plastic bag of trash she'd put at the end of the island to take out with her when she left.

Her hands smelled of grilled meat and grease, so she washed them at the sink and dried them with a paper towel from the roll she'd brought with her. He got up and came to wash his hands, too.

She passed him a paper towel. As he dried, she laughed nervously and said, "Now all we need is a breath mint."

He dipped a hand in his pocket and came out with a matched pair of candy-cane mints. "They were giving them out at the DQ."

She took one, twisted the wrapper off and popped

it in her mouth. He did the same. For a moment, they sucked in unison.

And then he reached out and touched the tip of her chin, a feather-light caress that she felt to the bottom of her soul. "You're not getting freaked on me, are you, Ava?"

She tucked the mint into the side of her mouth and confessed, "Yeah. I am, a little. I guess I didn't really think it all through. I mean, maybe this isn't the best setting for the start of this thing we're doing."

"Now it's a thing?" His mouth quirked at one corner. She wanted to rise up on tiptoe and kiss that faint smile, to trace that tempting bottom lip with her tongue.

Instead, she eased the mint back to the center of her mouth for a moment and sucked it some more. She had to tuck it into her cheek again before she said, "There aren't even sheets on the beds. And it just feels wrong. Kind of shoddy, you know?"

"*Shoddy*. Interesting word choice." He touched her hair. Her heartbeat ceased—and then started up again, heavy and deep. He ran his hand down the length of a curl and then rubbed the strands between his fingers. "Silky. I knew it would be. I always loved the color. Like summer wheat. And sunshine."

It was a beautiful thing to say, and she wanted to surge up, wrap her arms around him and kiss him hard and deep. But a second ticked by and then another, and she lost her nerve. She ended up blurting out, "I'm, um, on contraception. The shots."

"Ah."

"And I can't believe I forgot to bring a sandwich, but I did remember to bring condoms."

"Did you, now?" His eyes were a swirling combination of blues, like a whirlpool out in the middle of the ocean that could suck a girl down so very deep she might never find her way up to the surface again. He let go of her hair and then touched her left temple with his fingertips. Her skin heated. Burned. He pushed his fingers close to her scalp and then combed them downward, gently parting the long strands as he went.

A tiny gasp escaped her. "They're in my purse. A whole box." He cradled her chin, tipping it higher. Inside, everything was shivering and burning at once. She felt a definite heaviness down low, a longing so sharp, so immeasurably sweet. "Which is silly, right?"

He scanned her face as though memorizing her. "A whole box, you mean?"

"Mmm-hmm. Because there is no way we're going to use a whole..." Words deserted her as his mouth covered hers.

Holy cannoli. His mouth was so soft, just as she'd always known it would be. Soft and pliant, that bottom lip like a pillow. She gave it a little bite, because she'd always wanted to bite him there and at last she could. He made a lovely, low groaning sound in response.

And seriously, now. Who knew a kiss could feel this good?

For the longest, loveliest time, they just stood there at the sink with their lips locked together.

Now, this was more like it. This was just what she needed. Dare Bravo for Christmas, delivering endless, candy-cane-flavored kisses, his big hands cradling her head, stroking her hair as "White Christmas" played from the dock in the living room. He sucked her mint into his mouth. She let it go without regret.

And then, still kissing her, he started moving. Dazed

and delighted, she went where he guided her, backward, step by step, until she met the wall. He didn't stop there. Oh, no. Not Darius.

He kept on kissing her, moving in even closer, so their bodies touched, front to front, his so wonderfully big and hot and hard as he pressed her to the wall. She could feel his erection against her belly.

Wow. Just…wow.

It was happening. Finally happening, after way too many years. And with Darius, of all people. He kissed her so long and intensely and well that she didn't even care anymore that they were doing this in the perfectly staged home she would try to sell tomorrow.

And then those warm, knowing fingers of his strayed downward. He had the hem of her shirt in his hands, and he was sliding it upward. For the first time, the kiss broke.

But only long enough for him to take that shirt over her head and away. She felt the air of the room against her bare skin, and she almost got nervous.

"Shh," he said, moving in good and tight again. "Kiss me."

And she did, meeting his lips once more, drinking him in. She took his tongue into her mouth and wrapped hers around it as he went to work on her bra. Those knowing fingers skated lightly around between her back and the wall.

The clasp gave way.

She gasped in excitement and delight.

He went on kissing her as he slid the straps down her arms, so easily, smoothly, one and then the other, his fingers trailing along her skin, causing lovely little shivers to bloom wherever he touched her. He guided her hands down to her sides.

And then he eased a naughty finger between their bodies and unhooked the center gore of her bra, pulling it downward. The bra slid away, leaving her bare from the waist up.

He cupped her left breast. She moaned into his mouth as her nipple pressed into the hot center of his big palm. Had she ever been this turned on in all of her thirty-two years?

As her dazed, acutely aroused brain tried to ponder that question, a car door slammed outside.

The kiss broke. Her eyes popped open to meet his. They stared at each other. She wondered distantly if her mouth was as red and swollen as his.

Another door shut. Faintly, she heard voices. Feminine voices. She recognized Nell's throaty laugh and put it together: his sisters must have come home early from Denver. Any second now, they would burst in the front door—and find her here in the model-home kitchen, half-naked with Darius.

Get moving. Put your shirt on. The voice in her head knew what to do. But she was immobilized by...

She had no idea what.

Disbelief, maybe. Embarrassment, definitely. And shock that she'd chosen such an unsuitable location for lovemaking in the first place and then managed to get caught in the act.

Or maybe it was simply the bizarre, dream-like quality of the moment. To be about to have sex with Darius Bravo after all these years—and have his sisters walk in on them.

Whatever the sudden irrational affliction that had her

frozen in place unable to cover herself, it wasn't contagious. Because Darius had no such problem.

He was a blur of purposeful movement.

First, he scooped her bra and shirt up off the floor. Tossing the shirt across his shoulder, he dealt with the bra, sliding the straps up her arms, reaching around behind her and hooking it up on the first try.

"Come on, now..." He spoke to her so gently, without a hint of annoyance or impatience.

She blinked again. He held her shirt ready. Numbly, she stuck her hands in the armholes, and he eased it over her head and smoothed it down into place.

What do you know? She was fully dressed again.

She heard the front door open. "Ava!" Chloe called from the foyer.

Darius bent close. His lips touched hers, so soft, tasting of peppermint. "You've got my number in your phone. Call me." He breathed the words against her mouth, and then off he went.

Still leaning weakly against the kitchen wall, Ava watched him vanish down the short hall that led to the utility room and the four-car garage.

Chapter Four

"There you are!" Chloe led the group of women into the kitchen. "Everything looks terrific. You're a life-saver, Ava."

Ava straightened her shirt, smoothed her hair and tried on a smile. "Already done shopping?"

"We'd had enough," said Nell, "so we came to help out."

"Believe it or not, I'm pretty much done. Where's Jody?"

Elise shook her head. "She took a pass."

Clara said, "I think she's feeling down about poor Nick Yancy." There were sympathetic noises all around.

And Nell was watching Ava much too closely. "You look kind of flushed. What have you been up to?"

Ava knew she shouldn't say it. But she couldn't resist. "Having sex with Darius."

The kitchen went dead silent. Then everybody laughed. They all knew that he flirted with her shamelessly.

And that she never had sex with anyone.

That night, as soon as Sylvie was in bed, Ava sent Darius a text: Tomorrow night Sylvie has a sleepover at Annabelle's. You available?

He answered a moment later: A text isn't good enough. I want to hear your voice. Call me, Ava. Now.

Ava stared at the message on her phone. Her cheeks felt hot, and her core felt all melty. Who got turned on because a guy got bossy via text?

Apparently, she did. When the guy was Darius.

She made the call. "So, then? How about tomorrow night?"

"How'd it go after I left today?"

"It was fine."

"*Fine* tells me nothing."

She grinned to herself. "Well, Nell said I looked flushed and asked what was going on. So I told them I was having sex with you. And they all laughed because everyone knows that's never gonna happen."

"You're bad," he said, that voice of his in honey-dripping mode. "A bad, bad girl."

That melty feeling down low got more so. "Tomorrow night?"

"Tomorrow night is good. Come out to my place. I'll cook you dinner."

"Dinner." Was that wise? "I don't know. Dinner's a little too much like a date."

"Ava. I have to tell you. You're starting to make me feel cheap and used."

"Don't be ridiculous."

"What? Only women can feel used? Because face it, you are using me."

That gave her pause. After all, it was true. "I...well, I guess I kind of thought we were using each other..."

"Ava." He said it gently, kindly. "I was only teasing you. Sometimes you take things way too seriously."

Did she? Maybe so. And it really was very sweet of him, to offer to cook dinner. Plus, she'd always kind of wanted to see where he lived. "All right, dinner. Thank you. Seven?"

"Seven works."

"What can I bring?"

"Nothing. Just you. See you then."

She thought about that afternoon, the dizzying power in his kiss, the smooth, sexy way he'd half undressed her and then so swiftly covered her right back up again. Since she was a little girl and learned how precarious life could be, she'd been so careful to stay focused on the future, not to mess up and get distracted from what really mattered, which was to make a safe place in the world for herself and the ones she loved.

Was she messing up now, getting into this thing with Darius? "Dare, I..."

But he was already gone.

At the open house the next day, Ava served hot cider and Christmas cookies. She put the Christmas tunes on shuffle, and the house looked amazing.

Garrett, Nell and Chloe all stopped in to see how it was going.

And it was going very well, with potential buyers in and out all day and several couples talking about making offers. Bravo Construction had five other lots in that development. This house should go far toward getting them buyers for those properties, too.

Darius came by at a little after two. He ate a cookie and stayed out of the way as she chatted with potential customers.

She loved it, that he stopped in, loved pretending there was nothing going on between them, that nothing had changed, all while the awareness of the evening to come pressed in on her, making a rising feeling in her belly, putting a secret grin on her face.

It was exciting. Her doubts of last night didn't trouble her at all today.

Now, she felt really young, and that was a whole new feeling for her. She'd never felt young. She'd always been goal-oriented and determined to wrestle a little security out of life.

Well, she had security, finally, as much as anyone did. She had money in the bank, a college fund for Sylvie and a solid retirement plan. Her house was half paid for.

And for this Christmas season, with Darius, she could afford to feel like a girl again, to get all flushed and breathless, to have this secret sex thing between them. It made her smile to herself to think that nobody had a clue what would happen out at his place tonight.

Before he left, during a lull when there was no one in the house but the two of them, he pulled her into the master bathroom and shut the door.

"One kiss. And then I'll go."

She started to argue that she had a job to do and he was interfering with it, but why get on his case for something she wanted as much as he seemed to? So she tipped her face up to him, and his beautiful mouth came down on hers.

The kiss hollowed her out down low and left her wonderfully breathless. He tried to steal a second one.

But she put her fingers to his soft lips. "Tonight." He sucked those fingers into his mouth and swirled his tongue around them. "You say *I'm* bad," she accused.

He laughed then—and stole one more kiss before he let her go.

Dare's house on the edge of the forest was two stories, the porch wide and welcoming, sided in natural wood shingles and stone. He was waiting on the step, wearing his usual jeans and boots and also a heavy red-and-black plaid jacket, the collar turned up against the cold. Apparently, he'd been sitting there for a while. The brim of his black cowboy hat held a dusting of snow. A floppy-eared white dog sat beside him.

Ava stopped the Suburban in front of the porch, and he rose and came down the steps to her, pulling open her door and leaning into her, bringing the sharp, cold scent of snow and a hint of evergreen. "You made it." She nodded, feeling strangely shy and way too excited at the prospect of the evening ahead. "This is Daisy." The dog, who'd come to sit a few feet away, cocked an ear at Ava.

"Hello, Daisy."

"Now you can come meet my horses," he said.

She grabbed her wool beanie off the passenger seat and put it on, then took his offered hand. His fingers were surprisingly warm as he helped her down to the snowy ground.

Gathering her coat a little closer around her, she went where he led, across a cleared space, past a faded red barn to a stretch of paddock fence.

The horses spotted them and trotted over—three of them, a white mare and two geldings, one black, one a bay. "Josie, Clem and Sweet Sam, meet Ava." They greeted her with soft snuffling sounds. Dare had three small half-withered apples in his pockets. "Here. They'll love you forever." He passed them to her, and she gave each horse a treat.

Then she bent to pet Daisy, who'd followed them from the car. "In school, you always seemed like a guy who'd go to Yale," she said. "Preppy, you know? And a jock. I never made you for a cowboy."

He took her hand and pulled her to her feet again. "I've got three horses and a barn, but I wouldn't say I qualify as a cowboy."

She thought about kissing him and felt shy all over again. "What about the hat?"

He tipped the snowy brim at her. "The hat, least of all—and in high school I didn't know what I wanted, really. Now I do. I like horses, and I like a place with lots of trees. And I have a workshop in the basement. I do some mediocre carpentry when I have the time." He pointed off across the paddock. "I own twenty acres, most of it forest."

"It's a lot to manage, isn't it—I mean, what with running Bravo Steelworks, too?"

"I have help. His name is Corky. He lives in what used to be the foreman's cottage, on the far side of the barn. Corky does most of the cowboying around here. He works with the horses, mends the fence and takes care of Daisy when I'm not around."

"Sylvie would love it here." The words kind of slipped out, and she regretted them instantly.

"Bring Sylvie next time."

She stared off toward the barn. "I shouldn't have said that."

"Why not?"

"It's not a good idea. This is supposed to be a secret, remember? And it ends with the New Year."

"So?"

"So, it's not a good idea to drag Sylvie into the middle of it."

"Nobody's dragging Sylvie anywhere. I like your daughter. She and I get along. She's a great kid, and we're friends—as much as a grown-up can be friends with a seven-year-old. And that's completely independent of what's going on with you and me. When January comes, I'm not suddenly going to pretend Sylvie doesn't exist. So what's her coming here going to hurt?"

"I just don't want to put ideas in her head that are never coming true."

"You won't be. Believe me."

Ava so didn't want to be having this conversation. "It's nice of you to offer. And I'll, um, give it some thought, okay?" It was a lie. There was nothing to think about. She braced for him to keep pushing.

But he gave it up. "Fair enough." He took her hand again, his big, warm fingers sliding between her cold ones. "You're shivering. Let's go inside."

They took off their coats and hats and boots at the door, and he gave her a quick tour.

The house had four bedrooms, with a central great room and a big, modern kitchen. He had one of those

indoor grills, and dinner was simple and really good—
lamb chops, oven-browned potatoes, mixed vegetables
and a green salad.

They sat at the smaller of the two tables, in a nook
right off the kitchen area. It kind of was like a date, a
guy and a girl who'd known each other once, but not
very well, getting to know each other again.

She said, "You went to Las Vegas after high school..."

"My dad wanted me to get a business degree and
then take over at Bravo Steelworks. The steelworks was
always his baby. Most of the family fortune came from
my mom's side, but my dad had the steelworks before
they were married. He'd built that business himself from
the ground up. He eventually figured out that none of
us—none of my mom's kids, none of Willow's kids—
wanted to run a metal fabricating business, so he put
the pressure on me."

"Why you?"

"I don't know, really. Maybe because I'm the oldest. He wanted the business to stay in the family, so he
was determined one of us would take his place when he
retired. I rebelled and ran off to Vegas. I worked construction and in the casinos dealing blackjack. Eventually I moved to Los Angeles. Same thing. Odd jobs.
I got work with a landscaper and then a guy who built
decks and fences."

"But then you did come back to take over for your
dad."

"Yeah. After four years of knocking around, I realized I'd been rebelling just to prove that I could, that I
actually wanted what my dad wanted for me. So I went
to CU and then I moved home for good. I learned to run

the family business—and I know that look in your eye, Ava. You want to ask me something else, and you're not sure you should."

She fiddled with her water glass and reminded herself that she wasn't here to learn his life story.

But then he leaned into her and touched her chin with the tip of his finger, causing a lovely little shiver of anticipation. "Ask me."

And she did. "How come you never got married?"

"I almost did. Twice. There was a girl I lived with in LA. She wanted to get married. I didn't, but I liked her a lot, and I didn't want to lose her. I proposed. She accepted at first but then called it off. She said she couldn't marry a man who didn't really love her."

"*Did* you love her?"

He made a rueful sort of sound. "Got me there. No. I liked her, but it wasn't love."

"And the second time?"

"That was after I finished school and moved back to town. Marla Winston worked as a loan officer at the local branch of Dalton's bank." Dalton Ames, Clara's husband, was president and CEO of Ames Bank and Trust, which had branches all over Colorado, including one in Justice Creek. "Marla and I were together for three years. We were going to get married, but she got an offer for a great job in Oklahoma City. She wanted to take it. A lot. And I didn't want to move to Oklahoma City. I guess you could say I didn't love Marla enough."

She felt surprisingly close to him right then, felt that deep down, they were similar. He'd never gotten married—and she'd never wanted to. "I never planned to get married. I had big dreams to get out in the world and make lots of money all on my own and never be dependent on some guy."

"What changed your mind about marriage?"

"Craig. He just…never gave up. I met him over at the county fairgrounds, at the Summer Daze Rodeo. He was on leave from the marines and said he'd always wanted to see the Rockies. He asked me out. I went. I had fun with him. And then his leave ended, and he was gone. I never expected to see him again. But then he started writing to me—actual letters. I wrote back. Then there were calls, emails, texts. And over the next couple of years, he showed up to see me every leave he got. I guess I just couldn't help falling for him. It was like his love was contagious."

Dare smiled, but his eyes remained serious. "So you married him even though marriage wasn't in your plans."

"I did. And we were happy." *Most of the time, anyway.* "And he gave me Sylvie. And then…" It still hurt, after all this time, to say it. "He ran over a land mine in Afghanistan and died instantly."

Darius reached across the table, took her hand and rubbed his thumb across the back of it. A little spear of pleasure pierced her at his touch, but it wasn't enough to banish the feeling of loss.

She added, "So I packed up my daughter and came home to Justice Creek. There was nothing for me in San Diego. Craig's mom had died years before. I never even met her. His dad's remarried and lives in Arizona."

"I'm sorry, Ava. So sorry."

She gave him a wobbly smile and wondered what was wrong with her to be babbling on about Craig.

"Well." She pulled free of his hold and pushed back her chair. "We should clear off the dishes."

"Stop. Leave everything right where it is." He got up and came around the table to her.

"But—"

"I'll deal with it later." He claimed her hand again. "Let's go sit by the fire." And he led her out into the great room where he pulled her down onto his big leather sofa, hooked an arm around her and gathered her close to his side. Daisy, who'd followed them from the kitchen, stretched out on the rug with a long doggy sigh.

Ava rested her head on Dare's shoulder and stared into the fire. It was nice, sitting there with him. But then she tipped her chin up to look at him, and everything changed.

Desire. She saw it, right there in his eyes. A hot blue flame.

"Darius…"

"Ava." And he kissed her.

Oh, the man did know how to kiss. He eased himself back across the sofa arm, bringing his stocking feet up to the cushions, pulling her with him, guiding her to stretch out on top of him. He felt so good beneath her. She loved the solidity of him, the heat of him, the strength in his arms around her.

The kisses went on and on. She speared her fingers into his hair, stroked a hungry caress down the strong column of his neck, clutched the muscular bulge of his shoulder.

And she didn't stop there. She slid her hand down between them and cradled him through the front of his jeans. He moaned when she did that and palmed her breast, finding her nipple, rubbing it to aching hardness through the barrier of her bra and sweater.

She longed for more—for everything. To get out of her clothes and feel him, skin to skin.

But he didn't start undressing her. He just kept kissing and caressing her until she felt like she just might spontaneously combust.

She tugged on the collar of his soft flannel shirt and then tried to slip the top button free of the buttonhole.

But he caught her hand.

She broke his hold—and went for that button again.

Again he caught her hand. "Wait," he said in a rough whisper.

"For what?" She bit his lower lip. Because he tasted so good and he deserved a little pain for how crazy he was making her.

He lifted up from the sofa arm and caught her mouth before she could pull away.

And then they were kissing again. Kissing and kissing. She was on fire for him. He was ready, too, no denying that, so hard he had to be aching.

"Darius. Please…"

But instead of pulling off her sweater or unbuttoning his shirt as she longed for him to do, he only framed her face between his hands.

Dizzy with excitement and building frustration, she opened her eyes and glared down at him. "Darius, what is going on? You kiss me like you can't get enough of me."

"Because I can't."

"Then why do we both still have all our clothes on?"

He pulled her closer. She moaned as he caught her

earlobe between his teeth and worried it gently, sending sparks of need flashing across her jaw and then downward, all the way to where she couldn't wait another second to be filled with him.

He spoke into the ear he'd just bitten. "Yesterday, I almost took you up against a wall in a vacant house."

"Did you hear me objecting?"

"No, but since then, I've been giving this thing between us some thought."

"Oh, please don't," she pleaded. "No thinking is necessary. It's *doing* that's called for here."

"Uh-uh." He bit her earlobe again. She moaned and punched him in the arm. Not too hard, just enough to make her frustration crystal clear. And then he went and said something that tugged on her heart. "I wanted to kiss you so bad in high school."

Ava sighed. She couldn't help it. It was years ago. They were kids, and she'd hardly known him. But still. It touched her to hear him say he'd yearned for her kiss.

She laid her head on his chest and confessed, "I waited that whole school year for you to ask me out again."

He made a low, self-mocking sound. "I didn't have the guts. I knew you'd only turn me down."

A sharp laugh escaped her, one that skated a little too close to a sob. "And I would've, too."

"You were a hard case, Ava." She felt his lips in her hair. "Still are."

"Well, yeah. A little. Maybe."

"But I like you. I always have. And I want this Christmas to be really good. For both of us. I want it to be everything we never had, everything we *couldn't* have all those years ago, because you thought I was trouble for you and you wouldn't take a chance on me."

Her throat clutched. "I did think you were trouble. Things came so easy for you—plus, I had a future to make, and I couldn't allow myself to get distracted by a guy."

And speaking of distracting her, he was doing it right now, running his warm hands down her back, rubbing, caressing. It felt like heaven. She cuddled closer with another sigh.

He stroked a slow hand down her hair. "There's a lot to be said for getting right down to it."

"Amen."

"But sometimes it doesn't hurt to take your time."

She flattened her hands on his chest and rested her chin on them so she could look in his eyes. "I get that, if you *have* a lot of time. We don't."

"We have till New Year's. And that's a whole month away." With the pad of his index finger, he followed the line of her hair along her cheek. He just kept on touching her, as though he couldn't get enough of the feel of her skin. "I don't want to rush this," he said. "Anticipation is a good thing."

"Well, I'm certainly full of anticipation."

He traced the shape of her ear. "I just want to make it good, you know?"

"What you're saying is that you want to make me crazy."

"You're right. I do. I want us to drive each other crazy, so that when it happens it will be even better than if we rushed it." He cradled her face again, and then he kissed her. She savored the perfect feel of his lips under hers. "A little time, that's all I'm asking for," he whispered against her mouth. "Time for me to show you how good slow can be. Say yes to me, Ava."

Her throat burned, suddenly, the sweetest sort of ache. She remembered his words from all those years and years ago.

...someday you're gonna say yes to me, Ava...

And she realized she wanted that, longed for that, to say yes to him finally, this holiday season. And if he wanted to take his time about it, well, that sounded kind of beautiful, too. "All right then, Dare. Yes. We'll do this your way."

She stayed until after midnight.

They made popcorn and streamed a movie. There were more kisses. Lots of them. But finally, she said she had to go.

And then as soon as she got in her Suburban and headed for town, she wished she could turn the car around and spend the rest of the night with him. But she didn't. She resisted temptation and went on home.

The next morning, she woke up with a goofy grin on her face. Really, who knew that *not* having sex with Dare could turn out to be so much fun?

She stretched and yawned and went to the window to peek through the blinds. The snow had stopped. The sky was gunmetal gray—and she'd better get moving. She had to pick up Sylvie at Annabelle's at nine.

As she was filling the coffeemaker, she suddenly knew she'd forgotten something.

And then she remembered. Nick Yancy's funeral was at two that afternoon. And she'd promised her mother she would try to go.

Sadness—for Nick, for his family—weighed on her.

She thought of a number of good excuses not to go. There were always a thousand things to do on Sunday. And she'd hardly known Nick, after all.

But no. Really. Someone from the Janko family should be there.

And it should be doable. Janice was opening the clubhouse at one for any Blueberries and parents who could put in some time on the dollhouse project. Ava had signed up both her and Sylvie to pitch in for an hour or two. But Janice would understand if she dropped Sylvie off and went on to the service.

Dare wasn't at the clubhouse when Ava arrived with Sylvie—not that he should have been. He'd more than done his part on the project and had a right to a break now and then. But still, she felt a little tug of disappointment at not seeing him there.

"You go on," Janice said when she explained why she couldn't stay. "My condolences to the Yancy family…"

Sylvie had her own kid-appropriate Kurio smartphone, a present from her doting grandparents on her seventh birthday. Ava checked to make sure Sylvie had the phone with her. Then she got back in the Suburban and headed for the Community Church on Elk Street.

At the church, the parking lot was full. Ava ended up parking on nearby Marmot Drive. The church itself overflowed with mourners, and everyone in town must have sent flowers. There were urns brimming with them, wreaths decked with them, swags of them, everywhere.

Ava spotted Jody Bravo in the third row from the back. The pew looked full, but if people would just sit a little closer to each other, space could be made for more. And Ava hated seeing Jody sitting there all alone.

Scattering soft *excuse-me's* as she went, Ava wove her way to the end of Jody's row and then, murmuring more apologies, kept going until she made it to Jody's side. The lady next to Jody scooted over a little, and Ava claimed the vacant spot. Jody, who looked much too pale and tired, patted Ava's hand.

Ava leaned close. "Why didn't you get Nell or Elise to come with you?"

"They offered. So did Clara and Rory. I asked them not to come."

Ava had no idea what to say to that. And Jody didn't seem eager to chat, anyway.

There was shuffling from the other end of the pew, someone else jockeying for a seat. Ava glanced over and saw it was Dare. He edged toward them, and the man on Jody's other side slid over, making room for him. He sat down.

Jody gently bumped his shoulder with hers. "What are you doing here?"

"Nick was a great guy. Thought I'd pay my respects. How you holding up?"

"I've been better." Jody stared straight ahead.

Dare wrapped his arm around her. For a moment, Jody let herself lean against him, let her head droop to his shoulder with a sigh. But then she drew herself up and faced front once more.

Ava waited for him to glance her way.

When he did, he held her gaze just long enough to send a warm ripple of pleasure moving through her. "Ava."

"Darius. Hello."

The service began.

It was lovely, really, including videos and a photo montage of Nick growing up and riding in the local rodeos. They played several sweet and spiritual country songs—Nick's favorites, Ava assumed. She clutched a handful of tissues and dabbed at her cheeks whenever the tears got away from her.

Beside her, Jody stayed dry-eyed, back straight and gaze forward. Ava glanced at her now and then to see how she was doing. *Grim* was the word for Jody Bravo that day.

More than once, Dare looked over at the same time that Ava did. Their gazes would hold until one of them remembered to look away. Ava was so glad he'd come, glad that Jody had someone who cared on each side of her.

Afterward, the minister, Nick's stepdad and step-brother formed a receiving line in the narthex. Everyone began to file out, some stopping to pay respects to the family and the pastor, others skirting the line and moving for the doors.

Jody chose the line. Ava and Dare fell in behind her. Jody exchanged a few soft words with the pastor. She shook the hands of Nick's stepdad and his stepbrother, Seth, who'd been elected county sheriff two years ago. She said how sorry she was. Nick's stepdad, Bill, nodded and sadly smiled. The sheriff accepted Jody's gentle words with a single dip of his head.

"Ava, isn't it?" asked Bill Yancy when it was her turn to take the older man's hand. "Paul and Kate Janko's girl?"

"Ava, that's right. The family's out of town. My dad and mom and brothers send their deepest condolences."

"You tell them we do thank them."

"I will. Please take care."

And Ava moved on, nodding at Sheriff Yancy, murmuring words of sympathy. Dare followed behind her, speaking briefly with Nick's stepdad, then stopping to say something to Seth.

Out on the church steps, Ava looked for Jody and spotted her disappearing around the side of the building, walking fast toward the parking lot.

Dare came up beside her. "Did Jody say anything to you?"

"No. She just took off. Oh, Dare. I don't know if she ought to be alone right now."

"Come on. Let's go find out if she needs anything."

They went after her, catching up as Jody reached her Chevy Tahoe. Jody climbed in without saying a word to either of them.

Before she could shut the door, Ava asked, "Are you going to the gravesite?" When Jody shook her head, Ava offered, "How about some coffee?"

Jody sat so still behind the wheel, her door still wide open. "No. Thank you. No." She pulled the door shut.

Something wasn't right. Ava ran around to the passenger side and tapped on the window.

Jody didn't look happy about it, but she did unlock the doors. Ava got in. Dare climbed into the backseat behind Jody.

After that, nobody seemed to know what to do or say next. They just sat there, the three of them, for at least a full minute, the silence in that SUV hollow and infinite. Ava stared through the windshield at the gray sky and the muddy piles of old snow on the edge of the

parking lot, at the bundled-up people filing by to get
to their cars.

Jody finally spoke. "I'm pregnant," she said. "Three
months along."

Chapter Five

As Ava tried not to gape in bald surprise, Jody put her hand on her belly. If she was starting to show, Ava couldn't tell through the heavy winter coat she wore.

"It's Nick's," Jody said. "Nobody else knows right now, but I'll tell them all soon. I just haven't gotten around to spreading the news yet. And I would appreciate it if you would keep it to yourselves for right now."

"Of course," promised Ava.

"All right," said Dare.

Jody met Ava's eyes. With a soft cry, Ava reached for her. For a moment, Jody surrendered to an awkward hug across the console. When Jody pulled away, she craned her head and shared a quick glance with Dare. "You won't have to keep quiet for long. I really will tell them in the next few weeks. I'm starting to show, anyway. Winter sweaters hide a lot, but by Christmas it's a secret I won't be able to keep."

"Come to my house," Ava coaxed. "I'll fix us something to eat and we can—"

"You're sweet, Ava. But no. I just want to go home, crawl into bed and have a long nap."

"But are you sure you're all right?"

Jody looked away again. "Nick was a good person. I'll miss him. I'm sorry he'll never know his child. But yeah. I *am* all right, and I know what I want, which is to have this baby and be a good mom. So thank you. Both of you."

"For what?" Dare asked gruffly. "We haven't done anything."

"Yeah, you have. You're here and you care. And I'm grateful for that." She gave Ava a sad little smile.

Dare said, treading cautiously, "I, uh, didn't know you and Nick were together."

"We weren't." Jody gripped the steering wheel in her gloved hands as if to steady herself. "It wasn't like that. There was one night, that's all. He wanted to keep in touch, and we kind of got to be friends. And now he's gone and I'm having a baby and…well, I *want* this baby. I honestly do."

Ava couldn't help thinking of Sylvie. "Being a single mom isn't easy, but I promise you, it is so worth it— and are you sure you won't come to my house, just for a quick snack?"

Jody shook her head. "Nope. I'm going home."

"I don't like it," Dare said, "I'm not happy about leaving you alone."

Jody shrugged. "I *am* alone. And I'm okay with that. I honestly am."

"I'm calling to check on you later," Ava said. "And you know my number if you need anything."

"I have it. Thanks."

What else was there to say? Ava and Dare got out of the Tahoe on their opposite sides. They stood waiting as Jody backed, waved and drove off.

"Where's your car?" he asked once Jody was gone.

"Over on Marmot."

"Come on, I'll walk you."

Side by side but not touching, skirting dirty mounds of snow, they went back around to the front of the church. When they reached the sidewalk, they headed toward the corner of Elk and Marmot.

"You think Jody's told Seth and his dad about the baby?" Dare asked. "They acted like they barely knew her back there in the receiving line."

"Funerals are brutal, especially for the family." Ava thought of that windy day at Miramar, with Sylvie fussing in her stroller, the flag draped on the casket. She'd felt so empty that day. People spoke to her, and she didn't answer. She was quiet on the outside, but inside she was screaming. "I don't think we can draw any conclusions from what Seth and his dad did in the receiving line—and she's only three months' pregnant. Plenty of time before the baby comes to tell the stepuncle and step-grandpa."

One side of his mouth curved in a hint of that gorgeous grin of his. "In other words, butt out?"

"Pretty much. Plus, I clearly heard you give her your word that you wouldn't tell anyone."

"Jody's so hard to read. Always has been. She's the sister I could never really figure out. Clara has that big heart. She just wants us all to get along. And Elise is the busy, bossy one. And you know Nell. She makes it more than clear where she stands on any given issue. Jody, though, she's the quiet one, a still-waters type. She keeps a lot to herself."

"She's a private sort of person. I don't see anything wrong with that."

"I didn't say it was wrong. I just wonder if she's told Seth and his dad, if she even *plans* to tell them."

Ava decided she needed to make her point more strongly. "Dare. It's *her* news to share."

He slanted her a sideways glance and laid on the irony. "Gee, Ava. Tell me what you *really* think."

"All right. Keep your mouth shut. It's Jody's choice how she handles it."

He stepped in front of her. Walking backward, he put up both hands like she held him at gunpoint. "Don't shoot. I'll behave."

"Promises, promises."

They turned the corner. A moment later, they reached her car.

He opened the door for her. "I'll see you."

"When?" She slid behind the wheel and rolled the window down.

He shut the door, leaned in—and teased, "Can't wait, can you?"

She considered demanding a kiss, but he just might give her one. And how would they keep this thing between them a secret if she kissed him in broad daylight on Marmot Drive? "You're way too sure of yourself, you know that?"

"Tomorrow."

"What about it?"

"I'll see you tomorrow, Ava."

"What time? Where?"

"If I tell you, it won't be a surprise, now, will it?" He slapped his hand on the door and stepped back. Then his cocky grin faded. "You'll call Jody, you said?"

"Yeah. Tonight."

"Let me know if there's anything... I don't know. Whatever I can do." He looked honestly worried for his sister—and bummed that he had no idea how to help. And that made her want to kiss him all over again. "I'll check with you tonight, after you've had a chance to talk with her."

"That sounds good." She rolled up her window and got out of there before she jumped from the car and threw herself into his arms.

Ava called Jody as soon as Sylvie went to bed. Jody said she was fine and for Ava please not to worry about her, so Ava left it at that.

She got a two-word text from Darius at ten: How's Jody?

No news. She seems okay and says not to worry. I think we need to leave it alone for now.

Well, all right then. See you tomorrow...

Right. Tomorrow. Time and place of his choosing because the guy was determined to drive her crazy with unfulfilled lust. Good night, Darius. She turned the phone to silent mode and stuck it in her bedside drawer so he couldn't tease her anymore that night.

* * *

He showed up at her office at a few minutes after ten the next morning.

The receptionist, Myra, who also played secretary for the three other Realtors in the old Victorian that had been converted to offices, buzzed her. "Darius Bravo is here for you."

Her stomach went fluttery, and her cheeks flamed hot. "Thanks, Myra." At least she kept her tone calm and businesslike. "Send him back."

Thirty seconds later, he sauntered through her office door. "Miss me?" He shut the door behind him—and turned the lock.

Her knees went suddenly wobbly. She rose from her desk chair just to prove to herself that she could. "If I did, do you think I would actually admit it to you?"

"You're a hard-hearted woman, Ava."

"I have to be tough around someone like you."

He came toward her, circled the desk and pulled her into his arms. "Kiss me?" He made it sound like a request. And then he lowered those killer lips of his and kissed her anyway, giving her no chance to decide if she would or she wouldn't.

He tasted minty, and he smelled of leather and man. His tongue toyed with hers and his hands roamed her back. She clutched his big shoulders and moaned with enthusiasm, loving the smooth leather of his jacket and the hard muscles beneath. It was a long kiss.

But still, for Ava, it ended too soon. He lifted his head, and she opened her eyes to gaze up at him dreamily. "I have to show a condo in—" she brought her wrist up between them to check the pink-gold pre-owned

Rolex she'd bought to reward herself when she sold her third Bravo-built home "—forty-seven minutes."

"Then let's not waste any time." He pulled her close again, into all that wonderful hardness and heat, his left hand settling at the base of her spine as he guided her slowly over backward. She heard her chair roll away from her desk. And then he was laying her out across the desk pad, following her down.

She giggled like she was twelve or something. "You're lucky I keep a tidy desk. Pencils and paper clips would be flying."

"Tidy, huh?" He looked down at her as though he might eat her right up.

"I like things orderly." She tried really hard not to sound as breathless as he made her feel.

"I think I need to mess you up a little, Ava…"

She would have argued against that, but his lips met hers once more, and all the words flew right out of her brain. He left no room for anything but pleasure, his wonderful hands molding her waist first and then gliding upward to cover her breasts. She groaned when he cradled them. And groaned some more as he rubbed them, pinching her nipples through the fabric of her silk shirt and bra.

He started undoing her buttons. And she let him, though this was her place of business and it was nothing short of tacky to be doing this here.

But so what? She just couldn't stop herself—didn't *want* to stop herself.

Because Darius Bravo had mad skills when it came to upping the sexual ante between them. He really knew how to drive her crazy, take her higher, make her burn for the day he would finally be her lover for real.

One button undone. And then the next. And the next after that. He pulled her shirt from her skirt and spread it open, revealing her lace bra—and then breaking the kiss so he could tease her, "Pink. Very nice. Matches that fancy watch of yours."

He put those wonderful hot hands on her breasts again, and he used his thumbs to pull the cups of her bra down. And then he lowered his head and caught her nipple between his teeth. She cried out—and he reached up and put his hand over her mouth.

"Shh, Ava." He flicked her nipple with his clever tongue. "Shh, now. We don't want Myra to hear. This is our own sweet little secret, remember?"

So she pressed her lips together to keep the moans in, and she speared her fingers into his hair and held him close and let him kiss her bared breasts, one and then the other. He lavished endless attention on them, until she hovered on the verge of begging him to make this happen. All the way.

Right here on her desk.

Just like Saturday night, he was as ready as she was. She felt the rock-hard ridge of him, pressing against her right where she needed him so much. She even reached down between them, intent on driving him as wild as he was making her.

But he only chuckled in a rough, slightly pained sort of way, caught her wrists, one and then the other, and held them over her head, making her powerless to do anything but try to hold back her hungry moans and let him torture her with pleasure a little bit more.

It didn't last long enough.

Much too soon, he was lifting away from her, taking her shoulders and pulling her up to sit on the edge of the desk. She blinked at him owlishly as he straightened her bra for her and buttoned up her white silk shirt.

"There," he said at last. "No one would guess what you've just been doing."

She didn't need a mirror to know that she looked as aroused as she felt. "Liar."

He kissed her again. And then he said with real feeling, "You drive me out of my mind, Ava."

"I don't have a lot of sympathy for your suffering, being as how we both know there's an obvious solution to your problem. How much longer are you going to make me—make both of us—wait?"

He kissed the tips of his fingers and pressed them to her swollen lips. "Not much longer." The hot blue light in his eyes told her otherwise.

"You're a cruel man, Darius Bravo." And she was loving every minute of this torture, so what did that say about her?

He gently combed his fingers through her hair. "When it's over, I want you to remember me."

"As if I could ever forget you." She sounded desperate and adoring even to her own ears—so she added much more coolly, "I mean, I work with your family, I'm friends with your sisters and you're the king of my daughter's Blueberry troop."

He lifted her wrist and checked her watch. "Twenty minutes until you're supposed to be showing that condo."

She jerked her hand away to check for herself. "You're right. Go."

He caught her face between his hands and kissed her one last time, quick and hard. "Soon."

She gripped the top of her desk to keep from grabbing him and pulling that mouth of his back down to hers. "Get out of here."

With a low, knowing laugh, he turned for the door.

The Blueberry troop had its weekly meeting that afternoon.

When Ava came to get Sylvie, Darius was there supervising the ongoing work on the dollhouses. Janice announced that it was time to clean up. Ava pitched in. Gathering up art supplies, she headed for the storage closet.

She was stacking construction paper neatly back on a shelf when the closet door closed behind her. Simultaneously, the light went out, pitching the cramped, narrow space into total darkness.

She knew it was Darius. She could *feel* him there, so close. Moving in closer. She smelled leather and cedar shavings. His big, warm hands clasped her shoulders.

"Seriously? In the Blueberry clubhouse?" she whispered disapprovingly, though deep inside, she melted. "Have you no shame?"

"None whatsoever." He turned her around, pulled her against him and brought his mouth down on hers.

She kissed him back. It felt too good not to.

But only for a few seconds. Then she flattened her hands on his chest and pushed him away. "Enough. We've got to be out of this closet before the cleanup is finished and Janice starts talking again."

"Why?"

"You know why. Because when Janice starts talking, everyone stands still, and there's no way we can get out that door without somebody spotting us."

"Whatever you say, Ava." And then he kissed her

again. And she kissed him back with way more hunger and yearning than he deserved. He was the one who stopped it that time. He caught her hand, and she felt his soft lips brushing her knuckles. "Soon."

"That tells me nothing. When, exactly, is 'soon'?"

But, of course, he didn't answer. He stepped back. A split second later, the light popped on, the door opened and he was gone. Shaking only a little with nerves and unsatisfied desire, she turned and went back to shelving art supplies.

The next night, Tuesday, he called her at quarter after ten. "Miss me today?"

She couldn't help it. She grinned like an idiot. Luckily, it wasn't a video call and he couldn't see how happy she was just to hear his voice. "What have you been up to?"

"Working. We finished a copper backsplash for a new Fort Collins bar. It's a beauty if I do say so myself. And we're filling a lot of orders for our stainless steel toolboxes. They come in three sizes—and how about pizza? Tomorrow night. I'll bring the pies. I'm guessing Sylvie's a pepperoni girl."

Ava said nothing. Because the fizzy, bubbly feeling inside her had gone flat. He wasn't supposed to come to her house and hang out with Sylvie. And he knew that. Didn't he?

"Ava?"

"I'm still here."

"Great then. Tomorrow night. Is six good?"

"Darius…"

A silence. Then he asked too quietly, "What do you think's going to happen after New Year's?"

"What kind of question is that? We both know what's

going to happen. It's over at New Year's." *That is, if it ever actually even begins.* "Darius, how many times have we been through this?"

"I'm not talking about you and me. I'm talking about Sylvie and me."

"Sylvie and you? There is no—"

"Yes there is, Ava." His voice was suddenly as cold as the wintry night outside. "I like helping out with the Blueberries, and Janice has already asked me to help with another project next year. I like your daughter, and she's my niece's best friend. I'm not going to treat her like I don't know her anymore starting January 1—and haven't we already been through all this Saturday night when I asked you to bring her out to my place?"

"Yes. So why are we talking about it again?"

"Because you said you'd think about it, but you never planned to think about it, did you? You'd already made up your mind."

"Well, I…" She realized she felt guilty, which made zero sense. Why should she feel guilty for wanting to protect her child from heartache?

"Loosen up a little, will you, Ava?"

Why wouldn't he understand? "I don't want my daughter hurt."

"And how, exactly, am I going to hurt her?"

"She really likes you, and I don't want her thinking that you and I are together. That will only confuse her and possibly cause her pain."

Another aching silence from his end of the line. Finally, he spoke again. "You can't control everything, Ava."

"I know. You're right. I just…"

"Is Sylvie in bed now?"

"I don't—"

"Just answer the question."

"Yes. Sylvie's in bed."

"I'm coming over."

"Wait. What? You can't…"

But he'd already hung up.

Chapter Six

She tried to call him back twice to tell him not to come.

He didn't pick up.

Twenty-five minutes after he hung up on her, he was at her front door. And she was right there waiting in the entry hall, ready to answer before he could ring the bell and possibly wake Sylvie.

She heard his boots on the steps and pulled open the door. And then she just stood there, staring at him, feeling lost and awful and full of impossible yearning. "What are we doing?"

"Let me in, Ava." His voice wrapped around her, warming her all over in spite of how he wouldn't stop breaking all her rules.

"Where's your truck?"

His mouth was so soft, his eyes as dark as the night behind him. "Down the street so no one will see it parked in front of your house." He said it with resignation, playing her silly game because she'd asked him to.

She stepped back. He came in. She shut the door. "Go ahead. Hang up your coat."

He took it off and hooked it on the hall tree by the stairs.

She glanced down at the thick red socks on her feet. "Sylvie and I mostly wear socks in the house. So if you don't mind…" He sat on the bottom step and pulled off his boots, setting them at the foot of the coat tree. "This way," she said, when he stood again.

She led him through the living room and dining room to the kitchen in back. Somehow, the kitchen seemed safer—farther from the stairs that led up to Sylvie's room. And it had straight-back chairs, harder to get comfortable in. She gestured toward the table. He sat down. "A beer or something?"

He shook his head. "Sit with me. Come on." She took the chair opposite him. "Pretty house," he said.

"Thank you." She rested her hands on the table and then didn't know what to do with them, so she pulled them down into her lap. And then, for no reason she could understand, she started talking about her first home, the one she'd loved so much and lived in until she was nine.

"When I was little we had a house a lot like this. It's a few blocks away from here, actually, over on Primrose Lane. It was a little run-down, that house. But still, cozy and nice. A good house to grow up in, you know?" Dare made a low sound of confirmation and she added, "My parents owned it."

And really, why was she telling him this? She had no idea, and she ought to stop.

But she didn't stop. "It had been my dad's parents'

house. I loved that house. I felt safe there. I was a happy little kid. But I didn't get to grow up there. Mom got sick for a while, and Dad lost his job. Money was short. They had to sell the house. We moved to a rental. Dad still couldn't find a job. Frankly, he didn't look all that hard. He was worried for Mom and wanted to be with her. We got evicted. My brothers and I spent two years in foster care."

He regarded her so steadily. "I didn't know that."

"Yeah. Well, it was a long time ago, and it's not something I talk about much. Not something I really want to keep fresh in my mind. And at least it wasn't forever. I was twelve when my uncle Evan, who owns a used car dealership in Coeur d'Alene, gave my dad a loan to buy the double-wide at Seven Pines. My dad finally found a job, and they let us kids go back to living at home, which was now at Seven Pines.

"Somehow, we always managed to keep hold of that trailer. We all worked, doing whatever we could do—babysitting, yard work, house cleaning. I even did ironing for this lady whose husband wore white cotton shirts to work—the wrinkliest shirts I ever saw. I mean, honestly, who even *has* an iron anymore?" A tight laugh escaped her, one with way too much pain in it.

But still, she kept on. "Every spare cent we got our hands on went to keeping the trailer and keeping food on the table. None of us wanted to get thrown back in foster care." The story ran out on her. Again, she wanted to kick herself for telling it. At least she'd left out the worst part. He didn't even need to know about all that. Lamely, she concluded, "So that's why I always wanted my own house. A pretty house."

"Like this one," he said gently. And then he reached out.

She couldn't deny him. She didn't *want* to deny him. She put a hand on the table again and then slid it across to link her fingers with his. "Yeah. Like this one."

His hand engulfed hers, so warm, the skin a little bit rough in a way that seemed to her so manly, his grip confident. Strong. His thumb moved, stroking the heart of her palm, a caress that excited her at the same time as it soothed all the snarled and jumbled fears she could hardly put a name to.

"It will be all right, Ava," he said. "It *is* all right. I mean, look at you."

She glanced down at her baggy tan sweatshirt and leggings. "What?"

He gave her one of those smiles that could light up the darkest room. "It's only that you're so pretty it almost hurts to look at you."

"Oh, yeah. Right."

He put on a stern expression. "Take a compliment, Ava. It's not going to kill you."

She bit her lip to keep from grinning. "Ahem. Thank you."

"Better. And besides being smoking hot, you're smart and determined and you've made a success of your life against some tough odds. I get that you've had hard times. But things are good for you now. You have a beautiful, smart daughter, a job you seem to love and the house you've always wanted."

She thought about Christmas, suddenly. About how pretty her house looked once she had all the decorations up, with a big wreath on the door and her Christmas tree in the front window, the branches thick with lights and treasures she'd been collecting since before Sylvie was born.

And more than the tree and the wreath on her door, she thought about the light of the world, about hope in the darkness. About the glow on Sylvie's adorable face when she came downstairs last Christmas morning. About everything that she, Ava, had to be thankful for.

"I know," she said. "I've definitely had my fair share of good fortune. And I'm grateful, for my little girl, for my family and friends, for my prosperity."

"So what are you guarding? What are you afraid of? What bad thing do you think I'm going to do that you can't let me bring over a pizza and spend an evening with you and your daughter?"

She pulled her hand back to her side of the table. "Of course I don't think you'll do anything bad."

The way he looked at her said he *could* be bad. Deliciously so. And she already knew from personal experience exactly how good his badness could be. "So give it up then," he said in that voice with a growl in it, the one that rubbed along her nerves, striking off sparks. "Say 'Yes, Dare. Come over tomorrow and have pizza with me and my daughter.'"

"I...honestly, it's what I said on the phone." She lowered her voice to barely a whisper. "I just don't want Sylvie to start having expectations that won't be fulfilled."

"Even a seven-year-old can understand that her mother has friends."

"Well, of course."

"Why can't you tell her that? Just say that I'm your friend."

Ava folded her arms across her chest, realized how defensive that looked, and unfolded them again. "Why can't *you* just give up?"

He arched a sable eyebrow at her. "Say no one more time and I just might."

What did he mean by that? That he would give up trying to bring a pizza over? Or that he would give up everything, this magic between them, their secret Christmas fling?

She almost blurted out, *Fine, then. Go. Have a nice life.* But that would only be her past speaking, the scared voice of the girl she'd once been, the girl who'd lost her home for a while, had her family shattered, the girl who'd felt so very alone, so completely unprotected.

No. She didn't want him to go. He made her heart beat faster and her body ache with yearning. He was also patient and sweet and understanding.

And he was right. Sylvie already adored him. And when Christmas was over, Sylvie would still see him, at Blueberry meetings, at Bravo family gatherings. He wouldn't just vanish from Sylvie's life.

"All right," she said. "Tomorrow night."

He gazed at her across the table, a steady look that still managed to have her thinking of tangled sheets and secret nights. "That wasn't so hard was it?"

She answered honestly. "Actually, it was." Then she slid back her chair and stood. "We usually eat early. Five thirty?"

He got up, too, and came around the table to stand right in front of her. "Five thirty's good."

"No PDAs in front of my daughter."

"Ava." He made a tsking sound. "I am the soul of discretion." He tipped up her chin with a finger and kissed her, slow and oh, so sweet.

And then he turned and headed back through the dining room and living room to the front door.

* * *

Sylvie yanked the door wide. "Darius! Mom said you were coming—and with pizza. I love pizza!" She glanced down at the red-and-white pizza boxes in his hands. "You got Romano's! They have the best pizza." The landmark Italian place on the south end of Marmot Drive had been serving great food for as long as Ava could remember.

Dare frowned down at the boxes. "One supreme and one with pepperoni. Do you think that will work?"

"I'll take pepperoni!"

"I had a feeling you might."

Ava, behind her daughter in the doorway, shivered at the cold. "Sylvie, let Darius in before we all freeze to death."

Sylvie chose that moment to show off her good manners. "Please come in."

"Thank you." He stepped over the threshold. Ava caught the door handle and pushed it shut.

"Coat goes there." Sylvie pointed at the coatrack. "And if you don't mind, we wear socks in our house."

"I don't mind at all."

"Here," Ava said. "Let me have those pies." He passed the warm, pizza-scented boxes to her. "I'll just take these on into the kitchen…"

"Don't worry, Darius." Sylvie beamed up at him. "I'll stay here with you."

"Terrific." He was shrugging out of his heavy jacket as Ava turned for the kitchen.

She could hear Sylvie behind her babbling away. "The powder room's right here, so you can wash your hands before dinner. And then, when you're finished, I'll wash mine, too…"

In the kitchen, Ava set the pies on the table side by side and got the salad from the fridge. Sylvie had already set places for three and put out the salad dressings.

"And after dinner, I can show you my room and we can play 'Super Mario Kart' even though it's a school night—" Sylvie was still talking as she led Darius into the kitchen "—because I already did all my homework and when I do all my homework early, I get to play a game or watch a show."

"It all works for me." Dare was looking at Ava. She tried not to get lost in those gorgeous blue eyes.

Sylvie trotted over and pulled back the chair at the extra place. "Darius, you can sit here. Would you like some milk?"

Ava suggested, "Maybe Darius would prefer a beer."

"Ew. I *hate* beer—well, okay, I never had it. But you know it does smell bad and..." About then, Sylvie caught herself. She slapped her fingers against her lips. "Oops. Sorry, Mommy." And then she filled Darius in on the rules. "I'm not s'posed to talk about food I hate, and that includes drinks and that includes beer."

"I understand," Darius replied solemnly. But his eyes kind of twinkled when he added, "And yes, I would love a beer."

So Ava sorted out the drink situation, and Darius helpfully tore the tops off the pizza boxes so they could get at the delicious-smelling pies. Then they all dug in.

Sylvie talked nonstop, about school, about how much she'd enjoyed her Saturday night sleepover with Annabelle, and then about Christmas, one of her very favorite subjects. "Tomorrow night, we're going to start dec'rating our tree. Mom, maybe Darius can come and help us…"

Darius said nothing; he waited for Ava to give him his cue. She sent him a grateful glance and redirected her daughter toward the pizza and salad she'd barely touched. "Eat your dinner, Sylvie. That is, if you want to ask Darius to play a video game with you afterward."

That did the trick. Sylvie cleaned her plate and drank her milk. Then Ava let her drag Darius up to her room for a tour. Ava cleared off the table and wrapped the uneaten pizza in plastic for him to take home. When the two came back down, they played a video game in the living room for an hour, after which Ava joined them for a rousing—and endless—game of Uno. Finally, Sylvie went upstairs for her bath.

Ava and Darius barely had time to get second beers and settle in the living room before Sylvie came flying downstairs again dressed in flannel pajamas and asking if she could read Darius a story before bed. Just in case that might be okay, she'd brought the book of choice down with her. It was *Bear Stays Up for Christmas*, which was only forty pages. Sylvie knew that book by heart.

Dare said, "I'd love a Christmas story."

Sylvie jumped up on the couch beside him. "Mommy, come sit here." She patted the cushion on her other side. Ava took the offered seat, and Sylvie read the story.

After such a thrilling evening with Sylvie getting the Blueberry king all to herself at her own house, Ava half expected trouble getting her to bed. But Sylvie surprised her. Once she turned the last page of the story, she thanked Darius for coming over and said goodnight. Ava followed her up the stairs.

Sylvie waited until she was snuggled under the covers

before she made her move. Gazing up at Ava through big, hopeful eyes, she asked plaintively, "Mommy, can't Darius *please* come to help us dec'rate tomorrow night?"

Ava wanted to say yes. Because it *had* been a nice evening. Darius had been wonderful, and Sylvie had clearly loved every minute of it.

But Ava had to be careful not to give her daughter the wrong idea. One night was enough for now. "No, honey."

"But if you would only *ask* him, I'll bet he would say yes. I *tried* to ask him, but you didn't let him say if he would or not. He doesn't have any children, Mommy. He doesn't have a family at his house. Who's he gonna dec'rate with? I think it should be us."

"Let it go, Sylvie."

"Mom…" Sylvie stretched the three-letter word into at least four syllables.

Ava pressed a kiss to Sylvie's forehead and went to the door. "I love you," she said tenderly as she turned out the light.

Sylvie didn't answer. She shifted on the bed, rolling to her side and facing the wall.

Ava didn't push her. Sometimes a mother has to call a draw a win—but then, just as she turned from the doorway, a small voice said, "Love you, Mommy. G'night."

The slight tightness in Ava's chest eased. "Night, sweetheart."

Downstairs, she found Dare waiting in the living room. He patted the sofa cushion next to him, and she thought of Sylvie earlier, patting the cushion for Ava to sit by her while she read her story. They were both far too charming, her daughter and her would-be lover.

She went and sat beside him. "You're amazing with Sylvie."

"And why do you sound annoyed about that?"

"I'm not. Just cautious."

"Yes, you are. Always."

She opened her mouth to defend herself—and then thought better of it. Why argue with the truth? She *was* cautious, and she had no plans to change.

He wrapped his arm around her. She thought about Sylvie again, about the strong possibility that a curious seven-year-old might creep down the stairs to see what the grown-ups were up to.

Better to be somewhere Sylvie couldn't witness things she shouldn't. Ava got up again. "Come with me."

He rose without a word and followed her around through the dining room and into the master bedroom. "A cutthroat game of Uno *and* I get to see your bedroom?" He grabbed her arm as soon as she'd turned the privacy lock. "What a night." He pulled her close. And then he lowered his mouth to hers.

At last.

She wrapped her arms around his neck and gave herself up to the sheer perfection of his kiss, walking backward and pulling him with her as his lips worked their special magic, and she dared to hope that maybe this would be it—the night their Christmas fling finally really began.

She led him to the bed and pulled him down onto it. For several lovely, thrilling minutes, they made out like the teenaged lovers they never got to be.

But when she eased her hand down between them seeking his zipper, he caught her wrist.

She groaned—and not with pleasure. "You're kidding me."

He chuckled. A purely evil sound. "It's too soon."

"God. You're such a tease."

They lay facing each other across the bed. He pulled away enough to look at her as he ran his fingers along her temple, and then back into her hair the way he seemed to love to do. His touch felt so good.

She gave up pushing for hot, sexy action and let herself simply enjoy looking into his beautiful eyes, loving his rough-tender touch as he stroked her hair and brushed the back of his hand down the side of her throat.

And then he kissed her again, slow, deep and sweet.

She sighed when that kiss ended. "Maybe you have a point. Taking our time isn't half-bad."

He didn't say anything, just kissed her some more.

A little later, in the front hall, after he put on his boots and his coat, he said, "Rocky Mountain Christmas is Saturday." It was Justice Creek's big holiday season kickoff event. Every store on Central Street would be open at 8 a.m. "You going?"

"Wouldn't miss it. I have an open house that afternoon, so Sylvie and I will go early."

"I might run into you. Just, you know, by accident."

She liked that idea far too much. "And if you did, where would this accident happen, exactly?"

"I'm thinking coffee and a muffin at Bravo Catering at eight." Bravo Catering, which included a bakery, was Elise's shop. Elise and Jody had joined forces a couple of months ago, with Elise opening up her catering and coffee shop adjacent to Jody's flower shop, Bloom.

Saturday was three days away. Did that mean she wouldn't see him until then?

Maybe she should just go ahead and ask him over to help with the tree tomorrow night. Sylvie would be thrilled. And later, once Sylvie was safely tucked into bed, there would be more kisses. If she couldn't have sex with him, she needed lots of kisses, and she needed them often.

His mouth curved in that way he had—almost a smile, but somehow not quite. "So. Saturday at Bravo Catering?"

Today was almost over. So really, it was only two days before she'd see him again. She'd gone years of her life without seeing him, without kissing him. Two days wouldn't kill her.

"Eight o'clock," she said. "We'll be there."

Ava and Sylvie started on the tree as soon as Sylvie got home from school the next afternoon. At five, Ava's mom and dad dropped by. They volunteered to help. After a quick meal of soup and sandwiches, they all got down to work.

By Sylvie's bedtime, they had it all done, with the tree in the window, the big, lighted wreath on the front door, the holiday swags draping the staircase and the Christmas village scene on the mantel.

Sylvie wanted her grandma and grandpa to tuck her in, so Grandpa Paul hoisted her onto his shoulders, and the three of them went up the stairs together. About twenty minutes later, Paul and Kate came back down.

Ava offered coffee, and they sat at the kitchen table together.

"It was so much fun, honey," Kate said of the Thanksgiving reunion in Idaho. "Wish you were there."

"Sorry I had to miss it."

"Did you manage to make it to the funeral?"

"I did. It was a beautiful service."

"You gave Bill and Seth our best?"

"I did—more coffee?"

Her dad shook his head. "World Series of Poker main event at nine thirty." Her dad loved his poker tournaments. "We need to get going."

So Ava walked them to the front hall.

Just as she was about to usher them out the door, Kate remarked much too coyly, "Sylvie tells us you had company last night."

Ava was ready for that. "We did, yes. Darius Bravo dropped by with pizza. He's helping out with the Blueberry Christmas project this year, and all the girls are half in love with him."

"You went to school with him, didn't you?"

"We were both in high school at the same time for one year, yes."

"And now you're dating him."

"No, Mom. I'm not." *Or at least, not exactly.* "He came over, and he brought pizza. He played video games with Sylvie. It's called hanging out, and it is not dating."

"Ah. Well, that's nice."

"Mom, don't make a big deal out of it."

"Oh, I wouldn't. You know that." She absolutely would, and they *both* knew that. "So, then. It was just a friendly visit?"

"Just friends. Exactly."

"Well, Tom doesn't care much for him. I think your brother still holds a grudge because Darius fired him all those years ago. But Darius has always seemed like a nice young man to me. And so handsome and successful, too." Ava knew her mom didn't care in the least how *successful* a man might be. Kate just thought Ava cared, which annoyed Ava to no end.

"Mom. I make my own success." She tried to say it without heat.

But apparently, she failed. Her mom looked wounded. "I only meant that he seems like a fine man."

Ava's dad spoke up then. "Kitty Kat. Time to go."

Kate patted his arm. "All right, Pauly-Wally." Ava purposely did not roll her eyes at the corny pet names her parents had for each other. "So you're not going out with him? You're really just friends?"

"That's right, Mom. Just friends." It was only half a lie: She *wasn't* going out with him.

But they were so much more than friends—or they would be, as soon as Darius decided he'd driven her crazy enough with desire that their Christmas fling could finally start.

He was there waiting for them at Bravo Catering Saturday morning, wearing a leather bomber jacket over his jeans, his winter gloves on the table.

"Darius!" Sylvie ran to him. "Can we sit with you at your table?"

"As a matter of fact, I was hoping you two might come along."

"You were? Good, because here we are!" Sylvie threw her arms wide with excitement.

"Excellent. Hello, Ava." He gave her one of those looks that set fire to all her secret places.

"Darius. Great to see you." She pulled out a chair and dropped her giant red shopping tote to the floor beside it as Sylvie took off her hat and mittens.

Darius pushed back his chair. "Hold the table. I'll get the muffins and drinks."

Sylvie tugged on his hand. "I want to help."

So Ava ordered a cinnamon muffin and coffee, and Sylvie and Dare got in line.

Elise came out from behind the counter to say hi. Ava gave her a hug and started to ask how Jody was doing. But she had no clue how much Elise knew at this point, and it seemed wiser not to get into it.

So she settled for asking, "Is Jody next door?"

"Oh, yeah. She's here all day."

Darius and a starry-eyed Sylvie returned with muffins and hot drinks. They sat down to enjoy the treat, and Elise went back to work.

A few minutes later, Quinn, Chloe and Annabelle Bravo showed up. They grabbed extra chairs, and the six of them sat together. When it was time to hit the street and shop their socks off, they decided they might as well all go together—and Ava suggested they should drop in at Bloom first and say hi to Jody.

Dare shot her a knowing look. "Good idea."

They all filed through the open ironwork door between the two shops and found Jody behind the counter at Bloom. Ava thought she looked much better than the week before, with more color in her cheeks.

Was that the beginning of a baby bump beneath her red tunic sweater? If it was, nobody else seemed to notice. There were hugs and happy greetings all around. Jody had cute plastic dragonfly bracelets for the two girls.

Within a few minutes, it was time to go. Ava grabbed Jody in a final hug and whispered, "Call me if you need anything."

"Thanks. I will."

And that was it. They filed out the door and onto bustling Central Street.

In the next three hours, they went up one side of Central and back down the other, hitting just about every store. Darius and Quinn hauled around the ever-increasing number of shopping bags without complaint.

By noon, the girls were getting droopy. And Chloe suggested they all stop for lunch at Clara's restaurant, the Library Café.

Ava said yes, though the timing would be tight. She should get to her open house by one thirty to set up. And she had to drop off Sylvie at the Blueberry clubhouse before that. But she'd parked in the big lot in back of the café, so that helped. Darius put all her shopping bags in the Suburban before they went inside.

The restaurant was wall-to-wall with hungry holiday shoppers, but they got lucky and didn't have to wait long. A few minutes after Darius put his name in at the front desk, the hostess led them through the busy restaurant toward a cozy nook at the back.

Halfway there, Ava heard her mother call, "Well, hello, honey!"

She glanced toward the sound, and there was her mom waving madly. Her dad waved, too. They were just getting seated at a table near the two-story wall of bookcases that gave the restaurant its name. And Ava's parents weren't alone. They'd brought along her brother Tom and his family. Her mother spotted Darius in Ava's party and didn't even try to hide her gleeful grin.

"Gramma, Grandpa!" Sylvie crowed and then, more shyly to her ten- and twelve-year-old cousins, "Hey, Joe.

Hi, Andy." The boys granted her the barest nods of acknowledgment and Sylvie started toward them.

Ava caught her daughter's arm and kept her moving forward, simultaneously waving and signaling to her parents that she'd come back as soon as they were seated.

They made it to the table by the window a minute later. "I'm just going to run back and say hi to the folks," Ava said. "I won't be a minute."

"I'm coming," Sylvie announced. "And Annabelle needs to come, too. She likes Gramma Kate."

"Yes!" Annabelle agreed wholeheartedly. "I want to come, please."

Ava sent Chloe a questioning glance, and Chloe gave the nod that Annabelle could go. "Only for a minute," Ava warned. "We have to get back so the waitress can take our order."

"Maybe I should go and say hi, too," Darius suggested wryly. Ava sent him a quelling glance, and he shrugged. "All right, be like that. Go without me."

Which of course had Sylvie crying, "Mommy! Darius wants to come, too."

By then, Ava was wondering why they were doing this at all. She should have just waved at her mom and dad and left it alone, but she'd kind of freaked there at the sight of her parents and Tom. She didn't really want her mom to see her around Darius and get more ideas. And Tom didn't even like the guy, so she'd probably get grief from her brother for being anywhere near the rich Bravo who'd once fired him.

Ugh. Everything was getting way too complicated—and not just concerning the question of who would go and say hi to her parents.

At least Dare took pity on her and came to her rescue with Sylvie. "I was just kidding, Sylvie. I need to stay here and keep Quinn and Chloe company. You guys go ahead."

Ava made her move, herding the two girls ahead of her back the way they'd come.

Her mom got up as they approached the table. She hugged Ava and then bent down to greet Sylvie and Annabelle.

"Hi, you guys..." Ava gave a generalized wave to her brother, his wife, Libby, and their boys.

Tom just couldn't keep his mouth shut. "Hangin' with the upper crust, huh, Ava?"

Libby sent him a sharp look. He winced, which meant she'd probably kicked him under the table. Libby was a sweetie. She knew how to handle Tom. "So we'll see you tomorrow then?" Libby asked brightly. Tomorrow, the Janko family would get together for Sunday dinner at Seven Pines.

Ava gave her sister-in-law a grateful smile. "We'll be there—and Sylvie. Annabelle. Come on, we need to go order our food..."

Back at the table, the overworked waitress had already come by once to take their orders. She'd promised to return in a few minutes. It took her longer than that. But finally, they had their food and drinks.

Ava enjoyed her lunch and the easy conversation and forgot about the time until she glanced at her watch and discovered it was already half past one. She had to get moving.

"I'm sorry. The time got away from me." She whipped out her wallet and pulled out the cash she needed to cover her bill and a nice tip. "I've got an open house in half an hour, and I need to get Sylvie to the Blueberry clubhouse."

"We'll take Sylvie," Chloe volunteered. "Annabelle is going over there, too."

"And put your money away," said Quinn. "This is our treat."

"I couldn't—"

"Don't argue." Quinn, who'd once been a martial arts champion, used his tough-guy voice.

Ava thanked him.

Darius said, "I'm going over to work on the doll-houses, too."

Quinn gave a dry chuckle. "Right. They can't do anything over there without the Blueberry king."

Darius smirked. Ava had never cared much for men who smirked. But somehow, on Darius, a smirk looked just fine. "You think you're funny, little brother. But it's true. I'm indispensable—and Sylvie and Annabelle can ride with me."

"Yes!" exclaimed Annabelle.

"We want to ride with Darius!" Sylvie chimed in.

"Terrific," said Ava, and meant it. "Works for me." She pushed back her chair. "Sylvie needs her booster seat."

"I'll walk out with you and get it." Darius took her coat from the back of her chair and held it up for her.

In the parking lot, he led the way to the Suburban. He pulled the backseat door open and took out the booster.

"I really appreciate this," she said.

He turned and gave her one of those looks that made her wish they were alone someplace with a bed—scratch that. Who needed a bed? Any reasonably flat surface would do. "You're welcome." He spoke in that low, rough tone that made her want to do all kinds of naughty things to him and then have him turn right around and do them to her.

"Well, then..." Her voice sounded way too husky. And she didn't have time to sound husky. She had an open house in twenty minutes.

But then he lifted the hand that wasn't holding the booster, making the move very slowly, giving her plenty of time to duck away.

Yet she didn't duck away. On the contrary, she swayed toward him, her yearning for him stronger than her usual good sense. He brushed a slow caress along her cheek.

She should have been annoyed that he'd done that in public, but all she could think was she wished he'd do it again and this time that he'd also slide his fingers around the back of her neck, that he would pull her up close to him and kiss her until she couldn't see straight.

But he didn't pull her closer. "Soon," he said soft and low. And she stood unmoving, staring up at him, knowing she had to go, not wanting the moment to end. "Would you like me to kiss you, Ava?"

Her throat clutched. She croaked out, "What? Here? Now?"

He smiled then, slowly, a smile that made her think of tangled sheets and desperate, hungry moans. "Yeah, Ava. Here. Now."

And oh, my yes. She would. She would like him to kiss her. She would like that very much.

But of course, a kiss right here in the Library Café parking lot would be carrying it one giant step too far. "Better not."

"You sure? I personally think all these rules of yours are pointless."

Pointless? She frowned up at him. Silly, maybe. Childish. But there actually was a point to her rules, and the point was to keep her family out of her business—and okay, maybe also to keep this thing that was happening between them from getting too real, from spinning scarily out of control.

None of which she was even going to think about. After all, the whole idea of a fling was that you didn't spend a lot of time thinking about it.

If there even was a fling.

Because so far, not so much.

"My rules are not pointless—and yes, I'm sure that you shouldn't kiss me now."

He stepped back. "Well, I guess I'll just go on inside then."

She didn't trust herself to answer. At a moment like this anything could come out of her mouth. She just might start begging him to kiss her, after all. So she made herself nod.

The nod did it. He turned for the restaurant.

She watched him walk away. Too soon, he vanished through the back door—and left her standing there staring after him like some dreamy-eyed fool. She shivered, drew her coat closer around her and turned to pull open the driver's door.

That was when she saw her parents, her brother and his family standing in a huddle by her dad's Subaru five spaces down. Her mother waved and beamed her a big, pleased smile. Libby looked sheepish.

Tom only scowled.

Chapter Seven

Seven Pines Mobile Home Park hadn't changed much in the twenty years since Ava's uncle helped her parents buy their three-bedroom manufactured home there. The sign at the entrance declared it "A great place to live." And really, it wasn't half bad. Each unit had a little square of lawn in front and a tiny deck. Many had pretty container gardens.

Ava arrived before Tom and his family. Her other brothers, Pete and Brad, were already there. Pete and his wife, Laurie, had no children. Brad was divorced with two girls, both of whom were with their mom this particular Sunday.

Sylvie loved coming to Gramma Kate's. She helped set the table and babbled away about school and Annabelle, the Blueberries and how she couldn't wait for it to be Christmas. Ava's mom already had her small tree up in the corner of the living area, and Sylvie expressed her pleasure at the sight.

Tom, Libby and the boys arrived and they all sat down to eat. Ava was feeling pretty good about the afternoon. Sylvie had so far stayed off the subject of her hero, Darius. And Kate had not given her one single meaningful look. Maybe she'd get lucky and make it through dinner without a sarcastic remark from Tom or yet another dose of well-meaning romantic advice from her mom.

But her luck didn't hold.

Not five minutes into the meal, Tom said, "Pass the green beans, Ava—and what was that we saw yesterday in the Library Café parking lot with you and Darius Bravo?"

Ava opened her mouth to tell him to butt out, but Sylvie piped up with, "I *like* Darius. He's helping the Blueberries build special dollhouses for special children. He's nice and he's fun."

Ava smiled sweetly. "And mind your own business, Tom." She handed him the beans.

"Hold on a minute." Pete looked confused. "Something's going on between Ava and Dare Bravo?"

Tom turned to Brad and opened his mouth to reply. But Libby must have kicked him under the table again. He stiffened and muttered, "Never mind."

Brad, who sat to Ava's left, leaned close to her and asked, "Everything okay?"

"It's fine, honestly," she said.

Tom waited till dinner was over to come at her again. "Just give me a minute, okay? You and me, out on the deck..."

"Tom, really. Can't you just leave it alone?"

He wouldn't give up. "It's not going to kill you to hear what I have to say." So she put on her coat and followed him out there. He led her over to the corner farthest from the door and stuck his fists in the pockets of his bulky winter jacket. "Where to even start? Look, Ava. I just don't want you to get hurt is all."

Ava kept her voice even and quiet. "I'm not a child anymore. There is nothing for you to worry about."

"Yes, there is. I know the guy's a charmer, but that doesn't make him a good guy."

"Tom. He *is* a good guy. Okay, he fired you eight years ago. And then when you punched him, he punched you right back. But come on. It's old news. You've got a good job now. You and Libby and the boys are doing fine. It's time to get past all the crappy stuff that happened way back when."

He looked at her so intently, like he wanted to see inside her head and check for lies. "But are *you* past it? *Really* past it?"

Ava's mouth went dry, and her pulse ratcheted higher. "What, exactly, are you talking about?"

"Don't blow me off, Ava. You know."

She turned and leaned on the railing. "Wow. Okay, then." Staring hard at the gray wall of the unit next door, she tried not to grind her teeth together. "So how far back are we going here?"

"All the way," her brother said gently.

So she went ahead and reminded him, "I survived, Tom. I got over it. And I'll always be grateful to have brothers who looked out for me when times were really tough. But now you have to step back and let me deal with my own life."

"Not if you're messing it up."

"*Even* if I'm messing it up—which I'm not." *I hope*. "I mean, can you just try to view this situation objectively, please? Dare Bravo's got nothing to do with what happened to me in foster care when I was eleven years old. That you're even trying to equate the two..." She shook her head. "You're wrong, Tom. They do not equate. Not for me. If anything, what happened to me all those years ago has made it harder for me to trust a guy, to let him get close. It's made me less likely to let anyone take advantage of me again in any way, ever. Maybe too much so." She slid him a glance. He did seem to be listening.

And then he let out a long breath and leaned on the railing beside her. They studied the gray wall of the other unit together. "Well, okay," he said finally. "I see your point. Craig was a great guy. And he had to work his ass off to get you to even give him a chance."

She almost smiled then. "Now you're getting it."

"But Ava, I know how you are. Please don't take this the wrong way, because I respect how hard you work. Still, I know you want the good life."

She groaned. "Wonderful. Just when I'm starting to remember all the reasons I love you, you call me a gold digger."

"No, that's not what I said."

"Oh, you so did."

"Just hear me out. It's one thing to do business with the Bravos. I'm glad for you, I really am, that your partnership with Bravo Construction is a big success. But Darius is a bad bet. He never met a woman he could stick with. He mows them down and moves along."

"*Mows them down*? Tom, that's just mean."

"You know it's true. The guy's in his midthirties and he's yet to have a serious relationship with a woman."

"Wrong. He's been engaged. Twice. First, to a girl he knew when he lived in Los Angeles and a few years ago, to a woman who worked at Ames Bank."

"He told you that?"

"Yes, he did. Because we're friends. And friends tend to have actual conversations about what goes on in each other's lives."

He scoffed. "You and Darius. Friends."

"Isn't that what I just said?"

"I saw you in the parking lot yesterday. He was all over you."

"All over me? He touched my cheek."

"Exactly."

"You know, it's really hard to take you seriously when you won't stop exaggerating."

"Ava. That was not a *friends* moment the two of you were sharing. And you're just asking for trouble if you think there's a future with him. That guy will use you and dump you flat."

Oh, she was so very close. Right on the brink of telling her buttinsky brother the truth that if there was any using going on, she was the one doing it, that she was with Darius only for the hot sex.

Potentially. Eventually. She hoped…

But no. A revelation like that might be momentarily satisfying. In the long run, though, it would bring her nothing but grief. Tom just might freak if he knew that his precious baby sister could not wait to be Darius Bravo's Christmas-only lover. Plus, the whole point of a secret affair was that her family wouldn't be all over her case with warnings and advice—which was beyond ironic, now that she thought about it. The supposed affair hadn't even started yet and already she was up to her eyeballs in warnings and advice.

"I will say it once more, Tom. And then I'm going inside. Darius Bravo and I are casual friends and nothing more." Yes, it was a flat-out lie. And she refused to regret telling it. "I would greatly appreciate it if you would show me a little respect. I've been running my own life for a long time now, and I am doing a damn fine job of it, thank you very much."

Ava's doorbell rang at five fifteen the next night.

It was Darius, with one hand behind his back. "Nice wreath," he said when she opened the door.

"Thank you." She glanced over her shoulder. No sign of Sylvie. Yet. She stepped out to the porch and pulled the door most of the way closed behind her. "What are you doing here?"

"You're shivering, Ava. You should go inside. I'll come with you. In fact, I'll even stay for dinner." He brought that hand out from behind his back and showed her a pink-and-white bakery bag. "Cookies from Elise's bakery. For dessert."

She shouldn't be so glad to see him. It hadn't been that long. About half an hour, actually. He'd been there when she picked Sylvie up at the clubhouse after the weekly Blueberry meeting. He almost trapped her in the supply closet again, but she ducked out just in time. And he hadn't said a single word about appearing on her doorstep in the next thirty minutes.

He leaned a fraction closer. "Let me in, Ava." It was the same thing he'd said last week when he showed up without being invited.

She glanced past his shoulder. "You parked your truck right out there in front of my house."

"Ava." He wasn't actually touching her. It only felt like he was every time he said her name. He could hold her prisoner using only the sound of his voice—a much too willing prisoner, as a matter of fact. "If you let me stay for dinner, I'll move it around the block."

"Why bother moving it? My family saw us in the parking lot Saturday afternoon."

"Sorry."

"Oh, you are not—and you're right. It's cold out here. You'd better come in." She pushed open the door again.

And there was Sylvie, sliding to a stop in her stocking feet, her sweet face wreathed in smiles. "Darius! I thought I heard you out here…"

He knelt to greet her. "I came for dinner and I brought cookies."

"Good. Because we're having meat loaf, and cookies are a lot better than meat loaf." She shot Ava a wary look and added, "Not that meat loaf is bad. It's just not as good as cookies, okay?"

Ava tried really hard not to smile. "Okay. Go on in and set another place."

"Okay!" Sylvie whirled and took off for the kitchen.

After dinner, Sylvie did her homework in ten minutes flat, leaving time after her bath for some Wii bowling, a board game and *How the Grinch Stole Christmas*. And then she went to bed without stalling or complaint, whispering contentedly, "Night, Mommy," as Ava turned out the light.

"I think I'm raising the perfect child," Ava said to Dare when she joined him in the living room. "At least, today I am."

"She's a great kid, all right." He took her hand and tried to pull her down next to him.

She resisted. "Will there be kisses?"

"You'd better believe it."

"Then let's go somewhere more private."

"Great idea." He got up—and then held her back when she would have led him to the master suite. "Nice Christmas tree." He let go of her hand and slipped an arm around her. She felt his touch on her nape, rubbing a little in a lovely, companionable way as they stood there together and gazed at the tree in the window. "I should get a tree. And then I should go out and buy a bunch of lights and shiny ornaments. Then you should bring Sylvie out to my place and help me decorate."

She leaned into him, even put her head on his shoulder. But she didn't reply. Taking Sylvie to his place still seemed a step too far to her, and she didn't even want to have to think about why—let alone talk it over with him. She expected him to press the issue and tried to figure out how to gently say no.

But he didn't press.

And when she caught his hand a second time and turned again for her bedroom, he went with her, following her in there, even shutting and locking the door behind them.

Then he gathered her into his arms. "If you won't come out to my place, how about the party at Rory and Walker's on Wednesday?"

"Nell and Chloe both invited me. I'll be there." It was an annual Bravo family event, a tree-decorating party at the Bar-N guest ranch, which had belonged to Walker's family for generations.

"Are you bringing Sylvie?"

"No. It's a weeknight. Plus, I understand it's more of a grown-up party."

"Yeah, pretty much."

"I'll get a sitter."

He lowered his mouth a fraction closer to hers.

"Oh, Dare..." She went on tiptoe and claimed a sweet, slow kiss.

Eventually, he lifted his head and asked, "How about if we go together? I'll pick you up at seven."

"It's not on your way."

"You know I don't mind."

Why did he constantly refuse to take a hint? "Dare. Your taking me to Bravo family parties is not part of the plan."

"So change the plan."

She began the slow-walk backward. He came with her, and when they got to the bed, they stretched out on their sides facing each other. She tried to capture his mouth for another toe-curling kiss.

But he wasn't through talking. "Look. The whole secret-fling thing is getting old, don't you think? Not to mention, it's not even working. Everyone knows that we know each other. We've been seen together, and that's going to keep happening. And so what? It's not completely outside the realm of possibility that we could simply be friends. Why shouldn't friends go places together?"

What he said made way too much sense. Damn it. "Believe it or not, that's what I told Tom yesterday. That you and I are friends. I told my mom the same thing."

"So why don't we go with that, then?" He stroked his fingers into her hair, sending warm ripples of sensation moving out in a widening wave wherever his skin grazed hers. "And given that we *are* friends, I see no reason why I can't pick you up and take you out to Rory and Walker's place on Wednesday."

She totally surprised herself by answering, "All right, then. Thanks. I'll be ready at seven."

He kissed her again, those wonderful fingers gliding over her shoulder, drifting down the outside of her arm. Even through the bulky knit of her sweater, she felt his touch acutely. And then he asked, "So did Tom get on your case yesterday?"

"I got through it."

"You're saying he bad-mouthed me, right?"

"He's overprotective. And, well, you know he has issues with you."

"Should I talk to him?"

"Absolutely not. He resents you for firing him. But one of these days he'll get honest with himself and admit it was his own fault for being late or a no-show over and over. And frankly, you did him a favor by just punching him back after he hit you. You could have had him arrested for assault."

"I also could have been less of a jerk and given him another chance."

"Didn't he have plenty of those?"

"It wouldn't have killed me to give him one more. But I hadn't been with the company for all that long. I wanted to impress my father, show him I had what it took to keep the employees in line."

"Really, it all worked out. Tom has a good job with the county now. He's doing fine."

"So what's bothering you?"

"Bothering *me*?"

He ran his finger down the center of her forehead

and then stopped in the space between her eyebrows. "Something has you scrunching your eyebrows together."

She wished he didn't always seem to read her so well. "It's just...stuff happened. When we were kids."

"What stuff?"

She was not going to tell him. But then she asked, "You know how I mentioned that I spent two years in foster care?"

"I remember."

And all of a sudden, she just wanted it out there. She *wanted* him to know. "There was this boy, Trevor. He was two years older than me."

"In foster care, you mean?"

"Yeah. He was in the group home they put all four of us in first, me and my brothers. Trevor paid a lot of attention to me..."

Dare asked too softly, "What kind of attention?"

"Like a boyfriend—but really possessive, you know? I was only ten when it started, way too young for a real boyfriend. Especially one who kind of wanted to own me. I, well, I was having a hard time and at first, I liked it, to have Trevor's obsessive, undivided attention."

"I can understand that. You'd lost your home and you were away from your parents..."

"The whole world seemed scary and dangerous and wrong. I wanted someone to hold on to. At first, Trevor seemed like the solution to my fears, the answer to my lonely, desperate prayers."

Dare did the sweetest thing then, kind of turning her and tucking her so she was on her other side, facing away from him. He wrapped himself around her spoon-style. She felt cradled by him, by his body. Cradled and safe.

Plus, this particular story was easier to tell when she wasn't looking right at him. She tucked her arm under her head for a makeshift pillow and continued, "Then we left the group home. They moved us to foster homes. Brad and I went to one home, Tom and Pete to another."

"And what about that boy, Trevor?"

"He stayed in the group home at first. I was kind of glad for that. I'd started to realize that Trevor was...too much. My brothers had warned me off him. By then, I wanted to be away from him. There was another foster girl at the home where Brad and I went. But then she left. And Trevor took her place."

Dare made a low sound, a soothing sound. His hand closed over the outside of hers, cradling it. He wove his fingers between hers.

And that helped somehow. It gave her the strength to keep on. "Trevor kept trying to get me off by myself. He would kiss me. There was...inappropriate touching. I kept trying to let him down easy. But that wasn't happening. He wouldn't back off. Finally, I just told him in no uncertain terms that I wanted him to leave me alone. That made him mad. He cornered me in the basement when I was down there doing laundry. He attacked me and I fought him."

Dare muttered a bad word and held her even closer.

She went on, "But fighting him did no good. He just got rougher. He punched me in the stomach and in the face, hard enough that I couldn't breathe and I saw stars."

Dare smoothed her hair away from her throat, pressed his warm lips against the side of her neck. She took comfort from that, from his gentle kiss, from the reassurance in his touch.

And then she went on with it before she lost her nerve. "He didn't rape me, but I think maybe he would have if Brad hadn't shown up and stopped him. They fought. They were the same age, thirteen, Brad and Trevor. But Trevor was bigger. He was winning. Until I grabbed an old lamp off a stack of storage boxes in the corner and bashed him upside the head with it. He rolled off Brad and staggered up the stairs, stopping at the top to call me a rotten, disloyal bitch and threaten to 'take care' of me later."

"My God. What about your foster parents? Where were they?"

"I just remember they were always busy. They weren't around when it happened. And we were...damaged, I guess, me and Brad, by everything that had gone so wrong for us. And my mom was still sick and my dad had all he could handle, trying to take care of her and somehow get some money coming in. We had some idea that it would only make it all worse, to try to tell the grown-ups what had gone down. And I personally didn't want anyone to know."

"Ava," he chided, his breath warm in her hair. "You blamed yourself."

"Yeah. I did. At the time. But I don't anymore. I know better now. Later, when it was all long over, before I married Craig, I got counseling."

"Good." He wrapped his arm a little closer around her.

"I was a needy, messed-up kid who got taken advantage of by another messed-up kid."

"And you really told no one?"

"Uh-uh. Not back then. And since then, well, I've told Craig and my therapist. And you. We didn't even tell Tom or Pete, not at first. Brad and I cleaned up the mess in the basement and patched each other up. When our foster mom started asking questions about who beat up whom, all three of us kept our mouths shut, said it was nothing. Our social worker came and talked to us. We still didn't break."

"What about your parents? Didn't you have visits with them?"

"Yeah. And when they saw the bruises and cuts, they freaked. But Brad and I stood strong. We just said we were fine and it was no big deal. It's sad looking back now, but we were proud, Brad and me, that we didn't tell anyone. I have no idea why Trevor didn't talk. Maybe he came to the same conclusion Brad and I did—that nothing good was going to come from telling an adult what had happened."

"Especially for Trevor, being an abusing rapist and all."

"Well, yeah. There's that."

"And was that the end of it, then? Did he leave you alone?" He sounded hopeful. But then he sighed. "He didn't stop."

"No, he didn't. He cornered me again in the backyard one day. I got away, but not before he gave me a busted lip and tore my shirt. Brad said it couldn't go on. He went to Tom and Pete. They all jumped Trevor under the middle school bleachers. They beat him up pretty bad. That time he got the message. He didn't tell anyone, and he never came near me again." She tried a laugh. "I swear, last week when I told you I'd been in foster care, I was absolutely certain I would never tell you about Trevor, that it was a story you would never need to hear."

"Hey." He tugged on her shoulder. She went over onto her back again. Once she met his eyes, he said, "I'm glad that you told me—and I have to say I'm liking your brothers a lot about now."

She tried a smile. It trembled only a little. "Yeah. They're good guys. And you can see why Tom tends to be overprotective."

He asked, "So then is Trevor why you said no to me in high school?"

"Trevor and all of it, really. Mom getting sick, losing our house, being taken away from my parents for two years. You could say I had trust issues—and really, Dare, you were like some god back then."

"And yet you refused to even go to a party with me." He said it playfully.

But she was deadly serious. "I'm not joking. You had it all. The girls were all over you. I couldn't trust that, couldn't trust *you*. I couldn't be like any normal girl and just believe in love and hope and that some amazing guy was going to fall for me and love me forever and never, ever break my heart. I had to be careful. I had to watch my step."

"And you're still being careful." He wasn't teasing now.

Why lie? He saw right through her, anyway. "Yeah. I guess so. Some lessons you never unlearn. At least not completely."

He kissed the end of her nose. "Come here." And he pulled her on top of him. She rested her head on his chest and listened to the steady beat of his heart. He was warm and solid, so good to lean on. She tipped her head up to tell him so.

But then he kissed her, and she got thoroughly absorbed in kissing him back, in the taste of him, the delicious, manly scent of him, the feel of his big hands running over her shoulders, threading through her hair. He touched her so tenderly, those amazing hands stroking, soothing, sending all the old fears away, back into the past where they belonged.

He rubbed at the base of her spine, easing a knot of tension she hadn't even realized she was holding. Until it loosened and faded away.

And then he went lower, his hands sliding over her bottom, cupping her. Even with her jeans and panties in the way, she melted inside.

She eased one leg over him, straddling him. Groaning softly, he pressed his face into the curve of her throat. His breath flowed across her skin, and he moved both hands lower still, sliding them around the backs of her thighs and then inward. He touched the yearning core of her through her jeans.

She lifted away enough to gaze down at him, her hair trailing forward a little, a long curl of it brushing his rough cheek. The look of pure hunger on his upturned face told her everything she needed to know.

"Tonight?" she whispered, and she couldn't help grinning like a long-gone, love-struck fool. "Really?"

But he grew serious. "There's one more thing."

"Oh, God. What?" She searched his face.

His eyes went deep. "Even if he didn't actually rape you, that kid Trevor brutalized you. You said you got counseling. And with me, now, you don't seem the least reluctant or afraid..."

"Reluctant? About sex, you mean? I can't believe you haven't noticed that I'm about as far from reluctant as a girl can get." She said it lightly.

But he wasn't satisfied. "Ava, I need to know if you're past what he did to you."

She answered him seriously this time, with no teasing and zero equivocation. "I am, yes. It took some work, with Craig, to, um, get there. But we did. We had our problems, Craig and me, but not in the bedroom." She let out a slow sigh. "I hope that reassures you. Because I did love my husband, and I really don't want to talk about him anymore tonight."

For that, she got a nod and a seriously spoken, "All right, then."

"All right, then, what exactly, Dare?"

And that was when a slow smile curved that impossibly sexy mouth of his. "Still got those condoms?"

She drew in a shaky breath. "You bet. A whole box. Right here in the bedside drawer."

Chapter Eight

"Take everything off," he said, and then added fervently, "I will, too."

That sounded more than fair. "Done."

They broke apart, sat up and started pulling off their clothes, tossing them to the floor as fast as they could. It took about thirty seconds. She whipped off her last sock, threw it over her shoulder—and met his gleaming blue eyes again.

Had she expected to feel self-conscious the first time she got naked in front of him?

Definitely.

But somehow, she didn't. Somehow, it felt good and right—and about darn time.

And dear Lord, he was beautiful.

"Oh, Darius." She came up on her knees again and pressed her hand to his bare chest, all sculpted and hard, with a silky trail of hair leading down to where he was very much ready for her. "Just look at you."

"I'd rather look at *you*." His eyes were night-dark right then, all shine and shadow, full of the thrilling things he was going to do to her. "And I really want to touch you…"

For a long, lovely moment, they just stared at each other. "Yes," she answered finally. "Touch me. Please."

And he did. He reached out a hand and trailed the tips of three fingers across the top of her chest, causing a havoc of hot and prickly sensations all out of proportion to such a simple, seemingly innocent caress.

Would she ever have enough of feeling his hands on her?

Not a chance.

She pressed her palm to the side of his face, which was so warm, so wonderfully rough with just the right hint of stubble. Would she ever get tired of touching *him*?

Never.

She could so easily get addicted to touching him. To *being* touched by him. He could become her drug of choice. She would suffer painful withdrawals when this craziness ended.

And why was she thinking about the end now, when it was only finally really beginning? She needed to stop that.

And she would.

Right this minute.

She forced her lips to form words. "Is this really happening?"

"You'd better believe it." He brushed a lingering touch up the side of her throat.

"I almost gave up hope." She leaned in and bit the end of his chin—not a real bite, more of a slow scrape. That brought a chuckle from him. She stuck out her tongue and licked the beard-rough spot where her teeth had been.

And then he moved, grabbing her, scooping her knees out from under her. She let out a little cry of surprise as he laid her down with her head on the pillows. He stretched out beside her and covered her mouth with his.

It was one of those kisses, the kind that annihilate time. The world faded away, and there was nothing but the two of them spread out on that bed, nothing but pleasure. Her desire was a liquid pulse between her bare thighs, a singing rush along her nerves. Her blood seared and sizzled its way through her veins.

She grabbed his thick shoulders, her nails digging in. And she held on so tight as he just went on kissing her, a kiss full of hunger and heat and dark, delicious promise.

It was perfect, this moment. Just the two of them, naked together, touching each other, holding each other. Ava and Darius.

Lost in each other.

At last.

She scratched him, she knew she did. She made little red welts across his shoulders. And she didn't even regret it as she raked her fingernails down his back. He groaned a little, kissed her harder, his tongue sliding over hers and retreating, her tongue following, needy and insistent, only to be trapped between his strong, blunt teeth. She was the one groaning then.

And he never stopped touching her, stroking her,

those clever, rough-tipped fingers moving down and down—until he found her and dipped a finger in.

She cried out then, the sound muffled by his endless kiss.

He moved that devilish hand of his, slipping another finger into her slippery wetness, whispering lovely, dirty things, telling her how wet she was, how he knew now how much she needed him, how he was going to keep her naked all night long, that it was all right if she begged him, all right if she said please.

She did say please.

And she begged him, shameless and eager. She begged him for everything, all of him, inside her.

Right now.

Not that he listened, not that he took pity on her. Oh, no.

He wasn't finished making her crazy yet. He just went on stroking, touching, deeper, harder, varying the speed and the rhythm, driving her higher, to the brink and right over.

Her body lit up in ripples of light, little blasts of shimmery heat radiating out from his thrilling touch, making her bow right up off the bed.

And did he stop then?

Did he let her have a minute to catch her breath and collect her wits?

Not a chance. He just kept on touching her, fingers slowing but not stopping, catching the fire inside her as it flagged and stoking it to blazing life all over again.

He took his mouth from hers and trailed those wonderful, pliant lips of his downward, claiming one breast and then the other, rolling the nipples between his teeth, and then biting them. She groaned and tossed her head from side to side as pleasure skirted the sharp edge of pain. How could the things he did to her feel so exactly right?

It just wasn't fair. He had to stop, slow down, give her a break here. She couldn't take anymore.

But she did take more. And at some point, she realized she didn't want him to stop.

And he didn't stop. On down he went, kissing and nipping his way along the bumps of her ribs, into the hollow of her belly, where he lingered, dipping that tongue of his in and out of her navel.

That was just naughty, the way he strummed her navel with his tongue.

After which he went even lower, until he was right there at the center of her pleasure, rubbing his face in her wetness as he continued to stroke her with those evil, amazing fingers of his.

She hit the crest and went over again. That time she lost it completely and shouted out his name. He loved that. She knew he did. Because he gave a low, self-satisfied chuckle and put a hand over her mouth—a hand that smelled of her own desire.

"Shh, Ava. Shh, now..."

When the stars stopped exploding behind her eyes, she bolted straight up to a sitting position, determined to take back a little control. Because right now she felt like a hot mess of quivering sensation, pleasured within about an inch of losing consciousness—all that from only his clever fingers and his genius tongue and those teeth that knew how to take a little nip in the exact right spot at just the perfect split second.

"Baby, lie back down..." He said it gently, in that rough-tender voice of his that made her weak with yearning, had her ready and willing to do whatever he wanted.

However he wanted.

Any time that he desired.

Okay, she'd been getting a little impatient with all his stalling, with the way he kept putting her off.

But she sort of had to hand it to him. When the man got down to business, he sure knew how to hold up his end.

She was still sitting up, still telling herself that it was her turn to take the lead, choose the course of action, kiss *him* a little senseless, make *him* shout *her* name.

But then he did say her name—no, not in a shout. But quietly, soothingly. Just "Ava," kind of drawing it out, sweet and slow and tender.

That did it. She capitulated totally, surrendered unreservedly, flopping back against the pillows, putting her shaking body completely at his mercy. Little moaning sounds were coming from her mouth. Her eyes wouldn't focus. And what had happened to her eyelids? She couldn't lift them more than halfway. Each one seemed to weigh about a thousand pounds.

"What…? I don't…" Her words were gone, too. The ability to speak coherently had deserted her, along with everything else that made her the self-directed, independent woman she'd worked so hard to become.

Backbone? Somehow, she'd lost hers. Now she was a rag of a woman, totally limp, utterly boneless, lying there at his command. All she had left was this delicious pleasure he kept giving her.

Which was exactly what she'd fantasized about getting from him, now, wasn't it?

So she wasn't complaining.

Uh-uh. No way.

"Ava…" He rose up on his knees over her, all broad shoulders and deep chest and thick arms, the powerful muscles in his thighs flexing so beautifully. All he needed was a trident, a golden helmet and a shield. He could star in a gladiator movie.

He had the bedside drawer open, the lid up on the box of condoms and took one of them out. He took off the wrapper and put it on.

And then, at last, he came down to her. Gently, he nudged her legs wider, making room for himself between her thighs. He braced his forearms to each side of her, taking most of his own weight as he settled his big body all along her smaller one.

Caught and held in his eyes, she gazed up at his face above her. He stared at her so intently, as though he meant to drink her up with his eyes.

That was perfectly all right with her. She drank him up, too. He felt so right pressing into her, so heavy and male and exactly what she'd been missing for too many years.

She felt him nudging her, seeking her wetness and heat. She spread her legs wider, welcoming him with an eager sigh.

He sank home slowly, eyes still locked with hers.

There were no words. They didn't need them.

Not right now.

Right now, there was only the hot joy of him all over her, filling her so full and deep—and then somehow deeper still. There was his breath across her skin, his eyes rolling back when he hit that sweet spot within her, her own sharp, pleasured cry.

She twined her arms around him. He reached down

and wrapped those big hands around her thighs, lifting them, guiding them wider. She hooked her feet around him, too.

Now, she surrounded him and he filled her—so completely. All the way.

They were moving, hard and deep and fast.

And then, without a break in rhythm, he rolled them and she was on top, rocking her way to another explosion of bliss.

Or she would have been.

If he would only let her.

Just when she knew she would rock right to paradise, he gripped her hips and held her still.

She opened her thousand-pound eyelids and did her best to glare down at him. "That is just cruel."

"Shh…" He had this look. This smug, knowing, sexy, infuriating look.

"I think I hate you."

"Ava, don't say that. You know you don't."

"I think I…"

And then he moved. A sharp thrust upward.

And all she could do was groan in delight and roll like a river, tumbling fast, hurtling on toward the glorious fall.

Again, he rolled. They were facing each other. He wrapped her upper leg around his hip and pushed in so deep as he claimed her mouth.

An endless kiss, the two of them rocking in tandem, a slow pulse of energy sparking and flashing—from him, into her, forming a circle, a spinning ring of fire.

And every time she almost hit the peak, he knew.

He slowed.

He waited. Until the peak receded, became only a

beacon, a shining, heartbreaking possibility off in the distance.

At which point he would let her start moving again—and move with her, so perfectly, driving her onward, pushing her exactly where she longed to go.

Until he held off again.

It so wasn't fair. He made her want to bite him, tear him with her teeth, scratch him some more with her sharp fingernails.

Up was down and down was sideways. Everything shimmered. Her bedroom was some glowing, magic bower. Her skin was too tight, glossy with sweat, everything burning, her body in flames.

And then he was behind her, bending over her, so deep within her, she could feel him everywhere. His hand clasped her hip and slid in and under, finding her unerringly, stroking her higher again as he rocked her so perfectly.

"Ava." His voice like melting caramel in her ear. "Now?"

She couldn't believe it. He was actually asking her? "Yes," she answered eagerly. "Oh, Dare. Yes, please…"

"So sweet…"

"Dare. Please…"

"Come for me, baby. Come on. Do it now."

Oh, and she did.

And it was like nothing she'd ever experienced before, a slow, hot blooming, almost gentle at first, but then stronger, deeper and harder. It went on and on, the force of it growing, widening, opening, until she was shuddering, quivering from head to toe.

And he was there with her, surging into her, pulsing with his own completion, wrapping both big arms around her and lifting her, taking her upright, so they were both on their knees in the middle of the bed, his face in the curve of her neck, his mouth moving, branding words into her skin, rough, ragged words of pleasure, of satisfaction, of praise.

And then it was fading, going transparent, the hard, thrilling wonder easing into a warm, happy glow. He went down to the bed, taking her with him, gathering her into him, wrapping himself all around her.

She felt the rise and fall of his big chest against her spine with each breath he took, felt the hair on his thighs, rough and springy along the backs of hers. And his arms. Oh, they were so good and strong and solid wrapped around her.

She felt free in the strangest way.

Soothed and happy.

Cherished.

Taken care of in a way she hadn't been in far too long. A way she fully understood couldn't last.

And that was okay. Because this was just for the holidays, just for now. A lovely, secret, sexy magic to ring in the New Year.

He smoothed her tangled hair back from her forehead, brushed a kiss against her ear and whispered, "Merry Christmas, Ava."

And she reached back to wrap her hand around his neck, turning her head to him, whispering, "Merry Christmas, Dare," as their lips met.

Chapter Nine

"Black Russians," said Nell as she handed one to Ava. "It's a family tradition at Rory and Walker's Christmas decorating party."

"Oh, come on," Jody scoffed. "A family tradition? As I remember it, this is the third year Rory and Walker have thrown this party."

"So? I didn't say it was a *long* tradition—and here, Jo-Jo. Let me whip one up for you."

"No, thanks." Jody swirled the ice cubes in her glass. "Club soda's great."

They—Nell, Jody, Chloe and Ava—stood at the island that separated the great room from the kitchen area in Walker and Rory McKellan's gorgeous rustic ranch house. It was a good crowd that night, including all nine Bravo siblings, their significant others and also various friends. Christmas tunes played from the old-school stereo cabinet on the far wall, and Clara, Rory, and Elise were hanging ornaments on the tree. Ava glanced toward the fireplace where Dare stood with Walker, Dalton Ames and Elise's new fiancé, Jed.

Dare actually seemed to feel her gaze on him. He glanced her way and smiled. She got that heavy, throbbing feeling between her legs, and a series of knee-melting images from night-before-last flashed through her brain. She saw flames, she really did—each and every sexy mental image came surrounded in a ring of fire.

Nell nudged Ava with her elbow. "Something going on between you and Dare now—I mean, other than his usual nonstop flirting?"

Ava sipped her drink. "This is too good. Like an alcoholic fudge sundae."

"They are deadly," agreed Chloe. "Better watch out."

Nell stared at Ava steadily. "You didn't answer my question."

Ava played the friend card. "Dare and me? We're getting along great, even hanging around together now and then. Sylvie's crazy about him."

Nell snickered. "Be that way." She turned to Jody again. "One black Russian is not going to kill you. Lately, you're just beyond serious, you know? I mean you've always been too damn secretive for your own good."

"I am not secretive."

"Yeah, you are. I mean, who knows what really goes on with you? But at least you used to laugh now and then. Lately, you're like a stretched rubber band about to snap. You need to loosen up a little, have a little fun."

"Nellie, I love you." Jody sipped her club soda and sighed. "Leave it alone."

Ryan McKellan, Walker's brother, appeared at Nell's shoulder. "How's the Kahlua holding up? I have more in the car."

"So far, so good." Nell gestured at the bottles, garnishes and glassware set out in front of her. "Man the bar, okay?"

"I'm on it," said Ryan. He owned McKellan's pub in town and had probably brought most of the liquor and mixers arrayed on the island.

"I've had about enough of this." Nell grabbed Jody's elbow. "Come with me. We need to talk."

Jody set down her club soda and grabbed Ava's arm. "You're coming, too."

Ava laughed. "Oh, no. Uh-uh. I don't think so…"

Jody leaned close and whispered, "Moral support. Please. I need you."

Nell cast a knowing glance at Jody's hand on Ava's arm. "Well, all right. Ava comes, too. Whatever it takes, that's fine with me."

So Nell towed Jody and Jody pulled Ava across the great room toward the arch to the central hall.

As they passed the fireplace, Dare mouthed, "What?"

Ava widened her eyes and shrugged.

And on they went down the central hallway to the front entry and up the stairs. At the top, on the upper landing, Nell seemed to know right where to go. She led them along the upper hallway and into a bedroom that faced the back of the house.

"Well, this is familiar," said Jody when they got in there and Nell shut the door. She leaned close to Ava and stage-whispered, "A couple of Christmases ago, Nellie had a meltdown in this very room."

"Not relevant." Nell crossed her arms, tossed her thick ginger hair and set her lush mouth in a determined line.

Jody explained anyway, with relish. "It was old family garbage. We worked it all out that night, Nell and me, Clara and Elise and Tracy." Tracy Winham was a close family friend who'd moved to Seattle several months ago.

Nell said, "And we're working *this* out tonight. Sit down." Jody opened her mouth to argue. "I mean it, Jody. Sit." Jody gave in and perched on the bed. Ava took one of the two bedroom chairs. Nell went on, "Okay, now I just want to know—"

A tap on the door cut her off. "Nell? Jody?" It was Clara's voice.

Nell stared at Jody, who glared right back. Finally, Nell said, "Well?"

Jody made a wordless, angry sound. But then she got up and answered the door.

Clara, Elise, Rory and Dare were clustered on the other side. Clara said, "We just had to be sure that everything's all right."

"Come on in." Jody stepped back. The four of them entered, and then Jody stuck her head out the door and made a big show of peering down the upper hall. "No one else?" She turned and confronted them all. "Why don't we just invite the whole party up here?"

"Sorry," Clara said. "We've just been worried, that's all. And when we saw Nell dragging you up the stairs, we couldn't stand it. We couldn't pretend that nothing was happening."

Rory added, "You've been so withdrawn, and you won't talk to anybody."

"We just want to help," Elise chimed in. "And we were keeping it sisters only—well, and Rory, of course. But Dare wouldn't butt out."

Dare went to Jody. She looked up at him, misty-eyed. "I thought I should be here," he said, and wrapped an arm across her shoulders. "You know, just in case you need a brother to back them the hell off…"

"We don't need backing off," Nell huffed. "We need to *understand* so we can help."

"Thanks, Dare." Jody sagged against him. She gave Ava a weak smile. "You too, Ava. It really did matter to me the day of the funeral, it *helped*, that you two didn't let me just run from the church, that you stuck with me and you listened, that you were both so steady and kind."

"What is she talking about?" demanded Elise.

"And hold on a minute," said Nell. "Nick's funeral? You said you didn't want me to go with you to the funeral."

"She said the same thing to me." Elise looked hurt.

Rory and Clara both said, "Me, too."

Jody hung her head. "I'm sorry. I wasn't ready yet to talk about it, and I was afraid I might lose it completely during the service."

Nell gestured widely with both hands. "Which was exactly why you needed a sister there with you."

"We only want to help, all of us," Clara put in gently. "But how can we help if you keep shutting us out?"

Rory and Elise both murmured, "That's right."

And Jody just stood there in the shelter of Dare's strong arm, her sheepish gaze jumping from one sister to the next. "Fine," she said at last. "Okay." She drew in a slow breath and straightened her shoulders. "I'm having Nick Yancy's baby."

Clara cried, "Oh!"

Nell sighed as Rory and Elise made soft, sympathetic sounds.

Jody gave a tiny shrug. "It's true." She frowned. "What else? Let's see. I'm a little more than three months along. Yes, Nick knew. He was a total sweetheart about it and said he wanted to marry me. But, well, I just wasn't in love with him, and marriage wasn't going to happen. We had a couple of discussions about how we would work it out, the two of us, as coparents. They were tense, those conversations. He really thought marriage was the answer and I didn't, and, well, and then, he was gone." Her voice broke on that last word.

With a cry, Nell started toward her.

"Wait, Nellie." Jody huddled a little closer to Dare. "Just wait, please. Just let me finish."

Nell stopped midstep.

Jody swallowed hard. "It wrecks me, that he died. It's all wrong that he died. He was a great guy and so young. And I'm..." A tear slid down her cheek. And then another. She swiped them away with the back of her hand. "I feel awful about Nick. But not about this baby. No, I didn't expect to get pregnant. But I did. And I *want* this baby. I'm going to do this right, I really am. I'm going to be a single mom. And I am absolutely fine with that." They were all frozen in place. Nobody seemed to know what to say. Jody swiped another tear away. "That's it. That's all."

And somehow, that mobilized them. They went for Jody, who glanced up at Dare with a nod. Dare stepped back to give them room. They gathered around her, hugging her, saying how much they loved her, promising that they were there for her, whatever she needed.

Anytime. Anywhere.

It was after midnight when they got back to Ava's house. Darius pulled in at the curb behind the baby sitter's red Subaru.

Ava didn't want to let him go. "Come in. For a little while…"

He reached out and eased his hand under the curtain of her hair, his warm fingers settling on the back of her neck. "Come here." She leaned across the console, offering her mouth to him. He took it, rubbing warm little circles on her nape as his lips played over hers.

"So?" she asked when he let her go. "Want to come in?"

He traced a finger along the curve of her jaw. "Absolutely."

She led him inside. Maura Dell, who was sixteen and had been babysitting Sylvie for four years, came in from the living room as they were taking off their coats and boots.

Ava introduced Maura to Dare, tucked a few bills into Maura's hand and then saw her out the door.

She turned to find Darius waiting by the arch to the living room. A hot shiver raced just below the surface of her skin. "I need to check on Sylvie."

"Go."

"Some coffee or something?"

He shook his head. "I'll be right here."

She ran up the stairs. Sylvie was fast asleep on her side, both hands tucked under her cheek. Ava shut her door and went back down to Dare.

"All good?" he asked.

"Perfect."

He offered his hand. She couldn't take it fast enough.

In her room, he backed her up against the door and took all her clothes off. She just stood there and let him do it, reveling in the feel of his brushing hands as he pulled off her sweater and took down her jeans.

His voice was so wonderfully rough and deep as he instructed her to lift her arms, to raise one foot and then the other.

Getting undressed shouldn't be all that exciting.

But it was. When Darius undressed her, it definitely was.

When she was naked, he took both her hands and held them high against the door.

And there were kisses, his tongue stirring such exciting sensations, his scent all around her, the wool of his sweater and his black denim jeans rubbing her everywhere, a little bit rough and a whole lot arousing.

When he went to his knees in front of her, she almost collapsed to the floor in sheer ecstasy. But she pressed back against the door and managed to remain upright as he kissed her some more, nudging her legs a little farther apart, using that mouth of his and those highly skilled fingers to drive her completely out of her mind.

She came apart. Right there against the door, just shattered into a million fully satisfied pieces.

And then he picked her up and carried her to her bed and set about shattering her all over again. Eventually, he took his own clothes off. She pushed him back onto the pillows and ordered him not to even move.

For once, he actually obeyed and let her do what she wanted to him. His body was hers, he said. She took him at his word, kissing him everywhere, taking him into her hands, worshipping him with her eager mouth.

And then he took control again, sweeping her away to a place where nothing existed but the two of them, wrapped up tight in each other, rocking together in a hot, endless glide, until she came apart again. That time, he went with her.

It was past two when he got up to go. As she watched him pull on his sweater and zip up his jeans, she wanted to jump from her nest of tangled covers, grab hold of his arm and beg him to stay.

Which was completely contradictory and totally wrong. The whole point was he *wouldn't* stay. What they'd just shared—and would continue to share for three more glorious weeks—was exactly right. Just what she'd been needing. An amazing lover who *wouldn't* stay.

Best Christmas present ever.

"Friday," she whispered, when he bent close to kiss her good-night. "Sylvie and Brad's daughters, Cindy and Lisa, go to my mother's house. It's an annual thing. A Christmas cookie bake-off. The girls sleep over."

He sat on the edge of the bed. "So you'll be alone."

"Except I won't."

"Because you'll be with me." He bent close again.

She accepted his kiss with a smile. "I drop her off at six."

"Once you do, drive straight to my place. And bring your toothbrush. You're staying the night."

It was snowing again Friday afternoon, but not too hard. All the weather reports predicted the snow would end by midnight. The roads would be clear. Ava would have no problem getting back to Seven Pines in time for an eight o'clock breakfast with her parents and the girls.

She got Sylvie to her mother's at a quarter of six.

But then her mom wanted her to stick around. "Brad's dropping Cindy and Lisa off any minute now," said Kate. "You should stay. It'll be fun."

"Can't, Mom. Really."

"Tell me you have a hot date."

"Yeah. Me, a giant bowl of popcorn, extra butter, and my trusty DVD of *Love, Actually,*" she baldly lied.

"Sweetheart, that's just sad. You don't need a romantic movie. You need a man."

And she was going to get one. "Don't even start. Please."

"Someone has to remind you of everything you're missing."

"Well, you're doing a great job of it, Mom. I'm totally convinced. Feel free to stop now."

Sylvie, who'd tossed her backpack on her grandpa's pleather recliner and hit the sink to wash her hands, was already putting on the kid-size apron that Kate kept just for her. "Gramma! Hurry up. We have a lot of work to do. When are Cindy and Lisa getting here?"

"Soon," answered Kate.

"Love you, honey," Ava called from the door before her mother could start in on her again. "See you in the morning."

"Bye, Mommy." Sylvie flipped a quick wave over her shoulder, opened the door of a lower cabinet and started banging cookie sheets together. "Gramma!" she called, her head in the cabinet. "Come *on.*"

"Have fun, Mom." Ava pecked a quick kiss on Kate's cheek and got out fast.

* * *

Darius opened the door as she raised her hand to knock. "I thought you'd never get here." Daisy bumped past his legs and stepped out to greet her. Ava set down her tote and gave the dog a good scratch behind her floppy ears. "Come on inside before you freeze to death."

"Don't I get to say hi to the horses?"

"Did you notice it's snowing?"

"Not that hard." She rose and clapped her mittened hands together. "Come *on*."

He reached out, grabbed her wrist, and dragged her over the threshold. Daisy slid through behind her and he shut the door. "I need a kiss first."

"That's what I'm here for. To give you what you need."

He framed her face in his hands, slipping his fingers up into her hair, under the pom-pom ties of her knit hat. "Deliver."

So she did. By the time he lifted his head, she was ready to forgo the visit to the horses and head straight to bed.

But he only laughed, pulled on his boots, grabbed his coat and hat and led her out to the pasture. It was nice for a little while, out in the snow. She petted the horses and fed them the treats he'd brought out with him. But it was cold and getting colder.

They went back in, got out of their coats and left their boots in the front hall. He grilled them some chicken and she tossed broccoli and cauliflower in olive oil with salt and pepper and then roasted them in the oven.

They sat down to eat.

Neither of them had heard any news about Jody. Darius said that probably meant she was fine. If not, someone in the family would have raised the alarm.

Ava sat across the kitchen table from him and thought how easy it was with him, like they'd known each other forever—which, essentially, they had. But it wasn't only that sense of being a part of each other's worlds, each other's lives. There was something else, some deeper familiarity. Some feeling of connection she couldn't quite put a name to.

But that was all right. She didn't need to go defining her feelings for him, getting too deep into him. The deal was *not* to go deep. To keep it simple and pleasurable. Sexy, sweet and temporary.

He led her to his room at a little after nine, shutting the door when they got in there, leaving poor Daisy on the other side.

The bed was a California king. A natural stone fireplace blazed to cozy life with the flick of a switch. The floor-to-ceiling windows framed a view of the mountains—not that you could see much of them in the dark with the snow coming down.

They stood facing each other by the fire.

"Undress," he commanded.

She did, swiftly, without fanfare or pretension, pulling off her socks first. She shed her sweater and her thermal shirt. She unhooked and shrugged out of her bra. After the bra, all she had left were her heavy leggings and her panties. She shimmied them down and kicked them away.

"Ava." He said her name slowly, as though he liked the flavor of it on his tongue, as though he couldn't get enough of saying it.

So strange, so unlike her, to be so comfortable with someone.

And yet to be held on a razor's edge of need with that someone, too.

He reached for her. She fell into him, offering her mouth to him.

He took it. Her senses caught fire.

There was just something about him, about his kisses and the way he touched her, about his scent of wood and leather, about the feel of his skin under her hands. It scared her a little, how much she wanted him.

It scared her how much more this was beginning to feel like than what it had started out to be. So much more than the lovely, uncomplicated fling she'd bargained for.

As though every time he touched her, every time he put those too-soft lips on her, he was working her, working the lock on some deep, secret part of her, getting just that much closer to opening her up wide.

"Undress me," he said.

And she did, pulling and tugging and easing and unbuttoning, guiding everything off and away.

"Touch me."

She couldn't obey fast enough. She put her hands on him, caressing him, rubbing her palm against the silky trail of hair that led down to his belly and below it. She knelt before him on the soft rug in front of the fire.

And she took him in her mouth, played him with her two hands. For her pleasure and his—and for more.

For some safer place where she had control of this thing between them that somehow got stronger, more compelling, day by day. Because he wasn't supposed to be like this, so focused and sure, so coaxing and tender and...true.

He was supposed to be…less. Supposed to be just as she'd remembered him—defined him, really—back in high school. Not only killer-hot and oh, so charming. But also easy. Effortless at everything. With a short attention span, especially when it came to women. The kind of guy you could count on *not* to stick around. The perfect candidate for a steamy affair with a clear expiration date.

Should she have known somehow that he was so much better than she'd given him credit for?

Oh, who did she think she was kidding? Of course, she should have known. All the signs had been there. She'd seen his protectiveness when it came to his sisters. She'd watched him with the Blueberries—so patient and funny and kind.

And as for all the women he supposedly used and discarded, where were they? In the past year and a half, since she'd gotten close with his sisters, she hadn't seen him with a single one.

How could she not have realized that once she started in with him, it would only get better, that she would only want more?

"More," he whispered, as though he knew her inside and out, could see into her mind and pluck out whatever disjointed, hungry thought he found in there. His fingers threaded through her hair. "Yes. Like that, sweetheart. Just like that…"

She pushed all the scary thoughts away. She focused on giving him what he asked for.

And then he was bending over her, getting her under her arms and lifting her. One moment he filled her throat and surged between her eager hands.

The next, she lost him as he pulled her up. "Darius!"

"Right here, baby. Wrap your legs around me."

She did, and her arms, too. He carried her to the bed and laid her down on it. She tried to hold on to him, to drag him down with her, but he easily untangled himself from her grip to take a condom from the bedside drawer.

"Oh, hurry," she begged him. "Please..."

"I'm here. Right here..."

And then he *was* there, wrapping his big arms around her, easing between her open thighs and coming into her with one hard, possessive thrust.

All her thoughts spun away into velvet darkness.

There was only this pleasure. Only this man who had given her everything she asked of him.

Everything.

And so much more.

Darius Bravo lay staring up into the darkness with Ava in his arms.

She was fast asleep, had been for hours. Just before she dropped off, she whispered that she intended to keep him up all night, to kiss him all over, to have him on the big chair in the corner and up against the wall between the two bureaus.

"A tour," she'd whispered with a naughty giggle. "A sexual tour of your bedroom. We're going to make love in every square inch of it..."

He'd been all for that plan and told her so. They'd kissed on it, long, wet and thoroughly. And then she'd snuggled against him with a soft little sigh.

And dropped off to sleep.

He'd really liked the sexual tour plan. But she was a hardworking single mom. The woman never stopped, morning till night. She had to sleep sometime.

He smoothed her hair. Even in the darkness, it gleamed. Gold streaked with caramel and amber. He'd always loved her hair. And her eyes that were blue and green, swirled and blended together, so watchful sometimes. Too careful. Over the years, he'd frequently fantasized about seeing them glazed over and hungry.

And now, at last, he had.

He wanted to laugh suddenly.

Just throw his head back against the leather headboard and let the sound roll out. But if he did, he might wake her.

Couldn't have that. She needed her sleep.

However, the fact remained: there was a hell of a joke here, and it was on him.

Because he knew it now. He saw it now.

He was in love with her and had been for…how long? Since high school?

Not possible. He hadn't really known her then.

He'd only watched her from a distance, sensed a certain strength in her, a careful detachment that made him want to break through to her. She drew him like a beacon. The attraction she held for him had made no sense to him at all.

But he'd wanted to know her, even back then, though it was painfully clear to him just from the way she carried herself that knowing her wasn't going to be easy.

He'd made that one stab at it anyway. And she'd turned him down flat.

So he'd let it go, let *her* go. Because he was the guy who never really had to make an effort over anything or anyone. He worked hard at football and to get good grades, but that was it. The rest of life should be fun, right? Why knock himself out for some girl who didn't want him, even one he couldn't stop thinking about?

Still, he hadn't forgotten her. He'd compared every woman he'd ever met with her, and they all came up short. Which was patently ridiculous, given that he'd had exactly one conversation with her, the one in which she had told him no.

And as he came to understand himself a little better, he'd started to see that the memory of Ava Janko, who'd married some other guy and moved to Southern California, simply provided him with another excuse not to get too serious with any other woman.

The memory of Ava had helped him keep his life the way he liked it. Unencumbered. Free.

Yeah. By the time he came home to settle in Justice Creek, he had his mysterious ongoing yen for Ava Janko all figured out. He'd put his silly fantasy of her behind him.

And then he'd heard she lost her husband.

And then she moved back to town, same as he had. He'd seen her around a couple of times before she started working with Garrett and Nell. He'd felt the pull, strong as ever.

And told himself not to be a sentimental idiot. He didn't know the woman, and he never would.

If only she hadn't gotten hooked up with Bravo Construction, hadn't made friends with his sisters. If only he hadn't indulged himself in months of outrageous flirting with her.

If only he'd kept the hell away from her.

He could have gone on as always, never having to admit that she really was special to him, that she did something to him that no one else did, that she reached right down inside him, that she somehow had taken complete possession of his heart.

He never would have had to know.

But now he did know.

And now he wanted all the things he used to run away from.

Ava stirred in his arms. A soft little snore escaped her. He smiled at the sound as she settled once more. He held her loosely, her head pillowed on his chest, his arm resting in the curve of her waist. Dipping his head a little, he breathed in the scent of her—citrusy and summery, somehow. Like oranges and sunshine, clean and warm, sweet and fresh.

He wanted her, wanted Ava, in every way. He wanted her tight, limber little body. He wanted her mouth under his and her hands on his skin.

And he wanted a commitment with her, the beginnings of a future, eventually a family with her and with Sylvie. He wanted everything. And she was only in it till New Year's.

Somehow, he needed to change her mind about that, though he couldn't see how. She'd made it painfully clear that she'd loved her husband and she just didn't want to go there again. So taking a knee and declaring undying love would only send her running for the hills.

He needed to find other ways to convince her to stick with him after the holidays.

Clearly, he was going to have to up his game.

Chapter Ten

"I do not believe this." Ava wanted to scream. She stood on Dare's front porch in her big sweater and her stocking feet and glared at the snow that had piled up overnight. "It was just supposed to be a light dusting." Beside her, Daisy thumped her tail hopefully and gave a sympathetic whine. "It was supposed to stop around midnight. This is just wrong. I need to be at my mother's place in less than an hour."

Dare's warm hands clasped her shoulders. He guided her around to the open front door. "Come back inside where it's warm. I'll get the coffee started. You can call your mother and tell her you're going to be late."

"Late?" A whimper escaped her as she let him push her through the door. The dog followed them in, and Dare closed it behind them. "I might be stuck here for *hours*. Possibly overnight."

"What? You don't like it here?" He fake-pouted. "I think my feelings are hurt."

She hung back at the door to the kitchen just long enough to go on tiptoe and press a quick kiss to his scruffy jaw. "It's not that. And you know it."

"Good. Had me worried for a minute." He caught her hand and pulled her onward. "In the next hour or two, Corky will be getting out the snowblower to clear the driveway. Even if the main road's impassable now, the snowplow will be around by noon or so. And there's nothing to worry about, anyway—I mean, Sylvie's fine with your mom, right?"

In the kitchen, Daisy went to her water bowl to lap up a drink. Ava let Dare take her to the granite peninsula, where he pulled back a chair for her.

She hopped up onto it. "It's just...what will I say? That I'm stuck at home? It's not that far from my house to Seven Pines. If the streets in town aren't bad, she's going to wonder why I'm lying to her."

"She?"

"As if you don't know. My *mom*—and I need my phone." It was in her tote, and that was in his room.

He caught her arm before she could jump down from the chair. "Hold on. Why not just tell your mom the truth?"

Surely she hadn't heard him right. "Excuse me? Tell her I spent the night with you?"

"Yeah, tell her you stayed here. It doesn't have to be a major issue. You don't have to get too specific."

"You can't be serious. I mean, we had an agreement that no one would know. I can see going ahead with the whole friend thing. That way we can relax a little, and so what if people see us together? We just call ourselves friends. Boom. Done. But to tell my mother, who takes her ongoing quest to find me a new man way too seriously, that I spent the night at your place...?" How to even go on? "Dare, you don't know my mom. She's... innocent, really. She was eighteen when she married my dad, and neither of them has ever so much as looked twice at anyone else. If she finds out I spent the night with you, she's going to start planning our wedding."

"You're exaggerating."

"No, I am not. My mom loved Craig, and she mourned when we lost him. But now she can't stand that I'm a widow raising my little girl on my own. She wants a husband for me. She wants me living in my own personal happily-ever-after, and she'll never quit until she's made that happen."

He pulled out the chair next to her and sat in it, keeping his hand on her arm the whole time. As though he suspected she might jump up and run off—which, actually, she just might. "Friends often spend the night at each other's houses," he said in the patient tone of a man trying to talk some sense into a not-so-bright child. "Think Carter and Paige." His half brother Carter had married Paige Kettleman in August. For years before that, they'd been best friends—no benefits—and business partners, though just about everyone in town had believed that they were in love with each other and in mutual denial about it. "Carter practically lived at Paige's house for years. He'd go over there at the crack of dawn to walk her dog for her, and when he got back, he'd cook her breakfast. He had a key to her house, and she had one to his. Half the time, he'd stay so late watching a game or whatever that he'd just crash on her couch. Nobody thought anything of it."

"Oh, please. People did think stuff. People thought it was sweet and a little bit sad that neither of them had a clue they were in love with each other."

"So what? They did what they wanted, and nobody got on them about it. It was their business."

"We are not Carter and Paige."

"Right." His jaw had a knot in it. And his eyes were less blue. Less blue and more…flinty. "We're not them. But we are actual adults, single adults, who have every right to spend the night in the same house and not explain ourselves to anyone, not even your mother."

The really annoying thing was he was right. "Okay, now I'm starting to feel childish and whiny for wanting a little privacy around my personal life."

He held her gaze for the longest time. And then he asked, "But Ava, is this really about privacy?"

She tried to ease her arm out from under his hold. He didn't let go. And his question kind of echoed uncomfortably in her head. "Okay. You're right. It's not totally about privacy. I just don't want to have to think too hard about this, about us. I don't want to have to explain us to anyone. I want to love every minute of it. And I am. I want it to be…you know, lighthearted. I want it to be fun—and you're looking at me strangely." She tried a grin. "Is my hair on fire or something?"

He let go of her arm. And he didn't grin back. "Tell your mom the truth. You might be surprised. She might just be happy you're having a good time. She might just leave it at that."

Now she wished he *hadn't* let go of her. She wanted his touch again. She wanted too much from him, and that was starting to scare her a little. Which was why they needed to keep it simple and easy and light.

She asked sheepishly, "Are you angry with me?"

His expression softened. "Ava. No. I'm not angry."

Relief loosened the knot of tension that had formed under her breastbone. "Good."

And then he did touch her again. He eased his wonderful fingers up under her hair and clasped the back of her neck, rubbing a little, soothing her. The guy really did have magic hands. "True, we started out agreeing to keep it private, just between us. But sometimes things work out differently in practice. A plan can seem reasonable at first, and then before you know it the whole thing just feels silly."

"Yeah. Okay. I know you're right." She hung her head. "Ugh. The truth. To my mother. Really?"

He tipped up her chin. She looked at him, at his beard-scruffy cheeks, at his manly square jaw and the ginger lights in his brown hair. Just looking at him made her weak in the most thrilling way.

"The truth is generally better," he said. "Neater. Lies tend to get so tangled and messy. And then half the time you end up having to tell the truth, after all, which means that you've not only lied, you're a lying fool and now the people who matter to you have reason to mistrust you."

She couldn't help it. She laughed. "Well, that's not especially reassuring."

"Consider Jody."

"How's that?"

"Did you see how relieved she looked when she finally just broke down and told everyone what was up with her? I'll bet now she's wondering why she didn't tell them all earlier."

"But that was different."

"No."

"Yes. A baby isn't something you can keep to yourself forever. With a fling, no one really *has* to know."

He gazed at her way too steadily. "It's just the truth, Ava. That's all I'm asking you for."

She huffed. "When you put it that way, keeping us a secret just seems petty and ridiculous."

"You think?" He gave her the slow grin that made her want to drag him back to his bedroom and make love to him in that big chair in the corner. And between the two bureaus, too. And all the places they hadn't gotten to last night because she'd shut her eyes for just a moment and ended up sound asleep. "Go on," he said. "Get your phone and call your mom."

Ava returned to the kitchen after making the call and found that Dare had the coffee ready.

He held up a cup. At her nod, he filled it and handed it over. "So. How did it go?" He leaned against the counter.

She enjoyed that first delicious sip. "Nothing like I expected." Turning, she leaned back beside him. "My mother spent ten minutes telling me about each and every cookie she and Sylvie and her two cousins baked and decorated. They made fudge, divinity and Rice Krispies Treats, too. And they watched *Frozen* for the gazillionth time."

"Because when you're a little girl, *Frozen* never gets old."

"This is true. Once my mother had described yesterday's festivities in minute detail, she said she supposed I wouldn't be able to get over to Seven Pines for breakfast, with the snow. She said it wasn't a problem. She and the girls and my dad are planning a little sledding on the hill behind the double-wide. And Sylvie and her cousins want to build a family of snowmen—oh, and I should call when I'm on my way over."

"So you never even had to say that you weren't at home?" Did he seem disappointed?

She couldn't tell. Probably not. Her lying about the situation was what had bothered him. Wasn't it? "You're right. I never had to tell her." She let her smile show. "But then I just went ahead and did it anyway."

He swore low. There was real admiration in the sound. "You didn't."

"Oh, yes I did. I said I was out at your place on the edge of the forest fifteen miles southwest of town and it might take a little longer to clear the driveway here than at my house. And she said, 'That's fine, honey. Just call when you're on your way in.'"

He sipped from his mug before asking, "And that's it? That's all she said?"

"That's it."

One dark eyebrow lifted. "Kind of a letdown, huh?"

She set her cup on the counter and turned into him, slipping one knee between his legs so he widened his stance and she could step in even closer. "I do like being with you."

"And you have no idea how happy I am about that."

She leaned in and sniffed his neck. "I love the way you smell. Like leather and cedar shavings. Sometimes a little like pine."

"That would be my cologne."

"You're a generous guy."

"Thank you."

"And you're thoughtful."

"High praise."

"And so very, very sexy…"

"Keep talking, Ava. I like where this is going."

"However…"

"Uh-oh. All at once I'm not feelin' the love."

"It's just that I never expected to get ethics lessons from you."

He traced a finger down her cheek. "Some have called me shallow. Can you believe that?"

"No way. You are integrity personified."

"That's me, exactly—and are you in a hurry to get back to town?"

She leaned fully against him, and it felt so good. "My parents will keep my daughter busy for the whole day. And for once, I have no open houses and no appointments."

"So you'll stay?" His hands drifted down her back as he nuzzled her neck, which she stretched for him with a sigh.

"I would love to stay."

He used his teeth on her earlobe, and she swallowed a moan. "I need to feed the horses. Then I'll fix us some breakfast."

"I think before you do anything, you should kiss me."

Those supple lips slid up over her chin and settled right where she wanted them—on hers.

The night before, when he couldn't sleep, Dare had formulated a plan.

The plan was to take the high, thick, carefully guarded walls around Ava's heart and expand them.

It occurred to him that he'd started working on his plan intuitively, without even admitting to himself that he was doing it—when he flirted with her relentlessly for months. And when he chased her all over Clara's house at Thanksgiving, determined to discover what she wanted in order that he could be the one to give it to her.

Next, he'd talked her into telling everyone that they were *friends* in order that they didn't have to sneak around so damn much.

And after last night, when he'd finally accepted that he wanted a lot more from her than a few weeks of great sex, he was now going forward with conscious intent. He couldn't believe he'd actually convinced her to tell her mother she'd gotten snowed in at his house.

But he had.

Little by little, he was breaking her open. And he wouldn't give up until she let him inside.

She helped him take care of the horses. After breakfast, they went back to bed. And then to the chair in the corner. And after that, there was a mind-blowing interlude between the two bureaus.

Followed by some downright amazingness in front of the fire.

Later, she shoveled snow along the front walk while he spelled Corky on the blower. By two, they'd cleared all the way to the main road—which, by then, had been plowed clear of snow.

Before she headed back to town late in the afternoon, she'd agreed he could bring pizza to share with her and Sylvie Monday night. She'd also said he could drop in at her house anytime. She didn't qualify it, either, didn't remind him that, come January, everything had to stop.

Best of all, she'd promised to be his date Saturday for the Christmas Ball.

He took her new willingness to be seen coupled up

with him as a good sign. An excellent sign. Things were going well. Better than he'd dared to hope. He would show her in a thousand ways how good they were together.

Monday, he left work early to help the Blueberries put the finishing touches on the Christmas-project dollhouses. Sylvie was jazzed that he'd be coming for dinner. At Ava's, after the pizza, he and Sylvie played video games, and she told him all about the school Christmas show coming up Wednesday evening. She would sing in the school choir and play a bear in a skit.

Once Sylvie went to bed, Ava led him to her room. He stayed until midnight. Before he left, he wrangled an invitation to Sylvie's Christmas show.

Wednesday, he picked up Ava and Sylvie at six and drove to the elementary school. They walked Sylvie to her classroom and then continued on to the multipurpose room, where there was a Christmas tree in every corner. Rows of folding chairs had been set up facing the built-in stage at one end of the large space. Quinn and Chloe were already there with Quinn's longtime friend and former trainer, Manny Aldovino, who was like a grandfather to Annabelle.

Chloe waved them over and they all sat together. It was going great. Nobody seemed the least surprised to see him there with Ava. Ava's mom and dad appeared and took seats in the row in front of them. He shook hands with Ava's dad and said hi to her mom, who was sweet and friendly and bore zero resemblance to the wild-eyed matchmaker Ava had made her out to be.

Then two of Ava's brothers showed up—Brad, whose two daughters were still in elementary school, and Tom, whose younger son was in fourth grade. By then, the place was filling up. The brothers and Tom's wife, Libby, took seats several rows away.

Yeah, okay, Tom didn't look all that happy to see Ava sitting next to him. But so what? Ava didn't seem bothered by her brother's surly attitude.

The lights dimmed above them and came up on the stage. Dare took Ava's hand, and she let him. The program went on for two hours. There was a whole lot of carol-singing. And a long skit called "A Mountain Home Christmas" in which Sylvie played one of the daughters in a family of bears. Dare loved every minute of it. He could get into being a family man, attending overlong school presentations with Ava at his side.

Sylvie seemed to glow with excitement on the drive home. She sang snatches from the carols she'd performed and laughed over a gaffe made by one of the boys in her class. At the house, she had a quick bath and then came running downstairs.

"I need to read Darius his story." She waved yet another book with a Christmassy cartoon cover.

Ava chided, "It's past your bedtime, sweetie."

"Mommy, just one story…"

Ava sighed and gave the go-ahead. They all sat on the couch, and Sylvie began. When she finished that story, she hopped to her feet. "I think we need another one."

Ava rose, too. "Not tonight. Bedtime."

"Mom! Darius *wants* another story, don't you Darius?"

He'd been hanging around seven-year-olds enough lately to know when he was being worked. "Next time."

"Tomorrow?" Sylvie begged. "Please say you'll come tomorrow…"

Ava cut in then in a voice as flat as the Serengeti Plain. "Sylvie. Bedtime. I'm not saying it again."

Sylvie's little mouth twisted. But she did get the message. "Oh, all right." She whirled and flounced toward the stairs.

"Night, Sylvie," he called after her.

She sent him a sweet little pout and a grudging, "Night."

"Kids," Ava said under her breath and went up after her.

When she came back down, she took his hand and led him to her room.

"Sylvie okay?" he asked, once the door was shut.

"She'll live, though just barely if you ask her. And you'd better not come over tomorrow night. We can't have her thinking that you're moving in here."

Why not? he wanted to demand. Because moving in together sounded pretty damn good to him. But they weren't there yet, and pushing her too fast was not the way to get what he wanted from her.

"Sure. I understand," he answered mildly. And then he took off all her clothes and took her to bed.

The next day, he sent flowers to her office. Friday, he went in person. They put her big desk to good use. Before he left, she asked him if he would be helping transport the Blueberry dollhouses to the Haltersham Hotel the next morning for display at the Christmas Ball.

"Yeah, I told Janice I would be at the clubhouse at nine. We've got most of the troop and several parents signed up to help." He shrugged into his heavy jacket. "Sylvie's going, right?"

"Yes." She stepped close and eased her hands under the open sides of the jacket, sliding them up to link around his neck. Her fingers were cool on his nape, and she smelled so good. He wanted to scoop her up in his arms and carry her out of there, take her home with him. Forever. "I'm showing houses in the morning and afternoon, so I can't take her. My mom will pick her up and drop her off at the clubhouse, no problem. But then I was thinking Sylvie would love it if you drove her. And as long as you're going anyway…"

He couldn't say yes fast enough. "I'll be there to get her at quarter of nine."

Saturday afternoon, Ava got home just before Dare returned with Sylvie.

Her daughter came running up the front steps, gap-toothed smile a mile wide, Dare right behind her. "Mommy! We moved the dollhouses and put them at the hotel. It was a lot of work, and Janice says we did a t'riffic job and they make a beautiful display. And look! I got a Helping Hands badge." She held out the dark blue badge embroidered with linked hands. "Would you sew it on my uniform so I can wear it tonight?"

"Of course." Ava took the badge.

"Thanks, Mom. Dare, thanks for taking me."

"Anytime."

With a wave, Sylvie slid around Ava and into the house, leaving Ava and Dare alone on the porch. He smiled at her. She felt that smile all the way down to the core of her. How did he do it? He could melt all her girl parts with no more than a twist of those beautiful lips.

"I've got a job I have to check on," he said. "Be back to pick you both up at seven."

She wanted to throw herself into his arms.

And honestly, wasn't this thing with them getting

seriously out of hand, turning out to be way more than she'd bargained for?

Yeah. She kind of thought so.

But at the moment, she couldn't seem to bring herself to worry about it. She was too happy and having way too much fun.

"Seven," she confirmed softly—like a promise.

Or a prayer.

The five dollhouses, each on a specially built turntable stand beneath carefully positioned lights, had been set up in the lobby right outside the hotel ballroom.

They did look terrific, Ava thought. Each miniature house was in a different style: Victorian, Craftsman, Contemporary, Tudor and Cape Cod. Each had been painstakingly painted, furnished to style and period— and decorated for the holidays. Guests attending the ball could stroll the lobby before entering the ballroom, take their time admiring the houses and also pledge donations to the five children's charities to which the dollhouses would go.

The Blueberries, each girl in uniform, hair combed and curled and crowned with the trademark Blueberry beret, dragged their parents and grandparents around from one house to the other. They were all justifiably proud of the great work they'd done. Janice gave a little speech. Hotel staff offered sparkling cider and Christmas cookies to the girls and guests alike.

At nine, Janice herded the girls out to her van to drive them home. Sylvie's sitter would be waiting at the house for her.

Dare took Ava's hand. "Dance with me."

She followed him into the ballroom, with its glorious

tall windows topped with pretty fanlights. In daylight, the windows framed beautiful views of the mountains. But now, at night, they reflected back the warm glow of the ballroom's famous vintage Tiffany chandeliers, the twinkle of party lights and thousands of foil stars strung from the ceiling.

Dare took her in his arms. They danced by Nell, who stood at the gorgeous antique rosewood bar deep in conversation with Ryan McKellan. Nell winked at Ava. Ava smiled and waved. When they swayed past her mom and dad, who were visiting with another older couple near the doors that led out to the lobby, Ava gave her mom a wave, too.

"Our first dance." Dare pressed a kiss to her temple.

Their first, yes. And sometime tonight, they would probably share their last dance, as well. Because between now and New Year's, further opportunities for dancing were just about nil.

Then again, she could put on some Christmas music at home, couldn't she? Dance naked with him in her bedroom.

"What are you smiling about?" he asked.

She let a low chuckle serve as an answer.

The band launched into another holiday tune. Darius kept her close and went right on dancing. They swayed together, moving back and forth across the floor.

When the band finished that set, they ended up near the ballroom doors. Her mom signaled them over.

Ava went with some reluctance.

But as it turned out, it wasn't that bad.

Her dad asked Dare how things were going in the metal fabricating business, and her mom was charming and talkative—and minus that exasperating wily gleam in her hazel eyes. Was it possible Kate Janko had finally decided to give the matchmaking a rest?

Tom and Libby came by and joined the conversation. Ava tensed a little, expecting Tom to lob some hostile remark Dare's way. But nothing happened. Tom and Libby wandered off.

A couple of minutes later, Dare's phone must have gone off. He took it out and glanced at it. Then he bent close, "Want a drink?"

"Something bubbly?"

"Done. Be right back…"

He'd been gone for several minutes before she started wondering if he went after more than drinks.

When Dare entered the Haltersham's best restaurant, the Columbine Room, the pretty hostess beamed him a welcoming smile. "Good evening. Do you have a reservation?"

He didn't respond. Eyes straight ahead, he kept walking, headed for the swinging doors into the kitchen. When he reached them, he shoved them wide and went on through.

One of the prep cooks called, "Sir, can we help you?"

He ignored the voice and moved on, past the stoves and steel counters and walk-in refrigerator, down a narrow hallway and out the door at the far end.

Tom Janko was already there, standing by the Dumpster, his beefy arms wrapped around himself against the bitter cold. "I wasn't sure you got my message."

Dare crossed his own arms against the chill and wished he'd stopped to get his coat. "How'd you get my number?"

"Last Sunday, family dinner." Tom's breath came out as fog. "I borrowed Ava's phone to make a call."

"Sneaky."

"Yeah, well. She goes her own way and never listens to advice from the people who care about her. But she's still my sister, and I don't want anybody messing with her."

Dare made eye contact with him and held it. "I'm not messing with her, Tom."

"Oh, yeah? So what exactly would you call what you're doing?"

Dare stuck his hands in the pockets of his jacket and stamped his feet to keep from freezing to death—as he tried to decide how much to say. "I can't tell you what I'm not ready to say to her yet."

Tom swore low. "Man. What does that even mean?"

"It means I like her, okay? I like her a lot."

"Until you don't. Come on, Dare. We all know how you are. You get bored way too damn easy."

"Not with Ava."

"You say that now. But wait five minutes. We both know you'll be moving on."

"Listen. Can we just go back a little first?"

"Back where?"

"Eight years. I shouldn't have fired you. I should have given you a warning and another chance. And I was way out of line when I punched you."

Tom stared at him for a good count of five. Then a rumbling laugh rolled out. "I punched you first—and I had some issues then, issues that I was chasing to the bottom of a bottle. Another chance wouldn't have had much effect on the final outcome."

"Still. I was new on the job and out to show my dad
how tough and uncompromising I could be."

"I noticed. And at the time, I was seriously pissed at
you. Because it was easier to get mad at the boss man
than to admit I needed to lay off the booze and take my
work seriously." Tom put his hands together and blew
into them. "But I'm past all that now, and if Ava's told
you otherwise, she's got it wrong."

Dare hesitated, unsure how to respond. He didn't
want to cause trouble for Ava with Tom.

And then Tom waved a hand. "Never mind. Just take
my word for it. This isn't about what happened at Bravo
Steelworks way back when. We can leave all that behind."

Dare answered cautiously, "Okay…"

"No, man. It's not okay. My sister, she doesn't need
any more heartache. She may seem like she's got it all
together. And she's always telling Mom she's happy
and she's running her own life just the way she wants
it. That she doesn't want or need a man. But she hasn't
had it easy. She not only lost the guy she loved to a land
mine on the other side of the world, there were some
tough times back when we were kids. I'm not going into
any details. But there were bad experiences, you know?
Stuff happened that I'm still not really sure she's over.
Trust is a hard thing for her, and her toughness doesn't
go as deep as she wants everyone to think."

"When you say stuff happened…"

Tom shook his head. "Didn't I just tell you I can't
give you specifics?"

"And that's okay. I think I already know."

"Uh-uh. Not possible."

"Ava told me that the four of you spent two years

in the system where she met a screwed-up kid named Trevor."

Tom did a classic double take. He stopped blowing on his hands and let them drop to his sides. "My sister told *you* about Trevor? She doesn't talk about Trevor. Ever. Our *parents* don't even know about Trevor."

"So then maybe you've got this all wrong, Tom. Maybe she doesn't see me so much as the spoiled rich guy who never met a woman he couldn't walk away from. Maybe she feels safe telling her secrets to me. Maybe she trusts me more than you know—not as much as I want, but I'm working on that. Will I get what I'm after from her? Still can't say. But when you come right down to it, I'm not the one most likely to end up walking away."

Tom had been blowing on his hands again. But then he stopped. Leaning in, he squinted hard in Dare's face. "Good God almighty. You're in love with my sister."

To hear the truth right out loud like that from another guy's mouth? It shocked him.

And where to go from here? He hadn't even worked up the nerve to declare himself to Ava yet. No way he was telling her brother all about it first. He'd said way too much already.

But then Tom put up a hand. "Never mind. I get it. I finally get it. Wow. Does she know how you feel?"

Uh-uh. Not going there. "I don't know what you're talking about."

Tom wasn't fooled. "Right. So I'm guessing that's a no. You haven't told her."

"Look, I'd appreciate it if—"

"You know what? You don't even need to say it. Your

secret's safe with me. And I gotta hand it to you, Dare.
I never saw that coming."

"Yeah, well. You're not alone."

"Good luck to you, man."

"Thanks. I think."

"Because you're gonna need it." Tom laughed then.
It wasn't a reassuring sound.

Chapter Eleven

Dare found Ava more or less where he'd left her. Her parents had moved on. He handed her the glass of champagne she'd asked for.

"That took a while," she said.

"Sorry. I needed to clear up a few issues with an old friend."

"Who?"

"Your brother Tom."

She choked on a sip of champagne. *"What?"*

"Relax. Nobody bled—as a matter of fact, we made peace."

"You're joking, right?" She croaked. And then she coughed into her free hand.

He patted her back. "You all right?"

"Fine. Wonderful. Just answer the question."

"No, I'm not joking. I had a talk with Tom, and we put the past behind us."

She gazed up at him, blue-green eyes a little misty. "I...well, I don't know what to say."

"That's okay." He put his arm around her, bent close and breathed in the sweet scent of her hair, which she'd piled up loosely and held in place with a big rhinestone clip shaped like a peacock. Little wispy curls had gotten loose to trail along the silky skin at her nape. God, she was pretty, in hot pink satin that clung to every tight, tempting curve and ended a couple of inches above her shapely knees. He tugged on a curl. "You look beautiful. Absolutely beautiful."

"Keep talking." She twinkled up at him. "You just might get lucky tonight."

They got back to her place at a little after two in the morning. Ava paid the babysitter, and off she went.

Then they both shucked off their shoes. "Let's dance." He pulled her into his arms.

Her cheeks were flushed as pink as her dress, and her smile lit up the dim corners of the front hall. "There's no music."

"Oh, yeah there is. A golden oldie. Frank Sinatra. 'The Christmas Waltz.'" He tapped the side of his head. "It's playing in here."

"Well, all right then. I would love to dance—to whatever happens to be playing inside your head."

So they danced.

He waltzed her out of the foyer and into the living room, across the dining room and on through the open door of her bedroom. Pausing on the far side of the threshold, he kicked the door shut with his foot, simultaneously letting go of her hand just long enough to engage the privacy lock.

And then he had them on the move again. They circled the room, ending at the bed, where he finished by lowering her in a slow dip. When he guided her upright again, he claimed a kiss. "What do you think? Am I ready for my stint on *Dancing with the Stars*?"

She eased his jacket off his shoulders and tossed it on a chair. "I would totally vote for you."

"So you like me, huh?"

"Oh, yes. I do. I really do."

"I think you need to show me just how much." He unzipped her pink dress and took her down to the bed.

"Dare." Ava shook him awake. She switched on the lamp. He squinted at the burst of harsh light. "It'll be daylight before you know it. You need to get going..."

Get going. He rolled to his back and put his arm across his eyes. "Right." Because this was only temporary and Sylvie could never be allowed to find him here in the morning.

He pushed back the blankets, swung his feet to the floor and reached for his clothes. Ava stayed in the bed, covers pulled close. But already, in less than two weeks of being her lover, he knew the routine. She would get up when he left. Get up and trail him to the door for a last kiss before she locked up behind him.

It wasn't enough. He wanted more. He ached with the need to push for more—but they hadn't been together long enough for him to be pushing for anything.

Because she'd set it up that way. Fast and hot and festive. And done by the first of January.

He realized he was pissed off and getting angrier. Which was unreasonable. He needed to settle the hell down.

Dropping to the corner chair, he pulled on his socks as she pushed back the covers and slipped on her robe.

"Ready?" She wrapped and tied the sash. He just sat there, hands on his spread knees, staring up at her. "What is it, Dare?" He reached for her. She gave him her hand and he used it to reel her closer, until she stood between his knees. Her hair was a wild tangle, her eyes growing wary. "What?"

He brought her fingers to his mouth and kissed the tips of them slowly, all the while holding those aquamarine eyes. "Bring Sylvie out to my place today. We'll build a snowman, go sledding. She can meet Daisy and the horses. You know she'll love it. Did I tell you I cut down a Christmas tree? It's in a bucket of water in the front hall. Maybe you guys can help me decorate it, help me fix it up right."

"Dare…" She let his name fade away on her lips. He wanted to pick up the nearest lamp and hurl it at a wall. "Sundays are for dinner at my mom's."

He should stop. But he couldn't. "So tell her you're not coming. Or invite me along, too."

She did it again, said his name, "Dare…" and then let it wander off into nothing as she begged him with those shining eyes to tell her it was all right.

Well, it wasn't all right. And he damn sure wasn't going to help her to push him away. So he kept his mouth shut. He held her hand and stared up at her, waiting.

She took another stab at blowing him off. "It's not a good idea, okay?"

"No, Ava. Wrong. It *is* a good idea. What's bad is how you won't stop pushing me away."

That did it. She pulled her hand free, backed up and

dropped to the edge of the bed. "You're being unreasonable."

"I know. I can't seem to stop myself. I want you and Sylvie to come out to my place. And I'm not giving up on that until you say yes."

She fiddled with her robe, pulling it closer around her. "I don't know where to start. Yes, we've decided not to hide that we're together." She spoke with care, as though each word was dangerous and might suddenly blow up in her face. "But there have to be…boundaries. Lines we don't cross."

"Like Sunday dinner at your folks' house and Sylvie coming over to mine?"

She shifted, straightening her shoulders. "That's right."

"Why draw the boundaries there?"

Her soft mouth trembled. "I told you. The boundaries have to be somewhere. And that's where I draw them. That's where I just won't go."

"Why not?"

She folded her hands in her lap, lowered her head to stare down at them and sighed. "'Why' questions are not constructive."

"And that's no damn answer."

"I… Dare, I told you from the first that I didn't want to get involved. I loved my husband, and I don't want to get too serious again. I'm not ready for that." There was more. He could hear it in her voice, see it in the spaces between her words.

"Do you think you ever will be ready?"

There was a silence. A long, awful one. Finally, she answered, "I don't know. I doubt it."

"Look at me, Ava."

It took her a minute, but she did meet his gaze. Her eyes shone suspiciously bright. "Do you…?" She swallowed convulsively. "Is this it, then? Are we over?"

Never. "Do you want us to be over?" He was sure he'd have a heart attack waiting for her answer.

"No." She said it in a whisper. And suddenly he could breathe again. "No, it's selfish and I shouldn't ask it, but I want the rest of my Christmas with you."

"And after that?"

"Ahem. After?"

"Come on, Ava. You know exactly what I'm asking you."

"Can we just take it slowly, you know, see how it goes?"

"You mean take it slowly *after* the holidays?"

When she answered with a gulp and a nod, the knot of tension in his gut eased a little. She was offering him something, at least, taking another baby step in the right direction, granting another hard-won expansion of the walls around her guarded heart.

"Okay," he said. "If you won't bring Sylvie to my place and I'm not allowed to go to Sunday dinner with the parents, at least I want it agreed that we're moving on from the damn Christmas fling. That means we stay together after the first of the year. And we are exclusive for as long as it lasts."

"Exclusive? Who else would I be with?" She looked adorably bewildered. "I don't want anyone but you."

"Good. I feel the same." And marginally better about everything. At least she'd agreed to stick with him come January. Having more time with her mattered. They could work things out slowly, make their way toward a possible future day by day.

It astonished him how much he wanted that, wanted a chance for a future with her and Sylvie.

Sometimes, lately, he didn't even know himself. He'd never worked so hard for anything in his life as he was working to get Ava to see that she belonged with him. Loving her had changed him, rearranged who he was at the molecular level, made him into a different guy.

A patient guy, a guy who had what it took to stick it out until she told him her deepest truth and trusted him with his heart.

Or so he'd thought in the early darkness of that Sunday morning.

But later, alone out at his place, as he tacked up Josie to go riding alone, he just felt low. Disheartened.

What was her problem? Why did she have to draw artificial lines that couldn't be crossed? He spent every spare minute at her house. Why shouldn't she bring Sylvie here? It made no real sense to him.

Monday night, as soon as Sylvie was in bed, he led Ava to her room and shut and locked the door.

They took the argument up where they'd left it in the predawn hours of Sunday morning.

"What's the difference?" he demanded. "Why draw a line at bringing Sylvie to my place? Here or there, it's the same."

"Well, I *feel* differently about taking Sylvie to your house, and I'm just not going to do it."

That had him pissed off all over again. Maybe loving her hadn't gotten down to his DNA, after all. The newfound patience he'd been so proud of was already wearing thin. "You've got no realistic reason to call my place off-limits to Sylvie, and you know it. Except that you're afraid to get too close to me for reasons that still don't really make a whole lot of sense to me."

"You said yesterday that we could take it slow."

"So you and Sylvie come to my place. How's that not taking it slow?"

She put her hands to her head, as though she thought maybe her brain would explode. "Dare, you keep changing everything around on me, and I don't like it. This was supposed to be a fling, remember?"

"The fling." He said it like it was the dirtiest word in the English language. And by then, to him, it kind of was. "It's not a fling anymore, remember?"

"All I'm saying is that a fling is what I signed up for, and it's the nature of a fling that you *don't* get too close." She dropped to the edge of the bed. She looked so small and sad sitting there.

And now he was mad at himself for making her sad. He sat down beside her. "Ava."

She made a lost little sound low in her throat.

He put his hand over hers. When she didn't pull away, he laced their fingers together. And he seriously considered just putting it out there, just saying *I love you, Ava*. He wanted to do that.

But it didn't feel right. And he really didn't know why, just like he didn't exactly know how to do this, how to be the guy she needed, the sweet, patient guy who knew how to wait.

"I'm going to wreck this." Her voice was almost a whisper. "I'm wrecking it, aren't I, Dare? I know that I am."

False reassurances stuck in his throat. And then he just went ahead and gave her the truth as he saw it. "I hope not, Ava. But right now, this minute? I'm afraid that you are."

She looked up at him, soft mouth mutinous. "Will you just kiss me, Dare? Can we just forget all this relationship stuff, at least for tonight?"

So he kissed her. He pulled her down across the bed and slowly undressed her. He meant to take his time with her, to show her the patience and tenderness she needed.

But she wouldn't have that. Her kiss was frantic, her fingers rough in his hair. And something wild and angry inside him responded, catching fire from the desperate hunger in her touch. They crashed together, the need in him burning high and bright—all the way to a climax that turned him inside out.

He left a short time later. They could both use some sleep. Maybe everything would look better in the morning.

But it didn't, not really. He went to work, where his receptionist, Cathy, had the Christmas tunes playing and a miniature tree lit up on the corner of her desk. He went into his office and shut the door so he couldn't hear the music or see the damn tree.

That night, he waited till after Sylvie's bedtime and called Ava. They talked for a few minutes, carefully casual, two people who had way too much to say to each other with neither of them knowing quite where to begin.

"Tomorrow night?" she asked softly at the end. "Come for dinner? Six."

Hope rose through the sadness. "I'll be there."

Wednesday morning at Bravo Steelworks, he got a call from Janice Hayes. "School's out for the holidays," she announced. "So we're holding a special troop meeting this afternoon at one. It's almost Christmas, and the girls want a wrapping party. They'll wrap their craft projects, bring presents from home to wrap, too, if they want. One of the other mothers was supposed to help out, but she can't make it. How are you at wrapping presents?"

"I basically suck."

"Is that a no, you won't help me out here? Because I could really use an extra hand, even a hand that doesn't know what it's doing."

He hadn't been at the regular Blueberry meeting Monday. Now the dollhouse project was complete, they didn't really need him until late February when he'd agreed to supervise the making of birdhouses and feeders to help them all earn their Feathered Friends badge. Already he missed the happy chaos that could only be created by ten chatty, giggling little girls.

"There'll be cookies and juice in it for you," Janice coaxed.

"See you at one."

He got to the clubhouse right on time. Janice's van was there, in the adjacent parking lot. But the clubhouse looked deserted. Knocking the snow off his boots on the thick mat at the door, he peered in one of the windows that fronted the small porch.

There was no one inside that he could see, and the lights were off. He tried the door. The knob turned, so he pushed it inward. Warm air flowed out. The heater was on.

"Hello?" He went on into the entry area, which

served as a mudroom. Small coats and mufflers and little wool hats hung on the pegs there.

He was asking himself where the girls had gone when the lights popped on.

Ten Blueberries jumped out from behind chairs in the main room shouting, "Surprise!" more or less in unison. Rousing applause and a chorus of happy laughter followed.

"What in the...?"

Sylvie beamed at him. "It's a thank-you party, and it's for *you*."

"Because we love you, Uncle Darius!" added Annabelle, and all ten girls squealed and clapped some more.

"Take off your coat," instructed Janice. "Come on and sit down."

They had a special chair just for him, the back of it covered in cardboard, painted to look like a purple throne and positioned at the head of the longest worktable. Once he claimed his throne, they quickly rigged him out as usual, in a glittery paper crown, several fat strings of pop beads and a square of blue velvet for a royal robe. He also received a scepter made of PVC pipe topped with a plastic sphere, the whole thing spraypainted gold and studded with glued-on plastic jewels.

He played his part and waved the scepter. "Bring on the cake and juice boxes!"

The little girls laughed and clapped their hands some more. "We only have cookies!"

"With sprinkles?"

"Yes! Sprinkles!"

He waved his scepter again. "Then cookies it shall be."

So they had juice and cookies, and the girls gave him presents wrapped in colored tissue paper and tied with bright ribbons. He opened them. They were handmade Christmas ornaments—some of painted clay, others of cardboard and a few made from foam balls studded with beads and shiny rickrack. He loved every one and told the girls so, regret pulling at him for that tree in his front hall that he hadn't even put up on its stand yet.

But then again, to have ten sweet little girls praising him and calling him their Blueberry king? Worked for him, big-time. If only things were going better with Ava, he would be on top of the world.

Once he'd opened all his presents and they'd all enjoyed their cookies and juice, they got down to the work of wrapping gifts for the girls' friends and families. He helped where he could, holding paper in place while small fingers taped it shut, getting more paper and ribbons from the supply closet when they ran low.

By three, every gift had been wrapped. The girls cleaned up in a flash. Parents wouldn't be arriving for pickup until four. Michaela Rowe, who was Sylvie's age, but bigger and taller, a leader among the girls, decided they should build a snowman in the fenced yard beyond the porch. The rest of them loved the idea. Janice gave the go-ahead.

The girls knew what their snowman needed.

"We've got to have something to use for his arms…"

"And what about his eyes and mouth…?"

"And don't forget his nose…"

"And he's going to need a hat and a wool scarf and mittens so he won't be cold…"

Janice raised a hand for silence. "I'll see what I can find. Bundle up. Darius, will you go out with them and get them started?"

"I'm on it."

They all piled on their coats, hats and mufflers, and out they went.

Right away, it was clear that the girls were more interested in snowball fights and playing tag than in gathering snow to make a snowman.

Dare took off his gloves and whistled through his fingers to get their wandering attention. "We need three big snowballs." He put his gloves back on and scooped up a handful of snow. "Starting with the base, which is the biggest ball, we pack snow on it to make it bigger and bigger." He knelt to roll the ball and pile on more snow.

The girls went to work with him, scooping up handfuls of snow and patting them onto the growing ball. It went along pretty well for several minutes.

But hey, Christmas was coming and school was out. For over an hour, they'd worked hard at wrapping gifts. They wanted to play. He tried to keep the snowman project on track, but with minimal success.

Every time he called one of them back to work, another peeled off and ran giggling in a circle or used the snow she'd gathered to start yet another snowball fight. They were like puppies, rolling in the snow, jumping one another, falling all over each other. And the noise. Ten little girls could be downright deafening, laughing and squealing, screaming in surprise when they got snow down their jackets.

Janice came out of the clubhouse, arms full of snowman accessories, just as Sylvie jumped up and ran along the fence with Michaela Rowe chasing her. "All right, you two!" she called as the girls kept running, both of them laughing wildly. "Michaela, Sylvie! Stop running!"

Sylvie obeyed, freezing in midstep. But Michaela barreled on, plowing into Sylvie. Sylvie went down with a startled cry. Dare shot to his feet as her chin connected with a decorative rock poking out of the snow. He heard her teeth clack together.

He was running toward her when he saw the blood— vivid red against all that white.

And then Sylvie started screaming.

Ava had a closing that afternoon at Cascade Title Company a few blocks from her office. Halfway through it, her cell vibrated. She checked the display: Darius.

She let it go for now and concentrated on the job at hand. The phone buzzed again. He must have left a voice mail.

A half an hour later, she shook hands with her clients and showed them out the door. As they headed for their Escalade, she pulled up her voice mail, feeling more than a little apprehensive about Dare's call.

Would he bail on her tonight?

And if he did, could she really blame him? He wanted more from her than she knew how to give. She just wanted *him*, so much it made a constant ache under her breastbone. Hearts, really, were ridiculous things. And hers wanted to take her somewhere she'd vowed never to go again.

Where did that leave them? Nowhere very good.

She punched in her voice mail code.

"You have one new message..."

And then came Dare's deep, calm voice. "Hi, Ava. First off, everything's okay." *Okay?* What would be *not* okay? What was he even talking about? All of a sudden, her mouth tasted of dirty pennies, and she thought she might throw up. "Sylvie's had a little accident at her Blueberry meeting."

"Oh, God. An accident..." She realized she'd said it out loud when a woman coming out of the building behind her glanced her way in alarm. Waving the woman off, she concentrated on Dare's message.

"It's a cut, nothing too serious. But she's upset and she'll need stitches." *Stitches?* Ava swayed on her feet and stuck out a hand to steady herself against the wall of the building. "We're at Justice Creek General Emergency. And I mean it. Don't freak. She's shook up, but she's okay."

Ava broke every speed limit getting to the hospital. She'd called Dare back, but he must have switched off his phone. They made you do that, didn't they, in hospital exam rooms?

She got lucky and found a parking space near the entrance. Jumping from her car, she raced for the wide glass doors.

Inside, Sylvie sat with Darius in the main waiting area. Ava stopped stock-still to stare at them.

He had his big arm around Sylvie's narrow shoulders, and she stared up at him adoringly, her little chin bandaged halfway up each cheek and down her throat, a white beard of gauze and tape. Other than the bandage, though, she looked fine.

Until she saw Ava.

Then she burst into tears. "Mommy!" She bounced to her feet and came running.

Ava hurried to meet her, scooping her up in her aching arms and holding on tight.

Dare rose but hung back, giving Ava and Sylvie their

moment together. Ava nodded and made soft, encouraging noises, stroking Sylvie's brown hair as Sylvie babbled a mile a minute, about the snowman they were building, about how Michaela started chasing her and then ran into her, knocking her down.

"It was a big rock, Mommy. And my chin fell right on it. The doctor said I was a lucky girl and I'm going to be okay, but I needed eight stitches. Darius says I'm very brave." She caught her mother's face between her little hands. "Mommy, they gave me medicine, and it's all numb now. But before the shot to make the hurting stop, it really hurt a *lot*."

"Oh, sweetheart. I know it did. And you *are* brave. The bravest girl I know…"

Sylvie let out a long sigh and rested her head on Ava's shoulder. Ava's gaze found him then. She mouthed *Thank you* as she rocked her little girl from side to side.

After Ava filled out some paperwork and took care of the co-pay, Dare followed Ava and Sylvie to their house.

Sylvie wanted pizza. Ava said she would allow it this one time, even though it was the second pizza night this week. "Under the circumstances, how could I say no?"

Sylvie laughed. "You can't! Because I am very brave and with stitches—and I want pizza!"

So Darius ordered pizza. While they waited for the delivery guy from Romano's, Sylvie called her grandparents to say she was going to be okay now, but she'd had an *accident* and there were *stitches* and it really, really *hurt*. Then Annabelle called to see how Sylvie was doing, and Sylvie told her friend everything that had happened after Dare put her in his crew cab and headed for Justice Creek General. Sylvie sat at the kitchen table for the calls, and Dare and Ava sat with her. It was kind of an all-about-Sylvie evening, which was just fine with Dare.

After dinner, they played a board game. By the end of the game, Sylvie complained that her chin had started hurting again. And she kept yawning. All the excitement had worn her out. Ava gave her a mild painkiller.

A few minutes later, Sylvie dropped off to sleep on the couch. Ava carried her upstairs to put her to bed.

Dare sat in the chair by the Christmas tree and waited for her to come back down. He felt good—full of hope again. He'd been there when Sylvie needed him; he'd taken good care of her. And the way Ava had looked at him in the emergency room... Gratefully, yeah, but more than that, with acceptance, it seemed to him. With something damn close to love.

They were going to work through whatever was bothering her, work through it and come out strong, together.

He heard the whisper of her stocking feet coming toward him from the stairs and glanced toward the sound.

And what he saw when he met her eyes made the new hope inside him shrivel up and crumble to dust.

She led him to the bedroom and shut and locked the door.

Because they needed privacy. And he knew from the set of her shoulders and the bleak purpose in her eyes that it wasn't lovemaking they needed it for.

She sat on the bed. He considered sitting next to her. But he didn't feel welcome there, somehow. So he took the chair across the rug from her.

She gazed at him so somberly, her soft mouth drawn down. His gut twisted, the crappy certainty increasing that this would not be good. "You were wonderful today, with Sylvie. Thank you."

"You thanked me already, at the hospital. Once was more than enough."

"I just want you to know how much I appreciate—"

"Ava. What are you doing? What's going on?" It came out gruff, with a side of angry. Not the way to go here. This situation called for patience on his part. He knew that.

But he was kind of running low on the whole patience thing. He was getting really tired of trying to be understanding when she only pushed him away and refused to tell him what held her back from opening up to him.

Opening up. He'd actually believed he could open her up. He'd been patting himself on the back for finally stepping up as a man, for loving her and owning that love, for wanting only to give her the time and space to love him back.

He'd been so sure at the hospital that they were on the right track now, been certain that she loved him, too. He'd actually imagined for a little while there that she'd finally realized he only wanted to take care of her and her daughter, that she knew he loved her and she was ready to accept his love.

But he'd been wrong. Again.

And he was tired of getting nowhere with her. Right now, all his touchy-feely hopes of getting closer to her just embarrassed him. They made him feel like a fool, like a piss-poor excuse for a man. A man shouldn't be after a woman to open up to him. A man should have sense enough to let a woman run the emotional side of things. Women were so much better at all that.

Most women, anyway.

"Sylvie loves you," she said. "She's getting way too attached to you."

"I love her, too. I feel *attached* to her, too. And I fail to see why there's anything wrong with that."

"It's not what we agreed on."

"Agreed on when?"

"At first."

"So that's it, then? We're going backward now? You want me to keep my distance from Sylvie now, is that what you're saying?"

"I think it would be for the best."

The best? "You are so far past wrong I don't even know what to say to you."

"You're angry."

"You bet I am. And *you're* scared. Of you and me. Of what we could have together. Of letting me be there for Sylvie. You're scared, and instead of trying to figure out why and deal with it, you're shutting me down—the same as you did when you were fifteen years old. So that means you *are* right about one thing, Ava—right about what you said the other night. You're wrecking this. Wrecking *us*."

"You just don't see…"

He leaned toward her, braced his elbows on his spread knees and folded his hands between them. "So *make* me see. Explain it to me."

"I…I don't know if I can."

"Try."

She glanced away, toward the door. He kept his gaze squarely on her until she faced him again. "Fine." Her eyes had a spark in them now—a furious light. "When I lost Craig, I promised myself that I would never have

to hurt that much again. People think love is so wonderful, love is the answer, love makes life worthwhile.
But love—the kind between a man and a woman, I
mean—well, it hasn't worked out all that great for me.
My dad loved my mom so much that when she got
sick, he couldn't even function. He was out of work for
years, hovering over my mom, holding her hand, waiting for her to get better while we lost our house and my
brothers and I ended up in foster care—where I met
Trevor. Yet another example of love gone crazy bad.
After Trevor, I promised myself never again."

"Ava, you were, what? Twelve?"

"Eleven," she corrected tightly.

"You can't make a call like that when you're eleven."

"So *you* say, because, yeah, your family had issues,
I know, but you always felt safe, didn't you? You didn't
get thrown out of the home you loved. You didn't end
up becoming some psycho's preteen girlfriend in foster care."

"Come on, Ava. You did try again, with your husband. And everyone, including you, says that Craig
Malloy was a stand-up guy, that he loved you and you
loved him."

"Yes. That's true. Craig was a really good guy. And
he loved me, and I couldn't help myself, I fell in love
with him, too. Except he was in the service and his work
was dangerous. I told him straight out I wanted security—financially as well as just generally in life. I said
I couldn't marry a soldier, that I couldn't stand to spend
my days wondering if he was okay and if he would ever
come home. He said he would resign from the Marine
Corps. So I married him. And somehow, it was always
one more deployment and his guys needed him and why

couldn't I understand? So I told myself to get over it, that he bled green and what he did mattered. It mattered. And then he died. Died for what he believed in. Died when his little girl was just one year old. I guess I could kind of say he died for love, now, couldn't I? He died and left me to carry on alone. Well, okay. I'm alone. And I'm *used* to being alone. I take care of myself and my daughter. And I do a damn fine job of it, too."

"Yeah. Yeah, you do. But that's no reason not to want more."

"You don't get it. You refuse to get it. The reason is that it hurts, Dare. It hurts so bad, when everything goes wrong." She wasn't budging. Not an inch.

He should shut the hell up and leave. But somehow, he couldn't stop himself. He just had to keep groping for the words that would finally get through to her. "Look. It's a crap deal that your husband made you a promise he didn't keep. But he loved you and you loved him and…you know, that's all we get. A chance at love and happiness, and we need to grab it and hold it for as long as we can. Because no one can promise to live forever, Ava. No one can promise you will always be safe."

"I *know* that. I do. I just… I can't go there again. All the chance-taking is just wrung clean out of me. Something always goes wrong, there's always some catch I don't see until it's too late."

"That's just…"

"What? You tell me, Dare. You explain it to me. Getting your heart ripped out is just what?"

"Ava, it's life. Sometimes it all goes wrong. But that doesn't mean you just stop trying."

"It's different for you. You've never been married. You don't have any kids."

Was that a low blow? It sure felt like it to him. "Got me. On both counts. I suppose next you'll be playing the womanizer card."

"I'm sorry." Her voice had gone small and so very lost. "Really sorry." She wouldn't even look at him now. "But I can't. Uh-uh. I mean it. I just can't..."

"Damn it, Ava." He didn't know what else to do, so he went to her and pulled her up into his arms.

For a moment, she melted into him. It was right, exactly right, the same as it was every time he held her in his arms. He knew she felt it, too.

But then she braced her hands on his chest and pushed him away. He let go. They stood facing each other, not touching. His arms had never felt so empty.

She shut her eyes, pressed her fingers over them and let out a long, weary sigh. "I just want to make a decent life and raise my daughter. I can't...take any more big chances, in love, in relationships. I'm no good at all that, and I accept that I'm not. That's why this, with us, was just supposed to be a fl—"

He stopped her with a raised hand. "Don't say that word. I don't want to hear that word ever again."

"Whether I say it or not, you know what I mean."

He did know. She was doing it, wrecking it, just as she'd said she would.

Still, he waited like some lovesick, brain-dead fool, giving her one more chance to change her mind.

But she only stared at him, chin high, eyes full of shadows and bleak certainty. He heard her silent message: *We are done.*

Something shifted within him. He gave up. He was done, too. "I'll let myself out."

And that was it. He turned and left her there.

She didn't follow. And she never said another word.

In the front hall, he put on his boots, shrugged into his coat and went out alone into the freezing December night.

Chapter Twelve

"I need to call Darius." Sylvie crammed a giant fork-ful of scrambled eggs into her mouth.

Ava reminded herself that she'd done the right thing the night before, even if she felt flayed raw inside this morning, like she'd scooped her own heart out with a jagged spoon, leaving nothing but a gaping wound inside her chest.

But she would get over it. And better to end it now before she loved him so much she couldn't imagine her life without him—well, okay. She was already having a little trouble imagining her life without him.

But not to worry. She didn't *have* to imagine it. Because now she would be living it.

And she fervently hoped that by the time Sylvie chewed and swallowed her enormous wad of egg, calling Darius would no longer be on her mind.

No such luck. "So, Mommy. I need you to give me his phone number."

Ava knocked back another gulp of coffee and set down her mug. "What do you need to talk to Darius about?"

"Oh, lots of things. But mainly, I need to know what he wants for Christmas."

"Honey, I thought you were giving him that special bejeweled ornament at his thank-you party yesterday."

"And I did and he loved it, but I want to get him something else, not just an ornament. Something special to let him know that I'm so glad he's my friend—and that's another thing I need to do. He put me in his truck and drove me to the hospital, and he didn't have time to take his presents with him. I need to remind him that he has to go and get them."

"I'm sure he'll remember all on his own and that he'll call Janice and arrange to pick them up. Please don't worry."

Ava touched the bandage on her chin. "It doesn't hurt as bad this morning."

"I'm so glad."

"Kinda stings, though."

"Don't touch it. Finish your food." Were they done with the subject of Darius? Ava sent a selfish prayer to heaven that they were.

But no. "So just put his number in my phone, 'kay, so I can call him?"

Ava made a last stab at deflecting the question. "Come on. Eat."

Sylvie stuck out her bandaged chin. "You keep not answering me."

So much for avoidance. "Sylvie, Darius cares for you."

"I know that." Her voice was sharp with impatience.

"Honey…" There was just no good way to say it. "Darius and I had a long talk last night. You see, I think he was spending too much time here."

"No, he wasn't." Her little mouth was pinched up tight.

"Well, that is your opinion."

"And my 'pinion is right."

"I don't agree."

Sylvie set down her fork. "Humph."

Ava forged on. "What you need to know is that he won't be coming around to our house anymore. And I'm sorry, but I'm not going to give you his phone number."

"Did he do something *wrong*?"

"Honey, of course not."

"Then why did you send him away? Darius *likes* it here. He likes *you*. And he likes me, too."

"Oh, sweetheart. Of course he does."

"And maybe *you* don't want to see him so much, but *I* still do."

But I do want to see him. I want to grab him and hold on and tell him I had it all wrong. I do want to try again.

Except, wait. No. She didn't.

She *couldn't*. Never again.

Ava searched her brain for the right words and came up empty. "It's not the end of the world, Sylvie." Though it did kind of feel that way, everything gray and hopeless—and with that hole in her chest where her heart used to be.

Sylvie huffed in outrage. "It is *bad*, Mom. It's very

bad. He is my friend, and now I can never see him again."

"I didn't say never. You will still see him."

"When?"

"Well, now and then, whenever he works with the Blueberries. And occasionally, if you're at Annabelle's and he happens to be there, too."

"*Please*, Mommy." Sylvie flat out pleaded. "Can I just get him a nice present?" A hot flush stained her cheeks, and tears flooded her eyes.

Ava hesitated. Would letting Sylvie get him another present really hurt? Was she making it worse by not giving in a little? What was God thinking when he invented parenthood, and why was she so bad at it? "I'm sorry, honey. No."

Sylvie plunked her napkin on the table, hard. "That's not fair." A sharp sob escaped her. She sniffed, and the tears overflowed. They rolled down her flushed cheeks, and the white bandage absorbed them. "You make me want to say something really, really bad to you, Mom."

Ava felt the treacherous moisture fogging up her own eyes. Her kid was amazing. And dear God, she hated herself right now. "The decision is made. I'm sorry, but that's how it is."

Sylvie threw back her head and brayed her fury at the ceiling. "Aughgg! I am so *mad* at you, Mom!"

Ava gulped. "I can see that. I…" She had nothing at that point, just that giant heartless hole in her chest— a hole that was now filled with guilt as she stared at her unhappy child. "You will still see him, just not for a while."

"That's not fair!"

"You already said that."

"Why won't you *listen* to me?"

"I am listening, Sylvie. But *you're* not listening to me."

Sylvie let out a wordless little cry. And then she burst from her chair like a small, brown-haired rocket and bolted, disappearing into the dining room, headed for the living room. Ava let her go. She even bit her tongue to keep from calling out, *No running in the house*.

Ava heard her in the front hall. Little feet hit the stairs and pounded up them. Ava winced as a door slammed overhead.

And then she pushed her half-eaten breakfast to the center of the table and buried her face in her hands.

So much for breaking it off with Dare before anyone got hurt.

A half an hour later, Ava knocked on Sylvie's door. No answer. "Sylvie. Please open the door."

Again, there was nothing. Ava was about to call out that she was coming in anyway, when the door swung wide and her puffy-eyed daughter glared up at her.

"May I come in?"

Sylvie took a very long time to think that one over. Finally, she flounced to the bed and plunked down on the edge of it. "Yeah." Ava went and sat beside her and started to ease an arm around her. "Don't try to hug me, Mom."

Ava pulled her arm back. "Fair enough." She'd planned to go into the office today. But no. She worked for herself, after all. And buyers and sellers were busy with holiday plans anyway. Nothing was happening she couldn't work around—especially considering that her daughter was miserable. And with eight stitches in her chin, too. "I'm keeping you home today."

As a rule, Sylvie loved staying home from day care, which she considered kid stuff now that she'd reached the advanced age of seven. But not today, apparently. She slanted Ava a sharp glance. "I have stuff to do there and I don't want to stay home."

"We'll find something fun to do here."

"I don't really feel like doing things with you today, Mom."

Ouch. "Sylvie, I understand that you're upset with me. But I have to do what I think is best for you, and today that is to keep you home."

Sylvie pursed her mouth up hard—no doubt to keep herself from saying those very bad things she'd barely held back at the breakfast table. Then she sniffed. "I want to see Gramma and Grandpa. Can I go to their house, please?"

Terrific. There were so many ways that would not go well. Sylvie would tell her grandmother that Ava wouldn't let her see Darius anymore, and then Kate would...

Oh, what did it matter? Kate would know eventually anyway. And Ava felt so rotten and sad and broken-hearted now, how was one more well-meaning lecture from her mother going to make things any worse?

"All right. We'll go to Gramma Kate's."

They were barely in the door before Sylvie announced, "Mom said Darius can't come to our house anymore and I can't even call him on my phone."

Kate arched an eyebrow in Ava's direction. Suppressing a sigh, Ava nodded. Then Kate turned to Sylvie.

"Good morning to you, too, sweetheart. Take off your coat and hat and stay awhile."

"I *am*, Gramma." Sylvie hung her jacket and her red wool cap on a child-height peg that Ava's dad had installed by the door.

"Wonderful," beamed Kate. "Let me get a hug. I really need one."

Sylvie went to her grandma, who scooped her up and carried her to the kitchen area, where she sat at the table with Sylvie in her lap.

"There's coffee," Kate said.

Ava headed for the pot. "You?"

"Please." Kate smoothed Sylvie's hair. "Apple juice?"

"Yes!"

Ava poured the coffee and gave Sylvie her juice. Then she sat at the table opposite her mother and her daughter.

Kate said, "That is a big bandage."

Sylvie cuddled in closer, tucking her head under Kate's chin. "It's not so bad, and it doesn't hurt so much now."

Kate pressed a kiss into her hair as the door opened and Ava's dad came in.

"Grandpa!" Sylvie jumped down and ran to him. He dropped to a crouch and opened his arms.

And Ava's mom said, "I think we need donuts."

Wrong. More sweets were the last thing they needed. Kate had enough Christmas cookies and candy on hand to treat a small army.

But Sylvie loved donuts. "Cream-filled with chocolate frosting!"

"Pauly-Wally, why don't you take Sylvie over to the donut shop? She can help you choose."

"Yes!" Sylvie crowed. "I need to be there and make sure you get the good ones, Grandpa."

So Sylvie put her coat back on, and off they went.

"Smoothly done, Mom," Ava said the minute the door closed behind them.

Kate fiddled with the handle of her coffee mug. "We've got a half hour at the most. I'm getting that you broke it off with Darius. That's your business, of course. But I need to know how you're handling it with Sylvie so I can support you."

Ava felt a slightly unhinged laugh bubble up. "It's *my* business? Who are you and what have you done with my *real* mother?"

Kate got up, grabbed the cookie tin off the counter and set it on the table. "Help yourself."

"Just one." Ava took a green-frosted Christmas tree sprinkled with sparkly sugar stars. "I need to save room for the donuts."

"Good thinking—and it's occurred to me in the past few weeks that you're finally finding your way back from losing Craig. I realized I needed to butt out and let you do that."

"Finding my way back because of Darius?" Just saying his name caused a stabbing sensation in that ragged, hollow place where her heart used to be. Ava set down her cookie without tasting it.

Her mom was nodding. "However it's worked out for you with him, I think he's been very good for you. And I'm glad for that, honey."

But how good have I been for him? Ava's throat clutched, and her eyes swam with tears. "First, about Sylvie?"

"Tell me."

"They have…a connection, Sylvie and Dare. It's a strong bond. I should have thought all this through more, been more careful. I shouldn't have let him come to the house, shouldn't have let Sylvie get so attached. Now, I've told her she can't see him for a while. But I'm starting to think that's wrong. I'm realizing that the attachment is already there between them, and I have to find a way to let that play out and, well, I'm not sure how to do that yet. I'll probably have to talk to him, see how much contact he even wants with Sylvie."

"He does seem like a fine man."

"Oh, Mom. He *is*."

"And how about this? If Sylvie brings it up to me again, I will just tell her that everything will work out. That you love her and will take care of her and, of course, she'll see Darius eventually."

"That sounds good. And then she'll tell you how mad she is at me."

"And I'll hug her and spoil her and she will survive." Kate stretched her hand across the table.

Ava couldn't meet her reaching fingers fast enough. She grabbed hold. "Mom." The tears rose again, filling her eyes, stuffing up her nose. "Mom. I'm a terrible person."

"No."

"Yeah. I freaked, when I got to the hospital and saw him with Sylvie yesterday, saw the way she looked at him—like he was the dad she can't even remember. I saw that she loves him and… Mom, *I* love him, too. And that should have been a *good* thing, a *great* thing. But all I felt was terrified. And so I sent him away."

Kate turned and took the tissues off the little jut of counter behind her chair. She pushed them across the table to Ava. Ava snatched one and dabbed at her streaming eyes. Her mom shook her head. "You always did feel everything so deeply, just like your dad…"

"Oh, come on." Ava blew her nose, hard. "I'm tough and determined, and I can take care of myself. But when it comes to love, I'm a basket case, and we both know it."

"It's understandable. You had a difficult childhood, and I'm so sorry for that. And then you finally let yourself trust a man, gave yourself and your tender heart to him. And you lost him."

"That was six years ago. It's about time I got over it."

"And you *are* getting over it."

"Not fast enough, though. And Mom, about what happened when you got sick, I really don't blame you for any of that."

Kate tipped her head to the side, frowning.

Ava knew there was something she wasn't saying. "What?"

"Maybe you don't blame *me*…"

"I don't. Truly."

"But I think that you do blame your father a little."

Ava took another tissue, blew her nose again—and busted to it. "It's true. I've blamed Dad for not getting out there and getting work sooner, for getting so wrapped up in you and his terror of losing you that he stopped taking care of business. But right this minute, all I can think of is how much he loves you, how much he loves *all* of us. All I can see is him coming in the door a few minutes ago, holding out his arms so Sylvie could run into them. I see…that you're here, Mom, and you always have been, ready to listen to me admit what an idiot I've been. And Dad's driving Sylvie to

Deeliteful Donuts so that you and I can talk. I see that I'm a lucky woman, to have you and Dad for my parents. I see that we fought our way back from hell as a family and we're all still together, still looking out for each other, taking care of each other. And most of all, I see that putting blame on Dad or *anyone*, really, is just another way I've been a complete fool."

Now her mom's eyes were misty. "Honey, you are not a fool. And that was beautiful, what you just said."

"Yeah, well. Even a gold digger can have insights now and then."

Her mom started laughing—right through her tears. "You're no gold digger. A gold digger makes her money by sleeping with rich men."

"Hmm. So I guess I'm more of a money-grubber, then, huh?"

"Stop. You really are being too hard on yourself."

"You say that because you're my mom and it's part of your job description to believe I'm a better person than I actually am."

"No. I say it because it's true. Be gentle with yourself, honey. Trust yourself. It's all going to work out for the best. You just wait and see."

Trust yourself, her mom had said.

But really, how could she? She'd messed everything up so badly with Dare, messed everything up and at the same time failed to even consider how her screwing up would affect her own child.

If he had any sense at all, Dare would never get near her again. And if only she didn't miss him so much, she would simply give up now. Move on. Try to get over him, let him forget about her, hope that he would find a woman who knew how to appreciate a man like him.

But she did miss him, desperately. She wanted another chance with him.

She lay awake all that night trying to decide what to do, how to approach him, what in the world to say. She must have finally dropped off sometime after 4 a.m. And when she woke up at six, she was so tired, she decided to take another workday off.

And Ava Malloy *never* took a workday off.

But Christmas was just around the corner, she told herself. And a few days off would be good for her greedy little money-grubbing soul. She lay in her big bed alone between her silky-soft high-thread-count sheets and thought of her parents, of how they'd struggled all their lives to get by.

She'd wanted a different life, a safer life, with a nicer house and money in the bank. And she'd gotten what she wanted, hadn't she?

And her mom and dad? They just had what mattered most: each other.

Ava changed Sylvie's bandage for a much smaller one after breakfast. Her stitches already seemed to be healing.

"It doesn't even hurt today, Mom," Sylvie announced. "And can I please go to day care? Today's the Christmas party."

So Ava drove her over there. Then she met Janice at the Blueberry clubhouse to pick up the presents Sylvie had made and wrapped for the family and then left behind when Dare rushed her to emergency.

Janice unlocked the door and ushered her inside,

where the heater was turned down so low that both of them shivered, even in their heavy coats.

"I think I'll turn the heat up just a little so the pipes don't freeze." Janice went to the thermostat.

Ava wandered on into the main room, where a small pile of wrapped presents waited next to a larger pile of handmade ornaments. She spotted Sylvie's bejeweled creation among them.

Janice came up behind her. "The wrapped ones are Sylvie's. The rest belong to Darius. I keep reminding myself to call him and ask when he wants to pick them up."

"I'll take them to him." The words were out of her mouth before she could remind herself of the thousand reasons why she had no right to go there.

"Wonderful," said Janice. "I'll get you a box."

So Janice dug an empty box out of the storage room and found a separate bag for Sylvie's gifts. They carried it all out to Ava's Suburban.

She drove away feeling reprehensible. Like she'd not only dumped Dare because she was a total coward, but then she'd gone and stolen his Christmas presents, too.

And then she started thinking about him all alone in his house with only Daisy for company. Had he ever gotten around to decorating his tree?

She drove on autopilot, remembering all the ways she could have been a better girlfriend during the too-short time they'd had together. She could have taken Sylvie out to his place just once. It wasn't like keeping Sylvie away from where he lived had fixed it so Sylvie didn't get attached to him. Sylvie loved him and missed him without ever once seeing his place, without meeting his dog or petting his horses.

Ava drove right past the turn to her house and just kept on going, realizing she was actually heading out to Dare's only when she was almost to the long driveway that led up to his house.

Really, she had no business being there. She should give it up and go back home.

But she didn't. Her throat tight and her pulse pounding in her ears, she signaled, braked and entered the twisting driveway.

Stopping in the turnaround not far from the front porch, she jumped out and ran up the steps before she had a chance to lose her nerve.

But the house seemed too quiet, and she couldn't see any lights on. She knocked. No answer. No sign of Daisy, even. He was probably at work.

She peered in one of the sidelights next to the door and saw a big Fraser fir propped in a bucket against the wall in the entry hall. Not a single string of lights or an ornament in sight.

She actually thought about breaking and entering— and decorating his tree for him while he was gone. But did he even *have* decorations? The boxful in the car wouldn't be nearly enough.

Not to mention it was a truly bad idea. If she wanted another chance with him, she needed to call him or text him like any normal, sane person, to call him and ask him if they could meet and maybe talk.

And she would definitely do that, get in touch with him, get down on her knees in front of him and beg him to consider maybe taking her back.

Just…not right this minute.

Whirling, she ran back down the steps, got the box of ornaments from the car and carried it up to the door.

She should at least leave a note, but she had no paper handy, let alone a pen.

Maybe she should just text him about it: Hey. How've u been since I dumped u? Took those ornaments the girls made to your house. Left them on the porch ❤ u and miss u and I c now I was crazy 2 send u away. I wish we could…

Oh, no. Uh-uh. He didn't need a text from her.

When he got home he would find the box, and what did it matter who had left it there?

She went back down the steps again, slowly this time. Too soon, she was climbing up behind the wheel of her Suburban. She pulled the door shut and started the engine and made herself drive away.

When Sylvie got home from day care, Ava gave her the bag of presents. Sylvie carefully placed each one under the tree. She didn't ask about Dare's gifts from the Blueberries. Ava didn't tell her she'd driven them out to his place. It seemed downright dangerous to mention Dare to her daughter right now. Why invite a flood of questions she had no idea how to answer?

That night after Sylvie was in bed, Tom showed up at her door. Ava led him to the kitchen and poured him some coffee.

He said, "Mom told me you broke it off with Darius." Ava started to say that she didn't want to talk about it, but Tom didn't give her time to launch into denials. "I just want to say that I was a jerk about him. He's an okay guy."

"Well, thank you. And I know he is."

"I only want you to be happy, Ava."

"I'm working on it."

"Not hard enough, I'm guessing," her brother muttered into his coffee cup.

She didn't even call him a dirty name. Mostly because he happened to be right.

At ten in the morning on Christmas Eve day, Chloe dropped Annabelle off for a playdate with Sylvie. She came back at one to pick Annabelle up.

"How're you doing?" she asked, before Ava called the girls down from upstairs.

How much did Chloe know about her and Darius? There was no time to go into it now. "Long story," Ava said lamely.

Chloe touched Ava's arm, a little pat that spoke of friendship, of reassurance. "We should have a girls' night out. Get all the Bravo sisters together, see if Rory and Paige and Addie can come, too. We'll go out to the Inn." They all loved the Sylvan Inn. It was homey, with great food. "Maybe this coming week, before New Year's?"

Ava realized she wanted that, a night out with the Bravo women. She wanted to catch up, to check in with Jody and hear how she was doing. To ask Elise how the wedding plans were going. To listen to Addie rave on about her baby son. She wanted to tell them all everything, what a fool she'd been, how she couldn't seem to pull the trigger on her decision to reach out to Darius, to try for another chance with him. "A girls' night out. I'd like that."

"I'll set it up. Call you on the twenty-sixth?"

"You're on."

After Chloe and Annabelle left, Sylvie helped Ava prepare a couple of side dishes and a pan of Parker

House rolls to take to the Janko family Christmas dinner tomorrow. It was a quiet afternoon and evening. Ava kept the Christmas tunes playing. After dinner, Sylvie chose a Christmas movie to watch.

Bedtime came. Ava tucked the covers in around Sylvie and bent for a good-night kiss.

But before her lips touched her daughter's smooth forehead, Sylvie said solemnly, "Mommy, I know you don't like to talk about Darius. But don't you think he might be lonely without us? Friends need to tell each other to have a Merry Christmas."

Damn it. Sylvie was right.

Ava should at least let Sylvie call him.

She was just about to tell her daughter to go ahead and get her phone, when she had another idea.

Why not just bundle Sylvie up and head out to Dare's house?

Oh, please.

Bad idea. Because…crazy. Totally and completely insane.

How could she even be considering such a thing?

It could so easily backfire on her—which wouldn't be the end of the world if she had only herself to consider.

But there was Sylvie. If Dare didn't appreciate Ava showing up out of nowhere on Christmas Eve, that could be tough on Sylvie.

But then again, no.

Dare would never hurt Sylvie. Whatever his response to Ava, even if he'd already come to the conclusion that she wasn't worth the pain she'd caused him, he would be careful of Sylvie's tender heart.

"Mommy. Are you okay? You don't look so good."

Ava rearranged her expression into something vaguely resembling a smile. "I have an idea. You just said you want to wish Darius a Merry Christmas..."

Sylvie's mouth formed a soft O. "Yes," she whispered prayerfully. "Yes, I do."

"Do you want to do that now, tonight?"

Sylvie gulped and nodded, eyes bright with growing hope. "Yes!"

"Well, all right then. Why don't we drive out to his place?"

Sylvie popped to a sitting position. "Mommy, you mean it? Right now?"

"Right now. But remember, we aren't invited and we will be surprising him. He might not even be there. And if he is, it's very possible he will be busy, and we will just say Merry Christmas and then come right back home."

Sylvie's head bobbed up and down so fast it was almost comical. "I know we might not see him. I know he might be busy. I just want to *try*, Mom. If he's not there, I won't cry about it or anything. If he's busy, I will just say Merry Christmas and we can come home."

Were these the kinds of promises a seven-year-old could reasonably be expected to keep? Ava wasn't sure.

But the choice was already made. She'd held out hope to Sylvie. She couldn't snatch it back now.

It was snowing, the white flakes small and tight, hurling themselves wildly against the windshield. Ava played the radio, one Christmas carol after another. Intermittently, from the backseat, Sylvie sang along.

When they pulled up at Dare's house, the porch light was on. A wreath of pine and cedar boughs hung on the door. At the festive sight, Ava had to gulp down a surge of emotion.

She turned off the engine, ending "Frosty the Snowman" in midverse. In the backseat, Sylvie unhooked the belts on her booster. Ava unlocked all the doors, and Sylvie pushed hers open.

Ava got out, too. The snow was still falling. Ava tipped up her head and caught a few flakes on her tongue. Sylvie's mitten brushed her fingers. Ava took her hand. They went up the steps together, and Ava rang the bell. Deep in the house somewhere, Daisy barked.

"That's his dog," Sylvie whispered, as though they were on a secret mission and no one could be allowed to hear. "Her name is Daisy. She's a good dog. Darius told me all about her—and if he's gone, won't she be lonely?"

"There's a guy named Corky who has a house close by. He works for Darius. I'm sure he'll check in on Daisy if Darius isn't here to do that."

"Good. Because, Mommy, I don't think Darius is home."

"Should we ring again?"

Sylvie pushed the bell that time. The sound echoed on the other side of the door. Daisy barked some more.

But no lights popped on inside, no footsteps approached.

Ava peered through the sidelight. The tree was out of the bucket, up on a stand. Even through the shadows, she caught the shine of ornaments, the gleam of a star on top. The sight cheered her.

But then Sylvie said in her smallest voice, "Mom. He's not here."

Ava squeezed her mittened hand. "Sorry, baby." Sylvie's lower lip trembled. Ava bent and scooped her up into her arms. "I'll give you his number in the morning. You can call and wish him a happy Christmas."

"Thanks, Mom." Sylvie laid her head on Ava's shoulder.

Ava carried her down the steps to the car.

On the way home, they left the radio off. The snow fell harder, the flakes growing larger, spinning out of the night toward them as they rolled down the dark road. In the backseat, Sylvie was quiet.

Ava glanced at her in the rearview mirror to see if she'd fallen asleep. But her eyes were open. She stared out her side window at the snow whirling by.

Twenty minutes after they left Dare's dark house, Ava turned the Suburban onto their well-lit street. She saw the F-150 at the same time Sylvie did, and the heart she'd thought she'd lost turned over in her chest.

"Mom!" Sylvie's voice rang with excitement. "It's Darius. That's his truck at our house!"

He wore jeans and boots and a heavy jacket—and that cowboy hat he'd worn the first night Ava went to his house.

He rose from the front step as Ava swung into the driveway. She hit the brake and pressed the remote. The garage door started rolling up.

"Mom, unlock my door." Sylvie popped her belts open.

Darius was coming down the steps toward them. Ava punched the door locks, and Sylvie jumped out and ran to him.

They met in the middle of the snow-covered lawn. Ava rolled down the passenger window. And then she just sat there, the car idling, the garage door wide open in front of her, watching as Dare scooped Sylvie high and whirled her around. Happy little-girl laughter rang out, and the poms on her wool cap bounced as she spun.

Then he took her by the waist and hitched her over his head to sit on his shoulders. She laughed again, grabbed his hat and plunked it on her own head over her wool cap. The hat was so big, it covered half of her face, which only caused her to laugh some more.

He came and leaned in the passenger window—or at least, he did it as best he could with a seven-year-old on his back.

Their eyes met. Something inside her kindled and flared.

"I just wanted to stop by," he said in that deep voice that haunted her dreams. "To wish you two a Merry Christmas."

"And we went to your house to wish *you* a Merry Christmas!" Sylvie crowed in delight at the sheer wonderfulness of that. The big hat wobbled on her too-small head. She put up a hand to hold it in place. "But you weren't there. Because you were here at *our* house."

"Oh, yes I was." He never took his eyes off Ava.

"How about some hot chocolate?" Ava offered, breathless and eager and not caring in the least that he would hear the longing in her voice, see the light of hope and love in her eyes.

"I'm in," he said.

"Me too!" cried Sylvie.

Inside, they piled their coats and hats and wool scarves on the hall tree and got out of their boots. And then they trooped to the kitchen, where Ava made cocoa and Sylvie seemed driven to share every moment of her life since the last time she'd seen Dare. She chattered away about her playdate with Annabelle, the Christmas party at her day care, how well her stitches were healing and the deliciousness of the cream-filled donuts she'd enjoyed while at Gramma Kate's the other day.

At ten thirty, Ava cut into the monologue. "Tomorrow's a big day, and it's way past your bedtime."

"I know, Mommy—and I was wondering if maybe Darius can come up and tuck me in?"

A week ago, such a suggestion would have had Ava flipping out internally and firmly saying no.

But tonight, she simply turned to Dare. "What do you think?"

He gave her that smile again, the one that warmed her from the inside out. "Happy to." He scooped Sylvie up. "Give your mom a kiss." He dipped her sideways. She giggled and smacked a slightly sticky kiss onto Ava's cheek. "Off we go." And he aimed Sylvie like a rocket and headed for the stairs.

"Brush your teeth!" Ava called after them.

"I will, Mom!" Sylvie waved good-night as they vanished from sight.

Ava was there at the foot of the stairs when Dare came down twenty minutes later.

On the last step, he paused. Waiting. For her to reach out.

And she did. She held out her hand to him. He took that last step and gathered her into his arms.

Heaven. He felt so good all around her. The manly scent of him thrilled her. And then he kissed her, a slow one, wet and hot and endlessly sweet.

"A kiss at the foot of the stairs," he said when he finally lifted his head, "even though Sylvie might peek down and see us. This is real progress."

"You think so?"

"Oh, yeah. We've come a long way."

"God. I missed you so much."

"And I missed you."

"I... Oh, Dare, in case you haven't figured it out already, I want to try again."

He held her gaze so steadily. "Yes."

She breathed a slow breath of joy and relief. "That's the word. The *best* word. When we were kids, that day by the lockers, you said—"

"—that someday *you* would say yes to *me*."

Gladness filled her. "You do remember."

"All of it. Every word."

"Well, then. *Yes.* Yes, Dare. See? I am saying it. I'm saying it to you."

He stroked her cheek, smoothed her hair. "I swore to myself that I would be patient. And I wasn't. I couldn't stop pushing you for more than you wanted to give me. And the other night, I should have tried harder to get through to you."

"No. You needed to go. You needed to walk away and let me finally have to face my life without you. It was time for me to admit what we really are to each other, to be ready to stand up for what we might have together. I'm *glad* you forced me to get to work on that—well, I mean, now that you're here, now you've said yes to me, I'm glad. But the last few days...?"

"Not so good?"

"Worse. It's been completely craptastic, facing all my shortcomings and praying that someday I would have the nerve to go to you and ask you for one more chance." She took his hand again.

He let her lead him to the bedroom, where she shut and locked the door.

They fell into each other's arms. He claimed her lips in the sweetest, longest kiss. And when he lifted his head, it was only to swoop down and claim them all over again.

When they finally came up for air, he said, "I brought presents, but then I thought I should wait to ask you if that was okay. They're out in my truck."

"You always think of everything—and it's more than okay. We'll send Sylvie out to get them in the morning."

He swore low, a reverent sound. "*In the morning.* Because I'm staying overnight?"

"Will you?"

"Hell, yes."

She went on tiptoe for another kiss. "Also, I hope whatever Bravo is hosting Christmas dinner this year will forgive you if you beg off. Because I want you with us. Will you please come with Sylvie and me to the Seven Pines Mobile Home Park tomorrow to enjoy the Janko family holiday feast?"

"Best offer I've had in years."

"I do believe that was another yes."

He bent close. "Yes." He breathed the beautiful word into her ear. "Yes." He kissed it onto her cheek. "Yes." He pressed it into her hair. "I love you, Ava. You probably won't believe this, but I've compared every woman I've ever met to you."

"No…"

"Yeah."

"But Dare, I turned you down. We were only kids and you hardly knew me."

"Doesn't matter. There was just something about you. I never thought I'd get a chance with you. And the past few days, I've gone crazy thinking I blew it because I gave up and walked out."

"You didn't blow it. Not at all. And you didn't give up. I mean, here you are, ready to try again. And as for me, well, I've been working up the nerve to go to you almost since I broke it off. I took the Blueberry presents to your place."

"That was you?"

"Uh-huh. I should have left a note. But I didn't know what to say. I wanted to beg you to come back to me. And then I chickened out and just put the box there on your porch and ran away."

"Thank you."

"For running away?"

He grinned. "No. For the ornaments. They inspired me to get off my ass and decorate my damn tree."

She laughed. "I saw that you did. Tonight, I peeked in the window and there it was, all decked out in the front hall."

"It's pretty when it's lit up."

"I want to see that, your tree with all the lights on. Tomorrow, if the snow's not too bad, we can stop by your place before we go to Seven Pines."

"Good. I want so much from you, Ava. I want everything."

"Yes." She said it without hesitation.

"And to start, I want you out at my place more often."

"And I will be. I promise. And Sylvie, too." She studied his face. Never, ever would she get enough of looking at him. "What is it with you? I want to tell you everything, confess all my sins to you."

"And I want to hear them. Are they X-rated?"

"No, those are my fantasies. I'll share a few of those in a minute. But first…"

"Yeah?"

"I need to tell you…"

"What? Anything. Don't hold back."

"That day at my locker, back in high school?"

"Yeah?"

"That day I was terrified. I know I said I wasn't, but oh, I really was."

"You said I was dangerous to you…"

"And you were, but not for the reasons I gave you then, not because you were rich and I was poor, not because you went with one girl after another. Uh-uh. You were dangerous because I felt you could…" She sought the right word and found it. "…*know* me. I felt you could know me. You could see me. Really *see* me. And Dare, what you would see? It wouldn't be all that great. Because I was not only scared, I was desperate. Desperate to somehow make a life where nothing bad could ever reach me again. So I told you no. I told you never. I thought that refusing you would keep me safe. I was wrong. Doubly wrong, because this Christmas, when I had another chance with you, I refused you all over again. And this time, I've had to face the truth. This time, I've had to learn the hard way that refusing you hurts more than all my fears combined. Refusing you is the same as cutting out my own heart. So I'm done with never. I want more than safety now, more than security, more than the things that money can buy.

I want *you*, Dare. I love you, too. So much. Completely, with all of my heart."

He cradled her face between his big hands and brushed another kiss across her lips. "Damn. You mean it?"

"I do. I truly do."

"Good. Because I've been waiting."

"Oh, Dare. You don't have to wait anymore."

"I'm warning you. I'm not only talking about this Christmas, Ava."

"I know you're not."

"I want the next one."

"We'll share them, Dare, you and me and Sylvie, too."

"This year, and next year and the one after that…"

"They're yours, Dare. Forever and always, you and me together, for all of our Christmases to come."

* * * * *

Watch for Jody Bravo's story,
THE LAWMAN'S CONVENIENT BRIDE,
coming in May 2017,
only from Mills & Boon Cherish.

MILLS & BOON®

Cherish™

EXPERIENCE THE ULTIMATE RUSH OF FALLING IN LOVE

A sneak peek at next month's titles...

In stores from 15th December 2016:

- **Slow Dance with the Best Man** – Sophie Pembroke
  and **A Fortune in Waiting** – Michelle Major
- **Her New Year Baby Secret** – Jessica Gilmore
  and **Twice a Hero, Always Her Man** – Marie Ferrarella

In stores from 29th December 2016:

- **The Prince's Convenient Proposal** – Barbara Hannay
  and **His Ballerina Bride** – Teri Wilson
- **The Tycoon's Reluctant Cinderella** – Therese
  Beharrie *and* **The Cowboy's Runaway Bride** –
  Nancy Robards Thompson

Just can't wait?
Buy our books online a month before they hit the shops!
www.millsandboon.co.uk

Also available as eBooks.

MILLS & BOON®

EXCLUSIVE EXTRACT

When Eloise Miller finds herself thrown into the role of maid of honour at the wedding of the year, her plans to stay away from the gorgeous best man are scuppered!

Read on for a sneak preview of
SLOW DANCE WITH THE BEST MAN
by Sophie Pembroke

Maid of honour for Melissa Sommers. How on earth had this happened? And the worst part was—

'Sounds like we'll be spending even more time together.' Noah's voice was warm, deep and far too close to her ear.

Eloise sighed. That. That was the worst thing. Because the maid of honour was *expected* to pair up with the best man, and that would not make her resolution to stay away from Noah Cross any easier at all.

She turned and found him standing directly behind her, close enough that if she'd stepped back a centimetre or two she'd have been in his arms. Suddenly she was glad he'd alerted her to his presence with his words.

She shifted further away and tried to look like a professional, instead of a teenager with a crush. Looking up at him, she felt the strange heat flush over her skin again at his gorgeousness. Then she focused, and realised he was frowning.

'Apparently so,' she agreed. 'But I'm sure I'll be far too busy with all the wedding arrangements—'

'Oh, I doubt it,' Noah interrupted, but he still didn't sound entirely happy about the idea, which surprised her. Perhaps she'd misread his flirting earlier. Maybe he really was like that with everyone and, now the reality of having to spend time with her had set in, he was less keen on the idea. 'Melissa has quite the packed schedule for the wedding party, you know. She's right—you're going to have to find someone to take over most of your job here.'

Eloise sighed. She *did* know. She'd helped Laurel plan it, after all.

And, now she thought about it, every last bit of the schedule involved the maid of honour and the best man being together.

Noah smiled, a hint of the charm he'd exhibited earlier showing through despite the frown, and Eloise's heart beat twice in one moment as she accepted the inevitable.

She was doomed.

She had the most ridiculous crush on a man who clearly found her a minor inconvenience.

And—even worse—the whole world was going to be watching, laughing at her pretending that she could live in this world of celebrities, mocking her for thinking she could ever be pretty enough, funny enough…just *enough* for Noah Cross.

Don't miss
SLOW DANCE WITH THE BEST MAN
by Sophie Pembroke

Available January 2017
www.millsandboon.co.uk

Copyright © 2016 by Sophie Pembroke

Give a 12 month subscription to a friend today!

Call Customer Services
0844 844 1358[*]

or visit
millsandboon.co.uk/subscriptions

* This call will cost you 7 pence per minute plus your phone company's price per minute access charge.

MILLS & BOON®

Why shop at millsandboon.co.uk?

Each year, thousands of romance readers find their perfect read at millsandboon.co.uk. That's because we're passionate about bringing you the very best romantic fiction. Here are some of the advantages of shopping at www.millsandboon.co.uk:

* **Get new books first**—you'll be able to buy your favourite books one month before they hit the shops

* **Get exclusive discounts**—you'll also be able to buy our specially created monthly collections, with up to 50% off the RRP

* **Find your favourite authors**—latest news, interviews and new releases for all your favourite authors and series on our website, plus ideas for what to try next

* **Join in**—once you've bought your favourite books, don't forget to register with us to rate, review and join in the discussions

Visit **www.millsandboon.co.uk**
for all this and more today!

MILLS_WEB

